AMBER CASSIDY

First Surrender

First edition

ISBN: 979-8-9890036-5-5

This book was professionally typeset on Reedsy.
Find out more at reedsy.com

As I'm writing this, Western North Carolina and Eastern Tennessee are dealing with the devastating effects of Hurricane Helene. The flooding has destroyed the homes of so many in the Blue Ridge Mountains and many lives have been lost. The Chance Encounters Series is based in this area and inspired by the beautiful Appalachian landscape. The tragedy weighs heavy on my heart and my thoughts are with everyone who calls these communities home. Donate & Raise Awareness if you can <3

Preface

This novel is a little different than the previous two in my series, filled with more resistance and animosity among my main characters. Call it what you like, Hate to Love, or Enemies to Lovers, but Natalie and Jackson don't see eye to eye. They're pushed together despite their propensity for arguing and with that comes harsh words and actions. This is a romance but with hills to climb to get there.

Content warnings: Explicit Sexual Content, Pregnancy Loss, Assault

Mentions of: Past Physical & Sexual Assault, Drug Use, Coercion/Rape.

Chapter One

Jackson

The soft lull of a romantic tune slips through the windows surrounding the courtyard I'm hiding in. The newlyweds are making the rounds to greet each guest while I avoid socializing by checking my email. I have too much on my mind to make small talk.

Kidnapping, assaults, bombs, and drugs. Our home is suffering.

I've been the Sheriff of Rollins County for a year now and the workload has fallen heavy on my shoulders. I'm outnumbered and overworked. Overwhelmed.

We're low-staffed and low on funds with an uptick in dangerous crime in the area.

Dangerous crimes are not normal for a place as rural as Rollins County. I grew up here, went to school here, and formerly worked the roads here as a State Trooper. This is a quiet county with more mountain roads than highways. More mom-and-pop shops than nationwide chains. Many of the families in this community span generations.

I know the local business owners and am familiar with the county board members and other representatives. Where some places might've seen me as too young to hold the position, the people here know I'm more than qualified. The years of law enforcement experience I have far outweighed any of the other potential candidates. Egomaniacs more interested in the status and power the title of Sheriff came with instead of helping the people here.

Securing the office was a lot of work but relatively easy. I vetted the deputies and ensured that Sheriff Donahue was the only dirty cop and made the moves to get the Department back up and running the right way.

Unfortunately, more missing person cases have come to light since my time in office began. Rollins doesn't have enough of a population to be able to overlook disappearances. We're up to a dozen unsolved. All ages, genders, races. There isn't a pattern and it's keeping me up at night.

I want people in the county to be safe. I want kids to be able to walk to school without fear of being plucked off the street and into the back of a van. I want criminals behind bars.

Between that and the bombing this past fall, I've barely slept. I made it my job to fix things and I am not making progress.

"Hey, do you want a piece of cake?" Whitney asks from the doorway. Over her shoulder people are dancing in the library's interior under rows of string lights. The music is louder and more upbeat than before.

"No, thanks. I'm fine."

She nods and turns to leave, and I can't contain my sigh of relief. Whitney is a casual acquaintance but nothing more. A few nights spent together throughout the past few years is as far as it's gone. Every once in a while she gives off the impression that she would like me to give her more. A sly comment here or there, and more than obvious flirting that I let fly over my head under the guise of not noticing. It's not going to happen with her.

She's a nice girl, a pretty woman, but I'm not interested in wedding bells. Hell, I'm starting to wonder if I'm interested in anything other than this damn job.

The music's volume increases and even though my back is turned, I know that someone's invaded my hideaway once again.

"You know you can't leave until my sister sees you having fun, right?" I don't need to see him to recognize Nathan's voice. He and the groom are pretty much the only two people I would consider friends.

Callie is one less person on my missing person board because of him. Nathan is Army, ex-Special Forces, and I knew after he recovered her not to ask many questions. It was a safe enough assumption to tag it as a murder-suicide. Luckily, as a trooper, I was discouraged from looking into the case anyway. The state didn't want that type of "backwoods" crime to be their problem.

It motivated me to take the leap and run for Sheriff. I wanted to know more about the trafficking scheme that the late Sheriff Donahue was involved in and just how corrupt he was. I wanted to make sure that the person who proceeded with the position wouldn't be worse for the community here.

"I'm still trying to solve Callie's case you know," I state, ignoring his comment about the wedding. The people responsible for plucking Callie off the side of the road that day are dead but the person who was pulling their strings is still out there. They're most likely responsible for my other missing people and my sleepless nights.

"I know, man."

After he took some time off, he got into Army Criminal Investigations. We've talked shop on more than one occasion.

"I think I have a lead, but I'm not sure where it will take me. I can't stomach that it's taken me this long. The bombing at the 5k has been at the top of my plate."

"It's strange what's happened within a year of Callie's abduction. Any chance that it's all connected? Kidnappings, bombings?" He asks, voicing the thoughts that I've already had. We're more alike than either of us would ever admit out loud.

"Yeah, and now I'm looking into a drug dealer. The web of activity has to stem from one point. Everything happening is too prominent to be a coincidence. I just can't figure out which scenario would be better. Random violent crimes or a criminal mastermind." We stand in thoughtful silence until another person joins us.

"You lame asses going to stand out here all night?" Jesse, the groom, asks.

"Probably," Nathan responds, earning a punch to the arm from Jesse.

"Congratulations," I tell him, lamely. He did get married after all.

"Malec, smile, it's a wedding. You're supposed to be having fun," Jesse berates me. I don't feel like smiling. I never do.

"He's stressed about work, come on." Nathan ushers the half-intoxicated groom back into the party, letting me have some peace. That's the norm, Jesse tries to bring me out of my shell and Nathan understands my aversion to fun. They're good guys.

I wander back to my table where Whitney is finishing her

fourth glass of champagne. Her platinum blonde hair swishes just above her shoulders as she turns to look at me. Paired with her pink dress, she resembles a shiny Barbie doll.

Her looks have never bothered me but lately, I've felt more than an aversion toward her. If I had more of a social life then I'd stop inviting her to things, but selfishly, I can't be bothered to make new acquaintances. People exhaust me.

"I need to get going. Do you want to stay? Or do you want me to take you home?" I ask hoping she'll cut me some slack and say she wants to stay to dance with any other man at this wedding.

"You can take me home." She gathers her things while I groan internally. If I were a bigger jackass, I'd call her an Uber, but I'm not. Rideshares aren't very prevalent in this area anyway.

I'll make sure she's home and then never call her again. I wouldn't have this time but I didn't feel like coming to a wedding without a plus one. It'd been six months since I had last seen her, even longer since I'd slept with her.

We're a mile down the road when she starts stroking my arm. The same song and dance each time. She starts offering small touches then she'll bat her eyelashes and ask me up to her apartment for a drink. I know the routine.

Sometimes I would let her think it worked, sometimes I wouldn't. She's never caught onto the fact that I don't drink, ever.

"Do you want to come up for a bit? I have a new bottle of wine that I've been wanting to open." She purrs from beside me. Her voice rumbles from her chest like she's channeling Marilyn Monroe. It's too easy.

It does nothing for me. My blood hasn't pumped in that

way for some time now. Maybe I'm getting old. If 32 is the start of erectile dysfunction then I have a long sad life ahead of me.

"Not tonight." I ignore her sad eyes and the pout of her mouth, hitting the unlock button on my door so she gets the message. Thankfully, she does, climbing out onto the sidewalk. I should walk her to her door, but I won't. She'll get the wrong idea and I don't have the energy to care about being a gentleman.

"Call me?" She asks as she closes my door.

"Sure." I put it in drive and hit the gas before checking that she made it inside.

I think the next time that I arrest a drunk and disorderly, I'll let them have a free shot. I deserve a good punch to the face.

* * *

The fluorescent white lights of the courtroom reflect brightly off of the polished oak of the judge's bench and the wooden bar that separates the lawyers from the rest of the room.

I've spent many hours in this courtroom spectating cases being tried, testifying, and assisting with prisoner transport. Today I am one of the onlookers waiting for Declan Randolph to be brought out.

I readjust in my seat uncomfortably, dislodging my gun belt from where it's digging into my side. We're short on coverage today so I'm in full uniform in case I have to respond to calls. I prefer the days that I can wear a department polo, not twenty pounds of vest and gear. It seems that we're short coverage most days though, which leads to more after-hours work for me.

A man is led into the room with wrist cuffs chained to his ankles, his bright orange jumpsuit hanging off of his slender frame. There is excited murmuring among the audience as the deputy helps Declan Randolph to sit but just as the commotion settles, a woman enters the courtroom from behind me. Walking past my row and down the middle aisle, Declan's supporters go abuzz again, watching her pointedly as she strides confidently to the first row and directly into my line of sight.

Her long dark, almost black, hair sways down the middle of her back to her waist. Wearing a dark green sweater and a black skirt, with heels that are more than a couple of inches high, she flips her hair over one shoulder as she drops her purse and the long coat dangling from her arm onto the seat.

When she flips her hair again to fall down the length of her back, her eyes cut to the group of men on the other side of the aisle and they narrow.

I can only tell because of how long her thick eyelashes are. Her opinion is apparent even from my seat 15 feet back. A few of the young guys that she's staring at give it right back to her, cocking their heads and puffing their chests.

I'm not sure of the connection but their obvious disdain of the woman in front of me puts me on alert. Not only do they outnumber her, I'm sure a few members of that crowd have warrants. It's less about their appearance, though they do have a few crude tattoos and more about an attitude that projects unruliness.

Her dark eyes flick back in my direction as she sits but there is nothing but bored dismissal in them. On top of her petite facial features, she wears a hard mask. She hates the world and everyone in it.

It isn't the first time that I've seen her in the courthouse. It's been about a month, but my memory is sometimes painfully sharp and she's hard to miss. I don't forget a face, and I haven't forgotten hers.

The judge bangs his gavel and begins his spiel to the defendant. The hearing regarding Declan Randolph's case is beginning.

Mr. Randolph has a long rap sheet for various drug charges including Trafficking, Distribution, and Possession. He's a career drug dealer currently being charged with Aggravated Murder. That's a jump up from the other crimes but not unheard of in his line of work.

The victim was his wife, and now it's the court's job to find out if he did it on purpose as an act of domestic violence or if he's another uneducated, loose-cannon drug dealer who didn't know the heat he was carrying.

Lawson PD caught this case but I'm here anyway because it happened in Rollins County. We merely have a working relationship, not a great one, but it doesn't matter. Declan's crimes are a part of a big problem here and that means I have an interest in them stopping.

I want the overdoses to stop and the senseless crime. I need to know where Declan got the drugs that killed his late wife. The person who can supply drugs like that is powerful and doesn't belong here. Possibly powerful enough to orchestrate an entire epidemic of violent crimes against the innocent people of Rollins.

Unfortunately, Randolph has already been in jail for eight

months, his trial date continues to be postponed due to the run-around the Defense keeps pulling to dismiss the evidence and the charges. They haven't even made it to the pre-trial and the Prosecution's case is crumbling.

I look toward the bench just as Declan peeks over his shoulder and across the bar to the woman sitting in front of me. She's eerily still, her head turned just enough to glare in his direction. He winks at her cheekily, cockily, but she doesn't react. Her posture doesn't shift and I imagine her glare doesn't either.

Who is she?

An old girlfriend?

The victim's family?

I catalog each person around the room, habitually.

The five young guys who are seemingly here to support Declan are mid-twenties, three Caucasians, and two Hispanics. An older man with darkened transition lenses slowly stands from the last row by the window, shuffling over to exit the courtroom early. My auxiliary deputy is peddling lightly from his right foot to his left. He's old, retired, and only working in the courts part-time for extra money. I don't mind because I didn't want to waste one of my full-timers on it.

The Defense Council is speaking in hushed tones while Prosecutor Fulton stands, addressing Judge Reisner directly. He's tense, whatever is happening is not going in his favor.

As the shoulders of the woman in front of me become even more rigid than before, I'm suddenly curious to find out her involvement.

And these days nothing piques my interest.

Chapter Two

Natalie

That bastard murdered my mother.

It's almost nine months to the day that I got a text message from my mom telling me that she and her husband, my "stepfather", were fighting. She sent me one final text dreadfully stating that she thought he might kill her.

I was in New York and at the time I thought it was another dramatic stream of texts that I'd normally receive when she relapsed. All I thought was that it was happening again, her short-lived sobriety was over and my stent of being away from home was coming to an end.

Except, when the messages stopped rolling in and I couldn't get her to respond at all, I knew something was wrong. Within a week I dropped everything tying me to New York City and I was driving home to Lawson. To my brother. The only reason that I refused to cut my mother off was because of him.

By the time I got home, it was too late. My mother had been found in their apartment, overdosed. The neighbor saw her lifeless body as she was letting my brother in the door with her spare key after school. Thankfully she shielded him from the sight.

I immediately took emergency custody of Dec, it wasn't even an option not to. He is my brother and he's mine now. I'll take care of him until the day I die, unlike our mother. I loved her, or the version of her not on drugs, but I'll never forgive her for putting us both through that lifestyle. He turned seven two weeks after her funeral service.

She had me when she was sixteen. She got pregnant with Dec seventeen years later. She was so strung out that she didn't realize she was pregnant until she was six months along. It's a miracle Dec was born without complications, though he was a month and a half premature.

I had long given up on my mother being maternal toward me, but I was determined to make her the best mom for Dec. I helped her move into a new apartment and made sure she stayed clean. Most of all, I kept Declan Randolph away from her. He was ten years younger than her, closer to my age than hers, and a real piece of shit.

They were married before Dec was born even though he was in and out of my mom's life, she insisted he was the father. She named him Declan Jr against my advice. To me, he's just Dec because he's nothing like his father.

Dec is good and kind. He's a smart boy with a gentle soul. He has friends at school and makes good grades. I love him more than I've ever loved anything. When he started first grade, things were good. At least, I thought. That's why I took the opportunity to spread my wings and go to New York.

Unfortunately, my mom took the opportunity to let Declan back into their life. She started using drugs, again. The fighting started, again.

Then she was gone.

Just like that, within a few months, Dec's whole world evaporated. A repeating record of my childhood except this time my mom's gone.

I want Declan Randolph to die in prison. I want him to die for his crimes and for what he did to my mom. I don't want him to ever come near Dec again. I'll fight to my very last breath to keep my brother safe.

The posse of drug heads and criminal thugs that support the man I despise are also on my hate list. They're just as bad. They've been complicit in his crimes for years. All of them can go to hell.

The prosecutor leans over the bar in front of me and motions me closer. "Don't be alarmed by the Defense's tactics. They'll try to dismiss everything. They would attempt to suppress the tie I'm wearing if they could." He rolls his eyes, and I nod, observing the dark gray suit he has on.

He's wealthy, whether from his job or elsewhere. He's been kind to me so far during this past few months of proceedings and I do my best not to wrinkle my nose at his brand of aftershave. It smells too strong, too spicy.

As stated, the defense lawyer stands and starts speaking directly to the judge. Another man, a look-alike version of Morgan Freeman if I had to compare him to someone. His voice is low and slow, but his eyes are direct and harsh.

The testosterone in this room is suffocating but I'm not easily phased. I'm not in the business of letting men intimidate me. Not anymore.

"We're motioning to suppress the phone communication between the deceased victim and her daughter. It's hearsay." My head snaps to the defense lawyer. My text messages directly from my mother might be thrown out.

"It's a direct quote from our victim your honor. It shows a history of conflict and motive," Prosecutor Fulton drones with annoyance. He seems bored by these proceedings and it rubs me the wrong way. My mother is dead but this is only another day for all of these big wigs.

They go back and forth for a few minutes but it's all too quick to understand, their language of the law flies over my head.

"The texts will be dismissed. Let's get on with it. Set a date for pre-trial next month." The judge knocks his gavel on the podium and that's it—no more arguments.

Everyone begins packing up their paperwork as if they couldn't care less. Because they don't care. None of this matters to these people. They'll get paid regardless. It makes me want to scream.

I sit utterly still until the room clears. I ignore Declan as he's led out of the room, not giving him the satisfaction of putting my eyes on him for another second.

I know I need to leave. Dec will be home from school soon, but I can't find the will to move. I tap my four-inch knock-off Louboutins on the bottom of the bar in front of me. In another life, I'd have real ones. I wouldn't have had to raise myself and I'd be happily fed from a silver spoon.

Standing to leave proves difficult when it feels like an anvil is weighing down my shoulders but I do it anyway and shrug on my coat. As I grab my plain black bag, another rip-off from an off-price street vendor in Brooklyn, I realize I'm not alone like I thought.

The very large cop is still sitting in the back row of the pew-like benches. He's hard to miss in his dark green uniform and bulky bulletproof vest. His various tools of the trade tacked

13

onto his chest and belt make him look stiff and even bigger than he already is.

His eyes flash briefly toward me as I pass, barely acknowledging my presence. His haircut is clean and sharp. He probably goes to the barber every two weeks and I haven't been able to afford a haircut in over a year.

I trim my dead ends in the mirror every other month and Dec's shaggy blonde hair is way overgrown. Funds have been tight since I moved back home. I had to find a job that would work around Dec's schedule but it doesn't give me many hours.

I can't afford a sitter. Our apartment only has one bedroom but Dec has clothes to wear, a coat, shoes that fit, and books for school. That's all that I care about. He'll be eight in a few months and I've been putting cash away slowly to afford to get him a bike.

I push through the heavy doors to enter the lobby and my steps falter, but only slightly. Declan's goons are standing there, waiting. I steer past them but have no luck ignoring them.

"Hey, Ice Queen. How's our boy doing?" One of them asks. I think they call him Zeek but I don't care enough to confirm. I need to get home before Dec.

"He's none of your concern." I smile smugly, only so they know they can't intimidate me. Ice Queen has been their nickname for me since I started keeping my mother away from Declan. Unfortunately for them, it gives me a sense of pride rather than a complex.

"Ah, but he is. Declan wants to know what his only son is up to. It's our job to find out." Zeek steps toward me, but I don't budge.

"I don't give a damn. Declan is no concern of mine."

"Really? Seems odd you keep showing up then. Maybe you have a crush on him." The other four standing with him snicker at his comment. I roll my eyes and take a deep breath.

"I'm here to make sure he stays right where he belongs. Or even better, maybe he'll get shanked in jail." I shrug. It hasn't been the first time I've had that wish.

"You're a little bitch, you know that?" Zeek steps further into my space, his face inches above mine.

My hands stay planted on my hips, but a big part of me wants to push him out of my bubble. I can't stand to have him this close, but I would never put my hands on him because I know he would press charges. I couldn't do that to Dec. I'm all he's got.

The doors to the side of us open with grandeur, the strength behind the push making both doors swing fully into the lobby. Both our heads snap to the imposing man striding out of the courtroom that we just vacated.

Now that he's standing, his height is ridiculous and he looks more like a GI-Joe than a street cop. His hair isn't the only sharp thing about him. He's all hard lines and edges. His eyes especially, zeroing in on Zeek.

Instead of saying anything about our obvious conflict, he sits on a chair against the wall and folds his arms across his bulky chest. Those cold eyes stare at Zeek with disinterest, hardly blinking, but the tilt to his head screams "Try me".

"What the fuck do you want, Paul Blart?" Zeek sneers in his direction. The cop doesn't react, but his non-reaction is enough. Zeek steps back out of my face and toward him.

Again, the cop doesn't even blink.

"Come to save the little girl from the big bad wolf?" His

immaturity makes his gaggle of geese laugh.

The cop's gaze pings to me but back to Zeek so quickly that I almost missed it. "She seems fine but you need to leave. No loitering in the lobby." His casual tone doesn't match the seriousness of his eyes.

"What the fuck ever," Zeek leans in, "Sheriff Malec." He finishes after reading his uniform.

Is this the Sheriff of Rollins County?

He doesn't flinch at Zeek's language and the lack of conflict spurs the group to turn and leave. Spewing more nonsense from their mouths as they go.

"I had it handled," I snap. Something deep inside of me can't stand a helping hand when I didn't ask for it. Or, maybe I was hoping to elicit a reaction from him when Zeek couldn't.

There isn't one.

He doesn't even shift in his seat. I take pride in making men uncomfortable and I hate to fail.

"I know."

The lack of interest in his voice grates at me. Cops don't scare me and I can't stand a hero complex.

Now, I'm in the mood to fight with someone and he is too boring to challenge me. I turn and stalk out of the courthouse as quickly as my heels will take me.

I hate cops. I hate drug dealers. I hate men.

They're all pigs. All of them.

Chapter Three

Jackson

"The Motion to Suppress the warrant used to search the Defendant's residence is granted." Judge Reisner pounds his gavel once, punitively. The murmuring in the courtroom increases as he rises from his seat and dismisses everyone. It's only been a week since the last Motion to Suppress Hearing.

The judge pulled everyone in for an emergency session because he was tired of this case being dragged out. It barely gave me enough time to look further into the victim of this case, Nicole Halstead, and just how dangerous Declan Randolph is.

Not only is he a drug dealer, he has a rap sheet stemming back to his adolescence. Vandalism, graffiti, and drug possession before he turned twenty years old, and it only gets worse from there. He even had a report made against him for Domestic Violence from ten years ago, though no charges were filed and he was never convicted of the crime. It shows there is a history of violence but unfortunately, in the eyes of the law, it doesn't count.

The defense attorney slaps Declan on the shoulder while

the prosecutor gathers his paperwork silently. The dark-haired woman who has become my companion on this side of the courtroom is frozen behind him with her spine locked straight. Although her head remains high, I know this is a hard blow.

I've been in and out of this courtroom with my own cases enough to tell when certain evidence is crucial to an investigation. This news is devastating for her and this case.

Natalie Halstead. The victim's daughter.

Her mother was killed by Declan's drugs and I suspect that she, more than anyone, wants to see Declan go down for his crimes. Even more than I do.

Those text messages from the last Motion to Suppress were crucial. That's how they obtained the search warrant that the judge just voided. Now, it's up to the prosecutor to make a strong argument without them.

He leans over the bar, speaking low enough that only she could hear. I don't know what he said, most likely giving her some false hope for the future of this case, but she snaps her head to look at him directly and he leans back like she might smack him.

She doesn't. Instead, she gathers her jacket and purse and storms out of the courtroom, but not before shooting unsolicited daggers in my direction.

I ignore her look of disdain because it gives me a chance to look at her fully for the first time this afternoon. A dark purple top with a v only low enough to show off her sharp collar bones. Black pants that fit like a second skin and the same heels from last time.

She's a knockout even though her appearance screams venomous, I can tell that her attitude problem isn't strong enough to keep people from staring at her.

I'm not staring at her. I'm only gathering information.

The same way that I observe every other person in this room and their behavior. Judge Reisner's restlessness with this case directly correlates with the months ticking down to his retirement. Prosecutor Fulton isn't nearly as invested in this case as he should be and I suspect his personal life is taking precedent. He hasn't stopped checking his phone since the judge dismissed us.

The punks from last time jump up and make their exit after Declan is led out of the courtroom, and I keep my head averted as if I'm preoccupied with something else. As soon as they're through the doors, I'm up out of my seat because I've also had a chance to look into Declan's associates. They're younger than the man on trial but following in his criminal footprints.

My goal was to exit behind them so they wouldn't see me coming but as I enter the lobby, a squat middle-aged woman with harsh highlights stops me, nearly putting a hand on my chest. "Sheriff, I have been hoping to run into you." Vanessa Porter, the late Sheriff Donahue's widow, steps into my path.

"Ma'am. What can I do for you?" She's been calling me incessantly for months and I've been avoiding her.

"Ma'am, oh so formal. I have wanted to bend your ear about some projects I was working on when my husband was in office. God rest his soul." She motions the shape of a cross over her heart.

Over her head, I can see Natalie and Zachariah Keller, street name Zeek, arguing again. I believe she can handle her own, but I don't like disturbances in my courthouse and Zeek has a warrant.

"Right, I'll have to get in touch to set up a time to meet. Excuse me, I have business to handle." I skirt past her, dismissing whatever response she has. Bee lining to the raised voices.

"It's only a matter of time before Declan is out of here and we're getting the boy back from you. You might as well stop fighting it!" Zeek barks at her, mere inches from her face.

"I will fight for Dec until the day I die you rat bastard," she replies calmly, with all the malice in her small body.

As entertaining as it is to watch her, I've heard enough.

"Zachariah, you're under arrest." I pull out my cuffs, grabbing his wrist in a vice grip and twisting it behind his back before he can pull away.

"What the fuck? Why?" He cries, tugging his arms anyway with no success.

"You have a warrant, failure to appear."

"Good going, dumb ass," Natalie goads him.

"Not helping," I grunt as I cuff his second wrist.

The huff that leaves her chest is razor-sharp. "I'm not here to help you, Sheriff Small Dick. I don't care if he fights you."

I have him secure so there isn't anything stopping my focus from settling completely on the woman who just snapped a heinous insult at me. I don't know whether I'm shocked or offended, but I'm too dumbfounded to respond. Sheriff Small Dick? What did I do to deserve that?

It doesn't matter, she turns on her heel and struts away without a care in the world. The confidence oozing out of that woman is something else.

"That's why we call her the Ice Queen. She's a fucking bitch," Zeek whines. I jerk his hands so he has to move along with me. I don't like that type of language. Not toward her, not toward anyone.

Plus, even I can tell there isn't anything icy about her. She's full of fire.

Chapter Four

Natalie

"I need you to consider that this case might not go how you want." The words the prosecutor told me after the judge dismissed the warrant are at the forefront of my thoughts, harassing me.

Of course, it isn't going how I want because Declan Randolph is still breathing. I want him lined up in front of a firing squad.

I'm grumbling about it and the incompetence of every man that I've encountered today when I pull into the gravel lot behind my apartment. Dec's bus will drop him off soon so I sit in my car in the heat until it does. Even in the south, it stays cold in the mountains early in the year. Not nearly as cold as New York was, but there's still a chill in the air.

I never expected to be stuck living in my hometown, I always had big dreams to travel until my mom got pregnant. I hate the fake niceties of people that you've known your whole life who judge you behind closed doors. I hate that there are only two semi-decent restaurants. I hate that the only apartment I could find is on the second floor above a paint shop. If the fumes kill me one day I'm suing. Or rather,

I'll tell Dec to sue so he can get a nice goose egg to start a new life.

A police car drives by as I'm staring at the road waiting for the yellow bus to pull up and it reminds me of Sheriff Small Dick. I was pretty proud of the little nickname that rolled off the top of my head.

When he didn't react, I wanted to scream. He's like a robot, completely emotionless, and all I want to do is get under his skin.

Twice now he has interrupted me when I'm standing up for myself. Twice he has tried to be a savior to someone who has not asked to be saved. It's clearly a part of his God complex. Save all the women and children first. Blah, blah, blah.

He's probably used to women throwing themselves at him for that very reason and it makes me want to puke. He comes near me and I want to stick my hands in his objectively perfect hair and fuck it up.

The bus arrives before I can go off on another tangent in my head and I meet Dec at the bottom of the metal staircase that leads up to our door. "Hey, buddy. How was school?"

"It was okay, our class didn't get recess because some kids were being loud during attendance." His little shoulders are slumped as we ascend the stairs. My sweet baby brother and his big heart. It kills me that he misses out on fun because of some stupid kids.

"Well, it happens. I'm sure you'll get to play tomorrow," I assure him. I'm never as cynical to him as I am in my head.

"Yeah, I hope so. Can I have a snack in front of the TV today?" He asks as he dumps his Spider-Man backpack into the corner of the entryway. I don't have the heart to disappoint, so I agree and he gallops to the kitchen, completely forgetting his not-so-great school day.

I hope he can always keep that spirit. Let the bad roll off your back and move on. I want him to have a good future and to accomplish everything he wants. My only dream now is for him to accomplish his.

* * *

When I got the call from Prosecutor Fulton for another emergency hearing, I knew I'd have to leave straight for work. Normally I'd try to get someone to cover my shift, but I only had a day's notice and none of my coworkers are that generous. I don't blame them, we all have chaotic lives.

I hurry up the steps of the Rollins County Courthouse, tightening the belt on my only long coat. It hits mid-thigh and shows a lot of leg, especially since I'm wearing black nylons. I keep one hand pressed to the bottom hem to keep it from fluttering open in the wind while the other clasps the lapels together.

Just as I'm about to body check the door open since my hands are hard at work to conceal my work uniform, someone opens it for me with an arm stretched high above my head.

They hold the door ajar while I enter the lobby and take a second to correct my disheveled wind-blown hair. "Thank yo-" I start to say to the kind stranger until I see who it is. "Oh."

"Ma'am." He nods politely before breezing past me, his wrinkle-free black polo is stretched across his chest at my eye level.

24

"Don't ma'am, me," I retort, attempting to match pace with him. I don't know who entered us into the silent competition to get through the metal detectors first, but I'm going to win.

He steps up to the conveyor belt and pauses, so I cut him in line. I dump my purse into a tub and shuffle in front of him. He mumbles something but not loud enough for me to hear.

Not my fault that only one of us was prepared. The older-than-dirt security guard ushers me through the metal detector but it beeps. Shit.

"It's the buckle on my coat," I explain to him. He only raises his eyebrows and waves me to the side while Sheriff Small Dick steps around the metal detector without ever emptying his pockets.

As he begins waving his handheld wand around me like a sorcerer, I try my best to conceal my frustration. I don't have time for this. It beeps again, not on my coat.

"Miss, you need to remove the coat."

"What, no, I can't." My heart thunders in my chest. This is bad.

"I insist, or you'll have to leave the premises." The old man waits patiently for my response, though I can tell I won't be able to sweet talk my way out of this. I have to get to the courtroom. The Sheriff stands off to the side, waiting for me or waiting to see what happens. I'm not sure.

With my head held high and my back turned to the rest of the lobby, I let my belt go and flash what's underneath to the security guard. His mouth falls open and I'm convinced a fly buzzes in while he remembers he's supposed to be searching me.

"You're free to go on, miss. Thank you," he says a little too appreciatively while I roll my eyes. I stomp across the tiled floors, loudly clacking in my heels, cursing this day.

"What just happened?" The Sheriff asks from behind me, his long strides catching up to mine quickly.

"None of your business." He cuts in front of me before I can go through the tall wooden doors that lead to the courtroom.

"Natalie, this is my courthouse. It is my business."

The use of my first name like he knows me, or that he's sly for figuring it out makes me want to slap the smug look off his face. I mean his face looks as stoic as normal, but I imagine on the inside he's feeling smug.

"If that was true, you would have pulled me aside back there. You didn't because you have no real power. It's all in your little head. So, leave me alone." I cross my arms, tapping my foot obnoxiously because he won't take the hint and move out of my way. That's when I notice his downcast gaze.

From his height advantage over me, his line of sight is aimed directly down the front of my coat. I glance down, already suspecting what he is seeing and I balk. For Christ's sake. The lapels of my coat have separated and he can see exactly what I was hiding. A blood-red bustier.

"Yes. I have tits. Now, move!" I shove past him, righting my coat and wrapping it tightly around myself.

I can't make myself look him in the eyes but I refuse to be embarrassed. I'm doing what I need to do to ensure my brother is taken care of. Fuck anyone's opinion.

I plop down in my normal seat right behind the bar with a huff, rolling my neck to release the tension. Could this day get any worse?

Prosecutor Fulton enters and unlike the other times, he ignores me. Whatever. It means I don't need to hide my dislike for his overpowering odor. The judge enters and they run through the motions like they do each time.

I can feel *him* behind me and it irks me that I know he's there. Even worse, he knows what I'm hiding underneath my coat. Only paying customers get to witness it and it's the only way I can stomach it.

The judge starts speaking again so I focus in front of me, forcefully ignoring the aggravating pervert behind me with the superiority complex.

"What's the decision, Prosecutor?" Judge Reisner folds his hands in front of him, waiting patiently.

"We're offering the defendant a deal. If he agrees to supply information to the Rollins County Sheriff's Office, he can plead guilty to Involuntary Manslaughter. With his time served."

My jaw unhinges, dropping in disbelief. They drone about stipulations to the deal but I stop hearing them.

Declan's not going to be charged for murdering my mother.

Chapter Five

Jackson

I've been shot at four times in my career, hit in the vest once, and almost blown up by a bomb. But, when the woman six rows in front of me slowly turns her head 180 degrees to glare at me, I think it's the closest to death that I've ever been.

If it were possible, she'd have flames rolling off her back. She's pissed.

I knew the prosecutor would present the deal this afternoon and I knew that Natalie would likely have a problem with it, but I think I underestimated the power of her fury. The licks of it are reaching me all the way in the back row.

I wish I could say it scared me but it doesn't. It's worse, it intrigues the hell out of me. She's been a question mark since I first saw her but then I saw down her coat to what she was hiding underneath and it turned into full-blown curiosity.

All I can see in my mind is the two silver piercings that stared at me from the valley between her breasts. Nothing has held my attention in months but that did. As if I don't have bigger concerns in my life, I can't stop thinking about her cleavage.

She storms up the aisle and to my row as the rest of the courtroom disperses. "You. You son of a bitch," she lashes at me. More than a few heads turn in our direction, including my auxiliary deputy on the other side of the room. I wave him off.

"The prosecutor didn't have a case, he was going to lose if this went to trial," I attempt to appease her but I can see that it's not working. The poison she possesses in her soul is leeching out, attempting to suffocate me.

Her shiny black heel plants itself closer to me but I stay seated. Despite her anger, I have no reason to stand. Towering over her wouldn't benefit this situation, she can yell all she wants.

"That man murdered my mom. He did it on purpose and now he's getting a free pass. Do you even realize what you've done?" She seethes her venom at me but her eyes are filled with something deeper than anger.

There's fear in their dark depths.

My gut sinks with the realization. Prosecutor Fulton warned me that she'd be opposed to any type of deal but I stood my ground because I felt it was our best chance of getting more information, even if it meant he got off with lesser charges. I'm only doing my job but if I could do it properly then I wouldn't need Declan as an informant in the first place.

Now, I can see the thought of him being released is frightening her in some way. And, that bothers me.

"You can be mad at me all you want. Other people helped make this decision. We need to close cases. It's the way it goes sometimes." I shrug, trying to portray the indifference that I'm not actually feeling, but it only pisses her off more.

"If that man gets out of jail and tries to get custody of my brother, I'm going to make your life hell, you heartless piece of shit!"

I clench my jaw to stop myself from reacting. She knows how to hit below the belt, I'll give her that. Before I can attempt another shot at making this right, she blows out of the room like a tornado, full of fury and chaos.

Maybe she's the karma that I deserve for being rude to Whitney. Getting metaphorically kicked in the balls by a woman is way worse than any punch from a grown man.

* * *

"You understand that by accepting this deal, you agree to give me useful information, correct? If you refuse to do so, the deal is forfeit and you'll be fighting a maximum sentence." Declan Randolph is sitting across from me in a striped jumpsuit in the meeting room of the Rollins County Jail.

"I understand, yadda, yadda," he drones. This guy is a real piece of work.

"Where did you get the drugs?" I ask the question that has been bugging me since I learned of Declan's case. If someone is supplying deadly substances to people in my county then I need to know who and how much they have.

"I don't know."

I take a breath before I respond. I've dealt with people worse than this, he is not going to be the one that makes me lose my cool. He's not worth it.

"Declan, you have one chance. Is that the answer you're

going with?"

"The pills dropped from the sky. That's my final answer." He shrugs.

"You're prepared to serve the maximum sentence for Aggravated Murder by not complying with the terms of the deal, correct?"

"Well, hold on now, Sheriff. I believe my lawyer said there isn't a murder case." He looks at me smugly. He has no interest in this deal, he's wasting my time. He's still planning to have all of his charges dropped one way or another, that's the only explanation for the lack of self-preservation in this room right now.

The hair at his temples is balding and for being around my age, he looks much older. Despite trying to act indifferent to his circumstances, I can tell from his face that he's tired. It's exhausting to keep one eye open while you're in jail, surrounded by people that you can't trust. People that he's probably wronged in the past.

"Tell me what you know or I walk out of here and you go to trial." I fold my hands on the table as relaxed as I can. He's not going to get the tension from me like he wants.

He huffs. "You're lookin' at me, but you should be lookin' at bigger fish. I'm just a little fish." He pinches his pointer finger and thumb together to accentuate his point.

"Obviously." I know Declan isn't my criminal mastermind just by looking at him.

"Ahh. Maybe you should ask me *who* gave me the drugs, not *where* they came from."

This joker wants to play word games and I am in no mood. "Who gave you the drugs?"

"Oh, no. I can't tell you that. That would get me killed."

When I interrogated Thomas Jameson about his extremist group and the 5k bombing a couple of months ago, he had said the same thing. He couldn't tell me who funded his operation because it would get him killed.

"Killed by who?" I ask, impatiently.

He tsks at me. "Get me released, now, and then I'll tell you." He winks.

"Do you know Thomas Jameson?" I ask, hoping that even the simplest thread to these dangerous crimes will lead me somewhere.

Jameson is in this same jail, only he's awaiting to be transferred to prison because he's already been convicted for his crimes. His case was incredibly cut and dry, unlike Declan's.

He shrugs his bony shoulders and I can feel his ego rolling off him in waves.

"This is a small area Declan. Criminals run in the same circles. Everyone who lives here knows about the 5k bombing. Do you know anything related to the bombing?"

"I don't mess with explosives, Sheriff. I'm hurt that you think I would." He feigns offense but smirks.

I hate lifetime criminals like Declan. They have no moral code or sense of decency. They're willing to hurt anyone without remorse.

I place a piece of paper down as a last attempt to get anything useful from him. It's a compilation of photographs of our missing person cases but only those reported before he was arrested.

"Did you supply any of these people with drugs?"

He shrugs. "I don't think I should answer a question like that, Sheriff. It seems like... Hmm... What would my lawyer call it? Ah, entrapment." He eases the paper away from his side of the table with a single pointer finger.

"Information is what will get you out of jail, Declan. You haven't given me anything. You're going to rot in here."

"We'll see." The tilt of his lips is eerily confident.

It takes all my reserve to stand up and exit the room without tossing my chair across the suffocating space. This was pointless. Every lead is turning inside out before I have a chance to make a real connection to anything.

I thought I was getting somewhere but Declan Randolph is useless, and I have no other direction to go.

Someone in this county is orchestrating a human trafficking ring, funding extremists, and orchestrating a drug trade. I need to figure out if it's the same person and who the hell it is.

I don't care what happens to Declan Randolph but now I've stuck my foot into innocent people's lives. Natalie's words haunt me, and the fear in her eyes is stuck at the forefront of my mind. I might have just assisted in letting a criminal back onto the streets and there is a kid involved.

I slam the door to my suburban as I get in. I don't deserve the Sheriff tag branded on the body or any of the stripes. I thought I was equipped to handle this job but I'm failing every day that I don't put someone in handcuffs for their crimes against innocent people.

My phone rings and Vanessa Porter's name is on the screen so I hit ignore. I might as well have 'Do Not Answer' as her contact name since I always screen her calls. I'm not in the mood to hear about the old corrupt Sheriff's ideas for Rollins County or his flippant wife's fundraising ideas. The politics of this job are not important to me but I have to deal with

33

people like her every day.

The first time I ever spoke to her, she swore her husband's death was suspicious, that he'd never kill himself. She also swore that she didn't know he was involved in any illegal activity and failed to mention that they were one stack of paperwork away from a divorce.

Unlucky for her, since his death was ruled a suicide she didn't get to collect his life insurance. She also lost both of her brothers that day, both of which were menaces to society. I sympathize with her losses but I do not feel sorry that they're dead.

I should call her back only to appease her, but not today. Today I'm going to drive around until someone needs me, hoping that the answers I need will fall out of the sky like Declan's drugs.

Chapter Six

Natalie

"What was your favorite part?" I ask Dec as we walk side by side down the sidewalk, the street lamps guiding our way home. It was dollar movie night at the Olde Time Cinema downtown, but one dollar turned to fifteen pretty quickly after popcorn, slushies, and cookie dough bites were added to the bill.

"I liked it when the mummies were chasing everybody." He giggles, his little boy humor at full peak when it comes to scary, creepy, and grimy things. His happiness is worth the money spent, though I admit I didn't mind watching two hours of Brendan Fraser gallivanting through Egypt and saving the day.

It's a nice distraction from real life. I haven't had the heart to explain the entirety of the situation about his dad to him yet. Dec knows that our mom died from drugs. He's too smart for his age and he knew she had a problem that his friend's moms didn't have.

He knows that his dad gave her the drugs that killed her but not that I think he did it on purpose. He's so young, I've wanted to protect him from the dark realities that I can. He's dealing with the loss of two parents, no need to make it worse for him just yet with the full details.

Truthfully, his relationship with Declan was surface-level. He'd show up on Dec's birthday sometimes, and once or twice for Christmas. He would give him a gift and Dec would think it was the coolest thing ever, but he also knew that his dad wasn't around like he should be. Dec missed him a lot and still does.

He's young, hopeful, and sees the good in people. My mom would tell him elaborate lies like Declan was in the Everglades hunting crocodiles. Or, he was learning to fly airplanes in Alaska. I hated it, but it wasn't my decision to make. When Dec would ask me, I tried to stick as close to the truth as I could. Declan's job and his friends were keeping him away.

Being a drug dealer doesn't equate to a good family life and he was selfish for procreating in the first place. So was my mom.

I'm glad I have Dec, but I can't imagine what his life would be like if I didn't exist.

Would he have been taken from them? If things were different would Declan have tried to steal Dec away from my mom?

Sometimes I wonder if I wasn't around if my mom would have gotten her shit together without me. Maybe my presence was a hindrance to her sobriety because I was a scapegoat. She knew that I would take care of Dec when she couldn't.

That's why I went to New York. I decided to give her a chance to do it on her own and it was the worst decision of my life. But, in some twisted way, I think I was born so many years ahead of Dec just so I'd be around to take care of him.

At least I have that to hold onto. Neither of us has been

subjected to the system that would inevitably fail us like so many other orphans.

"Do you think you still want dinner when we get home or are you full from your snacks?"

"Umm. I might be hungry again," he says with uncertainty. He's still a little boy but he's growing fast and I am not ready for full-blown puberty to hit. I hope I get a few more years of my little brother being smaller than me but he's catching up quickly.

I have no idea how I'll handle it when he does turn into a man. I hardly know how to raise a child, let alone a man. One that will be good and kind. Someone who will take care of others and not hurt them.

"How about I make you one of my famous cheeseburgers?" It's his favorite and I always keep the ingredients on hand. I love to cook and I love when people eat my food. It's a shame that I'll only ever get to put that to use at home but Dec's a good customer.

"Yeah, that sounds good! It kind of smells like a barbecue out here already." He giggles. "Or, a bonfire. I think I want some marshmallows."

He continues to ramble on about other things that he could put on a stick and make over a fire as my senses pick up on what he's talking about. It does smell like a campfire out here... I guess there is some smoke in the air. I thought maybe it was fog.

We round the last street corner that takes us toward the little gravel lot below our apartment and that's when I see it. Smoke is billowing out the windows of our apartment, flooding the street lights and making it even harder to see this late at night.

My feet stay rooted to the sidewalk, frozen in disbelief. This isn't real.

We already have nothing, this can't be happening to us.

But, it is.

"Dec, stay here!" I shout at him, taking off and running toward our little home.

"Natalie! Stay back, honey! I already called 911," the neighbor from the next business over shouts at me from the street. I ignore her. Our life cannot go up in flames. It can't!

All of the stuff we own is in there. The court paperwork, guardianship papers, Dec's birth certificate, and our pictures. Our memories. I can't lose them. It's his identity, his life. I know what it's like to grow up without memories.

My mom lost my birth certificate and my social security card numerous times. She moved us around so much that I couldn't keep more than a handful of photos as evidence of my childhood. Dec can't go through that, I refuse.

I bound up the metal staircase, grabbing the door handle idiotically before checking it, but luckily it's only warm and doesn't burn my hand.

The basic principles of fire safety circulate in my mind but I can't be bothered to listen. As soon as my key jimmies the lock, I push the door open wide, getting hit full force with black smoke. It fills my lungs and burns my eyes, momentarily stunning me.

My only thought is to drop to my knees and crawl. A sane person would turn around and leave, but I'm not sane when it comes to my baby brother.

I drag my body across the carpet needing to get to the hallway. It's one box. All of the important stuff is in one box in the hall closet but each breath in is like needles down my throat, stabbing my lungs.

The coughing starts and it doesn't stop. I can't keep myself from sucking in lungfuls of putrid air. Hundreds of tiny needles penetrate my throat and chest from the inside out, desperate for clean air. There is none.

I'm diving deeper into the hellscape instead of away from it, stubbornly guiding my way to the closet by memory because my eyes burn too badly to keep open.

I don't see fire or feel the heat of it, I'm only drowning in smoke. Our apartment is tiny which means there is only one place it could be coming from. Dec's room.

Poor Dec. He's going to be so upset. All of his toys, his clothes. They're going to be ruined. I don't know if the tears streaming down my face are from the smoke or the guilt, but I don't cry, ever. It has to be the smoke.

I'm within arm's reach of the closet, my fingertips brush against the bottom lip of the door when I'm vaulted backward. My body slides against the dated shag carpet of the hallway as I'm tugged from behind by my ankles. "You have to get out!" A muffled voice shouts at me, dragging me back toward the living room.

"No!" I try to fight it but I am no match for the strength pulling me out of the hallway. I flip onto my back, kicking my legs out, and connect with a stiff firefighter's uniform.

"Are you stupid, lady? The place is on fire!" The mumbled shout lashes out at me.

The coughing overtakes me again and I can't respond, I can't fight. He drags me far enough into the living room that he can manage to grab one of my arms and throw me over his shoulder like a rag doll.

Like every other terrible moment in my life, I'm helpless to do anything but suffer. Powerless to the forces acting against me.

I beat on his back until my palms go numb. He has no idea how important that box is. He has no idea how hard I've had to fight for my brother already and now it's only going to be harder. I cough and wheeze, desperately wishing I had the lung capacity to scream.

This isn't fair. None of it's fair.

Chapter Seven

Jackson

"What in the hell were you thinking?" I direct my question at the blanket-wrapped woman that I'm furious with. I was almost home for the night when I got the call about a structure fire. I detoured here immediately in case the emergency crews needed backup.

Luckily the fire units responded quickly, working to subdue the fire in record time. The paramedics were blocking my view of the resident who dumbly went inside a burning building before I finally got a chance to see who it was. Natalie Halstead. The thorn in my side that wreaks havoc wherever she goes.

"Why are you here?" She removes her oxygen mask to speak, giving me a full view of her soot-stained face and hands, as well as the pissed-off glare that I'm becoming accustomed to.

"It's my job to be on scene. It's their job," I indicate to the fire engines, "to go into burning buildings," I snap. "What the fuck were you doing?" I shout louder than I intended and the outburst stuns me so badly that I practically stumble backward.

I never raise my voice.

Her eyes are round with just as much surprise, but when she removes the mask again, she's leveling me with another sinister look. "Awh, is Sheriff Small Dick afraid that he was going to find me dead? Too bad for you, you can't get rid of me that easy." She rolls her eyes, righting the oxygen over her face.

"Nat." I exhale, roughly. I don't even know how to begin to explain that I don't care how much she dislikes me. I wouldn't want to see her get hurt. I'm not that type of person.

"Don't call me that. No one calls me that," she bites out her words through the plastic. Before I have a chance to tell her she messed up by telling me that, because now it's a tool to annoy her, a little boy with yellow blonde hair pops around the doors to the ambulance.

"Look, sissy, they gave me a helmet." He giggles. His genuineness is pure and dissipates all of the anger in the air. "Oh, hi," he says shyly, noticing me for the first time.

"Hi, buddy. That is a cool helmet." I crouch to his level to admire it with him. At nearly 6'4, I've had the issue of scaring children with my size.

"Yeah. I thought so. The firefighters saved my sister. She was trying to save our box." He shrugs and I look at her. Her eyes stay averted but I notice her jaw is locked.

"What kind of box?" I ask the boy.

"Our memory box. Has all my papers. Pictures. My secret security card."

"He means his social security card," she adds from beside us.

"Oh. I see, so all the important stuff that makes you, you."

"Yep." He pops the 'p' on his word. Then smirks at himself for doing so.

42

I glance at Natalie and she's looking at me strangely, without the usual disdain. The sudden change makes me nervous as if she's trying to get my guard down. My hand hovers toward the holster on my hip, ensuring my gun's secure because I wouldn't put it past her to shoot me with my own weapon.

"What's the prognosis then? Are you okay?" I ask her to break the staring contest we're suddenly having.

"I'm fine." Except she starts coughing, painfully hard and loud enough that one of the paramedics jogs over to check on her.

"We're going to transport you to the hospital," the young paramedic says. She looks like she's still in high school and a little intimidated by Natalie's strong personality.

"What?" She and the little boy say at the same time.

"I'm sorry, it's protocol. Smoke inhalation is super dangerous. Your lungs could suffer if you don't get the right medical care," she explains meekly, pulling her stethoscope onto her ears.

Natalie lowers the blanket off her shoulders to allow the girl to check her lungs but all I can think about is her coat slipping open the other day and that red lace staring back at me. The piercing is still haunting me, too.

Today she's wearing a thick, frumpy sweater. It's not appealing in the slightest but it doesn't help to keep my eyes from wandering over her. It looks too big and distinctly masculine. She's wearing a man's sweater and I am annoyed that I noticed. Or, that I care.

No, I don't care.

"What about me?" The boy asks on trembling lips, looking at his sister with round fearful eyes.

I look to her because it is her brother after all, but I see fear in those eyes too. It's the same as when she was yelling at me in the courtroom, the common denominator for her fear is clearly her brother.

"What is your name, buddy?" I ask, still squatting to his level.

"Declan, but my friends call me Dec."

"Can I call you, Dec?"

"I don't know. I just met you, how do I know you're my friend?"

"Ah, smart kid. Well, I'm a police officer. The Sheriff, actually, it's my job to keep you safe. Could that be a start?"

"Where's your badge? All cops have badges."

I unzip my coat then ultimately decide to shrug it all the way off my shoulders so he can see my uniform. I unclip the badge from my shirt and hand it to him. "You can hold onto it, okay? That way if you ever need anything, you can tell anyone that I am your friend and they'll get a hold of me."

I don't know why I told him that. Maybe because I know who his father is. Or maybe because I've already been hearing quips from the fire chief in my ear, advising on the radio that it might be arson. Either way, I want this kid to be protected by someone.

"Here, I don't want you to get cold." I drape my Sheriff's jacket around him and roll the sleeves up to his wrists before he does a little spin to admire himself.

"Look, sissy." He's smiling big and I can't help but reflect it until I look at Natalie and notice the deadpan stare being leveled at me.

"Very cool, bud. Hey, will you go let our neighbor know that I'm okay? I can see her worrying from over here." Natalie motions to the older woman standing just behind the yellow tape.

"Sure." He takes off, proudly showing the woman his shiny new badge as he reaches her then spinning to show her the SHERIFF logo on his back.

"You shouldn't have done that." The familiar hateful tone is back and in full force.

"Done, what?"

"Don't get his hopes up that you're going to be his friend or that you are going to be around. He doesn't need another man to disappoint him in his life." Her words are like venom, but I know they aren't truly directed toward me. Declan Randolph has done a number on this family. The kid definitely doesn't deserve the hand he was dealt.

Natalie on the other hand, I don't know. She aggravates me enough that I don't quite feel sorry for her like I do the kid.

"Who said that I wouldn't be around? You live in Rollins County. I am the Rollins County Sheriff. Are you planning on going somewhere?" I throw back at her.

"Don't start with me, Small Dick. You know what I mean. If he thinks you are his friend and then you only show up during emergencies, he's going to associate his friends with bad things that happen to him. Leave us alone."

"Why do you automatically assume that I am a terrible person? Does it bother you that I might be telling the truth? That I have every intention of sticking around to keep that boy safe?"

"Why would you? I'm here. I'm taking care of him like I always have. We don't need you." She coughs through her final word but I can hear the anger regardless. This woman drives me crazy.

45

"Um, miss, we need to go, now." The paramedic is shuffling her feet awkwardly after watching our verbal wrestling match.

As soon as the words are fully out of her mouth, I see the fear again that I saw a few minutes ago. I'd almost believe that she has an aversion to hospitals if it weren't for her next question. "What about my brother?"

"Well, we can't transport a minor unless he's the patient. Is there someone who can take him?" The silence that follows is eerie.

She responds, "No." At the same time, I say, "Yes."

"What? No." She looks at me like I have three heads.

"I can give him a ride. Let him hit the lights. Distract him for a few minutes before I meet you at the hospital." Simple. It is an easy solution, she should be grateful.

"No chance. You could be a child molester."

This woman never quits. "Why would you think that? Why do you always assume the worst?"

"It's easy to assume the worst when you're always handed the worst."

The frustration of this conversation is going to give me a stroke. Luckily I'm saved from a gasket completely blowing when Dec skips over and skids to a stop next to us.

"Okay, Dec. Here's the deal, buddy. We're going to take my car, we're going to grab you some food and then we'll meet your sister at the hospital. Sound good?" I ask him, completely undermining his sister who is shooting more lasers at me with her eyes.

"Yay! I want a cheeseburger!"

"Great, my favorite." I glance at Natalie who has yet to say anything, realizing that she will do anything to shield her brother from whatever harsh realities that have happened to her in her life that have made her so pessimistic. Her eyes are cold and hard, glaring at me.

"Your sister knows, deep, deep down that you are going to have the best time with me. So, give her a hug. We'll catch up to her in about an hour. If we get lost for some reason," I say pointedly, speaking to her with my head cocked to the side so she really understands these next words. "She can send out the National Guard to look for us because I know she'll do whatever it takes to keep you safe." I finish sternly.

She huffs and looks away. I got her. She knows that I wouldn't do any harm to Dec and she's annoyed that she knows it. The paramedics start readying the ambulance to leave and I back up to give them space, putting my hands on Dec's shoulders so he stays put too.

Before they can close the doors, she leans forward from her seat. "Hey, Dec. Can you tell me how many fire trucks are here?"

He immediately stretches on his toes to start counting, looking off to the side and the rest of the commotion, while she flips me the bird.

This woman is going to kill me.

"See you at the hospital, fireball." I salute her by scratching my nose with my middle finger. Steam blows out of her ears as they shut the doors.

Chapter Eight

Natalie

58 minutes later, Dec and the big oaf accompanying him come strolling into my hospital room. He waited until two minutes before his hour was up on purpose just to goad me. I know it.

"Look, Natalie, I got a GI Joe with my kid's meal." Of course, he did. The GI Joe look-alike smirks smugly from the doorway while Dec shows me his new toy excitedly.

All I want to do is squeeze him, my sweet baby brother. He doesn't even realize how brave he's been tonight. I hated the idea of leaving his side and I hate to admit that the sheriff did help me out. I don't know what I would have done with Dec if I had to leave him with someone else. I have no one.

"Thank you," I whisper over Dec's head, but I'm not mature enough to look him in the eye.

"I'm sorry, what was that?" He asks just as immaturely. "I was almost blown up by a bomb a few months back, my hearing is a little messed up." He cups his ear in an exaggerated fashion to irk me.

"I'm not saying it again, forget it." I ignore the comment about the bomb. I didn't know that he had been there. Our apartment is only a block from where the blast went off.

It scared us but luckily we were far enough away from the damage.

"What did the doctor say?" He plops a brown bag with grease stains on my bedside tray. I ignore it.

"He wants me to stay overnight to be monitored and do a breathing treatment. If my lungs look okay tomorrow morning then they'll discharge me." I look at Dec as I say it so he knows that I won't be here forever.

"You got lucky," Sheriff Small Dick mumbles to me, not drawing attention to himself as Dec plays with his toy on the window sill.

"Really? I feel unlucky as hell, but thanks." I fold my arms over my chest like a child.

"You're welcome," he responds with fake niceness. Ugh, he is infuriating.

"You can leave."

"What about Dec?"

"What about him?"

"He can't stay here." He ambles around the small open space in my room, not caring to look me in the eyes as he speaks.

"Why not?"

"Because he's a kid. It's a hospital."

"Obviously, but what do you suggest that I do? I'm stuck here and he has nowhere else to go," I whisper-shout.

"He can stay with me tonight." He shrugs as if it's a no-brainer.

"You're insane."

He blows out a deep breath of frustration and crosses his arms over his chest, mirroring me. "This, again. Really?"

"Why would he go with you?" We're completely mimicking each others' stances, behaving too stubbornly for our ages.

"So, he doesn't have to stay here. I have the room. I live in a clean house. I'm not a fu-" He cuts himself off before he drops an f-bomb like he did earlier.

I was shocked when he yelled at me at the scene of the fire. I didn't expect it. He's been a brick wall every other time I've been around him.

"I'm not some pervert, criminal, or bandit that's going to hurt your brother."

I got under his skin with the pedophile comment earlier. Unfortunately, I am not feeling the satisfaction I thought I would for finally getting to him. I'm too exhausted and worried about Dec. He's right. Dec shouldn't stay here and I hate that he's right.

"How can I trust you?" I ask genuinely. My chest hurts, my throat's unquenchable, and I'm too tired to fight, mostly.

He pulls a slim wallet from his front left pocket and tosses two cards onto my bed, on top of my legs. I pick up his driver's license first, and then his Sheriff's ID, examining them closely.

Jackson Malec. His first name is Jackson. I didn't know that, nor care.

His hair is of course, perfect, in both photos. Cleanly shaven on the sides and longer on top. Barely long enough to keep pushed back. He probably rolls out of bed, slides his fingers over his scalp, and is good to go. Even without smiling in his photos, you can tell how authentically good-looking he is and it's nauseating. He's probably had everything just like that handed to him his entire life.

"Take a picture of both. It has my address. My height, and weight. My law enforcement credentials. Do you want my social? It's 232-"

"I get it, chill. I don't have a pen, anyway."

"Here is my phone number," he grabs a pen out of his vest pocket and writes his number on the back of his business card. He throws it on the bed with the other cards. I notice that he added his social security number, too.

"What if I want to talk to Dec?"

"Anytime you want."

I study him and the cards, snapping a picture of all of them with my phone. He stares up at the ceiling like he's praying for patience but doesn't say anything. "He has school in the morning."

"I'll take him."

"Why?" The disbelief in my voice cannot be hidden. I can't fathom why he is so willing to help us.

"Because he's too young to drive…"

This fucker wants me to fight him. Clearly, he has a death wish. "Yes, Jackson Small Dick, I know that. Why are you doing all of this?"

"Dec is my friend. This is what friends do. Now, eat your food. Get some beauty sleep because you need it." He doesn't even humor me by looking in my direction after that little dig. If he did, he'd get both of my middle fingers this time.

"You're a child, do you know that?"

"No, you can see that I am a 32-year-old man. You can reference the picture of my ID again if you miss my face after we leave." He puts his cards away, avoiding seeing my locked jaw.

"Give us a minute. I'm not asking." I bark at him. He looks at me finally, nodding his head before stepping out of the room. I ignore the pity in his eyes.

"Hey, Dec. You're going to have a sleepover at Jackson's house. Are you okay with that?" I look at my brother closely,

51

trying to gauge his response.

"Without you?"

"Yeah. He'll take you to school tomorrow."

"Okay."

"Just, okay?" I ask, softly.

"I like him but I'm sad you can't come." He shrugs his little shoulders.

"I know but I'll be okay. The doctors will get me out of here quickly. Then we'll be back to normal tomorrow."

"Where will we live?"

"I don't know but I'll figure it out. I always do, don't I?" I hug him tightly, hoping like hell it's not a lie.

Chapter Nine

Jackson

I step into the hospital with steel in my spine, preparing for the battle that I'm about to partake in at 8:30 in the morning. My house guest was a delight, the complete opposite of his sister. I sent him off to school this morning with a belly full of donuts and a flash of my cruiser lights, making him and his friends shout excitedly as they ran inside the school.

Natalie, however, has probably been fueling up all night to kick me in the teeth as soon as I walk through this door. Except, her back is turned when I walk in. She's dressed and looks ready to leave, sitting atop her blankets.

I place a cup of coffee down gently on her table, waiting for her to strike. It's supposed to be a cushion. A peace offering before we start this back and forth, but she still doesn't turn around. "Are you good to go?"

She doesn't respond, staring blankly at the windows that harshly light the room. I walk around her bed to see her straight on and her face is pale. Her normally darkly lined eyes are bare and hollow. She obviously didn't get any sleep last night. She's staring vacantly through me as if I'm not even here.

"Nat?"

"Go where?" She sighs. All the usual fire is gone. She didn't even react to me using the nickname she seemingly hates.

"I can take you to a hotel. Until you get on your feet."

"I can't afford that. I'm barely getting by as is. Now I'll need to replace all of Dec's stuff that got ruined."

"You didn't have renter's insurance?"

She huffs a sad laugh in response. "No. I didn't even realize that I needed it. I'm so fucking stupid."

She's not my favorite person. She drives me mad, but I don't like this side of her. I'll throw an insult or two at her but I don't like it when she does it to herself. It's not as satisfying.

"You'll figure it out. You always do, right? That's what you told Dec last night."

"You were listening?"

"I was only making sure you didn't advise him to put a frog in my bed or something." My attempted humor hardly makes her blink. I was hoping for an eye roll.

She blows a long breath out and stands up, but immediately sits back down. "I don't know what to do."

"I'm taking you to a hotel. The Sheriff's Department can cover it for a while. We have extra funds for situations like this. Consider it your taxes at work."

"How do you know if I even pay my taxes?"

"I know you would never take the chance of being arrested for tax evasion and leaving Dec to fend for himself." That snaps her out of her stupor. Her eyes flick to mine and she looks at me for the first time since my arrival.

"Was he okay?" She asks even though she already spoke to him on the phone.

"Yeah. He was fine. Kids are resilient." She nods her head, almost looking at me appreciatively until the nurse walks in and she blinks. The look is replaced by her usual disdain and I question if I imagined the sincerity before.

"Do you know where you're going, dear?" The nurse asks, politely. They must've already discussed this issue earlier.

"I'm taking her to a hotel. Are we good to go?"

"Yes, Sheriff. Here's the discharge papers." She hands them over, patting my hands excessively. It's always the older women who are touchy.

"Those are private." Natalie snatches the papers out of my hand after the nurse leaves. "HIPAA."

"Worried that I'm going to find out that you have seven toes on your left foot?"

"Meh-meh-meh," she mocks me as we exit the room.

"Very mature."

"Not all of us can be as mature as you, old man." Her comment makes me grit my teeth.

I'm not old but it makes me painfully aware that I've been arguing with and letting a woman seven years younger than me piss me off this easily.

"You're right. Respect your elders."

"Never."

* * *

"Why are you here?" The ever-pleasant Natalie greets me from the bottom of her apartment staircase.

This is the first time that I've seen her or spoken to her since dropping her at the hotel after the hospital. A part of me hoped we'd gotten past the ire-filled interactions. A sicker part of me is enjoying the familiarity of it.

"Nice to see you, too." I throw a garbage bag full of her clothes over my shoulder as I descend the stairs. The building was condemned after the fire but I convinced code enforcement to let me in to get some of their stuff. I didn't want it to be a total loss. "All of this needs to be washed but the smoke smell should come out."

"Are those *my* clothes?" She shrieks, following closely behind me as I cross the gravel parking lot. I throw the bag into the back of my SUV while she continues complaining at me. "You went through my stuff! That is so violating."

I ignore her comments. "There wasn't much else that could be salvaged."

"My brother's stuff..." Her tone is solemn suddenly and the shift forces me to meet her eyes. They're quickly cataloging the other bags I have piled back here, searching for Dec's belongings. I shake my head and her dark lashes squeeze shut in despair.

"He'll need new clothes, but the other stuff can wait. He's got you and a bed to sleep in for now. He won't care about the toys as much as you might think."

She nods her head stiffly and releases a breath. "I need to see if his box from the closet made it." She turns on her heels to go back toward the apartment but I stop her short.

"I have it." I pull it out of the backseat. It was the first thing I looked for.

She all but lunges back toward me, her hands dancing over the lid. "Is it okay?"

"Yeah, I had to wipe the soot off the top but it was safe enough on the floor of the closet."

She pulls the lid off, inspecting the contents to confirm what I observed. Her hands hover over everything but touch nothing as if not to disturb it.

"I have it meticulously organized for Dec's sake." She laughs sadly. "A few of the special items he kept of my moms are tucked away at the bottom for when he's older."

I don't know why she's voluntarily giving me this information but I don't mind. It's nice to see the sister side of her, the human side.

"I can keep it at my office if you want. Until you're settled somewhere permanently," I offer. "I have a safe and it's fire-resistant."

"It's not as if I plan to live through more fires," she argues, unleashing her usual side.

"Let's hope not." Max pipes in from over Natalie's shoulder. He's a firefighter and one of the volunteer fire marshals. He's the one who let me into the apartment.

I jerk my head in a quick "shut it" motion so he doesn't keep talking. I haven't told her about the arson yet because I don't want to add to her worry. His eyes widen in understanding and he changes the subject. "You guys all set in there?"

"I haven't even gone inside," Natalie responds, cutting him a cross look.

"There isn't anything else," I assure her, wanting to save her from seeing the extent of the damage. I meant what I said, there isn't anything else to be salvaged and I don't want the image of it to haunt her.

She ignores me, directing her full annoyance at Max as he speaks again. I try not to be amused by it.

"I pulled you out of the fire, ma'am." He tips his head, smugly. I think he intended for that to be a pickup line.

"Wow. Thanks. So brave." I almost miss it as she turns back to me, but there was definitely an eye roll attached to that bland response. Max is dumbfounded behind her as if he's not used to his firefighter shtick not working.

"Fine, take it to your office but if I need it at any point you have to give it back. Even if it's the middle of the night." She secures the lid over the box and gives it a small shove toward my chest.

"I wouldn't dare keep it from you, fireball."

"Don't call me that," she snaps.

"Okay, Nat."

"Don't call me that either. It's Natalie."

"Whatever you say, Nat."

Chapter Ten

Natalie

J ackson: Where are you going?
    Me: Excuse me?
    Jackson: My deputy said you just left in a random car.

Me: Why is your deputy watching me?

Jackson: They do extra patrol at the hotels.

Me: I don't believe you.

Jackson: Where's Dec?

Me: None of your business.

Jackson: Nat...

Me: Don't call me that. I'm busy, stop texting me.

Jackson: Busy doing what?

Me: I'm on a date.

Jackson: With Max?

Me: No, you're absurd.

I checked my phone a couple of times throughout dinner but convinced myself that it was only in case Dec needed something. He's at his friend Charlie's house tonight and is usually more than content there.

Jackson didn't respond again and I was hoping for more of a distraction by fighting with him. The local Mexican restaurant is good, but pretty basic like my date.

He might be worse than Max the firefighter who had the nerve to ask me out when we were still standing in front of my ashtray of an apartment. With a name fitting for a dog, I made sure to insult it and his mustache as I declined his offer.

Instead, I took a chance on a random dating app because I was starving and funds are incredibly tight right now.

I'd prefer to whip something up myself, but the single burner at the hotel can only accomplish so much. I also didn't want our room and clothes to smell like my meal for three days.

"You ready to get out of here?" Ty, my Tinder match, asks while he reaches for the bill. I know my answer will determine whether he pays the entire tab or asks to split, so I play the part. I'll be nice until we get back in the car. Then I'll tell him to take me back to the hotel and ruin his chance of getting laid.

The conversation has been polite but boring. No one with any sense would think that there was any chemistry between us, but I know guys only go out to get their dick's wet. He's not looking for romance and luckily for me, I'm not either. This is a simple bait and switch. He'll never see me again after our meal is over.

"Yeah, I'm ready. Thank you so much for dinner." I bat my eyelashes for extra effect. He smirks, shoving his card into the folder and I know he thinks he's got this in the bag. Dumbass.

As we're leaving, I throw another $5 down on the table because I noticed he left a shit tip. If this was a real date then that would turn me off for sure. I can't stand a bad tipper.

Only two minutes down the road, he reaches over and palms my knee over my jeans, wrapping his wiry fingers around it. "My place or yours?" He asks, channeling his inner Rico Suave.

"Um, you can drop me back at the hotel." I shouldn't have him let him pick me up. I wanted to drive but he was insistent and I was hungry. I figured he seemed harmless enough to get out of things by the end of the date.

We've been in the hotel for a couple weeks but to me, there's no end in sight. I can't find any other apartments for rent. I can't afford a house, nor do I have the credit or savings to buy one. A used RV either, I checked.

The clock is ticking down until my world implodes once again. I'm working as much as possible to get as many tips as possible, but it's not enough. It never is.

I refuse to leave this area. I am not making Dec move schools. His life has been turned upside down as it is without adding that social nightmare. I had to do it many times as a kid and it was traumatizing every time.

My mom would move us in with whatever boyfriend, drug dealer, or douchebag of the moment, and get drugs in exchange for doing housework. Or, sometimes worse.

Ty's fingers tighten on my knee and it's my first indication that he's not going to give up as easily as I thought. "Are you going to invite me up to your room or are you going to pay me back for your meal?"

"Excuse me?" How fucking bold, dude.

"Your choice, honey."

"I'm not your honey and I'm not inviting you up."

He scoffs, tossing my knee aside roughly. This is bad, I

might have screwed up here. I don't respond to his little tantrum, my self-preservation is strong enough to know when to shut my mouth most of the time.

I should have played nice a little longer, especially when he takes a left where he should have continued straight.

"You are taking me back to my hotel, right?" I ask in a last-ditch effort, hoping that I'm worrying for nothing.

"Just a shortcut," he replies in a clipped tone.

I don't believe him but we're not far enough out of town for him to be lying completely. He might be taking me there still in a roundabout way. It doesn't matter though because 30 seconds later, blue and red lights are lighting up the dark road behind us, reflecting brightly in the car mirrors.

"What the fuck?" Ty grumbles, shoving the car into park on the shoulder, huffing and puffing as he does.

We're both watching his driver's side mirror, holding our breath for different reasons. He's hoping to avoid a ticket and I'm hoping to vanish into thin air.

We both startle in our seats when a knock comes at my window instead of his. We never saw him approach which is hard to believe since he towers over everything around him, the car included. I don't need to look closely to know that it's Jackson. I don't want to see the smugness on his face.

"Evening, folks." Somehow his cop voice outweighs the triumph he's probably feeling right now for catching me in this predicament.

"What did I do, officer?" Ty asks way too defensively. He's like a kid who got the ball taken away at recess.

"It's Sheriff. You were speeding. I need both of your IDs."

"You're kidding." I cut him a glare, hoping he feels my wrath. He ignores me.

"I don't kid," Jackson says with all seriousness and I believe him. I don't think he's finding this as humorous as I thought.

We both hand him our license, but instead of taking them back to his car, he looks at them right there beside my door.

"Ma'am, step out of the vehicle." He opens my door before I have a chance to reach for my handle.

I didn't do anything wrong but whether it be because it's late at night or his red and blues are distorting everything, I'm feeling slightly off balance. He wouldn't actually arrest me, right?

I step out onto the side of the grassy shoulder but he doesn't move his arm from the top of the door, making me stand indecently close to him.

"Do you want me to leave?" He asks the question quietly so there's no way my date from hell can hear him but the depth of his voice vibrates through me, anyway.

There's a silence that follows and I realize that he's truly giving me a choice. If I asked him to leave, I think he would go. I'm not sure how that makes me feel but I know one thing for sure...

"I don't want to go with him."

Jackson studies me closely for only a moment, his eyes burning into mine. "Did he do something?"

I hesitate slightly and consider telling him that he is creepy and handsy but ultimately decide it's not necessary. I'll never see the guy again. "No."

His jaw locks and pulls out handcuffs. What the fuck?

"You're free to go, slow down." He tosses Ty's license onto the passenger seat and snags my purse from my seat.

"What about her?" Once again, Ty whines like a child getting his toy taken away.

"She's being arrested for theft. She stole her last date's wallet and car. Tried to cut his dick off, too." Jackson snatches my wrists quickly and twists them behind my back, easily holding them together in one hand while the other giant hand clasps the base of my neck where it meets my shoulder. Before I can protest, he's forcefully leading me from the car and toward his SUV.

The string of noises that comes out of my throat while we walk is nothing coherent.

"Don't fight me until he drives away. Or, I'll use the cuffs," he warns just before Ty's car pulls back onto the road, gunning it and leaving me in the dust. Jackson drops my arms immediately as if my skin's on fire.

"Did you have to make me sound like a psycho?"

"Did I? Oops." He folds his cuffs back into their spot on his vest.

"You're such an ass. Why did you even pull us over?" I huff and turn toward the passenger door, waiting for him to unlock it. "Can I sit up here? Or, would you rather throw me in the back with those cuffs on?"

The double meaning in my question was unintended, but when he steps up to me, closer than he had been before, he's looking down on me *deviously*.

My breath catches in my throat but I don't look away. I wouldn't want to give him the satisfaction even though my brain is mistakenly conjuring up all kinds of images involving me and Jackson in the back of his cop car.

His eyes track my facial features fiercely, reading every clue that he can from my demeanor like a predator about to pounce. I can't breathe, I don't even blink as he assesses me but I see the exact moment his thoughts shift and he reigns himself back in.

"I've been driving around in circles looking for you all night."

My jaw goes slack. "What? Why?"

He blows out a deep breath, softening his facial features altogether as his head tips back, staring at the dark night sky. A silent prayer before answering me.

"Things are bad around here. People are going missing. Being killed. Women are being picked up off the side of the road and barely making it out alive. I wasn't going to sit back and let that happen to you because you thought it was a good idea to go on a date with some random man."

I ignore the dark things he just told me, finding it easier to argue with him about the last part instead. "How do you know that I didn't know him? We could have gone way back. You don't know me and you certainly don't get a say in my dating life."

"Yeah, then why are you standing here with me right now and not with that loser?" He glares at me hard, daring me to challenge him.

"I'd rather walk." I turn my back to him but before I can take a step his arm shoots out to block me from walking away.

"I'd rather not be here. I'd rather you not need me at all but I *will* be here every time you need me." He steps back out of my bubble and unlocks the car, reaching past me to open the door.

"Get in before I change my mind about the backseat, *Nat.*" He enunciates my disgusting nickname on purpose, doing whatever he can to avoid any reverence toward me.

My ass plops into the seat, folding my arms dramatically as he shuts my door. When he rounds the front of the vehicle he looks as put together as he normally does. Even slightly pissed off and stoic as hell, he's a handsome bastard.

"Why do you insist on calling me, Nat?" I ask once he's driving.

"Because you hate it for some reason and you're like a pesky bug that won't leave me alone."

"You're such a dick."

"Yeah, well. So, are you."

I scoff. "Most men would refer to me as a bitch, not a dick."

"I would never call you that."

"But, you'll call me a dick?" I ask incredulously.

"Well, I'm not perfect." He shrugs.

If I wasn't so frustrated with him, I'd laugh. It only makes me more frustrated. Nothing good ever comes when we're in the same vicinity as each other but we keep ending up in the same place. Whether by chance or by choice. I think he's the pesky bug that won't leave me alone.

Chapter Eleven

Natalie

"Are there really people being kidnapped around here?" I ask him after a couple of minutes of suffocating silence. He doesn't have music playing, the only sound in the interior of the car is his equipment rattling around and frequent alerts from his police radio.

"Unfortunately."

"Kids?" My thoughts always go to Dec. It's a revolving door in my mind, especially since becoming his guardian.

"Mostly adults. One teenager." His flat tone is more deflated than usual but it doesn't keep me from pushing the topic.

"Sore subject?"

He scoffs. "Yeah, you could say that." There's a long pause of silence until he continues. "One of my friends. I didn't know who she was at the time, but she was driving through Rollins about a year and a half ago. She got a flat tire and ended up being kidnapped off the side of the road right outside of town. She barely survived but when she did they put a target on her head. They tried again and she made it out alive, again. That was my first encounter with it."

"Your first kidnapping?"

"The first time that I heard information about a supposed human trafficking ring running through here," he clarifies.

The gasp that leaves my mouth is unintentional but he glances in my direction anyway. "People from here are being taken and sold?" I ask in astonishment because it doesn't seem real.

He sighs again. "I don't know for sure, but that's my running theory. People are disappearing, not to be seen again. Drug addicts are overdosing left and right. We had a group of extremists try to blow up Main Street. Rollins is a mess."

"Wow. Maybe I should have taken Dec back to New York," I mumble.

"Maybe," he utters, distractedly.

"So, you think my mom is just another addict that over-dosed?"

"No, I don't."

This time I glance at him, surprised by his response. "You don't?"

"I think Declan did exactly what you accused him of. I don't know what will happen without the proof but I think he's as criminal as they get."

"Me too."

"I need to know where he got the drugs. The drugs that he gave your mom are still out there. They never recovered any more of his stash but people are still overdosing. That's why I've been butting into the case."

"Here I thought you were out to get me specifically." I huff, sadly. As validating as it is to hear him agree with me, it's hard to accept that I was right. Declan is as bad as I thought.

"I'm not out to get anyone. Unless they deserve it. Bad people, criminals, yeah. Everything else is... Draining."

His open admission stuns me silent and we stay like that, neither of us speaking until he pulls into the carport at the hotel. "You don't sound like someone who likes their job."

"I wanted Rollins to be safer. I didn't want the job." The dull tone of his voice suddenly sounds a lot less like indifference and more like exhaustion. "No matter what I do it's never enough."

"Your friend, the one who was kidnapped, is she okay?" I try not to let my thoughts run rampant on how good of a friend this woman might be to Jackson. I prefer to see him as a bully in a bulletproof vest, not someone with a family or love interests. I don't want to imagine him with some perfect life when he goes home.

"Yeah, she's fine, thankfully. She lives here now. She married the guy who saved her life, Nathan. I hang out with them from time to time." He shrugs before putting the car in park in front of the hotel entrance.

"Who knew you had friends?" The jab rolls off my tongue before I can stop it and even though I regret it, I don't take it back. I'm too prideful for that.

"Yeah and where are all of your friends?" He whips back without hesitating and now I'm glad I didn't take my remark back.

"You really are a dick." I shove out of the car and turn to grab my purse from the floor when a realization hits me. "Dammit," I sigh.

"What?"

"My leftovers are still in Ty's car. That's the only reason I went on that damn date." I groan into my hands until I remember that I'm being watched.

"You went out with a stranger because you wanted dinner?"

"A free dinner," I correct too quickly, regretting my admission.

He stares at me dumbfounded but I avert my eyes. I don't want to see his judgment. He has no idea what it's been like for me, learning to survive my entire life.

"Goodbye, Sheriff. Have a terrible night." The car door slams behind me as I march into the hotel.

I don't turn around until the elevator doors are shut safely behind me, staring into the mirrored walls' reflection. All I see is the broken girl that I've seen since I was a child.

For once, I want to know what it feels like to have someone to lean on. Anyone. Instead, I've always had to do it on my own. I fight so hard for Dec so he never has to feel the pain that I've felt. The abandonment that sets in every night when you're trying to close your eyes to sleep and realize that if you never woke up, no one on this planet would care.

If Jackson wants to judge me for doing what I need to so that I can ensure Dec has a meal to eat when he comes back from Charlie's tomorrow then so be it. His opinions of me don't matter. Except now I went on that damn date with no leftovers to show for it. I have to brainstorm where our next meal will come from anyway, even after dealing with two infuriating men tonight.

An hour later I'm still grumbling about my wasted evening when someone knocks on my door. I'm mid-brushing my teeth and not expecting anyone so I silently tiptoe to the peephole to check.

There's a set of broad shoulders in my view and I know they only belong to one person. "What could you possibly want?" I ask his back as I fling the heavy door open.

He turns quickly, his eyes cataloging the toothbrush dangling out of my mouth before pinging to the bird's nest on my head and then down to my exposed bare legs.

"I was getting ready for bed," I add defensively even though he didn't say a word. He only silently stares at me as I wipe my mouth with the back of my hand in case there's any lingering toothpaste.

"Here." He shoves a bag into my chest and it hits me before the smell does.

"What is this?" I can tell it's a bag of Mexican food but that's not what I'm asking.

"Your food."

"Did you go steal my leftovers back?" I snort.

"No."

The huff that leaves my chest is involuntary. He has no sense of humor. "I was being sarcastic."

"Bye, Natalie. Have a terrible night." He starts to walk away but I'm not finished.

"Jackson. This is enough for four people."

"Dec's a growing boy. He'll eat it."

"How do you even know it's something that we like?" I snip instead of being a normal human being and thanking him. Unfortunately, broken Natalie is an asshole.

"Go to bed." He never looks back, ignoring my rude behavior, continuing down the hall until he takes the corner and is out of sight.

I check the receipt taped to the bag and see that he re-ordered my exact meal from dinner, down to the substitutions, because Dec won't eat refried beans.

He's either stalking me and Dec, or he put more effort into this than he'd probably ever admit.

* * *

When the prosecutor calls me and asks me to come in for an important meeting, I have to rush back to the hotel from work to change my clothes. Luckily, Dec has been spending a lot of time with his friend from school so I don't have to worry about being here for bus drop-off.

I put on my favorite plum long-sleeve top and my usual black pencil skirt with heels, trying to give the appearance that I have my shit together, but I still end up half-jogging through the parking lot to get into my car.

Even in my haste, I realize the same Sheriff's Deputy cruiser sitting in the parking lot as when I pulled in. I saw it yesterday, too.

At first, I thought it was Sheriff Jackson Small Dick, but I haven't seen him since he dropped me off at the hotel the other night.

Dec and I ate our Mexican food for dinner two nights in a row while I did my best to forget where it came from. I have no plans to become friends with Jackson. He's still infuriating. And, a cop.

I roll my window down because this deputy is within spitting distance of my car and staring at me. Despite my nervous energy about the meeting I'm running late to, I can't contain myself. "Can I help you with something?" I shout at his window and he rolls it down.

"No ma'am."

"Why are you watching me?"

"Uh. Orders from the Sheriff to keep an eye on you." He glances away from me, nervously.

"Again, why?"

"Well, because of the arson, ma'am."

Arson.

Why wouldn't Jackson tell me? I knew I couldn't trust him. I knew it.

Within ten minutes I'm stomping up to the second floor of the Sheriff's Department. My heels threaten to crack with each frustrated step.

Following the directions on the wall to the Sheriff's office, I breeze by the secretary who tries to grab my attention, and pound on the wooden door with his nameplate. I try the handle but it's locked.

"Open the door, Jackson!"

"Um, ma'am," the secretary tries to get my attention but I cut her off with a look. The door swings open to a half-dressed giant. He's fully clothed, but to me, he's practically naked. He's not wearing his uniform or his black polo. He's standing in front of me in a white t-shirt with pants unbuttoned and no shoes on.

"It's okay, Roberta." He waves off the woman who is staring wide-eyed at me and him. "Are you going to come in or would you rather shout through the door until backup arrives? Crazy woman," he mumbles that last bit as I storm past him without acknowledging the remark.

Flinging my purse into a chair, I turn to stare him down. "Why are you naked?"

He glances down at his own body as he closes his door, clearly seeing what I see, that he is fully clothed. He's not even barefoot, he's still wearing socks.

"Did you hit your head or something?"

"Shut up. Arson?" I shout. "When were you planning to tell

me that someone set my apartment on fire?"

"Calm down," he starts to say something else but I practically levitate over to him. I hear the slap before I register that I actually slapped him across the face.

I slapped *him*.

Yet, *my* ears are ringing.

What did I do?

He's going to throw my ass in jail. His tongue works the inside of his mouth as if to check for blood and I hold my breath, preparing for whatever comes next.

He steps back to his door, opening it slightly. "Roberta. Go home for the day, put the Office Closed sign up in front of the lobby." The door shuts with a click before he turns to face me.

"One free shot, fireball. That is all you get. I hope you used it wisely." With his arms folded across his chest, his body completely blocks the doorway. I couldn't leave even if I tried. I'm not that stupid. I know I'm not physically capable of winning any altercation with him and he just sent away the only witness on this floor.

"Don't call me that."

His eyes bore into mine. Fiercely. I'm not scared of him. At least, I haven't been up until this point, but things can change quickly. Grown men can turn to anger in a blink of an eye and I was stupid enough to slap him.

He smirks but doesn't respond. That lift to one side of his mouth is the most intimidating look he's ever given me.

"Are you going to arrest me?" I ask boldly. I refuse to go quietly if so.

"No." There's a long pause until he adds, "I want you to move in with me."

"What?" I screech. "Did I rattle your brain? Are you insane?"

He doesn't react at all. He doesn't budge from where he's standing in front of the only exit. He doesn't want me to escape as much as I am desperate to do so.

"As I was trying to say before you hit me. I didn't tell you about the arson because I was on my way to meet you at the prosecutor's office to discuss it. You caught me changing out of my road uniform. I've been a little busy trying to figure out what the hell is going on in my county!" His voice became deeper and louder as he spoke but I'm still dumbfounded by the "moving-in" comment to care.

"I think Declan had someone set fire to your apartment on purpose."

"What?" I squeak out this time.

"Before you ask, no, I don't think I can prove it. I've been searching for any evidence that would confirm my suspicion but I've got nothing." He finally moves away from the door but I'm too stunned to move.

"You sent the deputy to watch over us because you think he'll try again?"

"Yes. No. I don't know." He plants his hands on his desk and hangs his head. For the first time, he looks like a man, not the Iron Giant.

My mind is running in a loop, not piecing any of the information together. My knees are weak and the only thing that will make me feel in control again is to retaliate.

"How can you let this happen? Isn't it *your job* to stop criminals?"

His head is hanging heavily but he nods it slowly, eerily. Then he laughs. A deep humorless laugh that startles me.

"I should have known. I've been working my ass off to keep you and your brother safe. I've been going in circles trying to solve this but you want to inflict pain. Fine. I get it. Hit me. Hit me, again, if it will make you feel better." He strides over to me, stopping so close that his toes touch the tips of my shoes. My chest rising and falling is the only movement between us.

"Nothing you spew at me will stop me from keeping Dec safe. Nothing you say is going to change the facts. So, instead of fighting me every step of the way, listen for once and play nice." His breathing is as ragged as mine, neither of us backing down from this.

"It's my job to keep him safe, not yours. We don't need you," I snap, drawing his eyes to my mouth. When they blink back to mine, they're darker and more menacing.

"You have no idea what you need, little girl."

Slap.

My hand stings.

Before I can blink, my chest is pressed to the oak tabletop and I'm face down on his desk. Both of my arms are twisted tightly behind my back and the entirety of the Sheriff of Rollins County is looming over me. Behind me.

No amount of fight will give me an inch. With hardly any effort on his part, he has me trapped and in a position to be cuffed. Despite his level of strength, he's not hurting me, and that annoys me more. "I hate you!" I scream, my cheek tightly pressed against the cool surface.

"Good. Feeling's mutual," he grits out, his head dangerously close to mine. My breaths are coming out roughly, impeding my hearing but I can tell that his mouth is inches from my ear.

I whip my head back as hard as I can, bucking my body to try to escape. It's an idiotic idea because he anticipates it, positioning himself firmly against me. And, that's when I feel it.

The *entirety* of the Rollins County Sheriff is planted firmly against my ass. Even from this position that I've found myself in, I'm pissed to realize that I have no business calling him Sheriff Small Dick.

"Is that how you show your anger, Jackson?" I ask, breathlessly as the angry fire in my belly spreads, turning to warmth between my legs.

"God dammit," he mumbles under his breath, pushing off of me and stumbling to the other side of his office. "Get out."

I stand up, slowly, adjusting my skirt that had ridden up to the tops of my thighs. I take my time, refusing to run away like he wants me to. When I look over my shoulder to gauge his feelings, his eyes are zoned in directly on where my hands are fixing my skirt.

All I feel is triumph. Mister high and mighty is only human after all. It's too easy. "If violence gets you worked up, you should consider anger management. Or, maybe it's a kink. That's how most serial killers start," I add cheekily, fully aware of how bold it is to harass him like this.

I start toward the door but pause as I grasp the handle. "What will the people of Rollins County think when they find out their Sheriff has a fetish for yelling at women." I shrug and start to open the door when it slams shut. An arm above my head braces it closed.

"You know you are the only woman who gets me this heated," he grits out. "I can't stand you and yet I'm hard as a rock every time you lash that pretty tongue at me."

My breath lodges in my throat. I wasn't expecting those words to come out of his mouth.

He's so close to me, his front to my back. If I leaned back even an inch, I'd probably brush against him. I'd feel the evidence of his hatred for me.

"Now, leave," he demands through a locked jaw.

Chapter Twelve

Jackson

My whole body is on fire. I'm frustrated with her and how I've reacted. My mind is begging me to get away from her but I can't seem to move.

"Fuck. You." Her whole body is vibrating with anger but I'm too worked up to get satisfaction from it. I want to shove her out of my office just as badly as I want to grab her by the hips and pull her back into me. Like I've imagined doing every time she's ever stomped away from me.

My attraction to her is the biggest burden of my life. I didn't get a say in it. She popped into my life, into my head, consuming my thoughts entirely. A lot of them are of annoyance and stubbornness, but more than a few are about the curves this woman possesses.

Her ass. God, I can't stop thinking about her ass.

I lower my hand from the door, finally backing up and away from her. What the hell am I doing?

I'm losing my mind.

"Go, Natalie. I am too tired to fight with you." I slump onto the small sofa on the far side of my office and close my eyes for a second. She doesn't bust out of the room like I suspected, instead, I watch from under heavy lids as she turns back toward me.

Maybe she'll strut over here and kill me. Put me out of my misery with a stomp of her heel.

She takes a seat in the chair that her purse was sitting in, crossing her arms over her chest. The way her leg rests over her knee with her foot tapping in the air is not the stance of a woman who is going to leave quietly. I blow a breath out, slowly. Here we go.

"In the interest of keeping Dec safe. Are we safe in the hotel?"

"I don't know, but-" She cuts me off.

"Surely he wouldn't be crazy enough to light a hotel on fire," she states, exasperated. She truly thinks I'm terrible at my job if she thinks I haven't considered all possibilities.

"I'm not implying that Declan is taking up a passion for arson, Natalie."

"Then, what are you suggesting?" She asks but I bite my tongue. I was hoping she'd come to this conclusion on her own and I wouldn't have to pull the wool from her eyes. When I don't respond, her eyes narrow.

"I need to call a ceasefire."

"A what?"

"I need you to promise that you will remain neutral toward me for a limited period of time."

"Why?"

"What I'm about to discuss with you is going to make you mad and I don't want you to run away from me because you hate me. I know I am not your favorite person, but this is serious and I need you to listen to me for the entirety of it."

"Why should I believe that you have my best intentions in

mind?"

Always the cynic.

"Because it's about Dec and I know he is your most important interest." I watch the defeat in her eyes. She knows I'm telling the truth. Her shoulders slump and I take it as a sign that she's giving in.

"Fine, cease fire."

"Declan is determined to get released. His lawyer is pulling out all of the stops. He's already tried to throw the prosecutor off the case, the judge."

"He can't get out, he-"

"I know. I don't want him to get out either. I terminated the deal because he didn't give me any information and now he's pissed. He's mad at me. He's mad," I explain as cooly as I can. I'm mad about all of it, too. This week has been hell dealing with it.

"You terminated it? So he isn't going to be charged with Involuntary Manslaughter?" She asks hopefully. I wish it were good news.

"He will be charged with Aggravated Murder but he won't be convicted... There's not enough evidence. That's why I pushed for the deal in the first place. The prosecution can't win this, the judge probably won't even take it to trial." She looks green as I finish that sentence, but I ignore it, needing to get the rest out in the open while I have her safe in my office.

"In the meantime, he's desperate to gain his freedom. I don't know why he's so desperate suddenly, but he is." Her eyes study me closely and I feel like an ant under a magnifying glass. There's no getting away from being burned.

"There's more, Jackson, I can tell. What aren't you saying?"

81

Like a coward, I'm putting off the final piece of information that will cut the deepest. I think this would be easier if she were still calling me Sheriff Small Dick.

"It's a long shot, but the reason that I think Declan had someone set fire to your apartment is because, with Dec dead, he would've been let out for extenuating circumstances. Like the death of a child."

There's a long silence as the blood drains from her face, her skin going porcelain white.

"Oh my God." She jumps up and as predicted, runs straight for the door. I launch up from my seat after her. She should not be leaving like this, not after that information.

"Nat, stop." I jam the door again with my arm above her head and she whips around to face me.

"Let me go. I have to go," she rambles.

"No, talk to me."

"About what? Declan wants to kill my baby brother!" She yells, her voice cracking. "I thought he hated me," she whispers. "I thought it was about hurting me."

"I don't know what he wants. I don't want this to be true, but I can't help but see the connection. I hope I'm wrong about this. I've never wanted to be more wrong."

She looks at me, finally. Her dark brown irises stare into mine. To her credit, she hasn't shed a single tear. Her eyeliner is as sharp as ever. "That's why you have the deputy watching us? Not because it was arson, but because you're nervous about what Declan might do."

"It's more than that. I don't want anything to happen to either of you."

"Is this a part of your God complex? You have to protect everyone?" She accuses, but the insult falls flat.

"I would like to protect everyone, yeah. Is that so bad?"

She rolls her eyes as a response and sets her jaw. There she is. "What do we do?"

"Move in with me. You'll be safer and I won't have to keep a deputy in front of your hotel. My house is safe." *I'll keep you safe.* I want to add but I don't. I've pushed her enough.

"Wouldn't it be safer to keep a deputy then? For Dec."

"I'll be there and won't need to pay anyone."

"Not enough tax funds?" She scoffs, but the sadness in her tone softens it.

"Uh, yeah." I move away from her again because it's suffocating to be too close and I need to keep my distance.

"You are still keeping something from me." Her perception of me is too knowing.

"I am not," I say without looking at her.

"You are."

"Really? Do you want to play this game?"

"No, I don't want you to keep secrets from me." She huffs.

"You don't need to know this one." I shrug. "Leave it alone."

"When have I ever listened to you? Why would I start now?"

Yep, I led myself into that one.

"Fine." I rub my hands across my face and over my head. This is a nightmare and we are long past the meeting time with the prosecutor. "Taxpayers aren't funding the deputy's overtime. I am."

"Right, well… You are the sheriff."

"No. Not as Sheriff, as me."

Her jaw drops. "What? Why?"

"The county can't afford overtime. We can't afford much of anything. I'm trying to fix it but I haven't yet. It will take time. I need to hire more people as it is and we have no money to spare."

"The hotel?"

I don't respond. I don't need to. She's smart enough to piece together what I'm saying. I couldn't stand the thought of her and Dec having nowhere to go.

"You bastard." Ouch. Okay, I should have expected that. "Is this some sick way of getting me to owe you? To have something against me."

"What? No. Not at all. Why can't you believe that I am a decent human being?"

"Most people aren't."

"I'm sorry that you feel that way."

"I am going to pay you back every penny for the hotel. I refuse to be in debt. Give me some time and I'll pick up more shifts."

"No," I say too quickly. I don't even want to imagine what she's doing for money in that red lacy bra that haunts me and all of the tiny smoke-covered clothes that I shoved into a trash bag at her apartment. She narrows her eyes again. "Don't worry about paying me back, you have enough on your plate."

"Stop trying to rescue me! I don't need your pity."

"It's not pity!" I shout, immediately regretting it. "Look, I'm sorry. I never yell, ever, but I can't seem to stop arguing with you." I blow out an exasperated breath.

"I bring out the worst in people. Call it a curse or a gift, I don't care. I appreciate you looking out for Dec but I do not want to move into your house. I don't want to keep disrupting Dec's life. I'll figure it out."

"Are we still in the ceasefire?" I ask, watching the decision play across her face.

"For the moment," she says softly. I recognize the exhaustion slumping her shoulders.

"For what it's worth. I think you're doing a great job with him. He's a good kid. All of his teachers had great things to say."

Chapter Thirteen

Natalie

"Why did you talk to his teachers?" A million scenarios play in my mind, none of which tell me why Jackson would be talking to Dec's teachers. I'm doing my best to ignore his first comment, the one making my jaw quiver.

I don't cry in front of anyone. The last time I cried was at my mom's funeral service. She wasn't even there unless you count her ashes in an urn as being present. I didn't cry for my mom, I cried for Dec.

"I spent a lot of the day at his school. I wanted to make sure the security was operating to standard. I asked all his teachers and the staff to call me if anything strange happens. I wanted to ensure everything was locked tight before I told you what was going on. One less thing for you to worry about," he admits.

He's so casual about it. He has no idea how bizarre this is for me. He has done more for me than anyone ever has and we can't stand to be in the same room with each other. I don't know whether to laugh or cry. I really don't want to cry but my eyes are burning. I turn to face the door so he can't see my face. Damn, this man.

"That goes for you, too. I don't care what time of day or night, if something feels off, call me. Even if you can't stand the thought of me, call me, please."

The desperation in his voice puts the nail in it for me. He is a decent human being. He wants Dec to be safe almost as much as I do and he hardly knows him.

"Still in the ceasefire?" I ask, my body still facing the door.

"Yeah."

As soon as the word is out of his mouth I take the leap, ignoring his confused expression as I close the gap between us and wrap my arms around his waist. I bury my head in his chest and breathe in his scent. This is the only time I'll ever do this, I want it to count.

"Thank you for caring about Dec."

He doesn't react at first, but after a few seconds his arms lift hesitantly and wrap themselves around my body, squeezing me into him.

I'll go back to ruining his life tomorrow, but for now, I can admit that he feels good. His arms are strong, his body is firm, and he towers over me, making me feel protected for the first time in a long time.

My body against his is enough to distract me from the tears that I almost shed. It's enough for me to regain my composure but I haven't moved away. Neither has he. This little bubble will burst soon enough.

When I breathe him in again, memorizing the fresh, masculine scent, I feel his lips atop my head. He kisses my hair and then smooths a hand down my back, over my grown-out locks.

When I raise my head to look at him, he's already looking

at me. His eyes filled with questions. None of which I'll be able to answer. I'll never be able to explain this or why I need it.

My eyes drop to his mouth and I can't will them away.

Would it be so bad?

"Nat." My nickname on his lips doesn't sting like it has in the past and I hate it.

"Jackson," I whisper in response.

He puts his finger under my chin, raising my gaze to meet his eyes again. "You're upset. There is a lot to process after everything that we've discussed. You should leave."

"What if just this once, I didn't?" My question shocks me, forcing me to swallow thickly. None of this makes sense.

"Are you asking for permission?" His words are soft, but his eyes are fiery, gravitating back to my mouth.

Pushing up on my tiptoes, I barely have time to whisper "no" as I seal my lips to his. I immediately feel his breath catch where my hands rest on his waist and the stillness that follows.

I think he's going to stop me or pull away, until his mouth suddenly moves against mine, delivering unrestrained tenderness that nearly knocks me back.

My heels sink slowly back to the ground, my legs turning to jelly until we're nose to nose. His head is bowed to accommodate my height as we wait for this to blow up in our faces, intimately breathing each other's oxygen.

It's pure frustration built up until I can't keep it in.

There is nothing more to this than getting it out of my system and burning off some energy.

My nerves are shot after hearing that Declan wants to hurt my brother and I need a distraction. That's it.

I need to feel something other than sadness, and fear.

"You don't have to be a good guy. Not right now," I plead after he doesn't move to take this further. I'm used to guys taking before I'm willing to give, but I've never been with a nice guy before.

His eyes widen slightly at my words and I watch the rest of his restraint snap. His lips fuse to mine as he hauls me off my feet, backing me into the door with a bang. My hands thread around his neck, into his hair, clinging to him automatically, but there's no need. Our bodies are pressed together so tightly that I can feel every hard line of his body. The hardest part digging firmly against my stomach.

My tongue snakes into his mouth, tasting him, and battling his. We kiss like we fight. Both of us wanting control. Both of us wanting to leave bruises behind. His tongue brushes my bottom lip and I suck it into my mouth before he can retreat.

His whole body tenses, pulling his head back suddenly to look at me. "Nat..." His voice is strained, his eyes begging for more.

"Just this once?" I breathe out.

His answer is another brutal kiss, owning my mouth entirely with his. His hands grasp my thighs roughly, wrapping them around his waist, and shoving the bottom of my skirt up to my hips. It positions my lace-covered core directly against his length. "Oh, fuck," I utter when he grinds himself against me, using his hands on my ass for leverage.

He doesn't speak, he doesn't need to. He's doing all of his talking with his body. Biting, sucking, and licking every inch of the exposed skin of my neck and collarbones while he desperately thrusts against my pussy, lighting up my nerve endings.

89

He's not struggling to hold me up against the door, but it still surprises me when he removes one of his hands from my ass to tug the v of my shirt down. The dermal piercings in the shallow valley of my cleavage are exposed with that extra couple of inches and he attacks.

His flattened tongue licks over them, up my chest, across my collarbone, and ends with a bite to the sensitive flesh between my neck and shoulder causing me to whimper. A full-fledged, embarrassing, whimper.

His head rears back and if possible, his pupils dilate to the point of totality, erasing his honey-colored irises. Dark is an understatement, he looks like a man possessed. We stare at each other for one full breath before it turns to utter chaos.

His free hand fumbles to get between my legs while I grasp for his zipper, roughly shoving the fabric until I can grab him through his underwear. There's so much of him.

Two of his fingers enter me the instant he gets my thong pushed aside making me gasp. He's inside of me and he feels so fucking good. I can't stand that it feels so good.

"Christ, sweetheart." The appreciation in his voice makes me whimper, again.

"Shut up," I tell him or myself, I'm not sure.

I'm losing all sense of control in this. Everything is happening so fast and even though I'm enjoying it, I don't want to give him all the power. I barely manage, but I'm able to get a hand inside his underwear, working his impressive length. I need him to be as fucked up by this as I'm going to be.

"Fuck me, Jackson." His eyes flash to mine, but he doesn't protest. His fingers leave me, shoving down his pants enough to let his cock loose and fall into my waiting palm. It's thick and heavy. It will probably hurt like hell but I deserve it.

He holds my hips open wide, still firmly pressing my back into the door to hold me up as I line the head of his cock up to my entrance. The tip is barely notched inside of me but he hesitates. I can feel his arms trembling and it has nothing to do with muscle fatigue.

This is too much, it's all too much but I can't stop. I don't want to.

"Say, please," I goad him, needing a sense of control before he fucks the living daylights out of me. His darkened honey eyes find mine and I see the challenge just as he shoves himself to the hilt inside of me. All the way home.

"Please," he grits out while the head of his cock is already crushing my cervix.

I'm too stunned to speak. It's like I can feel him in my stomach, stretching me uncomfortably tight. "Fuck, Jackson," I cry out. He did this on purpose and despite hating him for it, I fucking love it.

I've never been so consumed. I didn't even think dicks like this existed outside of porn and now I'm going to be ruined forever. Fuck him for doing this to me.

I think he mistakes my cry of pleasure as distress because after filling me, he hasn't moved. Our chests rise and fall quickly against each other, our breathing ragged and unsteady until he suddenly shifts us off the door and lays me down on his desk.

Of course, nothing to shove off in a flurry of passion because of how meticulously organized he is. If I wasn't so preoccupied, I'd make fun of him for it.

When he grabs the back of his shirt with an arm stretched behind his head and rips it off, throwing it across the room, my swollen lips hang open. He looks like fucking Hercules. Abs, pecs, all smooth skin. Sculpted from perfection.

I can't stand him.

His eyes are trained on my body, too. I'm laid out in front of him, impaled and at his mercy. My cleavage is spilling out of my bra, my top is still stretched low below the cups. My skirt is bunched at my waist and I watch as his eyes zero in on where we're joined.

I wasn't expecting this to happen with him or anyone. I haven't shaved and refuse to be self-conscious about it, but he also does not look like a man who cares. He's looking at me with nothing but obvious appreciation.

I try to ignore it. If this is only for tonight he can't keep looking at me like that, but he does more than look. He swipes the pad of his thumb over his tongue and draws it through my folds, reaching the peak and circling my clit. The sensation unleashes another whimper from me and I let my head fall back against the wooden desk. I need a muzzle.

When I look at him again because I can't not watch him, he's already watching me with fascination. It's analytical, the way he's touching me, toying with me. I make a sound and he documents it in his head for ways to use it against me later, I'm sure.

His thumb circles my clit again and I bite my lip, refusing to give him any more satisfaction, but he doesn't relent. He rubs me firmly, meticulously, and until my legs start twitching against his hips. He takes that queue to start moving inside of me.

He thrusts his cock in me slowly, only a few inches at a time, working my pussy like he owns it. I don't want that. I don't want him to figure out what makes me tick.

No man has ever made me cum. They either never cared to or weren't smart enough to figure it out. I don't want Jackson to have the satisfaction of being the first.

He would never know, but I would and I can't let that happen. I grab his hips and make him fuck me harder. I want brutal and rough, I don't want soft. He moves with me, letting me control the pace, his jaw slack with pleasure. It's going exactly how I want until his hand starts slipping off my clit with the momentum that I'm forcing.

His gaze flicks to mine and it's as if he realizes I'm taking control for the wrong reason. He takes my arms from his hips and yanks me up until our chests meet, kissing me senseless and stealing every bit of conscious thought from my mind.

The way he kisses me makes me tingle down to my toes.

No one has ever been able to read me so intimately, make me feel things so entirely.

"Don't fight me, not now," he whispers against my lips.

Before I can respond he flips me over like a rag doll, knocking the air from my lungs as I land in position on my stomach.

He doesn't hesitate to drive into me from behind, fucking me, ruthlessly. The grip of his hands on my ass is forcing my hips back as his move forward. It's too much, I can't catch my breath. The length of his cock is hitting my back wall without mercy, over and over. I can't stop the sounds coming out of me and with every thrust, I'm sure I'm going to split in half.

Tears are streaming down my face and my thighs are digging into the edge of the desk repeatedly, with biting pain. I'm going to be bruised and sore tomorrow. The last thing I want is to have something to remember this by.

His hand reaches under my hip and he starts working my

sensitive nub again, never letting up his rhythm. It only takes me a second to realize that it's over for me. The build-up of pressure is too strong, it feels too good. I'm not going to be able to stop myself from climaxing and I've never been more pissed.

Batting his hand away is my last ditch effort to regain my bearings to stop the inevitable, but my hand is wrenched away before I can and both of my arms are pinned behind my back while he fucks me.

My core tightens as my thighs shake, and all I can utter is "no, no, no," as I have the most explosive orgasm of my entire life.

Chapter Fourteen

Jackson

No amount of reason could stop me from driving myself into her over and over. Not even a gun to my head. From the moment she wrapped her arms around me and hugged me, I knew I couldn't fight her. I was going to give her every single thing that she wanted.

No one holds that type of power over me. I've expertly curated my life with absolute independence in mind, never letting a single person influence my decision-making, until her.

Whatever witchcraft she possesses has thrown my life completely off balance. I need the consistency, the logic. My attraction to her is anything but logical. She's rude and abrasive. She sees the worst in me and pulls it to the surface with every interaction.

This time is no different. Except, instead of screaming at each other, I'm fucking her on top of my desk. The desk that I worked my ass off to obtain. I'm practically destroying my career with every thrust of my hips but I can't stop. Not when she's making those little sounds that surge electricity directly into my bloodstream.

Her body is perfect. My deepest desires couldn't have done better.

My hands mold perfectly to the narrow part of her waist, giving me the best control of the hips that I've never been able to stop staring at and an ass that I finally get to appreciate.

It's still not enough, I want to bury my face in it and leave bite marks all over her backside. I want to mark her entire body so she can't ignore that this ever happened. I want her to wake up tomorrow and feel me everywhere. I want her aching for days.

When her tight cunt grips me with her orgasm, it steals the air from my lungs. I feel every part of her clenching every inch of me. My stomach muscles tighten and I know it's over, it feels too good to stop my release.

With great reluctance, I pull out just in time, coating her beautiful ass with my cum. The tip of my cock trails along the valley between her cheeks while I catch my breath, wishing this wasn't over.

That never happens to me. Usually, I finish with a woman and can't get away from them fast enough, whether it's disinterest in them or the commitment. Right now, I want to wrap her in my arms and go again.

I don't dare touch her, though. My brain is regaining enough clarity to know how stupid of an idea that would be. I just never imagined that the best sex of my life would be with a woman who hates the very air I breathe.

And, as suspected, as the last of the sex haze dissipates from around us, a thick cloud of smog descends.

The room is deathly silent, I'm not even sure if she's breathing, but the doom is suffocating. My chest heaves with dread.

Her hands brace themselves on the desk and she pushes herself up slowly before righting her black thong, trapping the mess I left. She doesn't turn around or say anything while she fixes her skirt, pulling it back down to where it belongs midway down her thighs.

It isn't until she smooths her hands over the top of her hair and down her neck that she turns around to face me. Her mascara is smudged, and the usual razer sharp wings of eyeliner are smeared. She looks thoroughly fucked and sexy as hell, but I'm not dumb enough to make that comment.

When her eyes stay averted to the side of the room, my stomach ties itself in knots. This was a mistake.

What the hell did I do?

She kissed me like she hated me, but her hands were in my hair pulling me closer. My mind can't make sense of what transpired but my dick pulses back to life anyway.

"Ceasefire is over. Goodbye, Jackson."

Her dismissal snaps me out of my thoughts and I watch as she retrieves her purse and walks out of my office. She doesn't look back and I don't say a word.

My pants are still around my thighs and she's gone. It's as if it never happened at all.

I licked across every inch of her chest, I was inside of her and I won't soon forget it.

It's already terrorizing me.

I analyze the last few minutes of our encounter. She was moaning, she was enjoying it. Every time a whimper escaped I almost came.

Now she can't even look at me.

She regretted it the moment it was over because she hates me. It's no act, she genuinely hates me.

The knife to my chest is scorching. I wasn't expecting to become allies after this, but I didn't think it would make our situation worse either.

Maybe I let it go too far but there are probably claw marks on my ass from her begging for more. When I flipped her over and fucked her harder than I ever have, I thought that's what she wanted.

My head's in my hands, desperately recalling every moment again. We fucked hard and rough, nothing she couldn't handle but she dismissed me so easily afterward that I feel like I have whiplash.

She came, powerfully. I felt it. She... *"no, no, no."*

She said no.

Jesus Christ.

I was working her with my hand, desperate to feel her orgasm...

She said no and I didn't stop.

"God dammit!" I roar, tossing my chair across the room and shattering a commendation plaque on the wall.

Holy shit I fucked up.

She said no and I kept going, I fucked her until I covered her in my cum.

Was she angry fucking me? Or was she angry that I was fucking her?

I'm reanalyzing every thought that I've had. Was she pulling me in or was she trying to push me away? Fuck.

Was she crying out in pleasure or pain?

I'm going to be sick. I barely make it to the small trash can under my desk before hurling.

Did I hurt her?

Did I take advantage of her?

Chapter Fifteen

Natalie

"Hey, Brax."

"Hey, sweetie," my manager greets me as I come through the door to our coffee shack. She's stocking the cups, preparing for the morning rush. She typically opens and I come right after Dec gets to school.

She's been managing the "Babe Shack" since it opened. It was the only job I could find in this town that would give me the hours I needed. The funds could be better.

Our customers are mostly male and usually generous with tips. I'm probably one of the more modestly dressed baristas but that's only because I'm terrified a parent from school is going to see me and judge Dec for it. I'd probably make more money if I showed more skin, but it's the sacrifice I make to help me pretend I'm doing this guardianship justice.

"Do anything fun last night?" Brax asks innocently but my heart skips a beat.

"Um, no nothing. Stayed in," I lie. I would never tell her that I was getting railed by an Adonis look-alike. Or that he knew exactly what he was doing and how to get it done. My legs are still trembling just thinking about it.

I accepted that he will always live in my memory as the only man to give me an orgasm but because he'll never know, I'm not wasting any time being upset about it. I will take it to my grave. Every time I see his face I will treat him like every other man in this world who pisses me off.

I'll pay him back for every cent he has spent on the hotel that Dec and I are staying in. I'll find somewhere else to live and then that will be the end of it. He can keep paying his deputies the overtime, that is not my problem.

I do my best to ignore the dark cloud over my head, the reason the deputies are watching over us in the first place. Declan might try to hurt Dec. That bastard is going to burn in hell before he ever gets to my baby brother.

Jackson's offer to take us in was ridiculous, but objectively kind. It softened me up enough to make the earth-shattering decision to sleep with him. I am so stupid. Nothing good was going to come of that and I practically took advantage of him. He's a man with a penis, of course, he wasn't going to turn me down.

After he finished, leaving me empty and instantly unsatisfied, I knew I was screwed. He made me finish but that's not what left me unsatisfied. I was disappointed not to feel him explode inside of me. I hated the thought as soon as I had it, but I had it.

I was terrified to look at him and see any disgust or regret on his face after what we did. My nerves couldn't take it. After everything, it's safer to go back to hating each other. Sex changes nothing.

I power through my shift, filling custom coffee and drink orders, and feeling every ache and pain from what we did. The soreness between my legs is a constant reminder and I am trying to ignore it.

When I looked in the mirror after getting dressed this morning, my eyes were drawn to the dermal piercing between my breasts and my whole body heated remembering his tongue on me.

He has stained my brain and it's not fair. It makes me want to scream every time I think about him unprompted.

Damn you, Jackson Malec. Damn you.

* * *

"I'm sorry, honey, he's still not here," the older secretary Jackson called Roberta the other night tells me. This is the second day in a row that I've tried stopping into the Sheriff's Department to give him money.

Regardless of what transpired between us, I have every intention to pay him back for the hotel. A little at a time, but I'll get there. I wanted my effort recognized but this is the second day he isn't in the office.

"Is he busy or something?" I ask, confused. What could make him be away from his office this much?

"No." She glances around to make sure no one is listening. A few people are scattered throughout the lobby and at other desks, but no one is paying attention to us. "He's at home, sick. The flu, I think. Poor guy."

"Oh. Is he okay?" I wasn't expecting that and it's a little concerning since I had my tongue down his throat a few days ago.

"I'm not sure. He's never, ever called off sick before. I'm

afraid it's bad if he's needed to be off this many days." Her sorrowful eyes tell me that she is genuine in her concern. She probably loves the man like a son. "Is there something I can help you with?" She asks, eyeballing the envelope in my hand.

"No, I need to give him this directly. Thank you, though. I'll try tomorrow."

The next morning I called the office number on the business card he had given me weeks ago and spoke to Roberta directly. She informed me that he called off for the third day. I assured her I'd check on him and she thanked me profusely. I didn't have the heart to tell her my reasons are mostly selfish.

I want to drop the money off and get the burden off my shoulders one block at a time. Making sure he is okay is only a ruse. If he's passed out, dehydrated on the floor, then I'll let someone know but only because I wouldn't want Roberta to have a heart attack if something happened to her precious Sheriff.

When I pull in, crossing over a small creek that separates his property from the road, the sun is shining down on the pristine white driveway. The house is no different, a modern cottage with a black roof and doors, the white siding looks brand new. It couldn't have been built more than a year ago. Everything's clean and perfect, but simple, boring even.

Huge, winding garden beds are the only outlier. Taking up a lot of the front lawn, they're all freshly mulched and beautiful, giving character to the yard. The trees are spread out enough that I imagine when the flowers bloom fully in the summer they're visible from the road.

Between the creek in the front and the mountainside behind the house, I can see why he said his house was safe. It'd be hard to sneak up on him here. Which is why I cringe slightly as my noisy Honda Civic makes its presence known.

An older woman with a short gray bob meets me in the driveway. She removes her gardening gloves to shield her eyes from the sun and watches as I approach.

"Hi, I am looking for the Sheriff," I tell her, kindly. She's older and thin, wearing a faded jean blouse and a gardening apron.

"Sheriff?" She asks, confusion marring her features. "I'm so sorry, you must have the wrong house."

"Oh, um." I check the picture I have of his ID, and the house numbers by the door match. Maybe she is the gardener and she's mistaken about who lives here.

"Do you like to garden?" She asks, not at all put off by my current predicament.

"Well, I've never had one to practice in, but I've always wanted to learn." I shrug and she smiles warmly, making me smile.

"What are you doing here?" My head snaps up when I hear his voice. He's striding down the driveway toward us, only wearing tennis shoes and athletic shorts that hit a few inches above his knee. His chest is bare, coated with a sheen of sweat. The garage door is open behind him and full of gym equipment.

He doesn't look sick. He's looking at me with guarded eyes, setting my defenses high. Is he offended that I would show up here? Is it supposed to be a secret that we know each other?

"Oh, Jacks. She's here to garden with me," the older woman says, grasping my hand. She must have been reluctant to admit who lived here. I'm sure he doesn't want random people to know where he resides.

"Mom, no, I don't-"

"Yep, I'm here to garden with your mom, *Jacks*." I let her tug me along and I stick my tongue out at him as I'm guided into the yard. He looks at me with utter confusion. Even as his mother gets me settled in front of a garden bed and I glance back at him, he's still standing in the same spot staring at us.

"He looks scared."

"Who dear?"

"Jackson. He looks afraid that you'll tell me embarrassing things about him."

She laughs softly but doesn't say anything as she starts pulling weeds from the dirt and pruning stems. Instead, she starts explaining the types of flowers she is growing, when their peak bloom is, and how to take care of them.

She speaks with such eloquent detail that I'm awestruck. I've always wanted to learn this stuff but I didn't have a mom who cared to try. She would have killed anything green before it even had a chance.

I don't even realize how much time has passed until Jackson comes over to us, shading me suddenly from the sun. "Mom, your ride is going to be here soon." He's wearing a t-shirt now and holding a water bottle.

His mom looks at me and tilts her head. "I'm sorry, dear, what's your name?"

"Natalie."

"Oh, how beautiful. You were meant to be a florist," she declares, happily.

"Mom," Jackson says again to get her attention. She ignores him.

"Are you one of Jacks' teachers?" Her brows are furrowed in confusion as she asks. She's looking at me like she's seeing me for the first time.

"No, Mom. She's my... acquaintance. Come on we have to hurry." He helps her up to her feet by her forearms, removing her gloves and apron and tossing them into a basket nearby.

"Acquaintance, huh?" I remark, subtly.

"I'll be right back," he mumbles as he guides her past me.

They go into the house and a few minutes later a small white bus pulls into the end of the driveway, giving a quick rap on the horn. Jackson comes back out of the house with his mom, hand in hand. He walks her to the bus and helps her up the steps before stepping back to wave.

After the bus backs out onto the road, his walk back to me is slow and reluctant. He nods for me to follow him and I do, tracing his steps to the garage, because my nosiness is getting the best of me.

He sits down on a workout bench, motioning for me to do the same on the box across from him.

"Why did you come here?" His tone is guarded like before, confused.

"You've called off three times."

He huffs out a breath and grumbles, "Roberta."

There's a silence that descends. I don't feel like talking about the money I brought, I'd rather ask him about his mom. Maybe it's because mine is dead now, but I have an overt curiosity about other people's family dynamics.

"Your mom-" I start but he cuts me off.

"She has Alzheimer's."

Chapter Sixteen

Jackson

16 years ago...

"Mom!" I run inside the house and skid to a stop in the kitchen, dropping my baseball bag on the floor. "You missed my game!" I grumble. This is the third game she's missed. Everyone else's parents are in the stands cheering for them when they get a hit and I have no one. It's embarrassing.

"Mom!" I yell, again, kicking off my dirty shoes. I stomp through the house looking for her. It's not that hard, it's tiny. Her bedroom is the only one on the main level, my room's in the attic upstairs.

I find her sitting on her bed, wearing her bathrobe. It looks like she just got out of the shower, but her hair is dry. "Mom, why did you miss my game? Again!" I whine in a way that I'd only let her witness.

"What, sweetie?" She looks at me with confusion. "Why aren't you at school?"

"It's nine o'clock, why would I be at school?"

She glances at the window and shakes her head. "Oh my. How did it get so late? I had no idea. I'm so sorry, Jacks." She rushes over and hugs me, squeezing me in a way that only moms can. She's a tiny woman, I've towered over her for a few years already, but she gives me the best hugs.

"It's okay. I want you at the next one though, okay? It's our last home game."

"Yes, dear," she scolds gently. She calls me dear when I try to boss her around, subtly telling me I'm too big for my britches.

"Love you, Momma." Sealing it with a kiss on the top of her head like she did for me when she could reach it, her absence at my game is already forgiven.

* * *

Natalie's presence is unsettling. First, she shows up unannounced and then sits on her knees in the grass with my mom for thirty minutes completely ignoring me. I don't know why she's here and I'm terrified to find out.

I'm so ashamed of myself. I haven't had the nerve to wear my badge for days because of how I treated her. I've continued to replay what happened in my office over in my head in every direction and I still don't know which way I've interpreted is correct.

She has every right to hate me, to belittle me if she pleases, but I need her to leave my mom out of it. She gets confused easily. The disease has eaten away at her for years and she's sensitive to conflict and to change.

"She seemed comfortable in the garden," Natalie murmurs, her normal edge is replaced with something softer.

"It's her happy place. She was a private gardener for years before she got sick. It seems to be deeply ingrained in there."

107

I motion to my head so she understands what I mean.

"You keep the garden for her?"

"Yeah. She lives in an Assisted Living Home a couple of miles down the road. On her good days, they arrange to let her come work in the yard." I shrug. I'm using my mother to avoid having a real discussion.

"Is she okay? Healthy otherwise?" She asks as if she isn't sure if she's overstepping.

"She's healthy as a horse despite her brain. It started with little memory slips. Then it became more severe and she couldn't take care of herself. The older I got, the more confused she was when I entered a room. She didn't recognize the man in her home and would get scared. That sucked." I sigh, heavily. "Still does."

"She still sees you as her little boy?"

"She only knows me as Jacks. Sheriff Malec doesn't exist to her."

"I'm sorry, Jackson." Her understanding is a nice change of pace but it's unnerving that she's being so nice. I'm waiting for the other shoe to drop.

"It's okay. I got the normal version of her through most of my childhood. She wasn't given the official diagnosis until I was a senior in high school. Thank you for being kind to her."

More silence descends, neither of us knowing what to say. I can't avoid it forever so I bite the bullet. "Why did you come here?"

"Why do you sound so offended that I did?"

"After what happened the other night I wasn't sure I'd see you again. You ran out on me pretty quick."

"So? We had sex. We agreed to one time. Did you expect

me to cuddle?" The fire in her eyes is back and I'm kind of glad. I can handle her anger better than her niceness.

"No, but I wasn't sure…"

"You weren't sure about what?" She snaps.

I stand up, pacing the length of my garage. I can't look at her when I say the next words. "I figured that you regretted it, but you did want it? Right?"

"What?"

"Christ, Natalie." I squeeze my eyes shut.

"What, Jackson? Spit it out." She huffs.

"It was consensual, right?"

"What?"

"Don't make me ask, again. Please." I stare at the ceiling, wishing I was anywhere else but having this conversation.

"Are you asking if I felt forced?" She seethes, the venom in her voice evident.

"Yeah."

"What the hell is wrong with you?" The volume of her voice bounces off the walls.

"I've been racking my brain, reliving it. I can't sleep because all I think about is you saying 'no.' I didn't stop when you said no."

Her head jerks back a millimeter and I watch her eyes dancing as if she's combing through her memory. Then she laughs. The least joyful laugh that I've ever heard.

"You idiot. You've been home sick from work because of your guilt? You thought that you took advantage of me?" She asks incredulously.

I'm glad she finds this so bizarre, it clears my consciousness slightly even though she's still yelling at me.

"You were in *my* office. I'm in a position of power. I'm a

man and you said no. I should have heard you right away and I should have listened," I explain consent to her like I would a teenager for my own benefit. It's black and white but I feel very gray about the encounter we had.

She stands up and jabs her finger in my chest. There might as well be an electric current striking me down. "I am going to say this one time and then we are never speaking of it again, clear?" She asks, her eyes narrowed to slits.

"Uh. Clear."

"What we did was completely consensual. We, two grown adults, had sex. You did not coerce me because you are a man of authority or because you are a man. I came on to you to scratch an itch. You would never be smart enough to convince me to have sex with you if I wasn't willing." Her finger jabs me with each punctuation of her sentences until I fall back to sitting on the workout bench.

She stands over me, glowering at me and despite the fury being directed at me, I'm so fucking relieved.

"Why did you say no?"

Her jaw locks at my question.

"It doesn't matter, forget it. Go back to work and stop feeling sorry for yourself. You are a grown man. Act like it." She turns and storms out of the garage grumbling to herself while I stay glued to where I'm sitting.

It was consensual. All of my grief has been for nothing. Sleepless nights and not being able to stomach food has been for nothing. I bury my face in my hands and breathe easily for the first time in days.

I hear her grumbling again and whip my head up to see her storming back into the garage with a bag in her hand. "Here. I brought you this because I thought you had the flu."

She shoves it into my hands and the savory smell hits me immediately.

"You made me soup?"

"No. I made my brother soup, you get the leftovers. Go back to work!" She shouts, stomping back to her car, peeling a u-turn in my driveway, and leaving tire marks in my grass.

I feel like I've been picked up and tossed around by a hurricane. I cannot get a read on this woman to save my life.

When I open the bag, there's an envelope with a hot pink logo in the corner. "Babe Shack." Huh. Inside is a stack of small bills.

Her first payment.

Chapter Seventeen

Natalie

I don't know why his interpretation of our sexual encounter has made me so upset, but I can't stop scream-crying into the interior of my car as I drive. Not actual tears, but full-blown crying out to the universe with my frustration.

He is just another man who has intruded into my life and tried to best me somehow. Every male of the human species feels like they have an automatic advantage over women as if our little female brains can't pick up on their gaslighting and manipulation tactics. Jackson is no different.

Instead of admitting that he partook in a consensual one-time fling, he twisted it in his mind that he coerced me. As if he is capable.

I am a grown woman and I know what coercion looks like. I've lived it. I don't need him to dumb it down for me. He made me a victim and I am no one's victim.

This is exactly why I am paying back the money for the hotel. I will never let anyone think they have something to hold against me. As if they have power over me.

Maybe I'm being irrational but I don't care. Jackson Malec

is never going to touch me again. He and his high and mighty horse.

Two more weeks living in the hotel and I am no closer to finding a new place to live. A few apartments I've looked into require more money for a deposit than I have in my bank account and the first month's rent upfront.

How do single mothers survive like this?

I've only been doing it a year and feel like I'm buried neck-deep in quicksand. I can't get a second job because I need to take care of Dec after school and on weekends. I can't afford childcare. I don't have a village to supplement the childcare. It's impossible.

Brax has been scheduling me every day during the week at the coffee shack, but by the time I ration my tips to put toward my hotel fund, I hardly have anything left. Dec and I have been eating a lot of doctored-up ramen cooked off the hotplate at the hotel because I refuse to go on any more bad dinner dates.

He hasn't complained because he gets different stuff at school, and a few times he's had dinner at his friend's house. I on the other hand have been living off of off-brand granola bars and peanut butter crackers during the day.

Sometimes I'll snag the day-old muffins from the coffee shack before they're thrown away and that's a nice little treat. The real prize is when someone's order is wrong and we take back their drink to give them a new one. No matter what kind of concoction it is, the caffeine is welcome.

Today has been one of those days that I need the boost to get through my shift. It's not even noon and I've been asked on two dates, hardly filled my tip jar at all, and spilled a hot cup of coffee down my legs.

"Woah, easy tiger." Brax laughs as I slam the dirty paper towels into the trash can.

"This day has been the worst," I utter.

"Well, it's lookin' up. Look who is pulling in." I glance at the monitor that shows us the cars as they approach and groan. No fucking way.

"Why is he here," I grumble to myself.

"The man is hot, hot." She raises her eyebrows suggestively and I ignore her. She has no idea that I know him so... Intimately.

"Good morning, Sheriff," she sing-songs through the window, leaning suggestively over the ledge and pushing her tits obnoxiously high. She wears nothing more than a few scraps of fabric to work, and it works for her. She's tall, hot, and has bleach-blonde extensions that get her plenty of compliments.

Her tip jar is almost always full.

My less-than-shining personality, dark hair, and pear-shaped body do not receive the same love. It's fine, I don't wish to garner male attention anyway, but I want the money. So some days I lay on my customer service thick. This is not a customer I will be doing that for.

Jackson is almost rudely staring out of his front window, not looking at Brax in the slightest, almost making me laugh. He's so uncomfortable that it's comical.

"I'm looking for Natalie."

"Natalie? She have a warrant or something?"

I roll my eyes from behind her.

"It's okay, Brax. He probably just wants to talk to me about my brother's dad."

She nods in understanding. I've told her tidbits about the

case but not all the details of my life. We're not necessarily friends.

"Okay, I'll go take my break." She winks at Jackson as she leaves our little shed, but his eyes are focused on me now. They trace my body with intense accuracy and I wish that he didn't know what my vagina looks like. Ugh.

"What do you want?"

"What? You can show up to my house uninvited but I can't show up to your job?" He asks, finally tearing his eyes off my low-cut black halter top. I don't know why he's looking, there is a lot less to see than on Brax.

"How did you even know that I was here?"

"I put a BOLO out on your car," he states seriously.

"You did what?!" I screech.

"I'm kidding. The envelope you gave me came from here and I took a lucky guess that you would be working." He looks at me like I'm dense.

"You're such an asshole."

"It's an interesting uniform."

"Shut up, I don't need your opinion. Either order or leave."

"Coffee, black." Of course, he has the most boring drink order. Instead of doing what he asked, I pull out the caramel drizzle and steam some milk.

When I glance back at him to see if he's noticed that I'm making his order wrong, his stare is glued to my ass. Men are too simple to be allowed to function in society.

I shift my apron around my waist, twisting it so the pockets hang down the back and cover my cheeky velvet shorts. His eyes snap to mine and I smirk.

"I should call in and complain," I threaten lightly. I never would, not after jumping him in his office, but I might be tempted if he pissed me off anymore.

"Complain to who?"

"I don't know. The Mayor. Judge Reisner."

"They don't care if I'm looking at your ass. They probably would too."

I gape at him, searching his eyes for the joke. He's absurdly serious.

"Maybe I'll tell Roberta then. Your nice little secretary would probably scold you." His jaw clenches because he knows I'm right. "Here."

He grabs the hot drink from me and sniffs it. "What is this?"

"Caramel macchiato. $6.00"

His eyes bulge. "For a cup of coffee? It's not even the one that I asked for." I only shrug.

"This is ridiculous. I knew I'd regret coming here." He digs out his wallet anyway, shoving his card into the machine that I'm offering out the window to him.

"Why did you come here? Just to get a glimpse at the butt you'll never get to touch again?"

He scoffs but otherwise ignores me, getting to the tip screen on the card machine.

"Both guys who asked me out today left me the biggest tips, just so you know. In case you're worried about me comparing *tips.*"

"What is wrong with you?" He looks at me incredulously and it makes me laugh with triumph. It's not always easy to rile him up, but I do notice that he hit 20%.

"I came here because there has been an update in Declan's case and the prosecutor wants to meet with us. I told him I would let you know and that neither of us would miss the appointment. This time."

I ignore his remark about missing the appointment because my mind is already coming up with all of the reasons there might be an update. "Is it good or bad?" My heart is suddenly beating out of my chest.

"I don't know. Either way, we'll figure it out."

Six hours later, we're seated across from each other at a long wooden table in the prosecutor's office. Neither of us speaks, staring at each other blankly.

"Do you guys need time to process this or..?" Prosecutor Fulton asks from the head of the table.

He just got done telling us that the Lawson PD Detective who was the lead investigator on Declan's arrest, had just been arrested himself for planting evidence on a different case two years ago. All of his cases are being looked at.

"Declan's case will be dismissed then?" Jackson asks, never taking his eyes off of me. It's as if he's waiting for me to explode. He's assessing my internal temperature increase by the second.

"There is a strong possibility. Yes. Nothing is set in stone as of now, but we'll meet with the judge next week. You should be prepared for that scenario," he directs to me, but I ignore him.

Declan is going to get out. He's getting away with murdering my mother. Dec's mom. He is going to be released because some mother fucker screwed up. This can't be happening.

I push up from my seat and nearly trip over my feet exiting the room, throwing the door wide with a crash. "Nat!" Jackson calls after me but I keep walking.

When his footsteps get heavier, catching up to me, I break into a run. I can't do this.

I smash the elevator buttons, desperately. Please, open.

117

Please.

As soon as the door slides open a crack I jump in, hitting the close door button, but it's no use. Jackson stops the doors from closing with a meaty palm and steps inside with me.

"Go away."

"No."

"Why? Go discuss this with the prosecutor. You know, one of your fellow bigwigs that hold all the power and whatnot. I'm just one of the ants you people get to stomp all over."

"I told you we'd figure it out."

"There is no we! I am going to take care of Dec like I always have. You are going to go back to shooting people or whatever the hell you do all day."

"That's not fair."

"Life isn't fair! Obviously!" The doors open to the lobby and I sweep past him. "Time and time again, I learn that all cops are assholes. They don't know how to do their job and they screw everyone over. Including you!" I scream.

Luckily it's after hours and the building is closed. There aren't any witnesses to this.

"Don't lump me in with all cops. Some are bad, yes. Some shouldn't have a badge, agreed. I can't control the actions of all of them. I can only stop the corruption in this department. Lawson PD does not correlate with me. I can't control what happens there but I can try to fix this."

"You can't. Declan's case will be dismissed and then he'll be a free man. The criminal justice system has failed me once again." I turn my back and walk away. I walk away from him. I walk away from this case.

All I can do is focus on Dec, now. If Declan's getting out then I need to protect him even more.

Chapter Eighteen

Jackson

"Mrs. Porter, I cannot meet with you today, I am slammed with a case. I apologize but I'll have to get in touch with you when things slow down." I end the phone call as painlessly as possible and continue staring at the wall in my office-turned evidence board.

A kidnapping off of I-83 a year and a half ago uncovered a trafficking ring.

Four more people have been declared missing since then.

A domestic extremist group attempted to set off a bomb in the middle of a local race in downtown Lawson.

The boy who wore the backpack that day had been drugged for weeks and used as bait... Where did Thomas Jameson get those drugs?

From the same place as a long-time criminal, drug dealer, and user who supplied his estranged wife with a pill that was laced with fentanyl and ultimately killed her?

It's too hard to prove.

Declan Randolph was in jail, but could he have done it? Would one of his associates have given Jameson the same type of drugs that Declan had a supply of?

He's been in jail for almost a year already so why the big rush to get out now?

The investigator on his case was arrested for planting evidence, leading to all of his cases being investigated and overturned. Declan's included.

What are the chances that would happen right after our deal fell through?

Who would Declan be in contact with that would have the power to set a fire and leave no trace of themselves behind, as well as outing a veteran Detective for an old screw-up?

All my questions continue to lead me back to the same place. There is someone who is controlling all of this. Is it the same person who orchestrated the trafficking scheme and funded Thomas Jameson's bomb-making extremist group?

But, who?

I start combing through every name I have on the board. I need to find out who their known associates are, who they're related to, where they grew up, and where they lived before they were arrested. I need to know every detail and find out every single thing that overlaps.

I start with Declan, my most recent subject. Running his known associates, my database comes up with a list of names I'm already familiar with. His posse that comes to sit in on his court hearings and harasses his stepdaughter are all nonviolent, low-level offenders. I go through each person anyway, checking their known associates, and come up empty.

Possession of drugs, Intent to traffic drugs, Possession of drug paraphernalia, etc. are not typically crimes that prelude to committing arson or killing your wife. Except for one charge of Domestic Violence that was dropped years ago.

Nicole Halstead, Natalie's mother, is listed on the report but the victim is redacted because they were a minor.

My blood starts to heat. Who do I know that would have been a minor then and related to Nicole Halstead?

Son of a bitch.

No wonder Natalie hates Declan. He hurt her and then her mother stayed with the man. No one has protected this girl, ever. I can see why she is so protective of Dec.

That starts me on a path of researching Natalie. She's 25 which I already knew, her birthday is two days before Christmas and she probably hates that. She was born to Nicole Halstead with no father listed on her birth certificate. Huh, I guess we have something in common after all.

She has a recent ticket out of New York City. A parking ticket that has not been paid. Christ, Nat. The last thing Dec needs is for her to be forced to appear in court in New York.

I pull up the website and pay it before she gets a warrant out for her arrest. This woman, I swear. She will be the death of me in some way.

Having my card out already reminds me to call the hotel and extend the reservation for her and Dec another week.

"She's already checked out, sir," the front desk clerk tells me politely.

"What?" I ask way too loudly.

"She checked out yesterday morning. The leftover room balance will be refunded to your card."

"Did she say where she was going?"

"Uh. No, I don't think so. I don't usually ask those kinds of questions," the clerk sounds startled, probably because I'm using my cop voice on her.

"Right, I'm sorry. Have a good day."

Where the hell did she go? And why hasn't my deputy checked in with me to tell me that she's disappeared?

He's my next call. "Stew, what's Miss Halstead doing?"

"Well, she's hanging out in her hotel room I reckon," Stewart draws, sleepily.

"Uh-huh. Would that be the hotel that she is no longer a guest of? Since she checked out yesterday!"

"Uhh. I guess so?"

"Get back to the office. I'm docking your pay for today unless you get on the road and accomplish some real police work."

"Yes, Sheriff."

I rub my head, cursing myself for ever taking this job. What was I thinking? I know what I was thinking but did I have any suspicion that it would turn me gray prematurely? No.

Where the hell are you, Nat?

Instead of calling her which would be the sensical thing to do. I dial Lawson Elementary and confirm Dec's attendance. He's where he is supposed to be, so she's not far. That's a guarantee.

I'm finally diving back into my suspect names when my office door flies open. I'm about to reprimand whoever just did that when I take in a disheveled Roberta, looking at me with concern.

"What is it?"

"It's your mother."

Chapter Nineteen

Natalie

W hy are tampons so expensive? Even the generic ones without all the pretty wrapping are hardly cheaper than the name brand. I could start using a diva cup but I am not messing with a cheap one if that's the case. It will suction out my uterus or something.

I'm about to pick up the smallest box of generic tampons when raised voices reach my ears. It's the middle of the afternoon and the drugstore was relatively dead when I came in, so it's not hard to hear the commotion. Mirrors along the highest part of the wall show me the reflection of the rest of the store.

The altercation is taking place in the pharmacy and the owner of the raised voice is eerily familiar-looking. When the pharmacist takes his turn, raising his voice back at the gray-haired woman who I now recognize, I can't stop my feet from moving.

"My pills. I need my pills. You have them back there, I know it." Ms. Malec cries out, smacking both of her frail hands on the counter repeatedly. It's not loud but it screams desperation.

"I have no idea what you are talking about, ma'am. We have no pills for you, you're causing a scene. You'll be trespassed if you don't leave." The man is middle-aged and his scowl is hardened by those years.

"Please, I need them. I need them." She begins to cry, obviously confused, and his dismissal is only making her more upset.

"You aren't getting anything from me. Go," he scolds her like a child and that's enough for me.

"She's only trying to get help. You don't need to be rude," I accuse the balding pharmacist.

"Please, she's the rude one."

"Excuse me? She has issues with her memory. I'm sure the medication she's asking for is related to it but you're being too much of an ass to check. Right?"

He glances at his screen and purses his lips. "I'm just the manager here. I don't have access to the pharmacist's logs."

"And, you're doing a bang-up job, asshole."

He scoffs, steam blowing from his ears. "Doesn't matter. The cops are already on their way."

"The cops? You called the cops on a confused old woman? You should be ashamed of yourself." I turn, dismissing the dumbass manager entirely. "Ms. Malec," I speak gently to her. "Let's go, we can wait outside and away from this mean ugly man." He grumbles something rude but I ignore him.

"I'm sorry. I didn't mean to cause a fuss. I need my medicine," she pleads quietly. Her eyes are wary and sad.

"I know. I'll figure it out. Come on." I grab her gently by the hand and lead her away from the pharmacy counter.

"You're banned, too!" The manager yells. I turn around and launch my box of tampons toward him, not close enough to hit him, but close enough to make him flinch. If I'm banned, better get my worth out of it.

"What's your name?" She asks me as we exit the store. It's a nice spring day and I'm glad. There is no way I could let her stay in that store to be berated.

"I'm Natalie. I know your son. We met once and you showed me how to plant some flowers."

"Oh." She doesn't remember me but she also doesn't let go of my hand as I ask her about gardening. We sit together on a bench and I let her talk until the first police cruiser arrives. Lawson PD, of course.

The officer approaches us but I hold my hand up to stop him. "We aren't talking to you. Call Sheriff Malec."

"The Sheriff doesn't come to calls like this. It's my jurisdiction and you both are being trespassed for disorderly conduct."

"Call the Sheriff."

"You don't get to tell me what to do, lady." The cop huffs.

"Call him. I'm sure he would like to hear directly from you that his mother is being trespassed from a store for being discriminated against." The officer balks at my use of discrimination or because I told him that Ms. Malec is Jackson's mom. Either way, he backpedals, leaving us alone.

Ms. Malec continues telling me about all the beautiful gardens she has worked on and her favorite flowers to plant while I keep an eye on the parking lot. Two more Lawson PD cruisers pull in but no one approaches us.

It's an unsettling feeling. I've never been a fan of law enforcement, but I've never truly been on their wrong side either. As their numbers and power outweigh me significantly, I'm using Ms. Malec as a crutch for strength.

If I'm arrested, I'd gladly take my charge if it means I was standing up for what's right. Helping Ms. Malec out of this situation is absolutely the right choice.

Finally, after ten minutes, the Sheriff Suburban comes flying into the parking lot and I breathe a sigh of relief. His tires screech to a halt right in front of the curb before us. Ms. Malec curls into me slightly, startled. She doesn't know that he's here to help us, or her rather.

"Mom, what are you doing here?" He asks before he's even out of his car all the way. Her shaking body pushes into mine further and I realize it's because she's truly scared of him. He's wearing his full uniform today, a vest and belt with all his go-go gadgets attached. She doesn't recognize him.

Jackson realizes it too because he rips the Velcro from his sides and shoulders, tossing the Kevlar off over his head. It lands with a heavy plop on the sidewalk as the Lawson PD officers watch on, shaking their heads in obvious annoyance. Their judgment of the Sheriff's approach is displayed clearly, and filled with contempt.

It doesn't matter, I can only focus on the man in front of me. His hair is disheveled and his face is lined with worry. He looks... Tired.

"Mom, it's me. Jacks."

"No, no. Jacks is my boy. My baby boy," she mumbles against the arm she's grasping. My heart is fracturing into little pieces for her, I can't imagine her confusion and fear.

Jackson looks at me directly for the first time with so many questions in his eyes but all I can do is shrug for now. "Ms. Malec, remember when I said that I knew Jacks? He'd want me to take care of you so I'm going to make sure you get home, okay?"

"Okay." She nods softly against my shoulder.

Jackson hangs his head for a second before standing up and retrieving his vest. He holds his hand out for his mom but she shies away so he drops it limply. That has to hurt but he doesn't say a word.

"Do you think you can get her into my car?" He asks, dryly.

"I'll try." I take her by the elbow and shuffle her toward the Suburban but as soon as she sees the big bold letters she stiffens. "It's okay, he's going to take you home."

"No. Don't leave me. He's going to put me in jail. Please, don't leave," she begs and I don't know what to do.

"I can take her in my car if you'll lead the way," I offer. He only nods stiffly.

I buckle her into my passenger seat without a fight and we make the five-minute drive with no more difficulty while she talks of the importance of planting bulbs in late autumn. Luckily, she never needed a word from me because my eyes stayed glued on my rearview mirror and the man driving behind me. His seriousness reflects harshly, but I imagine it's covering a great deal of sadness over his mother.

Unlike mine, his loved him and treated him kindly, and now she's gone in her own way. An ideal maternal figure snatched away by a disease while my mom chose to destroy her life. And, to neglect me. His mom never chose to abandon her son.

As we pull up to the curb of the assisted living home, nurses are rushing out to greet us.

"Bye, Ms. Malec."

"Thank you for spending time with me, dear," she tells me kindly as she's led inside. She has no idea of the ruckus she caused.

"Why were you with her?" Jackson spits his question at me as if I'm the scum on the bottom of his boot.

"Excuse me?"

"She wasn't where she was supposed to be, she was missing. And, with you!" He flings his hands out toward me, the *you* in question. As if I am the worst person his mother could ever be seen with.

"She wasn't with me, you insufferable pig. She was alone and scared! I stepped in to help her because I just so happened to be in the right place at the right time. So, no. She wasn't with me until I held her hand and walked her away from the grown man yelling at her. I held her hand while I told off the cop who was trying to trespass her. I let her cling to me while we waited for you!" I scream, embarrassingly loud.

He doesn't flinch and no one in the assisted living center comes out to check on us. Probably a good thing because I would give them a piece of my mind too for losing Ms. Malec in the first place.

"Here is a bright idea. Instead of accusing me of conspiring against you, walk your tight ass in there and yell at them!"

His jaw locks, his teeth undoubtedly grinding together. "Sorry," he mumbles.

"What? What was that? I couldn't hear you because of how big of an asshole you were being."

He exhales roughly. "I'm sorry. I am an asshole."

I wasn't expecting him to admit that so easily and I'm not ready with a witty comeback. I can only stare at him blankly.

"I was scared out of my mind when they said she was missing. I wasn't thinking straight. I'm still not. If something ever happened to her I'd..."

He doesn't finish his thought. His dejected stare at the

ground keeps me from badgering him anymore even though he might deserve it.

"We're even okay. Dec and your mom are innocent. We might hate each other but neither of us is that insane. Our family is irrelevant to whatever argument you and I might be having. Okay?"

"Family ceasefire?" He suggests.

"Don't ever use that terminology again. It's what got us in trouble last time. Family is off-limits. That's it." I turn to get in my car.

"Thank you, Nat," he calls out after me.

"Don't call me that!" My door slams and I can only fight the urge to scream until I'm out of his earshot.

Chapter Twenty

Jackson

"Where have you been?" I ask the seething barista who saved my mom the other day.

"Will you ever leave me alone? I want to go one day without seeing your ugly mug." Her insult doesn't bug me because I know she doesn't think it's true. I think.

"I am being neutral toward you only to tell you that the judge will make his ruling tomorrow." I don't have to elaborate. She knows I'm referring to the decision that will mean Declan gets out of jail and back on the streets.

"Great. See you tomorrow. Bye." She dismisses me but I don't move my foot from the break. Instead, I put the SUV in park. She rolls her eyes at me.

"Where did you go after you left the hotel? It's the third day I've wondered where you're laying your pretty head at night."

"Awh, you think I'm pretty," she says sweetly, dripping with sarcasm.

"It was an expression." I think she's gorgeous but she does not need that fuel added to her fire. "I could call child services and ask that they provide me with your current whereabouts, assuming you've been checking in with them as Dec's guardian."

The look on her face is nothing short of murderous. That was a low blow on my part and I am aware. I'm also desperate to know where she's been.

"You wouldn't dare."

I shrug in response but I wouldn't. I think she's doing a great job with Dec.

She turns her back to me momentarily when a machine behind her starts beeping incessantly and I grind my teeth together to stop from making any audible noises.

She's wearing a pair of black spandex shorts that start at her waist and end midway down her ass. The rounded exposed skin is a reminder of what we did and will never do again. Though, I've thought about it every single day, multiple times a day since then.

I peel my eyes away just in time for her to turn around and hand me a coffee I didn't ask for. "What is it this time?"

She snorts. "It's black coffee. I only fucked with you last time because I thought you'd give it back and I'd get it for free."

"You don't get free drinks here?"

"No. Only the mistakes and stale leftovers."

"Tell me where you've been the last few days and I'll buy your drink for you."

Her eyes narrow but she eyes my cup longingly. "I've been staying with a guy."

"What?!" I sputter, almost spilling the hot coffee I had started to drink. "You moved Dec in with some random guy?" I'm suddenly disagreeing with my previous opinion of her caretaking abilities.

"He's someone that I met casually online. Why is that a

problem? You wanted us to move in with you and you're some random guy, too."

"I'm not random and I'm a cop. It's different."

"Yeah. Whatever."

The thought of her being with some strange guy makes my blood boil, especially with how her last date ended. "How could you do that to Dec?"

"Okay. You're done. You are overstepping. I'll see you tomorrow." She waves a hand dismissively and turns around, ignoring me since I still haven't moved.

"What's his name? Let me at least run a background check on him."

"No," she says into the interior of the shack.

"Fine. Here's your money." I hand her a twenty.

"Would it make you feel better to know that he also started coming here regularly to harass me?" She pouts dramatically.

"So, he's a stalker. Great. Real good role model for Dec."

Her eyes narrow again, the same way they do every time I mention her brother.

"Fuck off, Sheriff."

* * *

I planned to spend the day in the office. I didn't want anything to keep me from the emergency hearing regarding Declan's case. It'll be dismissed, there's no doubt in my mind but I want to be there to hear it myself.

Unfortunately, someone called in and requested a parole check on Second Chance Sanctuary and now I'm driving deep into the mountains on the other side of the county to waste my time.

Lochlan Dane, the owner of a black bear sanctuary, employs convicted felons but is nothing but above board. Each of these checks is time-consuming and unnecessary because he keeps his boys in line.

I pull through the gates to his property and the grizzly of a man greets my vehicle before I can put it in park. If I didn't know better, someone like Lochlan would normally keep my spine locked and my defenses on alert, but the 6'6 giant of a man has been nothing but respectful toward me since I've had the badge. He's had a rough history with law enforcement and I wouldn't judge him for holding a grudge, but luckily, we've never had any issues.

"Mr. Dane, sorry to come out here and disturb your day. We had another anonymous call to check on the parolees." I shake his hand, not bothering to waste any time with ego checks.

"I figured. The guys are in the barn." He accompanies me down to one of the larger barns on the property and stands idle while I do what I need. Weapons checks, drug checks, the usual. As with each time, there are no issues, but checking their bunks and living spaces is time-consuming. It takes me half the afternoon.

"Thanks for your cooperation, as always. Hopefully, I won't see you for a while." I turn to get back in my cruiser, already calculating how fast I need to drive to make it back to the courthouse in time but he clears his throat, stopping me.

"We've had some issues with harassment, not sure it's a problem but since you're here." He shrugs, not giving much of anything else away. He's a man of few words but I understand his language.

"Violent?"

"Not yet."

"What's happened so far?"

"Hate mail. Garbage is being thrown over the fences. One night on the farther side of the property it sounded like someone was trying to pull one of the gates down with a tow chain. They were gone by the time we got there but they left the broken chain behind."

"You have any idea who it is?"

"We aren't short on enemies, Sheriff. Anyone who hates what we stand for has made it known."

I look at him, slightly puzzled, because I wasn't aware he was receiving any backlash. He rehabilitates felons and bears, it's not exactly devious.

He notices my confusion and enlightens me. "People in town don't like rubbing elbows with felons. They hate that I have the largest property in Langston and they don't get to profit off of it. They hate that they can't exploit the bears."

"Ah. Well, you're doing everything right in my eyes. I've got your back if things get worse. If anything else happens document it the best you can. Get some cameras if you don't have any but call me if there's a new incident. I'll keep an official log and if the harassment becomes a bigger issue, we'll nail down who is responsible."

He seems surprised by my response. His eyes widen subtly but he quickly covers it and reaches out to shake my hand. "Appreciate it, Sheriff."

By the time I make it back into town, I've broken multiple speed limits. After a quick pit stop in my office, I'm in the clear to get to the courthouse. To Natalie.

Not that she cares if I'm there, but I'll feel better being there when she hears the bad news. I might have to stop her from hitting someone.

As I pull my office door closed and lock it, I immediately feel someone's eyes on the back of my head.

"Sheriff, there you are!" The chipper voice belongs to one singular person and I am not in the mood for fake niceties.

"Mrs. Porter." I acknowledge her with a nod but continue walking past her toward the elevator. I should take the stairs then I'd lose her quickly.

"I know you're a busy man but I wanted to let you know some exciting news."

"Yeah, what's that?" She follows me into the elevator.

"My son is running for Mayor."

"Of Lawson?" The current mayor is a long-timer who will probably be strong in his position for a few more years. It'd be a losing battle to run against him.

"No, no. Langston."

"Ah. Okay." It's the smallest populated city in the county but has the largest land area. Langston is where I just was at the sanctuary, and Thomas Jameson's farm was. They were practically neighbors, if you can call it that, with miles between them.

"I would love it if you could back him. Show your support since his daddy is no longer with us."

We've made it outside the Sheriff's Department building and I'm striding across the walkway to the courthouse when her statement stuns me immobile. Why she would think I would ever align myself with her late husband is beyond me.

"Mrs. Porter-"

"Vanessa, please."

"Vanessa. No." That's the nicest way I could put it.

"What?" She gapes at me like a fish.

"I cannot back your son. I do not know him, nor do I care to get involved with politics. I will not be backing anyone's campaign."

She doesn't like my answer, her shoulders square and her chest rises with displeasure. "Your position is an elected position. I hope you realize the impact this will make."

That gets me moving again. "I don't think it will and honestly, I don't care," I shout loud enough for her to hear because this time she doesn't follow me. I have more important places to be.

Chapter Twenty-One

Natalie

I settle into the unforgiving wooden bench like I have every time that I've been in this damn courtroom, adjusting to the cool lacquer under my fingertips, and forcing my wound-tight muscles to relax.

I'm not much of a prayer warrior but I've spent all morning hoping like hell that something will go in my favor and I'll learn that Declan is staying in jail. Or better yet, being sentenced to life in prison.

That won't happen but I'll plead with the universe regardless.

Declan's posse arrives and I ignore them. I don't have the energy to deal with their shit today. When the prosecutor and the defense lawyer get settled, I know Declan will be led out soon. My back stays tight with tension preparing to see him.

I have beef with most men I encounter and obviously can't stand Jackson, but I've never hated anyone more than I hate Declan Randolph. He will forever be the worst person who has ever entered my life. The only reason that I don't wish that he was never born is because I have Dec. Dec is the one good thing that Declan and my mother's sham marriage ever did.

Judge Reisner enters and the deputy asks us to rise but as usual, the judge quickly seats us again. In that minute gap of time that my butt leaves the bench I peek over my shoulder to see if Jackson is in the back row.

He isn't.

I assumed he'd be here as he has the last handful of times but it doesn't matter. I'll stake a claim on this side of the room, being the only advocate for justice and the only person who truly cares to see Declan Randolph rot.

The proceedings continue and my gut feels increasingly hollow as the judge allows Prosecutor Fulton to update the courtroom on the issue with the Lawson PD detective before he makes his announcement.

Sometime during his spiel, the air shifts. I don't know how I can tell. There wasn't a disturbance behind me, no noise to indicate someone had entered the courtroom, yet somehow I know Jackson's here now.

If I turn my head and look, I guarantee that he'll be in his usual seat in the back row and his eyes will be on mine as if he anticipates all my movements. Despite the nerves tingling the hairs on the back of my neck, I keep it locked tight and don't allow myself to turn to confirm if he's here.

It doesn't matter if he is or not, it won't change the outcome that's about to take place in front of me.

"As of today, the defendant's charges will be removed. His case is dismissed and in the eyes of the court, he is innocent." The room erupts. The posse of thugs to my right hip and hooray while I claw at my stomach and try not to puke.

This can't happen.

All of the willpower in me to overcome whatever comes next drains from my body until I'm lightheaded. The fight to put Declan behind bars was the only thing keeping me going besides Dec.

How can this man get away with murdering my mother?

The tension in my neck uncoils, forcing my attention to the back row without any energy left in me to stop it. The familiar honey eyes are already staring directly at me and the breath stills in my chest. The spot was empty a few minutes ago but I knew I was right.

He's here.

The defeat and the horror are evident in his gaze. Or maybe it's a projection of my own inner turmoil, I don't know.

"Order, order." The judge pounds his gavel ordering the room to quiet and I have to force myself to turn back to the front of the courtroom, slowly tearing my stare from Jackson's until I'm locking eyes with the monster who killed my mother.

Then Declan winks at me. The fucker winks.

My stomach fills with acid and I think I'm going to be sick. All I can do is sit painfully still and breathe through it.

Alongside the noise of the room dying out is an unmistakable one. It's the creaking of a wooden bench, the jangle of metal, and the rustling of fabric as someone approaches me from behind. The wood creaks again and the same noises happen as the person sits directly behind me.

I don't need to turn around to confirm who it is. He is always right here. No matter how many times I yell at him, or how mad he gets, he is the only one who keeps showing up for me.

For Dec, I amend it in my head.

I hate that a part of me trusts him. I hate that I know he's not as bad as the other men in my life.

I hate that he sees me at my worst even though I love seeing him at his.

It's an endless cycle that ends today.

Declan will be released. There is no reason for Jackson to keep showing up. His involvement, law enforcement's involvement with him, is over. These courtroom appearances are over.

"Miss Halstead. Are you listening?" The judge calls to me directly. That has never happened before.

"Yes." There is no way he could hear me as much as he saw my mouth move.

"Mr. Randolph will be a free man and because I understand that you currently have guardianship of his son, Declan Randolph Jr., I assume we'll be seeing you in family court."

"What?" My brain isn't processing what he's telling me. I feel everyone in the room's eyes on me, including my "stepfather's."

"Declan will be pursuing custody of his son as his rights as his biological father."

The world is spinning, suddenly.

This can't happen. He's going to try to take Dec from me.

"Miss Halstead, I suggest you have your priorities straight and your ducks in a row. You'll be joining us in court soon. This is me extending a courtesy to you. Obtain a lawyer.

"Mr. Randolph, I hope you learned your lesson during these proceedings. A criminal record will not help you keep custody of your son if that becomes the case. I suggest you stay away from this side of the justice system."

"Yes, your honor," Declan replies with false sincerity. He

hasn't learned his lesson. He is not a changed man. He might be wearing a cheap suit instead of a jumpsuit but he is still a criminal.

"Go home, Mr. Randolph. Court dismissed." The gavel bangs and my shoulders jump.

The pack of men behind Declan break out into celebration again but I do my best to ignore them. My ears are ringing enough that I can't tell what they're shouting anyway.

As they all start to file out, Declan stops at the end of my row to stare at me. I sense Jackson standing up from his seat behind me as if the shadow of a mountain blanketed me. Declan's eyes flick to the giant of a man but return to mine quickly.

"Be seeing you real soon, Nat." I flinch at his voice. At the nickname.

"Court's over. Get out," Jackson snaps. His voice is laced with more malice than he's ever used against me, and I want to weep.

Declan chuckles, all of his gaggle does, but they ultimately leave. The only two remaining are me and my supposed enemy, bracing his hands on the back of the wooden bench on either side of my shoulders. If his thumbs moved mere centimeters on either side he'd be touching me but the empty space feels like miles.

"Listen to me, Natalie. We're done playing this game. You and Dec are moving into my house. You are going to get a damn good lawyer and you aren't going to stress about surviving every damn day. You are going to let me help you. No more paying me back, no more working at that damn coffee shack. Your only focus from here on out is to keep Dec."

141

His words are fuzzy in my brain and I know it takes me longer than necessary to process what he's saying, but he doesn't rush me. He doesn't say another word as the minutes tick by.

There are a million reasons that I should protest, a thousand reasons I should scoff in his face, but only one reason has me nodding my head up and down in the hollow silence of this courtroom.

I will do whatever it takes to keep my brother safe and now I know that Jackson will too.

Chapter Twenty-Two

Jackson

"This is my house," I announce awkwardly as Natalie squeezes past me through the door into the entryway. Dec's been here before so he flies past her, launching onto the gray sectional that takes up most of the living room.

"Dec, be respectful," she scolds quietly.

"It's okay, this is your home now. He can be himself." I wink at Dec as he plops back into the oversized cushions with a Cheshire grin.

"It's temporary." She cuts a glare at me before continuing her assessment of my space. "Everything is so... Neutral." She spins in a slow circle taking it all in.

The living room opens directly into the kitchen. A large white marble island sits in the middle and the sink overlooks the backyard. The dining table is off to the side where it stays unused.

The walls are white, the furniture is gray, and the appliances are stainless steel. I understand her comment. I don't have any pictures or color. I'm not home often enough to make it look lived in.

"Um. The fridge is empty so we'll have to order groceries but, you're free to use whatever. Dec knows how to work the remote to the TV already." I stand uneasily in front of the hallway, letting her look around before I show her to their rooms.

"The oven still has plastic on it," she ponders out loud, looking at the film on the oven door.

"Yeah, I don't cook much," I admit.

She looks at me after I speak and there is undeniable curiosity in her eyes. "You have this beautiful kitchen and you don't cook?"

"It was pretty standard with the build." I shrug.

"What the hell is this?" She asks after opening the refrigerator doors.

"What?"

"It's empty, empty. There isn't *any* food in here, just Tupperware."

"Yeah, I really don't cook. Ever. I order a meal service, coffee, and protein bars."

She looks at me with her jaw slack. "Oh my God," she finally mumbles.

I feel my cheeks heat with foreign embarrassment and turn away from her quickly. "Come on, I'll show you to your room."

She follows behind me, Dec zooming past us once again. "Look, Natalie!" He goes into my computer room first so we veer left.

"Jackson has a dragon, too!" Dec shouts excitedly, bouncing on the futon.

"Dec! Feet on the floor you barnyard animal." Her words trail off as she glances at the figure sitting high on a shelf.

"You made all these?" Her eyes trail across the shelf full of miniature models and LEGO builds.

I'm more uneasy the longer she stares at my silly craftsmanship, feeling overwhelmingly put on the spot. Even as a grown man I can't comfortably talk about myself, especially when it's about something that most people wouldn't consider mainstream. And, incredibly nerdy.

I haven't felt this kind of spotlight since I was a child being picked on by the older kids at school.

"It's just a hobby. I built the computer myself, too." I motion to the multiple screens set up off to the side, hoping for a distraction. Not that it helps the nerd persona. I am waiting for her first jab at me about it.

"Are you a gamer?" There isn't any mockery to her tone but she could be setting up for the punchline.

"No, not really. I just like the challenge of piecing something together until it works."

She stands still for several seconds, looking at each model on my shelf until she finally turns back to face me. There's no joke, no insult, she only looks at me curiously. She doesn't say anything and I don't either. Dec takes that as his queue to start remarking about all the cool things that he would like to build.

"Why did he say that you have a dragon, too?" I ask her between his spiels of chit-chat.

"Oh, he was just being silly. Probably something we had at the apartment." She exits the room quickly and I follow her across the hall.

"This will be your room, sorry about the cheeriness." The walls are a pale yellow, the comforter is a yellow floral print, and the curtains correspond. It's the only room in the house with color. "This was supposed to be my mom's room before I accepted that she needed round-the-clock care. Yellow is supposed to be calming."

"I'm sure she would have loved it," she says quietly, observing the space.

Once again, her niceness is putting me on edge. I handle it much better when she's smart and snippy with me. I don't know what to do with her gentle side.

"Dec can sleep in here with you, or I can put the futon in here, but he's more than welcome to stay in the computer room. You guys can use the computer if you need to," I explain, trying to erase the tightness in my chest that I've felt since she stepped through my front door. This situation is awkward for both of us.

"My room is on the other side of this wall," I motion to my left. Right next to where you'll be sleeping, I add in my head.

This might be harder than I originally anticipated.

After they get their bags out of her car and get settled, Dec gets comfortable on the couch watching an old Spider-Man movie while Natalie and I work out the kinks of our living arrangement.

"You don't want me to pay rent?" She asks skeptically.

"It's not necessary."

She eyes me questionably as I sit on one of the bar stools. She's opposite me, standing on the other side of the island.

"Groceries?"

"Not necessary."

"Jackson, this is ridiculous. Seriously?"

"I want you to save all of your money for a lawyer. I'll ask around for a good one, the best one. That should be your only focus."

"I still need to pay you back for the hotel." Her head is tilted and her arms are crossed, preparing to battle. I should be worried, but if anything it eases me.

"Consider it settled. Okay? Stop worrying about money."

"That is an insane thing to ask me to do. All I've been doing my entire life is worrying about money. Especially this past-" She lowers her voice out of earshot of Dec. "Especially this past year," she whispers.

"I know. Let me help you now. Only until you get full legal custody of Dec. Then you can ride off into the sunset flipping me the middle finger."

"Two middle fingers," she corrects under her breath.

"Fine, whatever. You need to quit your job, too."

"What? I thought you were joking about that!"

"No. The last thing we need is for Declan's lawyer to bring up your occupation in court. It wouldn't be the first time they've tried to smear a woman for her profession."

"I make coffee! I'm not a stri-" She pauses again to collect herself. "I'm not a stripper," she whispers.

"I know that but one photo of you in your underwear at work and they could use it against you. I'm not saying that it's right. I'm telling you the reality."

"This can't be real." I see the lack of color in her face. She understands what I'm saying but it doesn't mean it's fair. "It's the only place I could find around here that would let me work between 8 and 3. I only know food and bev. I don't even know where to begin looking for something else." She hides her face in her hands and all I want to do is comfort her. I don't though, it would only unleash her fury.

"I can cancel my housekeeper. Pay you instead?"

She blinks rapidly at me but doesn't say anything at first.

I can't tell if she's considering it or if she's about to bite my head off for suggesting it.

"No. No, we'll clean up after ourselves but I don't want to be your housekeeper," she replies quietly. Her eyes wander around the kitchen, stopping on the fridge. "I can cook."

"What?"

"You don't have to order your meals. I can cook."

"That would be a lot of work. I eat a lot."

She shrugs. "I love to cook. I went to culinary school in New York."

It's my turn to be stunned. I had no idea that's why she was in New York but I guess I don't know much about her at all.

"You're a chef?"

She laughs sadly. "No. I was two weeks from graduation when-" She glances at Dec and I read it loud and clear. She had to come home for Dec.

"I'm sorry."

"It's okay. He was worth it."

"That might be the case but if it was your goal..."

She waves me off. "My dream was to work as a private chef on big expensive yachts. I wanted to set out for months at a time and leave everything behind." She sighs. "It was only a dream though. My goal now is to give him a childhood that he doesn't have to recover from."

"Nat- Natalie," I plead with her. "Once everything is settled, you should pursue it again. Maybe no yachts, but you could still make a living, and be happy."

She shakes her head in response but mumbles, "Maybe."

She shouldn't have to give up everything. She deserves a life too.

"I'll give you $1000 a week to cook breakfast, lunch, and

dinner for six days. I'll cancel my meal service and whatever you don't use for groceries, you keep. Deal?"

Her jaw drops. "That's way more than I made at the coffee shack a week."

"Good, then you won't miss it."

"Are you sure this isn't just about people seeing my ass?"

My jaw clenches even thinking about other people seeing her ass, but no, it's also about Dec. "If you're worried that the change will be too sudden, you can always wear your uniform here." I motion to the kitchen.

"You're a pig."

Chapter Twenty-Three

Natalie

"I've never seen this fridge with so much in it," Jackson mumbles after we put all the groceries away. We got a late-night order delivered before I helped Dec settle for bed.

"I don't understand how you've survived without cooking. You look like you eat well."

He whips his head toward me. "Was that a fat joke?"

I roll my eyes. "No. It wasn't a fat joke, Hercules."

Anyone with two eyes can see how built he is. There isn't anything pudgy about him. He is all hard, toned muscle. Under all that, there seems to be more to him than I ever realized. I never would have guessed that he'd come home and build computer systems or sit meticulously for hours and create such incredible things. It makes him seem endearing somehow and more human.

It's easier seeing him as a one-sided coin, a stiff robot who wears a badge. Getting to know him only makes him more likable and it aggravates me.

Why does he have to be perfect at everything that he does? I'm not perfect at anything.

I pull the plastic containers out of the fridge and crack open a lid. The smell of old processed chicken and rice hits me like a brick and helps me humble him in my mind. "Oh my God. That's bad. That's really bad." I gag, literally. A loud, unladylike reaction that I could not have prevented if I tried.

"It's not that bad once it's warm, you're being dramatic."

"No, I'm not. That's rancid." I chuck all the containers into the trash. It's been a long time since anything has grossed me out like that. I know how to de-feather chickens and de-bone fish, I thought I was past the food heebie-jeebies.

"My mom cooked a lot when I was growing up but I was too busy outside playing to take notice. Then she started having memory issues. She couldn't remember recipes or steps and would burn everything. After I graduated high school, I stayed home and went to the community college so I could work full-time in the evenings. I wasn't home enough to cook for myself. Now I'm so busy, cooking is the last thing I want to experiment with when I get home. I don't have the energy for it."

"What did your mom do when she was home alone so much?"

"She could make sandwiches and use the microwave. One scary situation with the stove being left on was all it took to pull the cord from the wall. It stayed like that for years."

I glance at his brand new top-of-the-line oven and suddenly see it in a new light. It is completely untouched because he existed without one for so long. I almost bet if I looked behind it I would find the plug lying on the ground collecting dust.

"When did she get really bad?"

"Uhh, maybe three years ago now. I was making decent enough money as a trooper to hire a home health aid while I worked. That helped.

"Eventually, though, I decided to build this house because I needed everything on one level. At night, in the house I grew up in, I couldn't hear her if she needed me because my room was upstairs. Once she tried making a break for it in the middle of the night I knew I needed to find a safer place for her to live." He shrugs.

"She didn't get a chance to live here at all?"

"No. Six months before it was completed she took a turn. She couldn't take care of herself at all it seemed like. She needed help 24/7 and I wasn't able to do it. I painted her room, just in case, but once I looked into the assisted living home, I realized it was the best choice for her. It still makes me feel guilty."

I can't believe he's telling me all of this, but then again, we did enact a truce regarding our family. I guess it's safe territory.

"That's a lot of responsibility for a teenage boy to sign up for back then, even if you didn't realize the commitment at the time. I'm sure she is proud of you and grateful for all that you've done. You could have left her hanging a long time ago."

"I would have never done that." He shakes his head incredulously as if the idea itself doesn't belong in his brain.

"I know." My words soften him immediately.

He looks at me thoughtfully, appreciatively, as if he hasn't had many people in his life recognize the sacrifice he has made.

"How did you deal with all of it? I've only had Dec for a year and I'm drowning."

"You're doing better than you think. Trust me."

I shrug off his compliment. It makes me feel too... Good.

CHAPTER TWENTY-THREE

When he says nice things to me, I forget we aren't supposed to like each other.

"Dec didn't luck out in the parent department... I have to be better than them for his sake," I explain.

"I didn't have a dad growing up," he admits, surprising me. "I knew that I was going to make something of myself and prove the unknown man wrong I guess. Dec will do the same, he'll be fine." His assurance shouldn't matter but it does feel nice to hear.

"Did you always want to be a cop?" I ask while the opportunity is here to get more information out of him.

"No, I wanted to work in sports medicine and be a trainer on the field at professional football games."

"You didn't want to play? You look like a linebacker."

He squints his eyes as if he's trying to decide if that was an insult or not. It wasn't, but I like that I can keep him on his toes.

"Being good at sports was the only thing that made me fit in as a kid but after a couple of my own injuries, I realized that I was more interested hanging out in the training room or on the sidelines than on the field. Fixing people up seemed more enticing than getting concussions for another decade."

I glance at his head and consider making a joke about having a concussion or two, but I recognize the sincerity in his story and I change my mind. I tuck my bottom lip into my mouth and simply mumble, "Hmm," to encourage him to continue.

"With my mom sick though, law enforcement was the best option. I didn't need a ton of schooling, the pay and insurance were decent, and I could stay around here for her.

"When the opportunity to run for Sheriff came about, I realized it was the only way I could get to the pinnacle of my career without leaving Rollins County. As a state trooper, I would have bounced all around the state eventually if I wanted to work my way up."

"So you accidentally found yourself as the Sheriff of Rollins County." I laugh to myself. How annoying that he's so good at everything. Except cooking.

"I guess. I want to fix all the messed up stuff happening but it's been a long year. I can't keep up with paperwork and working the road when we're short-staffed. It's been a nightmare, honestly."

"Finally, he's human. I wondered all along if you were a cyborg."

He laughs, mockingly. "It takes too much energy to show emotion. The only problem that I have with that, is you. So thanks, you're exhausting."

I give a dramatic bow, making him do that thing where he looks up toward the ceiling as if he's praying for strength.

The next day, I'm cooking and it's the best I've felt in a long time, being back in the kitchen and in my element. Our apartment was not even close to as nice as this though. It's almost comparable to the professional equipment I used in culinary school. I had to stop what I was doing multiple times to unpeel plastic wrap from utensils and the appliances.

Me: Do you want me to bring your lunch to you?

I accidentally threw away his lunch last night while purging the gross meals from the fridge. It wasn't until I was cooking that I realized my lapse and that he went to work without food. I like the arrangement we made and I am not going to screw it up this early on.

Jackson: I'm in the area, I'll stop home.

I look around at the chaos that I've created. It's probably

the messiest his house has ever been. I think about tidying up quickly, but I'd rather see the shock on his face.

Only twenty minutes later he strolls in through the front door in his full uniform. I hate to admit how appealing he looks, I avert my eyes so he doesn't catch me staring. I can't find a cop attractive, it goes against my moral code.

"Wow. It smells good in here." He doesn't say anything about the mess in the kitchen or the dirty dishes. He plops down on the same bar stool he sat on last night and glances around at everything I've prepared.

"Do you want a plate?" I ask hesitantly. I assumed he'd pack it up and leave again. I wasn't expecting him to eat here, with me.

"Yes." His eyes haven't left the spread laid out on the counter.

I dish up a seasoned chicken breast, roasted Parmesan Brussels sprouts, and a butter garlic orzo. "I wasn't sure what you liked so I kept it simple."

"This is simple?" He asks, astonished.

"Um. Yeah, for me. I can make all kinds of stuff. Do you have a preference?"

"No, I like anything."

"Okay. Well, I'll get more creative if you don't mind but I'll mix in some of Dec's favorites too. He usually asks me to pack his lunch for school."

Jackson digs into the plate I handed over and I watch in ample fascination as he eats. I've always loved seeing the reaction to my food. I get high on creating food that people can't get enough of. The way Jackson is eating, I'm not even sure if he's come up for air. It makes me giggle.

That's when his head snaps up to look at me. His eyes blink

a few times but he just stares at me.

"What?"

"I have never heard you make that sound."

"You mean, laugh?"

"It was more than that. It was happy."

I turn my back to him and start working on packing Dec's lunch for tomorrow, ignoring his comment. I can't seem to wipe the smile off of my face though.

* * *

Our routine continues for a week. I spend my days in the kitchen, preparing fresh meals and packing lunches. Some days, Jackson leaves without his lunch and comes home to eat it. Some days, he doesn't. He's always home for dinner, though, and we've all been eating together at the table.

The new routine is different for me but it's been relatively painless. Aside from being in the kitchen, Jackson and I skirt around each other. We only seem to speak to each other if I'm cooking. He's either watching me cook or he's eating, but the kitchen has turned into neutral territory.

Dec's made himself right at home. The bus picks him up and drops him off at the end of the driveway now. I make him do his homework while I cook dinner and he usually convinces Jackson to play with him after he eats.

It's a weight off my shoulders not needing to entertain him constantly, but I'm still worried about how all this will affect him. He's been bounced around to different homes. His dad is out of jail. His mom is dead. I still lie awake at night and worry.

I guess this is what it feels like to be a mother. I can't imagine that it's going to get easier.

I'm sitting on the couch, scrolling on Jackson's iPad to order groceries when a sale ad pops up for feminine hygiene products and my stomach drops like a rock. My world is suddenly tilting on its axis.

I never bought the tampons the day that I ran into Jackson's mom. I should have needed them by now.

I stand up slowly and move down the hall on wobbly legs. When I reach the computer room, I lean my head in. "Hey, I need to run to the store. Is it okay if Dec stays with you?"

"It's late, you don't want us to come?" Jackson asks in his completely normal, hasn't just experienced a mind-numbing realization, voice. They're building a LEGO rocket.

"No, I'll be quick. Dec, behave."

* * *

Positive.

My hands are shaking uncontrollably holding the little plastic rectangle. Two blue lines.

It's positive.

I'm hyperventilating in the drugstore restroom that I was almost trespassed from a few weeks ago.

It's positive.

How did this happen?

Jackson pulled out. I remember it vividly because I scolded myself afterward for being disappointed that he did. I was horny enough that I didn't care about the consequences. I'm not on birth control. I haven't been for years.

It's positive.

I'm pregnant.

How did this happen?

I know how it happened. I've already gone over this but my brain cannot fathom it. I'm pregnant. With a baby. Jackson's baby. Oh my God.

My racing mind attempts to backtrack to when we had sex. When my cycle last started. I can't think straight but I think I'm a week late. Which means I'm three weeks pregnant? Four?

Or, I don't know. I don't know how it works. I've never been pregnant before. What do I even do? I don't have insurance. I don't even have a doctor.

I suck all the air that I can into my lungs. I'm pregnant with a baby and there is nothing I can do about it right now except get up, go back to the house, and pretend like nothing is wrong.

Is it wrong?

It feels wrong to call a baby a mistake. I know how they're made but it was clearly a mistake to get pregnant.

A baby.

I'm going to have a baby.

A few sobs break loose while I'm in my car but I don't allow a single tear to escape. This is a result of my actions. I will not blame this on the baby.

I can't believe I let this happen though. I swore after my mom got pregnant with Dec I would never put myself in a similar situation. It worked, I have practically sworn off men for years. If I did hook up with anyone, there was always a condom used. Until this time, with Jackson.

Oh my God. Jackson.

What is he going to say? Is he going to blame me?

Fuck him, he doesn't get to blame me and I don't need him. I'll do this on my own. There is no way that I will let him make me feel guilty.

He doesn't need to know.

No. I'll tell him. I can't keep it from him, that would be terrible.

I'll tell him and let him make his own choice. Eventually.

I'm not telling him tonight or anytime soon. I need time to process this before I can handle the implosion when I tell him.

What if he kicks us out? He might back out on his deal to help us if he thinks I did this on purpose.

I'll keep it to myself until after I get custody of Dec. It should only be a few months, I can hide it.

Hopefully.

Chapter Twenty-Four

Jackson

The first week that my house guests were here went too smoothly. When everything went off the rails during week two, I was only slightly surprised.

I had been under the impression that Natalie and I had come to some sort of understanding. We hadn't fought, we were communicating effectively, and I was starting to pick up on more details about her than I had ever known or suspected.

Aside from being an amazing cook, she is ethically ambiguous in her music tastes and cuisine choices. Whatever region the dish she is making comes from is the music that she'll play over the Bluetooth speaker.

I caught her smiling more times in the first week than I had the entire time I'd known her. Then week two hit and it all shifted. She wouldn't look me in the eye, she hardly spoke two words to me at a time and spent most of her time in her bedroom. She'd only stay in the common areas if Dec was around or needed her for something.

She still packed my lunch, but when I'd come home to eat, she'd disappear to her room. Dinner would be served quickly and she'd start washing dishes before me and Dec were finished.

I guess I shouldn't be offended, but after thinking we were past the mortal enemy stage, I feel like I have whiplash. Why can't we be civil?

I get that she doesn't like me but if she hates me that much, why did she agree to move in here? Or to cook me meals? She could have told me to fuck off.

Except that she wouldn't. Not when Dec is at stake.

Once again, when it comes to her I'm an idiot. She was never growing fond of being around me, she was only securing her place here so that I'd help Dec. I get it and won't fault her for it, even when it stings a little.

When my cell phone rings in the middle of the afternoon, I ignore it. I want to keep digging into all these cases until I find the connection that I haven't discovered.

Thomas Jameson, the 5k bomber, is the next person I'm studying up on. Born in Rollins County to a Vanessa Jameson. Maiden name, Porter. That's odd. The Vanessa Porter I know is close in age to Thomas Jameson.

It only takes a little deep diving to find the blaring connection. Vanessa Porter is named after her aunt, Thomas Jameson's mother. They're cousins.

I jump up from behind my desk and stride to my investigation board.

Anthony and Benjamin Porter are Vanessa's brothers.

Sheriff Donahue was her husband.

Thomas Jameson is her cousin.

Which means... Kyle Jameson is related to her also. The kid that I shot and killed when he was holding Jesse Callahan hostage six months ago.

Holy shit.

161

This could be it but how is Vanessa involved in this? She looks like a typical housewife from the south. She has no criminal record. There is no way she would knowingly be involved in all of these criminal acts.

Right?

I've been blowing off her phone calls for months, blowing her off in person, and the connection was right there all along. The only one that doesn't draw directly back to her is Declan Randolph. He's from the area and went to school here, but that could be a coincidence.

I plop back down in my chair and stare at the ceiling. Until I know I can connect Vanessa to Declan, I need to keep this close to my chest.

"Sheriff," Roberta grabs my attention from my door. "You have a personal call."

"About my mom?" I ask, instantly standing.

"No, it's about a student at Lawson Elementary. She wouldn't give me details."

I'm grabbing the receiver and picking up the line before Roberta can finish her sentence.

"Sheriff Malec."

"Hi, Sheriff, uh Sir. I'm the principal at Lawson Elementary and we're having an issue with Declan. *My name is Dec!*" I hear the shout from the background.

"What? What is it? Have you called his sister?"

"Yes, a few times. It seems her phone is off. Decl- Dec asked me to call you."

"I'll be right there."

Mere minutes later, I'm striding right into the Principal's office. I've been here a few times and know my way around quite well. I've made it a point that all of my deputies are familiar with the layouts of all the schools.

"Sheriff, they're right through here." The secretary ushers me through a door and I stop dead in my tracks. Dec is sitting in a chair with tears streaming down his face but that's not what makes my cool snap.

A chunk of his shaggy blonde hair is missing. Cut clean off the side.

"What the hell is going on?" My voice is loud, and more authoritative than I usually use. I'm not usually fueled by emotion and ready to throttle someone. Dec starts to cry harder as I kneel in front of him.

"What happened, buddy?" I ask him softly as he falls into me, leaning his head on my shoulder. I rub his back until he settles enough to sit up and wipe his eyes.

I turn to the woman sitting behind her desk with her hands crossed, watching a little boy weep. "What happened?"

She looks relatively put off balance by my presence, but her hesitation only makes my defenses strengthen.

"There was an issue in gym class. Dec talked back to the gym teacher and he reprimanded him." She stops talking as if that's all there is to it. As if this little boy hasn't had his hair forcibly cut.

"And?"

"Mr. Wheeler took him to the locker room and attempted to give him a haircut as punishment."

"Where is he? Get him down here. NOW!" I yell, thunderously and she balks.

"He's already left for the day. He'll be on administrative leave until further notice."

"I want him fired."

"Sheriff, I-"

"If I see him around children at this school ever again, I will get you fired, too. Dec. Let's go." I can't think straight, my gut is begging me to get him out of here and in a safer place. Away from this uncaring woman.

Once we're in my SUV, and far away from the school, I pull over on a random shoulder and turn the car off. "Will you tell me exactly what happened? Please, buddy."

"Mr. Wheeler was being mean to me in gym class. He kept yelling at me to get my hair out of my eyes. We were playing wiffle ball and my hair would cover my eye when I tried to bat." He sniffles and I give him a second, rubbing his back until he can continue.

"He said I looked like a girl. That I needed it cut. But, I don't want to cut my hair. I haven't cut it since- Since Mommy died. She always cut my hair." He cries, a full belly heaving cry, and my heart breaks into a million pieces for this little boy.

I jump out on my side and round the hood, throwing open his door and pulling him into my arms. "I am so sorry, buddy. So sorry." I squeeze his small body, rocking him back and forth until his tears soften.

"He tried to cut more off but Charlie ran and got another teacher. He got this part though." His fingers brush the side of his nearly scalped head and his little chest heaves like he might start crying again.

"Hey, it's alright. I know it's scary, but how about I take you somewhere I like to go so we can fix it? We'll take pictures that way you can remember it longer. Would it be okay if we fixed it?"

He nods sadly and I pull him in for another hug. "You did a good thing by telling them to call me, Dec. You did good. Anytime you need me, I'll be here."

* * *

"What the hell did you do?!" Natalie screams at me as soon as we step through the front door. All I can manage to do is take a deep breath before I lose my damn mind.

"Sissy, no don't-" Dec tries to intervene.

"Dec. Go to your room. Now." She can hardly look at him with his new hairdo.

"Natal-"

"Now, Dec."

He hangs his newly trimmed and faded head but complies. While she's waiting for his door to click shut down the hall, I step outside. I need the open air to stop me from flying off the handle when she lays into me.

As suspected, she stomps out after me, shoving me roughly when she reaches me. "What the hell did you do? Why did you cut his hair?" Her voice cracks as she yells.

"Go ahead. Get it all out of your system. Yell at me, hit me, scream at me, I don't care. There's nothing you can do to me that will make me feel worse than what happened today."

"What the hell does that mean?"

"I don't know, let's start with why you were unreachable today. Hot date? Booty call? What?"

"You're insane. You're literally insane."

"Dec's school called me, they couldn't get a hold of you."

"What? Why?"

"How about you tell me where you were today first?"

"I had an appointment. The lady doctor, you asswipe."

That cools some of my anger but it doesn't put it out completely. "Dec's gym teacher cut a chunk of his hair off. As a punishment."

"WHAT!" Her volume pierces my eardrums and all but rattles the windows of the house.

"He was upset. I took him to my barber to get it fixed, okay?"

"No, not okay! I'm going to kill him. How dare he!" She scrambles to open the front door, grabbing her purse from the hooks on the wall before storming back out.

"Stop, you are not leaving." I block her path before she can make it past me.

"Jackson, move out of my way!"

"No. Dec needs you. I have everything else handled."

"Bullshit. I need to talk to the principal, the fucker should be arrested."

"Dammit, Natalie! I said that I have it handled!" I shout.

She steps back at my tone as if I slapped her but I continue. I'm too riled up and tired of being seen as her enemy. As if I'm nothing but a nuisance to her.

"You know that I would never stand by and let someone hurt that innocent little boy. Go inside and be with him! Now!" I bark at her.

She looks at me like I'm the biggest villain in her story but I don't care. I'm done proving myself.

She turns slowly and marches inside without looking back. I sit on the concrete steps as it gets dark and attempt to calm my rage before I do something stupid.

Even as I get in my SUV and leave, I know it didn't work.

Chapter Twenty-Five

Natalie

After talking to Dec, I learned exactly how well Jackson handled the situation at the school. Dec and I have always been close so I know he was being honest about everything. From Jackson yelling at the principal, to holding him while he cried, and then taking him to the coolest barber in town to fix his hair.

The guilt has been eating at me since then. My hormones have been off the charts. I cried while Dec told me what happened. I've cried myself to sleep almost every night since I found out I was pregnant.

My OB appointment confirmed that I'm almost five weeks along based on my last period. She still encouraged me to get scheduled for an ultrasound at the free clinic to confirm the timeline.

It's after midnight but I stayed up to apologize to Jackson. I hate saying sorry, it's my least favorite word in my vocabulary, but he deserves an apology. He took care of Dec when I couldn't and it's the only thing that matters to me more than my pride.

He drops his keys on the counter, the loud clatter echoing

in the silent house. "I'm not in the mood, Natalie." He turns to start down the hallway.

"Jackson. Please."

His steps halt but he doesn't turn back toward me yet. His chin drops to his chest and he takes a deep breath before he finally comes back to stand at the kitchen island, completely avoiding eye contact with me. I take it as my queue to keep going, anyway.

"Dec told me everything that happened. Thank you for taking care of him. I will never be able to express how much it means to me." I take a deep breath to ward off the tears burning my eyes. These stupid hormones have turned me into a baby and I hate it. "I'm sorry for yelling at you and for doubting you. I am so, so sorry." My voice breaks and he finally looks at me, right as the first tear rolls down my cheek.

He watches it travel the length of my jaw but then his eyes remain downcast. He doesn't want to look at me. I've finally done it. I've managed to push him away. He doesn't even want to argue with me anymore.

"I understand that you're angry at me and I deserve it. I don't deserve the nice things that you've done for me. I know I'm a fuck up. From here on out, you won't have to deal with me. I'll cook and take care of Dec. I won't step on your toes or get on your nerves anymore. At least, not on purpose." I slide off the bar stool on trembling knees, hoping he'll say something. Anything.

He doesn't.

The dam doesn't release until I crawl into bed. I can't tell him that I'm pregnant with his baby. He'll resent me for the rest of my life. Resent what we made.

He'll only ever hate the thing that is half of me.

I sob into my pillow until I lose consciousness.

The entire weekend passes and I don't get out of bed.

Part of it is the sudden exhaustion that I've convinced myself is a pregnancy symptom. Part of it is a pathetic state of depression. I don't want to go into Jackson's kitchen or living room and say something that will anger him. I don't want to do anything that will put Dec's living situation in jeopardy.

There's only a month and a half left of the school year. If we can make it to summer, I'll start over then. I'll find us somewhere new to live in his school district. I'll get a new job. I'll figure it out.

I don't know, maybe I can make it as a private cook without a culinary certification. I'd only need a few people to take a chance on me.

Jackson did but look where that's gotten me. Feeling sorry for myself while I watch reality TV reruns in a bed that isn't mine. Too sick to my stomach with nerves to eat.

Maybe when I go to the free clinic for my ultrasound they'll have information on programs that will help single mothers. I mean, that's what I'll be. There is no way that Jackson would take one look at my baby and love it.

"Alright, that's it." The voice that booms from the hallway makes me startle. "Are you sick? Do I need to call someone?"

I stare at him for more than a few seconds, trying to make sense of what he's asking me. His arms are crossed as he stares back at me with narrowed eyes.

"What?"

"You've been in bed for three days. I've never seen you stay still for more than thirty minutes."

That can't be true. "It's only been two days," I correct him.

"No, it's Monday."

"What?!" I screech, launching out of the bed. How did I lose track of time?

"School. Oh My God! Dec!" I scream into the expanse of the universe, frantically searching for pants.

"I made sure he got on the bus this morning."

"What?"

"Stop saying what."

"Why didn't either of you wake me up?" I pause what I'm doing, a pair of shorts dangling from my fingers.

"Because we voted and neither of us wanted to wake the sleeping bear. I also wasn't sure if you were sick and wanted Dec to stay clear."

"I'm not sick." Not yet at least. It might only be a matter of time.

"Okay. I'm going to make lunch." He disappears from my doorway.

"It's already lunch time," I whisper to myself. Holy shit. I need to snap out of it, I cannot live this way.

It isn't until I pull on my weathered athletic shorts I've probably had since middle school that I realize what Jackson said. He's going to make lunch?

Nope. That man is not going to suddenly enjoy the art of cooking and put me out of my job. I run to the kitchen and gasp when I see him throwing random ingredients into a pan. A super nice stainless steel pan that needs to be heated properly before it's used or everything will burn.

"Stop. Jackson. Stop." I reach for the handle of the pan but he moves it out of my way. "You'll ruin it."

"It's a pan."

"It's a nice pan, nicer than I've ever had. Don't mess with

it unless you know what you're doing." I reach again but he moves it out of my reach again. The jolly green giant has a great advantage over me. "Please!"

I watch his eyes widen slightly with my use of the p-word and victory sweeps over him. This asshole. He leaves the pan on the stovetop and backs away with a sweeping motion with his hands as if saying, "All yours."

"This was very unnecessary," I grumble.

"Nah. I think it was necessary. Now that I got the taste of hearing you say please, I like it just as much as I like arguing with you."

My head whips toward where he's taken a seat at the island. The last time he told me how much he liked my anger, we had a catastrophic night in his office.

"Don't get used to it," I mumble, not knowing what else to say.

"I wouldn't dare, fireball."

"I don't know what that nickname means, so don't do that either." I turn back to my tasks at the stove, thankful that all he dumped in the pan were precut veggies that I had in the fridge already. I can make quick work of them.

"Who's shirt is that?" He asks from behind me.

"I don't know," I answer honestly.

"Jesus Christ," he murmurs in an exasperated tone. I have a smart remark ready but I'm trying to behave, so I ignore him.

I have a big ask of him and I need to be on his good side to do it. After a few moments of silence, I ask him if he wants a drink from the fridge but he only stares at me in confusion.

I grab myself a coke because I need it. Somehow I know that the caffeine will give me strength but I take my time popping the tab open in the silent kitchen and pouring it into a glass. "I have a favor to ask. Feel free to say no, but I have to ask anyway."

He nods for me to continue as his eyes assess me.

"Dec's 8th birthday is in two weeks and I was wondering if you would be okay with me inviting a few of his friends from school over for a few hours. Not this Saturday but next. The other moms will probably come and stay. I guess that's standard, I don't know. My mom always dumped me at any parties I wanted to go to until they stopped inviting me." I'm rambling but I can't seem to stop.

"I'll clean up before and after, and you won't even know it happened. You can come or leave for the day if you don't want to be around a bunch of crazy boys. Up to you."

He stares at me, not acknowledging my request and I wonder if I was talking too fast for him to interpret what I said until he goes, "Huh."

"What does that mean?"

"Sometimes I forget that you were a kid once." He squints his eyes as if trying to imagine it.

"What the hell does that mean?"

"I don't know, I guess I assumed you started your life as an angsty teenager and got more rage-filled from there," he says dismissively, shrugging.

He's doing this on purpose. He's trying to rile me up. I can see it in the way he's tilting his head arrogantly.

"My rage stemmed from very early childhood trauma and progressed from there. Nice try though."

He laughs and it shocks me. A deep and loud laugh that I'd never heard before. I think I've entered the wrong dimension. This is not the same man who yelled at me the other night and then ignored my apology.

CHAPTER TWENTY-FIVE

"You can have Dec's party here. I don't care. What are you going to get him?"

"Um. I don't know yet. I've been thinking about it a lot, but I'm so worried about disappointing him that I haven't pulled the trigger on anything."

"I think he wants a bike."

"I know that, but how'd you know that?"

"He told me he wants to learn how to ride a bike."

My finger taps the spatula I'm using rhythmically against the pan, thinking. "I was going to get him one. I saved up but had to use the money to get him new clothes after the fire instead."

"We'll go in on one, from the both of us," he offers, generously. On one hand, I hate to get any more help from him than I already have. On the other, getting a bike for Dec is important and his happiness is the only thing that really matters to me.

"Are you going to teach him how to ride it, safely? I haven't ridden a bike since I was probably Dec's age. My only bike was from a garage sale. It was stolen from our driveway and I never got a new one."

He stares at me briefly, in concerned disbelief over my childhood misfortune, before responding. "Of course, I will."

"Okay. We'll get him a bike." We might as well have shaken hands and called a truce.

Chapter Twenty-Six

Jackson

She had hidden away in her room all weekend long, and I couldn't stand it. I could handle fending for myself in the kitchen, though I missed her cooking. It was the silence.

The boredom I experienced being in my home without her to talk to, to bug while she cooked, left me empty.

My brain was desperate for stimulation I couldn't get from anywhere else. I tried to build a LEGO baseball with Dec but that turned into me watching him while simultaneously staring off into space.

I worked out three times and didn't even break a sweat. All I could think about was the singular tear rolling down her cheek late Friday night. I didn't realize that she possessed the emotions to cry. I thought she was invincible to sadness because of her capacity for anger.

I should have known that anything involving Dec would bring that out in her but I still caught myself worrying that it was all for show. That her apology wasn't as genuine as it seemed and she was fooling me into thinking she was actually sorry.

All day Saturday without her had knocked all those thoughts out of my brain. I knew something was wrong when she was still holed up on Sunday. Monday morning I stayed home long enough to get Dec on the bus and then left for work assuming things would return to normal eventually.

But when I stopped home on my lunch break to see her still in bed, the dread in my gut amplified. She wasn't the fire-filled woman I knew and it was startling to realize how deeply I cared.

Getting her out of bed was the only way I could ignore the ache in my chest that she undoubtedly caused.

Then I saw her ass. God, her ass. That perfect round skin peeking out the bottom of her t-shirt about killed me.

Luckily, she put on shorts before coming into the kitchen. Unluckily for me, she isn't wearing a bra and the way the shirt hangs on her body is worse than a strip tease. I can see the outline of her petite chest and the points of her nipples.

Her hair is pulled up in a sloppy bun and the neck of the shirt is stretched enough that I can't stop staring at the expanse of skin between her throat and shoulder that I have a vivid memory of biting.

The sound she made when I did still haunts me. I'm straining against my zipper behind the cover of the kitchen island just thinking about it.

Now I'm sitting here like a pervert, watching her cook, and imagining what it would be like to have her. Not for a moment, but to really have her.

Will she ever accept that I'm not out to get her? Can she?

I don't know the answer to that and I'm too afraid to ask. If she could never truly trust me, I'd never be able to live that way. I'm fine with the arguing, her temper won't scare me away, but I would need to know that she won't run from me when she gets mad. Right now, I sense her need to run after every conversation, every look.

She's one foot out the door and struggling to remember the plan from the start.

Is all of this going to be temporary?

Will I have to say goodbye to Dec one day and expect not to see him again? And, her?

Now that they're in my life, I can't imagine not having them in it in some way. I don't want to go back to the time when I didn't know either of them, when I didn't get to watch her shuffle from foot to foot, humming along to the music playing while she cooks.

"Where are you from?" I wonder out loud, admiring the contrast of her dark lashes against her ivory skin and the fullness of her lips. And the way her eyeliner always accentuates the brazenness in her eyes like a siren luring me in.

"Uh. Here?"

"No, I mean your heritage."

"Oh. I don't know—a mix of things I guess. My mom had blonde hair, and blue eyes like Dec but I got the dark features from my dad. I never knew who he was. My mom would never tell me."

"My mom refused to talk about my dad, too." Our poor single mothers.

"Your mom is so small, he must've been a giant." She laughs softly at her statement.

"One time during a bad episode my mom rambled about her time working at the Governor's estate. She let it slip about sneaking around with him, but that's all I got from her. She might have had me from an affair with the Governor." I laugh but Natalie looks at me like I've sprouted three heads.

"You never looked into it?"

"No, I'm sure it was crazy talk. I never took it seriously. It's easier to pretend like my father never existed at all."

"Have you ever thought about doing a DNA kit?" She asks, her eyes wide with wonder.

"No. Have you?"

"Yeah, I've looked into it. I had a classmate in culinary school who was this beautiful Eastern European girl. She had dark hair and high cheekbones, dark cat eyes. People would get us mixed up until she stood next to me. She was like 5'10 and a model." She laughs. "I always kind of hoped that I had something cool in me. Greek, Native American, something Latin, I don't know.

"I was too afraid to send off my DNA though and find out that I have a bunch of half siblings out there. I can barely manage to take care of Dec. If anyone else was out there in a worse situation I don't think I'd have the capacity to handle it," she admits.

"Yeah, I've thought about that too. There could be a whole family out there that I belong to and they don't even know I exist. Or worse, they knew I existed and chose to ignore me." I've never shared that fear with anyone.

"Exactly," she whispers, plating the food.

"I'll do mine if you do yours," I challenge her.

"You're kidding?"

"Why not?"

"My heart can't handle it right now." She shakes her head, dismissing the idea.

"Because of Dec?"

177

She bites her bottom lip, hesitating. "Yeah, I guess."

I give her the benefit of the doubt and drop the conversation for now. If she changed her mind, I'd help her navigate whatever dirty secrets she'd discover with her ancestry. I'd probably ignore mine.

"I have a lawyer that a friend recommended. She's said to be one of the best."

"Really?"

"I even think she'd give us a friendly discount, too. I'll set up a meeting." She might not give a discount, but I'd also cover whatever she can't afford. I can't stand the thought of her going with someone less reputable because she can't afford the best.

"Thank you, that'd be great. I've been holding my breath waiting for the phone call about Declan filing for custody. I haven't heard a peep."

"Maybe he'll give up before he starts."

"That doesn't sound like him," she huffs incredulously.

"Will you tell me what happened between you two?"

She drops the utensils she's cleaning in the sink with a loud clatter before turning off the water. As she turns slowly to face me, indecision plays in her eyes.

I hope one of the choices is that she'll trust me enough to tell me. The other one is probably to tell me to fuck off.

"You don't have to-"

"It's okay. I had just turned 17 and my mom had already been with Declan for a while when she told me she wanted us to live with him. I couldn't believe it. I mean he was degrading toward me, creepy, and he was in his early twenties. It was weird for me and my mom didn't understand. She refused to accept that she aged after she turned 30 or that she was

178

supposed to be the responsible one.

"Then she told me she was pregnant and as you can probably imagine, I flipped out. Like screaming, cussing, and blaming her for being so stupid." She pauses for a moment, squeezing her eyes shut for several seconds.

"She accused me of being jealous." She scoffs at the thought but continues. "It was absurd and it only made me furious... I told her to get an abortion." She hesitates before continuing, staring at the ground for a moment. I don't say a word, giving her space to continue.

"We were inches from each other's faces, screaming, and then suddenly I was thrown back. I landed on the couch but Declan jumped on top of me and started-" She grasps her own throat as if to show me so she doesn't have to say it. My fists are clenched together painfully on the counter.

"He squeezed until I was seeing stars. I couldn't breathe but I was more concerned about what would happen after I passed out. His body was on top of mine and I couldn't stand feeling him on me. I was afraid he would rape me if I lost consciousness. I knew my mom would probably let him.

"The police came because the neighbor heard the fight. They ignored the marks on my neck and listened to my mom when she said that I was a bad kid. She swore I was making it up and they believed her. I tried to push it further but they dismissed my complaint.

"I tried to leave, I wanted to but then my mom had Dec and I knew I couldn't stay away. It was hell, though. He never physically hurt me again but he would still mock me or threaten to hurt me any chance he got. My mom never stood up for me, not even when she was sober."

"You didn't deserve any of that," I utter, truthfully. Now

I can see her as the younger version of herself. Lost and abandoned, not taken care of by the one person who should have always kept her safe.

She nods her head stiffly, squeezing her eyes shut again, and all I see is pain. Pain in her heart and in her memories. "The police never saved me. I needed help so badly when I was growing up and they were never there when I needed them... They'd pull my mom over when she was driving under the influence, ignoring me in the backseat and letting her go because she'd bat her eyelashes or flash her cleavage." Her eyes burn into mine as she tells me her story, begging me to understand.

"We'd get evicted from someplace and they'd be there to escort us out, but ignore the little girl who was living with a drug addict." She chokes back a sob, her eyes fluttering as if she's reliving the memory.

Before I know what I'm doing, I'm around the counter. I want to hug her but stop short because I don't know that she'd want me to. She eyes me up and down, wondering what I'm doing, while I stand in limbo, not knowing if I should take a step forward or back.

Instead, I open my arms to indicate my intentions. She huffs a sad sound and melts into me, wrapping her arms around my waist. She doesn't let go and neither do I.

"I'm going to do everything in my power to get Declan behind bars. He'll slip up, I'll get him on something. I'm never going to let him get to you and Dec again," I vow against the top of her head, punctuating it with a soft kiss.

She starts trembling and warmth floods my shirt. Maybe she is a crier and I had her pegged wrong from the beginning.

I'm still thinking about it when I get back to work in the

afternoon. It takes more than a few tries to dive back into my case files.

I'm so close to catching a break in all of these crimes but all I want to think about is the woman living in my home. The way she fits in my arms when she lets me hold her, the sadness in her eyes that I want to ease.

The quicker that I can get Declan back behind bars, the better.

Chapter Twenty-Seven

Jackson

I t's a dark drive home by the time I put the case files down. My job is my life but I had to fight the urge to come home all evening. I've never been so desperate to find out what I'm eating for dinner.

Even though it's late, there's an un-belonging car in my driveway and two silhouettes in the front doorway as I park my SUV. I recognize the car before I recognize the silhouette blocking Natalie's.

This can't be good.

"Whitney? What are you doing here?" I ask a little too defensively as I quickly approach the two women at the door. Decency would say I should invite her in but I never have and don't plan to start now.

"I stopped by to ask you to an event but you weren't here. I didn't get a chance to bring it up when you came over the other night," she croons, attempting to touch my arm as I pass by her. The blonde woman I've known for years suddenly looks like a stranger, as if I've never truly seen her at all.

"I'm busy," I respond dismissively to Whitney but my eyes stay on Natalie. She's standing deathly still, watching the interaction but not saying anything. She looks like a ghost of herself.

"I didn't even tell you when the event was." She laughs, not seemingly put off.

"Doesn't matter. I'll be busy. Have a good night, Whitney." I brush past her and into the house, hoping she gets the hint. I'm an asshole but I don't care. I'm more worried about the only woman I've ever invited into my home than the one on the porch.

"I see. Bye, Jackson."

I don't turn to see her leave as I empty my pockets by the door. Once it's clicked shut beside me, my breath comes a little easier.

"Dinner is in the microwave if you want to warm it up." Natalie starts walking away and I grab her gently by the forearm.

"Wait."

"Don't!" She snaps at me. There she is.

"Talk to me," I beg.

"Why?" She tugs her arm but I don't let her escape an inch. I'm done allowing space between us.

"Whitney is no one."

"It doesn't matter who she is." She doesn't look at me as she speaks.

"It matters."

"Why?" She still won't look at me and it's killing me.

"Because she means nothing to me," I explain, my chest burning with dread. I like that she seems jealous, but not if it means we'll go back to how things were before, with her shutting me out completely.

"Obviously. Since you went running to her arms after our

fight the other night. Seems like something you would do with a nobody. While I waited here like an idiot for you to get home so I could apologize." She scoffs and tries to shrug me off again but I pin her to the backside of the couch, caging her in and forcing her to look at me.

"That's not what happened." I plead with my eyes.

"Then what happened?" She does everything in her power to look away from me but I don't let her.

"I went to see Mr. Wheeler the other night to make sure he knew he was fired. I threatened him within an inch of his life for hurting Dec. I could have killed him because I was so worked up from fighting with you. I knew I wasn't ready to come home because I was so mad at you. I couldn't think straight because I was so mad. I drove around for hours and only ended up at her house because it seemed easy. And it was. She let me in after not hearing from me for months. Before that, even longer between calls."

"I don't want to hear about this." Her voice is breathy but undeniably sad.

"I don't care. You need to listen to me for once in your life."

She harrumphs but doesn't say anything.

"Yes, she's an old hookup but I haven't had sex with her in almost a year. I didn't have sex with her the other night even if she made you think that we did."

Her pretty lashes blink rapidly and I know I hit the nail on the head. Whitney must've tried to stake a claim on me that she has no right to. "Doesn't matter," she mumbles weakly.

"It matters. The only reason that I ended up at her house is because I thought that easy would be good and it'd get you off of my mind. I only had to step through her front door to realize there was nothing that I wanted from her. She had nothing that I wanted because what I wanted was to come home to you."

"Jackson," she whispers my name, painfully. "Don't."

"Why? Why not? I can't tell you how I feel?"

"No. Not when you shouldn't feel that way. We argue all the time. Nothing between us is a good idea. You deserve someone perfect like her."

"Is it because you're seeing someone else?"

"What?" She finally looks at me with her normal, pissed-off face. "What the hell are you talking about?"

"I've ignored the fact that you've seen other people. Going on dates and staying with some guy when you left the hotel. You could still be seeing him, but I'm condemned because of Whitney?"

"I don't know what you're talking about. I think you've dropped too many weights on your head." She pushes me off and stalks into the kitchen.

"Tell me that you don't think about our night together. Tell me that it's history and I'll move on."

She glances over her shoulder at me briefly but doesn't say anything. Her brows are furrowed as if she's contemplating her next words.

"Tell me that I'm no better than any of the other guys you've been seeing."

She turns to look at me fully and her eyes are shooting flames. "Jesus, Jackson. I only ever talk about other guys to get under your skin. The customers that flirted with me at the coffee shack sucked. I only went to dinner with Ty because I was using him for a free meal."

"And? You stayed with some random guy after leaving the hotel," I include childishly.

"Dec and I stayed in an Air B&B for a few days, that's all. Theodore was the owner's name if you're worried about it, he has gray hair, walks with a cane, and so kindly rents out his garage for cheap." She rolls her eyes and grumbles to herself. "There is no one. Okay? I'm as alone as I've ever been. Drop it."

"What about your shirts?" She's changed since this morning, but the wildcat football t-shirt is engraved in my mind.

"What shirts?"

"The ones you were wear to bed. Or, you know, if you can even remember which guys they belong to."

Her eyes zone out for a moment like she's struggling to remember what I'm referring to then she sighs. The thing that has given me so much grief makes her sigh in annoyance.

"I haven't been with anyone since I lived in New York. The shirts that I sleep in are thrifted. Most of my clothes are second-hand. Happy?"

Am I happy? Honestly, I'm fucking thrilled. All this time I've been cringing at the nightmarish thought of her with anyone else and it was all made up in my mind.

Before she can register it, I'm on her, scooping her up by her thighs and setting her on the kitchen counter. She lets out a squeak in midair but doesn't fight me.

"You have no idea how happy I am."

"Why?"

"Because, Natalie. I want you. So, desperately. I want to kiss you and touch you like I did when you gave me a taste the first time. I think about it every day, every night. Don't tell me that you haven't thought about me."

She looks away again, but I pull her chin back with my finger. My body is crowded between her thighs, she can't go anywhere.

"Jackson, I can't."

I don't know if she means that she can't tell me what I want to hear or that she can't do this, but I'm not letting her run from me.

"Why, sweetheart? Tell me why we should fight this?"

She makes that sweet noise. The one I've been dreaming about and I grasp her hips in my hands. I want her so bad. I always have.

"Tell me that you don't hate me like you say you do." I run my nose along her collarbone and up her neck until I feel her shiver. My fingers dig into her soft flesh harder, tugging her to my body tighter. "Tell me."

Her hands thread through my hair and I sigh in relief until she uses it to pull my head back. "I can't do this, Jackson. Please." She pleads with watery eyes.

I'll never take that word for granted. Please is her safe word whether she realizes it or not. I have to respect it.

What the hell have I done to this woman to make her cry so many times in so many days? Maybe I am a bigger asshole than I ever realized.

I pick her up by her hips and set her feet gently on the ground. As much as it pains me to, I step away.

She hates me and I have to accept it. The need that I feel is one-sided and it always will be.

She's here for one purpose, to secure her future with Dec.

A heavy silence settles between us but I don't want to wake up tomorrow with a canyon between us like before. Even if we always remain in neutral territory around each other.

I have to clear the thickness from my throat before I can speak. "It's supposed to rain the next few days, do you think you could make me that soup again? The one you brought when you came here for the first time," I utter my question, needing to leave this moment on good terms.

"I can make it on Wednesday since Dec will be at Charlie's house." Her voice is small and tight but relieved as if she's grateful for the conversation shift.

"I thought Dec liked it."

"No, he only likes soup if it has ramen in it," she admits as I turn to leave the kitchen. It isn't until I reach the hallway that her words register.

"You made that soup for me because you thought I wasn't feeling good?" I ask, turning back to look at her.

"It's not a big deal," she mumbles almost too quietly to be heard.

"I think it is."

I swear I see the breath catch in her chest before she turns her back to me but I walk away anyway.

I'll give her the space she needs for now but I'm holding onto that little thread of hope with all my might.

Chapter Twenty-Eight

Natalie

I've never been more confused in my entire life. It's as if an imbalance in my brain forces me to see every good intention as a fallacy. I've convinced myself for months that Jackson is someone I could never get along with. We're too different.

He has this amazing career and success in his life, while I have struggled day in and day out for years. Even before I had guardianship of Dec, I struggled. I didn't know what I wanted to do for a living, and then when I decided to turn my love of cooking into something I had to bust my ass to afford school. School that I never got to finish.

I've been taken advantage of and mistreated by every man that has ever come through my life. The very first is the father who never bothered to exist. How am I supposed to take 25 years of these preconceived notions and change my way of thinking for him?

I should because he's kind to Dec. He's given us an opportunity to get back on our feet and succeed at something. He argues with me toe to toe and I love that he doesn't back down. He fights with me without making me feel less than.

So, why can't I tell him the truth?

Hey, Jackson. I'm carrying your baby and have been lying about it for weeks because I didn't trust you enough to tell you. Hey, Jackson, I'm an idiot and was convinced I hated your very existence and you hated mine. I'm too much of a chicken to tell you the truth about either of those things.

Yeah. I can imagine that the conversation will go great.

I've had so many opportunities to tell him but I can't. It's easier to pretend it isn't happening at all. I'm still acting as if everything is normal and fine, but I've realized that I hate myself more than I've ever hated him.

I'm having a hard time remembering why I hated him in the first place when he's redeemed himself so many times.

His ex-girlfriend, or whoever she was, showed up and bragged about him showing up at her doorstep the night we fought and my world crumbled. I was suddenly the other woman.

The fool who got knocked up.

When he dismissed her so easily and insisted that he wanted me, I couldn't process it. All I could think about was my dirty secret.

Did he really care about me or was he lying to get out of a confrontation?

If I told him the truth was he prepared to go from being a bachelor to a parent of two?

The number two still makes me nauseous to think about. I have a baby inside me and Dec will have a niece or nephew. One that I'll have to raise alongside him.

What if Dec hates me for bringing a baby into his life and disrupting it further?

How do parents of multiples cope with sharing their time

and attention? What if I'm not capable?

I'm running to the bathroom, puking my guts out before I can stop myself. I don't know if this is from my stress or the pregnancy sickness finally made its debut, but I puke until there is nothing left in my system.

I'm supposed to be getting ready for the appointment with the lawyer that Jackson set up but my stomach rolls again. I breathe through it and attempt to put on a brave face.

"Natalie?" Jackson's voice sounds from the other side of the bathroom door.

"I'm ready, I'll be out in a minute." I smear some concealer under my eyes to fix the bags and ensure my eye makeup is up to standard. It is but I don't feel like myself. I'm seeing a stranger in the mirror.

I fling the door open, preparing for what lies ahead of me, but what's ahead of me smacks me right in the face. Jackson was waiting on the other side of the door and catches me as I full-body slam into him.

"Ow, why are you standing so close?"

"I don't know, I was afraid you were in there panicking."

I was panicking but he doesn't need to know that. I scoot past him and out to the kitchen in the safe zone, busying myself with prepping stuff for dinner. I need to keep my hands busy or I'll be a nervous wreck.

"She's pulling in. Are you ready?"

"Yeah. Let's do this."

The lady that walks through the door is not what I was expecting. I thought she'd be old and frumpy. Instead, she's an Ivy League hair model. Her pantsuit is navy blue and crisp, but her hair is chestnut brown and billowy, catching the light perfectly. She looks cut straight out of a Law &

Order crossover episode with America's Next Top Model.

Liv Greenwood. She introduced herself and dove right into it, outlining what we should expect with the proceedings. I don't miss how she refers to Jackson and me as a 'we' throughout her spiel. Or, the sparkling engagement ring on her left hand.

I ignore how relieved I am that this beautiful perfect woman has seemingly no interest in the man that I'm secretly impregnated by.

"We'll want character witnesses. As many as you can get. Once we're in Family Court you'll want any and everyone there to support you. It looks good."

Her technical language was one thing because I didn't understand it, but asking me to have a village when I don't have one... That terrifies me. My wide eyes search for Jackson's across the island. His are already on me and he gives me a subtle nod, as if I know what that means.

"Declan will try to assassinate your character. He'll try to negate all the work you've done so far with Dec. The biggest thing in our corner is that you are a damn good guardian and Declan was never present in the first place. We'll destroy any argument he has. Do you trust me?" She asks the loaded question as if I've been able to give anyone my trust, ever.

I look to Jackson again and he nods his head again. My eyes linger on him as I reply, "I trust you."

"Okay, all we have to do is wait for the petition of custody from Declan and then we'll be summoned to Family Court. We've got this Natalie." She leaves a few minutes later and I'm left staring at the wall.

"Are you alright?" He raises his hand slightly as if he's going to touch me, but it clenches into a fist, dropping before he makes contact.

"Yeah. I'm fine."

"We will get this done. I'll write you a letter, help Dec write one, and we can ask your old manager. Dec's teachers, Dec's friend's parents. Anyone who has seen how well you've done with that little boy."

I had never even considered all of those people. Of course, he thought of it. All I can do is swallow the lump in my throat.

"I have to get back to work, will you be okay?"

"Of course. I'll be fine."

He looks at me worriedly but nods. As soon as he's out the door, I run to the bathroom and hug the toilet.

Two days later we get the call and the first court date is scheduled.

Chapter Twenty-Nine

Jackson

The Porter Family tree goes back a hundred years in the Rollins County Census. The tree is as wide as it is high. Ties weave throughout every town within twenty miles. Is it a coincidence that the crime in my county is connected back to this family?

I've been delving into it nonstop for days and this afternoon I'm finally meeting Mrs. Porter for lunch. Even after how I acted toward her last time it wasn't a hard sell. She accepted my invitation quickly.

It doesn't mean that I'm looking forward to it. I rinse my razer in the sink and wipe the excess shaving cream off my face like I do every morning before walking down the normally dark hallway as I leave for work. Except this morning the hall bathroom is illuminated.

When I peek in the doorway, Natalie's sitting on the countertop doing her makeup with her bare feet resting against the sink. It's a small counter and her legs are bent to her chest but she looks perfectly content.

"You're up early."

She looks at me through the reflection of the mirror as she

finishes a swipe of eyeliner. "I have an early appointment. I'm leaving as soon as Dec gets on the bus."

"Everything alright?"

Her eyes ping to mine again as she tubes her mascara. "Yep. I'm trying to get all my appointments out of the way before school ends for the year."

"I have a working lunch, and won't be back until this afternoon."

"Okay. You'll be home for dinner, though right?" She asks, hesitantly.

Her voice is small and I blame it on being too early for her. We've barely talked the last few days. I've been neck-deep in these cases and she's been calling her acquaintances about writing letters.

"Yeah, definitely." It's not obvious but I see relief sweep over her face after I answered. I don't know what it means. Is she happy that I'll be home for dinner? Does she like it when I am?

We haven't discussed anything personal between us, not with the custody case looming over our heads. It's selfish of me to keep hoping that things will change but I've never let myself be a selfish man ever in my life.

Is it so bad to start now?

* * *

"Sheriff, I am so glad you've reconsidered my proposal," Mrs. Porter sings my praises over the lunch menu.

I don't correct her about being here to reconsider anything

195

but I smile politely anyway.

"How long have you lived around here, Mrs. Porter?" My question interrupts her out-loud decision-making over what to order.

"Vanessa, please." She smiles, sweetly. The makeup on her face is thick, the texture evident in her crow's feet and around her mouth. "I've lived in Rollins my whole life. I was raised in Langston, but we moved to a bigger house here in Lawson when I was in elementary school."

"Ah, I see. Your family has been around here a long time then?"

"Oh, yes. Generations. We take pride in our community, Sheriff. That's why my husband ran for his position. The one you hold now, obviously." She smiles, sweetly again but I see something else in her eyes. There's a coldness behind them that differs from the expression on her face.

"I am sorry for your loss. Losses," I correct, purposefully.

"Yes. My brothers were quite the troublemakers. I'm only sorry that they dragged my poor husband into it."

"And, the other troublemaker, your cousin is it?"

Her eyes widen slightly but she tilts her head in question. "I'm sorry, who do you mean?"

"I learned recently that your cousin is in prison for the bombing. Thomas."

"Oh, yes. Tommy was my aunt's son. He was raised with us after she passed away. I guess he might've been the one to pass on his troubles to Benjamin and Anthony." She fidgets uncomfortably with her silverware and I'm only getting started.

"That's why you moved to the bigger house in Lawson?" I ask gently, giving her the false confidence that this isn't an interrogation but rather me getting to know her. Technically, it's not an interrogation but I'm definitely prying for information.

"Yes, my daddy insisted on doing right by his sister. He took in Tommy and his sister, Margaret. Though she ran off years ago, right after she graduated high school."

"Kyle's mom. Right?" I hadn't brought him up on purpose yet. I wanted to see her reaction when I said his name. The only person that I've killed in the line of duty and it was in the papers for days. Somehow no one ever connected him back to the prominent Porters.

She pales noticeably but doesn't refute it. The waitress chooses this moment to get our food orders, though I think Vanessa's appetite is gone.

"I must say, I was saddened by his death but you must know that I did not have much of a relationship with the boy. Tommy is the only one who kept in contact with Margaret and Kyle. I didn't even know what he looked like until his picture was in the paper next to yours."

She might be telling the truth. If I'm right, she seems to be embarrassed by the connection. I was hoping to catch her like a deer in headlights but that doesn't seem to be the case.

"I guess it is unfortunate that your family has had such negative press in the last year. I'm surprised your son is running for Mayor. What's his name, again?"

"My boy, Randall, he's a good man. He's bright and intelligent. He went to college and has stayed far away from the bad seeds. He wanted to run for Sheriff like his daddy but I can tell you're doing a fine job. With your experience in law enforcement, I understood that he wouldn't have a chance to beat you."

At least she's being realistic.

"I think he'll be the Governor of North Carolina one day. I can see it."

Okay. Maybe she's not being realistic. The Governor is the same man now who was running things when my mom worked at his estate decades ago. He's close to retirement but I've heard rumors that his son is next to run for office. I don't have high hopes for Vanessa's son.

"Let me ask you a question and maybe this is totally out of left field…"

She eyes me skeptically as she takes a drink of her sweet tea.

"How do you know Declan Randolph?"

Her eyes don't even flinch, they don't widen, or give anything away. "I'm sorry, I'm not sure who that is. A colleague of yours?"

"No, not quite. He was an associate of Tommy's."

Her eyes widen this time and she sputters. "Well, that has nothing to do with me. I was not involved with Tommy and his shenanigans in the slightest. Just who do you think that I am, Sheriff?"

"I'm not quite sure, Mrs. Porter."

Her jaw sets and I see the coldness in her eyes that she hides so well. "I have tried to give you the benefit of the doubt. You're young, cocky, and you flubbed my husband's case as a trooper. But do not forget who pays your salary, young man. You are correct, my family goes back a long time in these parts and we have more power in this county than you ever will."

"Enough power to get convictions overturned? People out of jail? Start apartment fires?" I ask, boldly. She stands up and tosses her napkin on the table.

"You're out of line. Have a good day, Mr. Malec."

She stomps out of the restaurant with a flurry, huffing the whole way. It's about how I expected it to go but I still don't have any concrete answers. If her family is the root of the crime then who runs it?

Vanessa Porter? Not likely.

I ask the waitress to box the food to go and stew on my thoughts all the way home. It's as if the answer is right in front of my face but I'm missing a piece. There is something else that needs to come into play.

Why Declan Randolph?

He's not related to any of them. He supposedly has never even met Thomas Jameson and I believe Mrs. Porter when she says she doesn't know him. So, where does he fit into all of this?

Someone helped him get out of jail. I know his defense lawyer isn't that good. An old detective just so happened to get slammed with planting evidence at the exact right time to dismiss Declan's case... But, why?

Who would have set Dec's room on fire?

Who is the mastermind?

It's dampening my mood entirely and I know it will only be a matter of time before I lose more sleep over it. I thought I was getting somewhere but I don't feel any further than I did a month ago.

When I walk through the front door, I expect to see Dec on the couch but the house is silent. He should be off the bus by now but I don't usually get home until after 5, so maybe I'm mistaken.

"Natalie?" If she's not in the kitchen, she's normally in her room but when I go down the hallway, the bathroom light is on like it was this morning. The door is closed but it's not soundproof. I can hear muffled sobbing.

"What's wrong?" The sobbing only intensifies. I try the handle but it's locked. Something's not right and my usually calm reactivity is flying out the window. All of my issues at work are suddenly the furthest thing from my mind.

"Open the door." I plead gently, but nothing happens. "Natalie, open the door or I'll bust it down. I swear to God."

"I can't," she cries, heartbreakingly sad.

"Yes, you can. Please, sweetheart," I beg. I can't stand knowing that she's in there alone and crying. The door is only a barricade. An obstacle that I will easily go around if it means I can get to her.

I step back, preparing to kick it in until I hear the lock click.

Chapter Thirty

Natalie

There is no point to my existence. I was a mistake when I was put on this earth and I've been a mistake ever since. I was a burden to my mother and I was a burden to myself. Now, I'm a burden to Jackson.

He opens the door quickly, blinking rapidly as he takes in the scene. I'm standing in front of him in my favorite plum shirt, pantsless, with my jeans crumpled up in the sink.

The blood stains on my pants match the blood on my inner thighs and my underwear.

My heart is bleeding out of my chest already but looking at him trying to register what the hell is going on is only making me sob worse. He never even knew. He never had the chance to know that his baby was inside of me and now it's over. My baby is gone.

"What's wrong?" He asks, tenderly, but it only makes me heave a rasping breath painfully through my throat. My mouth tries to form a word but I can't, my jaw only trembles.

"You have to tell me what to do. How can I help you?" He reaches for me but I brush his hands away.

"You- You can't fix this." I don't know what is wrong with

my brain. I don't know why I'm so quick to anger when I'm emotional, but it ignites in me whenever I feel trapped.

Standing in the bathroom of his home, in the blood of my miscarriage that he fathered, I am a caged animal.

"You did this to me," I grit out through clenched teeth. My whole body is trembling. My teeth chatter incessantly from the adrenaline, filling my head with noise.

"What?"

The pain that I'm feeling lashes out of me and I start beating on his chest with the sides of my fists manically. "You did this to me!" I scream, hitting him over and over.

He lets me for several seconds, standing like stone, not reacting. It only makes my blood hotter. "Your fault!" I blubber, borderline hyperventilating.

He finally grabs my wrists in a vice grip, keeping my enclosed fists pressed to his chest. "What the hell do you mean? What did I do?"

"I lost it," I breathe out a sob, my voice cracking.

"Lost what?"

"Our baby." I can't look at him. I can't. My heart is already shattered and I can't see the disappointment on his face when he realizes what I did.

I betrayed him. All of his kindness. All of the trust he might have had in me is gone now. I lost his baby.

"You were pregnant?" His tone is brittle, unlike anything I've ever heard from him, and his whole body sinks until we're both slumped on the floor. His arms cradle me, keeping me plastered to his body as I nod against his chest, letting my tears fall freely.

This is when he's going to yell at me, call me a whore, or a bitch for keeping it from him. It's all going to implode because

I failed.

"You were going to have my baby…" He whispers the words atop my head and instead of pushing me away as I suspected, he pulls me impossibly closer. It only makes me cry harder.

"I'm sorry that I didn't tell you. I'm so sorry, Jackson." My words are almost nonexistent because I'm speaking directly into his shirt but I'm not brave enough to look at him.

He doesn't say anything for several minutes but his arms never loosen. He holds my trembling body with all of the strength in his even though I don't deserve it. He should be mad at me, yell at me, anything other than gentle.

"Why didn't you tell me? Is it because you thought I'd be a bad father?" His voice breaks and my head snaps up to his. The stronger-than-life man who saves everyone has his back against the door with tears in his eyes, desperately searching for my response.

I had never considered that he would be a bad father because when it came down to it, I knew he'd be the best.

"I was afraid that you wouldn't love it because it would be mine," I whisper, hardly able to say the words aloud.

His jaw drops and he shakes his head in silent disbelief. "I would have loved it," he finally utters. "I would have taken care of you. Both of you."

I bury my head into his neck, selfishly seeking comfort from the man who owes me nothing, but he wraps his arms around my back anyway, holding me to him as tightly as he was before.

"I know you would have," I admit against his neck. I realized he would do the right thing no matter what and I decided to tell him. "I was so afraid at first and needed to come to terms with it. I went to get an ultrasound today and was going to show you tonight at dinner. But-" I sob into his neck and his arms hug me until I can hardly breathe.

"My levels were low and they couldn't find a heartbeat."

I couldn't believe it. I was sitting in the clinic with my world turning upside down and all I wanted was Jackson. I wanted him there with me like he has for every other difficult moment since I've met him. "They warned me that I could start bleeding at some point but I didn't realize how soon." I hiccup a sob.

"I'm so sorry, sweetheart." His term of endearment for me cracks my heart wide open but in the worst way. I don't deserve it.

I'm such a disappointment.

"I always wanted to be a mom. Not like this, but I wanted to be the best mom, the one that I never had." My tears flow silently down my face while I feel like I'm on the verge of dissociation. My brain can't handle this, my heart definitely can't.

"You would be," he assures me even though I don't deserve it.

"I've already messed it up. How am I supposed to get custody of Dec when I couldn't take care of my own baby? I couldn't even keep her alive."

"Her?" He asks, breathlessly.

"I don't know, I always thought I would have a baby girl one day. It's how I imagined the baby in my mind," I explain, pathetically.

"You will be a good mom someday. You're the best mom to Dec already. You're his sister but you are a damn good mom. You didn't mess anything up." He leaves no room for argument with the intensity of his words. I want to believe him, I really do, but I'm so defeated.

"I failed you," I murmur the words I've been dreading.

He pushes me back, taking my face in his hands. I can only assume that my eyes are swollen and makeup is streaked down my face, but all I can focus on is his honey-brown eyes searing into my soul.

"This is not your fault. We will mourn this baby. Our baby." He stands up, pulling me up with him. "But, we're doing it together. We can go back to how things were tomorrow, but for tonight, let me take care of you. Okay? You can hate me again tomorrow." He sweeps me up and off my feet, curling me to his chest.

I don't have the energy to tell him I don't hate him. I don't want to go back to how things were but I'm too afraid to admit it. It was easy living with someone I thought I hated, but now I am terrified to be close to someone that I might actually care about.

He sets me on the counter in his bathroom. Dark gray floor, gray walls, silver faucets. It's much bigger than the hall bathroom, with a double vanity, a big glass walk-in shower, and a white tub. It's stark and clean.

While the tub fills up, he disappears momentarily before returning with my makeup remover wipes. I sit there like a statue while he wipes my cheeks and gently under my eyes. I close them to let him do my lids and feel a kiss on my forehead when he's done. His lips vanish by the time I open my eyes.

This is just for tonight. He's taking care of me tonight because we're sad. That's all.

His hands expertly twirl my hair into a twisty bun, something I imagine he's had to do for his mom a time or two.

When the tub is ready, those same hands help me off the

counter and delicately remove my shirt from behind, giving me a veil of privacy.

There's a sudden intake of breath when my shirt crests over my head and I feel him freeze behind me. "Your dragon," he whispers in astonishment as he unclasps my bra.

In the middle of my back, between my shoulder blades is a fine line tattoo of a black dragon. The ink weaves in and out expertly, giving the illusion of being wrapped around my spine.

I'm silent, letting him look. It's the first time anyone has seen it since I got it done in New York. Aside from Dec who tried to expose my secret the day we moved in here.

I got it for me, I didn't want anyone else to know about it, but I'm glad Jackson does. He'll have a little part of me forever anyway.

He respects my silence and instead of asking me about it, he cups my hips in his big hands, right on the sides of my underwear. "I'm going to get these off but I'll keep my head turned so you can get in the tub."

We've had sex, it seems so silly to need privacy but my emotions have been rubbed raw enough for one day. I've had enough exposure for a lifetime, and somehow he knows that already.

The same way he knows to chuck my bloodied panties into the wastebasket as I climb into the tub. I never want to see that underwear again.

The water is hot and there are just enough bubbles that I could lay back if I wanted to, but I don't. All I can do is hug my knees. Being tucked into myself makes me feel less alone.

Less empty.

Chapter Thirty-One

Jackson

She was pregnant. With my child…

My logical mind can't handle the information. I have to put all of my energy into taking care of her because otherwise, I'd spiral into a very dark place.

I rub a lathered wash cloth gently over the skin of her shoulders and back, faintly tracing the lines of her tattoo. Her dragon. It suits her. The powerful, fire-breathing creature carries a likeness to the fire that burns in her. My fireball.

It's hard for me to see her so broken after I've known her to be so strong. The unanswered questions that have bothered me for the last few weeks have clicked into place. The reason she's been crying so much and the long weekend she wouldn't get out of bed.

I should have been beside her, taking care of her from the beginning. *I was afraid you couldn't love it because it would be mine.*

If anything, I failed her. I should have never made her feel like she couldn't tell me the truth. She didn't trust me enough with the truth and that kills me.

The washcloth in my hand continues its journey down one

arm and then the other, doing everything in my power to put the woman I know back together. She's so small in this big bathtub and the way she's hugging her knees to her chest isn't giving me any sign of hope that she's okay.

"I'm going to drain the water before it gets cold."

She nods subtly against her knees and I move as fast as I can, grabbing the biggest fluffiest towel I own and some clothes from my closet, not wanting to leave her alone for more than a few seconds.

"It's white," she murmurs as I hold the towel up as a partition. "I might still be bleeding."

"It doesn't matter. I promise." I hear the water falling off her body as she stands and I have to remind myself that I'm a decent man even though every molecule in me wants to see the water dripping off of her skin.

She steps onto the tiled floor and I fold the fabric around her, covering her from her shoulders to her knees. When she doesn't move to dry herself I wrap my arms around her toweled body and she sinks into me instantly, making my chest tight.

She doesn't say a word as I dry her off and I can only hope that she hasn't because she's starting to trust that I'll always do the right thing when it comes to her.

"Do you want me to help you get dressed?" I hold my breath waiting for her response. I don't think she's incapable but it's too fulfilling being able to take care of her like this. For once, she's letting me take care of her without a fight.

Her head nods against my chest and I'm simultaneously relieved and worried that she's letting me. Her devastation over this situation radiates out of every poor, reminding me how big I know her heart is. She tries to hide it, but I knew the second I saw how she worried over her brother that she was a big softy on the inside.

I drop to one knee in front of her and line my underwear up at her feet. She raises one delicate foot and then the other, letting me slide them up to her calves, and then up her thighs. My fingertips skim her soft skin while I remind myself to inhale and exhale.

I tug them up until they're high on her hips because they're way too big, but they're black and they'll be comfortable. Once less thing of hers to stain.

She's watching me closely as I stand back up with a little more warmth in her face.

"Turn around, I'll put my shirt over your head," I offer.

Her eyes stay on mine as she drops the towel where she stands. I can feel the muscles in my neck straining to keep my head from tilting downward. This woman, I swear.

If she's in the mood to challenge me then she must be feeling better. I don't mind, as long as it means she's okay.

I loop the shirt over her head and she raises her arms, allowing me to slide them into the arm holes. Somehow I get the shirt on and remain a gentleman at the same time.

The first time I see her beautiful body without anything concealing it won't be by accident. I want her fully on board even if it means a lifetime of waiting.

My t-shirt looks like a dress, hanging to her mid-thigh, but I like it much better than the ones she normally wears. I have nothing against second-hand clothing, only against her wearing men's shirts that aren't mine.

"Come on, into bed."

She shuffles out of the bathroom and hooks a right before I navigate her back the other way and to my bed. She is not going anywhere. She's mine until tomorrow at least.

She sits on the edge of the mattress as I change into shorts, her eyes widening slightly when I come out of the closet without a shirt on. Maybe it makes me an asshole because she's had an awful day but I don't regret it in the slightest.

One of these days I'll get her to admit that she's attracted to me. Won't be today, but hopefully one day because I'm sure as hell attracted to her.

She comes quietly as I pull her against me, tucking her body against mine in the middle of the bed. I carefully tuck each blanket around us, cocooning her in warmth, encapsulating our bubble of sadness.

No words are spoken as I watch her eyelids get heavy. I keep watching as her long lashes flutter softly closed and the tension from her brow disappears. Her head rests on my arm but she's leaning on me fully. Finally.

My thoughts drift in and out, contemplating all of the ways I can erase her burdens permanently. I'll shoulder it all to maintain her serenity.

* * *

Jackson - Six years old

"Mommy. Why don't I have a daddy?"

It's Saturday morning and Mommy just made me her big weekend breakfast. It's our tradition and I usually eat two plates.

"Well, honey. Um. What makes you ask that question?" Mommy sets her fork down on the kitchen table and looks at me as I stab my pancake.

"The kids at school have dads." I shrug my shoulders and keep tearing up the pancake that I don't think I'm hungry for anymore. Yesterday was Dad's Lunch Day at school and I was one of the only ones who didn't have a lunch buddy. Mommy is the best but I don't understand why she is always alone.

"You do have a dad, honey. One day, I think I'll tell you about him but it's not anything you need to worry about now. Okay? I'm sorry if you feel like you're missing out." She reaches out to hold my hand, stopping me from destroying my pancake.

"But, where is he?"

"He's a very important man. He's busy working for the President of the United States."

"The President?"

"He has an important job and has to be there at all times. That's why he isn't around." She smiles but her eyes are watery.

"Oh. Okay. Will I ever get to meet him?"

"I don't know, Jacks. I don't know. Maybe when you're older." She shrugs her shoulders and takes her plate to the sink. I don't ask any more questions.

I don't want to make Mommy sad.

* * *

I startle awake, confused, and disoriented. It's daylight, I never wake up in the daylight. It isn't until I blink a few times, and feel the warmth wrapped around my body that I remember. It was only a nap and it's still early evening. The sun won't set for another few hours.

The body pressed to mine in every spot possible is all-consuming, giving me more comfort and peace than I've ever thought possible.

However, impossible for me to remain decent in these conditions. She feels too good. Especially when she starts to wake up and instead of rolling away, she rolls even closer, plastering herself to me entirely.

Her hand searches for something, tapping the pillow by my head, then my shoulder, until she finds my neck, sliding her palm until it cups my jaw. The way that her thumb brushes against my cheek is a loving caress that she probably has no awareness of doing.

I don't care. She can touch me any way she pleases, in her sleep, awake. It doesn't matter, I'm at her mercy whenever she wants me.

Have been for quite some time.

Chapter Thirty-Two

Natalie

Five years old...

Fi "Mommy! Will you play princesses with me?" I'm bouncing up and down outside of the bathroom door while Mommy cleans the bathtub.

"Can't you tell that I'm busy? I've gotta have this whole house clean by the time Ricky gets back or we'll be homeless again. Do you want to be homeless?"

"No, Mommy." I don't know why we don't have our own house. We always stay with Mommy's boyfriends. They never let me have more than one or two of my toys because they say I'm messy and annoying.

"Go be useful and make yourself a PB&J. Make me one too."

"Okay, Mommy." If I make the best PB&J ever, maybe Mommy will play with me for a few minutes. I skip to the kitchen in my Pooh Bear sneakers, making the charms on the ends of my shoestrings jingle.

Mommy's last boyfriend bought them for me, he was nice to me, and always wanted me to play special games with him, but then she said we had to leave. We came here the next day.

I'm almost done with the peanut butter when the front door

swings open and Ricky walks in. He takes one look at me but doesn't say hi. He's not very nice. He never talks to me.

"Nicole!" He finds Mommy down the hall and they go into their room together while I eat my sandwich alone at the table. Mommy's sits on a paper towel beside me.

It's still sitting in the same spot the next morning when I'm getting ready for school. The bread is crusty but I pack it in my backpack anyway. If I ask real nice then the lunch lady might give me a new one. She usually does.

Ten years old...

"Mom!" She's sleeping on the couch, her head lying on the arm of the sofa at a weird angle.

"What, Nat?" She grumbles but doesn't open her eyes.

"Someone's at the door. They're asking for money."

"Oh, hell." She pushes herself up and crosses the living room. We're in a trailer now, one owned by someone else. I'm not even sure who. I don't know if she knows either. "What can I do for you, sir?" She asks the man standing on the other side of the screen door on the tiny wooden porch as she fluffs her hair.

"No one's paying the lot fees. You're behind by four months. I've tried being reasonable seeing you've got a child and all, but I run a business here. Someone needs to be payin'."

"There must be some sort of misunderstanding, truly. My boyfriend's driving a truck and won't be back for another two weeks. He said he'd been calling and trying to pay." From my spot across the room, I can tell she's lying.

There hasn't been a boyfriend here. It's the only place we've lived in a long time where we don't have to share it with a man.

"I'm sorry, ma'am. That's not the case. If no one pays, you'll have to leave."

"Is there anything that I can do for you, instead? I clean. I'll clean your house for free if you'd like."

He looks at her closely, his eyes traveling the length of her. My mom's a pretty woman even though she looks so tired all the time. Everybody always says it's a shame I didn't get her blonde hair or blue eyes. I used to like my brown hair but not much anymore.

My mom told me that I looked like my dad. I've never met him because she said he was no good. She wouldn't tell me about him but she told me how much she hated him.

"Alright, you come clean and we'll work something out."

That got us another month in the trailer but we were moving again after that.

Fifteen years old...

"Connor, I don't want to go to the party. I want to go home." My date ignores my plea, driving the opposite way from my apartment building. Mom doesn't know that I went to homecoming. She told me I didn't deserve to go because I'd been back-talking her so much.

I only talk back because she makes me so angry. I don't know why she's made our life so hard. I've been at my school for two years and now she's saying we have to move. I don't want to move again and I don't want to change schools. I have two more years of high school left and I've made some friends. Life's been easier with friends.

"We'll stop at the party for a few minutes to say hi then we'll leave, I promise." He puts his hand on my knee while he drives and I don't hate it, but it's not super comfortable either. It's weird to have a boy touch me but he's the first one who has ever shown me any real attention. He asked me to the dance and to be his girlfriend in the same week.

The party is at someone's house but I don't know them. They're from a different school. There are kids everywhere wearing their homecoming clothes, but I don't see any parents.

"Are you sure we're allowed to be here?" I ask Connor as he tugs my hand along.

"Definitely. Come on." He pulls me down some steps into a basement with fewer people. A few boys drinking beers are sitting around on a sofa.

"Hey, Connor." One of them holds out his hand and instead of shaking it like I thought, Connor hands him a $20 bill.

"First door on your right." The boy points to a door and Connor drags me to it.

"What are we doing?"

"Come on, Nat. I wanted us to have some privacy for once." He pulls me into the half-darkened room. There's a mattress on the floor and a table lamp in the corner.

"Connor, I don't want to be in here. I want to go home."

"Come on, sit with me for a minute. I only want to talk." He pats the bed and I sit down stiffly.

It only takes a few minutes for his talking to turn into leg rubbing. His hand goes higher and higher up my thigh until he reaches the hem of my tulle skirt. My dress is a hand-me-down from a local church, but it's sparkly and pretty. I only got it because it was cheap and Connor offered to buy it. Plus, my mom didn't have to know. She'd tell me how hideous I look in it anyway.

"I don't want to do anything, Connor."

216

"It's okay. We're boyfriend and girlfriend, this is what we're supposed to do." He kisses me sloppily and even though I don't have any other experience, I know it's not like this in the movies.

His hand moves until he touches my panties, his fingers fumbling with the material. I don't want him to do this, but I don't want him to be mad. He's my first boyfriend, maybe I am supposed to do this.

When a finger finds my opening, he shoves it in and I squirm away. That did not feel good. Again, I don't think that's how it is in the movies. The women are always moaning and smiling, this doesn't feel like that.

"Come on, Nat. Let me touch you." He kisses me again and pushes my shoulders back until I'm lying down. He takes my panties off and I turn my head to the side so I don't have to look.

He fiddles with me, pushing a finger in and twisting, then another. It doesn't feel good. When something blunt pushes at me, I tense. "What are you doing?" I try to squeeze my legs shut but his body is in the way.

His hip bones are jabbing into my inner thighs and his pants are shoved down to his thighs.

"We're making love Nat, like boyfriends and girlfriends, remember?" His penis nudges me again but doesn't enter me. It can't, everything's too dry.

"I don't want to."

His eyes narrow and he huffs. "I took you to the dance, didn't I? Asked you out? I've been real good to you, right?"

"Um. Yeah," I whisper.

"All of that and you won't do this for me? Why are you being so selfish?"

217

He's mad. I don't want him to be mad at me. Am I being selfish?

He has been the only boy to ask me out. Maybe no one else will ever like me...

I nod my head and turn it to the side again. My whole body trembles as he shoves his way inside of me. It burns. Each time he moves it hurts but I hold my breath to avoid making a noise until I can't stand the pain.

"Connor, it hurts. Can we stop?" My distress doesn't even slow him down, I want him to stop but I'm afraid to disappoint him. "Please!"

He doesn't stop. Not until his eyes roll back in his head and plops back on his heels. The condom that I didn't even know he was wearing is filled with his release and coated in my blood. He only looks at me for a second before he pulls his pants up and leaves the room.

If he is my boyfriend then why doesn't he care that he was hurting me? Why didn't he stop?

The tears stream across my temples and dampen my hair as I lay in regret. That's not how it was supposed to be.

Present.

My calf is cramping. My knee is bent at an off angle, so I stretch it, trying to ease the ache until I realize my leg is draped across something hard and elevated, making my eyes ping open.

A hip. My leg is draped across Jackson's hip.

Not only that, my entire body is lying on top of his with my hand plastered to his face.

I peel myself away but not subtly enough because he blinks awake and looks at me. There is no immediate surprise on

218

his face, he's not at all concerned by my body on his.

My other leg is tangled in the sheet and I can't get loose. I thump back onto my pillow in defeat, too exhausted to fight it. My eyes sting from all the crying.

There's a soft cramping in my stomach but I'm not feeling as fragile as I was before. I'm still sad, but I think the nap helped.

"What time is it?" I ask the ceiling.

"Six." His voice is low, sleepy. It makes me want to curl back into him, but I refrain. "Should I be at all concerned by Dec's wellbeing?"

I snort. "No. He went to Charlie's after school. His mom will bring him back here first thing in the morning before his sister's ballet recital." Charlie's mom, Sienna, has been my saving grace since Dec's been in school this year. She's saved me on more than one occasion.

"See, told you that you were a good mom. I was worried that he was standing outside waiting for us to unlock the door." It's a silly comment and it makes me huff a laugh, but then a sad sound escapes my throat and I don't stop myself this time from rolling back toward Jackson. He welcomes me with open arms, pulling me close again. "I'm sorry, that was stupid. I shouldn't have said that."

"It's okay," I whisper against his neck. It was a lighthearted comment, I'm just emotional. I settle against him and sigh with contentment, suddenly feeling something against my thigh.

"I'm sorry about that, too." He reaches down and adjusts himself so his dick isn't poking me.

The worry in his voice makes me laugh. This time a real, from the belly, laugh. I have to take a few deep breaths to regain my composure. A few more stray giggles escape before I can completely contain myself.

"Do I amuse you?" He asks sarcastically, making me sputter another laugh.

"Yes, actually. You do," I reply honestly. In one way or another, he always amuses me. That's why it's usually so fun to fight with him.

Chapter Thirty-Three

Jackson

"How did we conceive a baby? It nearly killed me but I pulled out. That has to be a one-in-a-million chance," I ponder against the top of her head.

"4 in 100. I looked it up." She sighs. "It probably wouldn't have happened if I took some sort of birth control, but I haven't in years. I went on it after-" She hesitates. "I went on it when I was 15 and it made me suicidal. Not an exaggeration. The synthetic hormones and the shit show of my life combined to be almost fatal."

I squeeze her body tighter. The thought of her leaving this world in that way, and so young, makes me want to hold onto her and never let go. "But, you're okay, now?" I ask, hesitantly.

"Some pretty dark thoughts were going through my mind earlier today, but I would never leave Dec that way. I'm better, now."

I grasp her hand in mine where it was drawing faint circles on my chest and kiss her fingers. "Can you promise me something?"

"I can try."

"Come to me next time, whatever it is. You don't have to handle everything on your own. You can lean on me."

Her silence worries me slightly, it's a big ask but I mean it. We both know what it's like to carry everything on our shoulders without support but it doesn't have to be that way.

"I promise that I'll try," she finally responds.

"I knew you'd warm up to me eventually," I brag with a contented sigh. She scoffs before laughing gently.

"You are different than any other man I've ever met," she whispers suddenly, sobering me.

"How so?"

"Well, you show up and you're consistent. Even when you're a pain in my ass you're inherently kind to me. I know that I can be hard to be around, it's why everyone leaves. Or, calls me a bitch." She laughs humorlessly and it makes me squeeze her tighter.

"You're allowed to be angry with all you've been handed in life. That doesn't make you a bitch and any guy who tries to call you one isn't a real man."

"Guess I've never been around any real men before," she teases but I hear the sadness in her tone. I could be that man if she'd let me, but I don't dare say it. That's not a thought she needs to worry about right now.

"I don't know what it takes to be a dad, but I would have been a good one. I would've helped you with every step. Gone to every appointment. Even if that's all we were, kick-ass coparents, I would have been happy to do it with you. I hope you know that." It's probably not the time to bring it up because I don't want to upset her, but I need to get it off my chest. Her words about not thinking I would love our baby are torturing me.

"My dad didn't love me enough to stick around and my mom didn't love me enough to be a good mom. I guess it was a deep-rooted fear that I was projecting onto you. I'm sorry, Jackson. I do believe you'd be a good dad. The best." She squeezes my wrist where her hand has been resting before she continues.

"I always thought being a mom would be the best job in the world. I couldn't understand why my mom was so bad at it. When she had Dec, I doted on him. He was so sweet and innocent, I did everything in my power to give him the childhood that I didn't have. I took his picture all the time because I wanted him to have the memories.

"I've already started making photo albums for him, documenting everything. That's what I'd do for my kids. I'd cook big family dinners on Sundays like they do in TV shows, decorate for Christmas every year, and just take care of my family. Make their lives better, not harder."

"You should have had all of that, you deserved that type of life," I insist. "You can still be that type of mom someday."

"Honestly, I gave up that dream a long time ago. Going to culinary school was my way to secure a career that I could always fall back on because I knew Dec would need me. I wanted to be prepared because I knew my mom would inevitably fail him like she did me. It just happened sooner than I planned. She relied on men her entire life and it never did her any favors."

"You're not your mom," I state definitely without even knowing the woman who ruined Natalie's outlook on life. Who destroyed any chance she might've had at a real family growing up.

I would love a life like she described and I've never realized

223

it until now. A house full of kids. A home, with her.

She'll make me work for it, but I'll do whatever it takes to earn her. I'll show up every day until she chooses me.

"Thank you for taking care of me," she whispers the words as if they're stuck in her throat.

"Thank you for letting me." We lay in silence for a few more minutes as the sun sinks in the sky, darkening the room, until her stomach growls.

"Hungry?"

"Uh, yeah I haven't eaten all day. I should go make something." She starts to get out of bed and I stop her.

"Stay here, I've got it."

"You're going to cook?" She asks, skeptically.

"Not quite." I make a quick trip to the kitchen and return with the to-go boxes from my lunch. "My lunch meeting was cut short. She practically ran out of the place," I laugh to myself but when I look up, Natalie's gone still.

"She as in Mrs. Porter," I clarify. "Who is like 50 and might be into some shady business."

Her shoulders relax and she opens the box in her lap. She looks at her Club sandwich but her eyes flick to my Reuben and she switches the boxes. I have a feeling that no matter which way I placed the boxes the first time, she would have made me switch.

I'm still stuck on her little display of what I hope is jealousy when I mentioned having lunch with a woman.

I'm right here, sweetheart. All yours.

She starts cramping again not long after we eat but insists she only needs ibuprofen. The doctor told her that some pain is to be expected but I'm a worried mess.

Luckily, she doesn't resist when I crawl back into bed with

her and is actually the one pulling me closer.

I end up spooning her, cradling her body while she cradles her aching stomach. Her head rests on the bulge of my bicep while my other hand massages the soft curve of her waist. I dig my thumb gently into her lower back attempting to help give her some relief.

She moans quietly and mumbles, "Harder, please."

That word is the most powerful weapon she holds against me and she doesn't even realize it. There is nothing that could stop me from doing whatever she asks. This time it's simple because I'm desperate to make her feel better, but I imagine that one day it won't be. She'll plead for something that I can't give her and she'll leave.

Massaging her skin is all I can offer her for now so I do it diligently, rubbing her body until her muscles ease and she relaxes deeper against me. Just as she's about to drift to sleep, she clasps my hand in hers and tucks it against her belly.

She holds our hands together against her aching womb, where our baby grew for a short time.

With her safely asleep, I let myself feel the loss fully for the first time.

Chapter Thirty-Four

Natalie

I wake to an empty bed but I welcome the privacy. Today is a new day but I don't know what that means for me and Jackson. Are we going to pretend like it never happened? Are we friends now?

There are too many questions and not enough answers in my mind. There never are.

Rolling out of the king-size bed is painful only because I think I could sleep for two more days. My cramps have subsided and after a quick bathroom stop, the bleeding seems to be done as well. It's as if it never happened at all.

Except that it did and I'll forever hold the memory of being a mom for six weeks. Having a little piece of Jackson.

There's a weight on my heart thinking that it might be all I'll have. He's proven that he's a kind man, but that doesn't mean I deserve him. He has more options out there than me, a girl with no job, a brother to take care of, and a boatload of childhood trauma.

Voices draw me out to the kitchen but I stop short and listen before they see me.

"I thought you knew what you were doing?" Jackson asks.

"I do. Natalie does this all the time and I watch her," Dec replies.

"But you haven't actually done it?"

"No, I'm only 7."

"You'll be 8 in three days," he states dully. I'm pleased that he remembered Dec's birthday.

"You're like 40," Dec counters.

I have to cover my mouth to stop from laughing out loud.

"Take that back. I'm 32."

I peak just in time to see Dec shrug. They're making pancakes. Or, attempting to.

"Does she even like chocolate chips?" Jackson asks and is met with silence. "Am I going to have to make another batch?" Dec only shrugs, again.

"I like chocolate chips," I announce myself, saving him from his cooking-induced panic attack. They both turn to me, smiling wide, and it's quite the welcome. I've never walked into a room and felt such… Belonging.

"We're making you breakfast!" Dec announces proudly.

"I see that. Thank you. Do you need help?"

"Jackson does," Dec whispers but it's heard loud and clear.

"Hey," Jackson scoffs in betrayal.

"Here, let me help before you burn them." I lower the heat on the burner and bump them both out of the way with my hips. Dec takes off and bounces onto the couch but Jackson stays next to me. Very close.

"How are you feeling?" His words are meant to be discreet but his nearness sends a chill down my spine regardless.

"I'm good as new." It's not a complete lie. I'm still sad, but I do feel way better than I thought I would. "Thanks to you," I admit, softly.

His smile spreads slowly across his face and it makes me smile but I look back toward the pan to hide it.

"Glad you're back, fireball." He sneaks a kiss against my hair and steps away to gather plates and utensils.

Little actions like that are too confusing for me. I like it but it scares the hell out of me. The second I believe that he's the real deal everything will disappear. It always does.

"The apartment fire was not my fault. I don't know why you call me that." I feign annoyance. In reality, I'm starting to like all the little nicknames he gives me.

"That is not why I call you that." He laughs from inside of the fridge, fetching the butter.

"Why, then?" I'm plating the pancakes and can't look up but I sense his amusement. "You're not going to tell me, are you?"

"Maybe someday."

"You are such a pain in the as-"

"Are the pancakes done?" Dec interrupts and cuts off my insult to Jackson. An insult that does not hit its mark because he just winks at me.

"He looks like you now," I comment about Dec's hair for the first time since our big fight. It's short on the sides, and longer on top. The blonde isn't as bright anymore, now it's darker and more similar to Jackson's.

"Is that bad?" The big twin asks.

"No, it's not bad."

"Did you just compliment me?"

"Um, no. He just looks like a teenager now, not my baby brother."

Jackson isn't the worst person in the world to look like but I'm not ready to say nice things like that to his face.

As the day progresses we go back to our usual routine. I do my thing, he does his, and Dec bounces around the house like a maniac. Our only conversation is surface level and in the safety of the kitchen. I don't know how I'm supposed to handle my feelings toward Jackson now that they're taking over my thoughts.

I need to pick a fight with him so I can distract myself from all the "what are we" questions in my head.

I won't fight with him unless he starts it first. Then I'll win for sure.

"What's for dinner?" Dec asks.

"I don't know, what does it smell like? What kind of music am I listening to?" This is our usual game. I make him work for it to challenge his brain a little bit.

I've always loved feeling the culture while I cook, imagining that one day it would click and one of them would feel right. I could find a small way to connect with my unknown heritage.

"It's spaghetti," he states with confidence.

"It's not spaghetti, but close."

"Lasagna!"

I smile at his correct answer. "Yep, where do you think lasagna comes from? Think about the music."

"It's Italiano!" He shouts enthusiastically, pinching his fingers and thumb together in that stereotypical way that I know he learned on TV somewhere.

"Good job, Dec," Jackson says, startling me. I didn't realize he was watching the interaction. He snuck in and sat on one of the barstools without me noticing.

He gives me that knowing look, pointing out the secret conversation that he and I are the only ones in the world who know about.

"Dec, go wash your hands," I tell him like I do every day, regretting it as soon as he leaves the room. Jackson studies me and my heart rate picks up. His eyes cover me inch by inch, from my head to my toes.

"I like you in my shirt." His voice is low and husky, it makes my toes curl. I changed into shorts earlier, but I'm still wearing the t-shirt he put on me last night. I'm not wearing a bra because I hardly ever do, my chest isn't big enough to need one unless I'm out in public. Sometimes even then I skip one.

I probably should wear a bra if my nipples are going to react every time he speaks to me because he notices. He definitely notices.

I should turn around or cross my arms to cover my chest, but part of me is still too stubborn to back down first.

"It's an okay shirt." I shrug, instead. His eyes narrow and I see the challenge in them, and it turns me on beyond belief. Part of me wishes the kitchen island wasn't between us but a bigger part is glad for the distance.

The oven beeps, distracting me from our standoff just as Dec comes back into the room. Jackson and I go back to avoiding eye contact, or at least I do.

We eat and close out the evening as usual until I'm suddenly lying in bed, staring at my ceiling. The normalcy of the day is long gone from my mind and in its place is bounds of negativity.

My guilt, my failures, and my loss.

There's a gaping hole in my heart that can only be healed by time, but I'm too impatient to accept that. Women have miscarriages. I had a miscarriage and I have to move on. Except, I'm not ready to. I'm not ready to be alone again.

Before I can talk myself out of it, I'm silently braving my way down the hallway toward Jackson's room. It's dark through the crack in his door and I don't know if he usually leaves it open or if I'm taking it as an invitation, but I enter quietly in case it's not.

He seems to be sleeping soundly with the blankets wrapped around his waist and his arms tucked under the pillow, beneath his head. His muscles have muscles and I never thought the overt masculinity was something that I was into, but apparently it is.

The warmth in my belly cannot be mistaken for anything other than scorching attraction, which is a nice reprieve from the pit of cold sorrow I felt moments ago.

He doesn't stir as I climb onto his bed, settling along the edge in case I need to make a quick escape.

The air feels lighter in here, the atmosphere isn't so suffocating and relief washes over me because I might actually get some rest tonight.

A sigh escapes me as I nuzzle into the pillow and shut my eyes, willing sleep to come. Except, almost immediately an arm latches around my waist, dragging me backward across the sheets.

It's so comically simple to accomplish that I don't fight it as he tucks me against his body. His slow and steady breathing resumes over my head, distracting me from my uncertainties, and lulling me unconscious before I can worry about what all of this means.

Chapter Thirty-Five

Jackson

We've found our new routine. She waits until she thinks I'm asleep at night then sneaks into my room, never resisting when I pull her into my arms, but in the morning as I wake up, emerging from either my bathroom or closet, she's gone.

During the day I go to work, she cooks, and Dec goes to school. We eat dinner together and then she disappears into her room after Dec goes to bed. I pretend I don't expect her each night and she pretends it isn't happening at all.

I welcome her presence and appreciate any bit she gives me, but it's frustrating that she's still fighting it because I know how good it will be once she's all in. Once she feels safe enough to let go of her fears and trust me.

I'm afraid she'll heal from her heartache and be done with me, the chapter we have together will close. I enjoy our platonic nighttime sleepovers but I don't want this to be it. I want to give her the life she wants, the Sunday dinners, and the traditions. She deserves it all. So does Dec.

They're a packaged deal and I'm the one lucking out.

I never realized how alone I was. Even as a kid growing up

with a single mom and no siblings, I was used to doing things by myself. Now that I have a taste of family life, I don't want to give it up. Hell, I want to give Dec a big family. Add on a couple of siblings? Nieces/nephews? Whatever he wants to call them, I'm down.

It would help if Natalie could stand to be around me in the daytime but we'll get there. Hopefully.

One week after the miscarriage we have our first day in Family Court. Well, Natalie does, I'm only here for support. She sits next to Liv at the table and I sit behind them in the first row.

Judge Reisner is presiding as normal. He's the only judge in the county for Adult, Juvenile, and Family court. Declan's lawyer isn't anyone I recognize, nor do they look as put-together as Liv. I got her name from Thea and Jesse. Liv is her best friend and one of the best independent lawyers in the state.

"Today we're only discussing our options, okay? Nothing will be decided in this session. We'll lay out the information and then decide the best option for Declan Jr.," Judge Reisner explains and I watch as Natalie's shoulders shutter at the name. She hates it when people call Dec that.

"Mr. Randolph, what have you done to ensure a good home for your son?"

"My client has an apartment and is currently working in a factory. He is looking forward to bringing Declan home where he belongs." His lawyer provides his information with very little flourish.

"The apartment that the council is referring to is the same apartment that Dec's mother died in. Mr. Randolph was not a resident of that home when they lived there and there is no record of him on the lease currently. I checked with the landlord. There is also no substantial work history to confirm that Mr. Randolph will hold down his job permanently or refrain from going back to his less-than-legal income stream. He hasn't been employed long enough to get a pay stub." Liv drowns Declan's lawyer's points but she's not done.

"Mr. Randolph did not have a consistent visitation history before Mrs. Halstead's death and it's unlikely that he knows basic information about his son, his school, or his medical history. My client has taken care of her brother since his birth. She has been his sole guardian this past year and has maintained a residence for him, ensured his academic success, and allowed the boy to prosper during this difficult time. She is the best choice for custody and I think your honor will see that."

I should clap. I want to. Liv is worth every penny and we've just begun. Natalie's remained relatively still during the entire monologue but I can tell she's shaking with nerves.

"That was a very impressive argument Miss Greenwood, but save it for the ruling day. My main concern is the lack of support in Miss Halstead's corner. She's young, there seems to be no other living family, and I'm concerned that she might be taking on more than she realizes," Judge Reisner says.

Declan leans over and whispers something to his lawyer. "We have reason to believe that she's an irresponsible fit. There has been a suspicious fire at her place of residence and she has moved multiple times since gaining guardianship. There is also reason to believe that she is involved with sex work."

"Objection." Liv shoots up out of her seat. "My client is a private cook. Her last five employers are all in the food and beverage industry. My proof and references are labeled in yellow." She drops the folder on the table to make her point. "That is a farce of an argument."

"I agree. We're not throwing around rumors today gentlemen. What is this about the living situation? Where is the boy living?" Reisner asks, gazing over the top of his glasses.

"My client and Dec have been living with a trusted friend."

"And, who would that be?"

"Me, your honor." I stand to address the judge directly because he knows me well.

"Ah. I didn't realize you were a close friend of the family, Sheriff. Nice to have you here in my courtroom under any circumstance, but if you don't mind, tell me your involvement." He motions to Natalie. I don't know if this is personal curiosity or professional, but I oblige.

"I've been friends with Miss Halstead for a few months. I assisted when the fire that was ruled as arson condemned their apartment. The arson was investigated and none of the evidence points to Miss Halstead. You can trust that Dec's well-being is a top priority for me."

"Ah, I see." He eyes me knowingly but doesn't question me further.

"Miss Halstead, are you sure you're ready to be the custodial parent if it comes to it?"

"Yes, your honor."

"And, if Mr. Randolph is found to be unfit and something happens to you, have you thought about what happens to him then?"

"Of course, your honor."

"You don't have an emergency contact listed on these forms in front of me. What happens in an emergency?"

She hesitates to answer. I am screaming at her in my head to pick me, choose me, but she needs to come to that conclusion on her own. Liv leans in to say something to her and Natalie nods.

She turns to look at me briefly as Liv confirms that the emergency contact sheet with *my* information has already been added to the folder she brought today.

The folder was created way before this hearing started. My name was already listed. I breathe a sigh of relief.

I don't know what comes next for us or if there is an us, but she trusts me with her brother. That is the biggest honor she could ever give me.

* * *

Me: Going to be home late, sorry sweetheart
 Natalie: I'll leave a plate of food in the fridge

* * *

After the custody hearing, I went back to work for the afternoon but it turned into a hellish day. When I drag myself through the front door into the dark house, I consider stopping in the kitchen to eat, but there's only one thing I want.

I head straight into my room but hit the brakes as soon as I see an empty bed. That's not what I wanted.

My shirt and pants are tossed off to the side and I resume my mission. A few quick steps to an unlocked door, and my arms are lifting the pain-in-the-ass woman who won't get the hint. I want her in my bed, dammit. Even if I'm not here.

"I wasn't sure..." she utters softly. There isn't a hint of sleepiness in her voice, she was lying wide awake because she was too stubborn to go to sleep in my room and give away that she wants to be there too.

"Always my bed, fireball."

"Don't call me that." She yawns.

"Go to sleep." I situate us on the bed and before I can pull her to me, she's laying her head on my chest, and draping her leg over my thighs. I needed this desperately after today.

Thomas Jameson was found shanked in his cell.

I spent hours at the jail trying to make sense of what happened and there are still no answers. No guards witnessed it, no cameras picked it up, and as usual, none of the inmates were speaking.

Thomas Jameson was killed, but I don't know by who. My mess of a county just got messier and I'm doing a terrible job of cleaning it up. Mrs. Porter's son could probably do just as well, might as well pass off the reins.

Natalie's sleepy sigh snaps me out of my spiraling thoughts and I hold her closer, kissing the top of her head. She'd tell me to get the fuck over myself if she heard my pity party, so I take her assumed advice and shove my problems aside until morning.

When I wake up, a short six hours later, she's still in my arms but we've maneuvered into a spooning position. Every morning I wake up as hard as steel but this morning my cock is pressed directly against her ass and for the life of me I can't move. I don't want to resume my problems, I want to stay right here and soak in the feeling of her body against mine.

So, I do for a while. I cuddle with this sweet woman who has fire in her soul and love in her broken heart, wishing she might spare some for me one day so I can heal it. I memorize the way her curves feel against me and how her hair smells, hoping each day we wake up like this won't be the last.

A shrill noise sounds from down the hall and she groans awake, stretching haphazardly and grinding her backside into me further making my teeth clench. It's bliss and agony at the same time.

"That's my phone alarm," she grumbles. Her phone is still in her room, not making the journey during my abduction of her last night.

"Do you want me to get it?"

"No, I need to get up. I have to get ready for Dec's party."

Shit. "I need to tie up a few things at work this morning, but if you need me I can stay," I offer.

"On a Saturday?"

"Yeah, yesterday was a rough one. I probably would have worked through the night but-" I stop midsentence, not wanting to finish my thought.

"But, you didn't want me to be alone," she assumes, correctly, with a defeated sigh.

"I wanted to come home to you," I insist.

Her alarm is still going off down the hall as she scoots off the bed and away from me. "The party is at 4:00 if you can make it. If not, no biggy."

No biggy. Why can't she just tell me that she wants me there? Because she wouldn't risk the disappointment if I didn't show.

Chapter Thirty-Six

Natalie

"Sissy, can we do cake now?" Dec begs with over-the-top enthusiasm. He rarely calls me sissy anymore, usually only when he's overly happy or sad, and even though his party just started, I can tell he's having the best day of his life.

All his friends have arrived and are taking turns launching themselves across the couch onto the balloon-covered floor. The four moms here are in the kitchen with me, watching them go wild, and laughing at their antics.

"Let's wait just a little bit." I ruffle his hair at the top where it's still long and he nods, quickly jumping back into the chaos.

Little boys are energy-filled monsters, but funny monsters.

Jackson didn't say when he'd be home, but I hoped he'd come to the party. We had Dec's favorite dinner on his actual birthday the other day and gave him his bike, so it's probably too much to expect him to be here too.

"Natalie the party is great. Dec's so happy." Sienna is the mom that I know the best. She's the one that has been the most kind and helpful since I've had Dec. The other three moms seem to have their own little group dynamic.

"Thank you. I was afraid I wouldn't be able to pull it off. Last year we didn't get to have a party, things were still pretty chaotic." She knows more about the situation with my mom than the other three, so I don't expand further.

"You have a lovely home," Kelly, I think, says.

"Oh, it's not mine. We're only here temporarily."

"That's right. The Sheriff lives here, right?" She asks the question to which she clearly knows the answer.

"Yeah. Jackson was kind enough to let us stay here after the fire."

"He is something else, isn't he?" Jennifer adds.

"Uh, yeah. I guess." I must blush because Sienna jumps and tries to steer the conversation away, bringing up the weather. It's a beautiful day so it doesn't distract the moms much.

"Are you guys together?" Kelly noses.

"Oh, um no. We're friendly. I mean we're friends."

"Oof, I'd love to be friends with Sheriff Malec. I heard he doesn't date." Maryanna is the one who speaks up this time. She doesn't beat around the bush.

"Aren't you married?" Sienna asks her. She shrugs.

"JACKSON!" Dec shouts from the living room, running full speed at the man as he's barely stepped through the door.

"There's the birthday boy!" Jackson matches his energy, strong-arming Dec before he can react, body slamming him on the couch WWE style.

The giggles echoing out of the room make me want to cry. Dec deserves all of this.

I look back to my guests but only Sienna is looking at me, her face full of knowing. I bite my lip to keep from smiling and bless her for not saying anything out loud about my obvious crush on the man who is tickling my brother to death.

I busy my hands tidying the plates and napkins to avoid looking at him as he comes into the kitchen. "Ladies, thanks for bringing your boys over. We appreciate it," Jackson greets them. The formality makes me want to laugh.

When he passes behind me toward the sink, I feel his lips on the top of my head at the same time his hand brushes my waist. His whole body stills for a nanosecond as he does it as if he realized that he shouldn't have. My body is on fire regardless.

Not only did he openly touch me in front of these women, but now they're staring at me while he washes his hands in the sink, avoiding their nosey gazes. I have to clear my throat before I can speak. "Are you hungry?"

"Always for you," he replies casually, making me squirm internally. He is backing me into a corner with the gossip committee and he doesn't even realize it. "I think I've gained ten pounds since she moved in with me," he says directly to our audience, ignoring my side eye begging him to shut it.

They all collectively look at his still perfectly flat stomach, aside from Sienna who is becoming my new best friend. I don't miss how he phrased my living situation. I moved in with him, not that he offered to let me and my brother stay here because we were homeless.

"Here you go." I shove the plate into his hands.

"Thanks, sweetheart." My jaw slackens. "Let's go boys, I have Nerf guns in the back of my SUV." He ushers all the kids outside, leaving me to the wolves.

"Oh my." Kelly fans herself with an empty dessert plate while Maryanna pouts and watches him out the window.

"Yeah, you guys are so hooking up," Jennifer states boldly.

I choke on the soda I was drinking as a distraction. "We are not."

"Something is going on. I bet you've kissed. Ugh, I bet he is an amazing kisser," Kelly croons.

My mouth is opening and closing like a fish out of water.

"What's it like? Come on! We're living vicariously through you," Maryanna begs.

I don't know if it's because I want them to like me or because I want them to know that I have kissed him, but I decide to spill a little while they all stare at me in amazement. Even Sienna looks like she has hearts in her eyes.

When all of the kids and the moms have left besides Charlie and Sienna, she insists on helping me pop all the balloons. I spent so long blowing them up that I never wanted to touch them again, so I accepted her help graciously.

Dec blindsides me while I'm straightening the pillows on the couch, snapping a candid photo of me. "Where did you get that?"

"Jackson got it for me. He told me how to use it and everything. Said I could take pictures of anything I want and he'll get me a new one when it's full." He holds the disposable camera up to show me, waving it like a maniac.

"Wow." I can't even begin to express what that means to me. My brother has no idea of the giant green flag we just waved in front of my face on Jackson's behalf. He is going to make sure Dec has memories.

"Can Charlie stay the night? Please, please!" Dec begs.

"Uh. I don't know, we'd have to ask Jackson." He's outside picking up Nerf bullets and I don't know how to remind Dec that this isn't our house without bursting his bubble.

"Dec how about you come to our house, yeah? That way your sister can relax after throwing you the world's best party."

243

Sienna offers, looking at me for confirmation.

"Are you sure? You just had him last weekend."

"I'm sure, Dec's a great kid. Plus, I know you're doing it all alone. I've had my parents to lean on after Ray died. I know how it feels to need a break." Her husband passed away a few years ago from cancer. She doesn't talk about it much, but I can tell how much it's affected her.

"Okay, if you don't mind. Thank you for everything, really."

"Take the night to figure some things out." She nods toward the back patio where Jackson's igniting his propane firepit. "Life's too short to miss out on things because you're scared," she tells me thoughtfully as heat rushes to my cheeks.

Dec says goodbye and they pull out of the driveway, leaving me to my thoughts. Life is short but what if I make a huge mistake? I could put myself out there and be crushed. And then potentially homeless. No, God. Jackson wouldn't do that. Why can't I ever give him the benefit of the doubt?

Hopped up on too much cake and a little bit of adrenaline, I change into my new favorite bed attire before joining him outside. "Can I sit with you?" I ask from behind him.

"Of course." He turns to look at me and his eyes widen a fraction when he sees me in just his t-shirt.

His gaze stays heavy on me as I force the nerves away and sit on his lap instead of the chair beside him. His hands settle comfortably, one on my hip and the other around my waist, cradling my body against his naturally, while my legs dangle over the armrest.

"Thank you for showing up today." I melt against his chest, hoping he can't hear my heart beating.

"I'll always show up for you," he whispers sincerely, his lips barely brushing my temple.

"I know." My lips skim his neck lightly making his grip tighten. When I kiss his jaw next, he looks at me with his brows furrowed slightly.

My hand trembles softly as I cup his cheek and pull his face to mine, kissing him for the first time in almost two months. His lips are everything that I remember. Soft and urgent, fitting mine perfectly.

He pulls back an inch, blinking his hooded eyes open. "Where's Dec?"

The way this man cares about my brother does me in every time. Everything I feel for him would cease to exist if he treated him as a burden.

"He went to have a sleepover with Charlie." The fire's reflection dances in his eyes as he searches mine. "The moms asked me what kind of kisser you were."

"And?" His focus is on my lips, waiting for my answer.

"I told them you kiss like a man on the edge of losing control. As if at any moment your perfectly curated behavior will snap and you'll forget all sense of right and wrong. In the best way possible," I tell him honestly, watching as the first thread of that control snaps.

He crushes his mouth to mine again, consuming me like no other. The hand gripping my hip travels, sliding along my waist and then down to my backside, squeezing the flesh roughly over the top of my panties.

My hands bury themselves in his hair, desperately pulling him closer, and begging for this kiss to continue. As my body wriggles in his lap, I feel his hardened length against my thigh, and without a second thought, I'm eagerly repositioning myself.

As soon as I settle back onto his lap with my legs straddling his hips, we both sigh into each other's mouths, our lips never missing a beat. His fingers slip under the lace edges of my underwear, taking two full handfuls of my ass while I grind my body against his with forceful desperation.

"Jackson," I utter his name against his lips as he thrusts against me, the material covering me is thin, the barrier not keeping me from feeling each movement intimately.

"You're so beautiful, sweetheart. So beautiful," he whispers against my mouth before dragging his lips down my neck. I want more. I'm desperate for more.

I whip the shirt off of my body before he knows what's happening, exposing my naked chest to him fully, and he's taken aback, literally. His upper half falls against the back of the chair as he stares at me in shock, blinking rapidly. His mouth hangs open like a kid seeing a nude magazine for the first time.

Grasping his wrists to snap him out of his haze, I force his hands to my chest to cup my breasts for the first time. When we were together in his office, my top stayed on, my bra too, and when he was helping me with my bath after my miscarriage, his eyes stayed above my neck the whole time. I watched intently then, waiting for him to slip.

This is a first for us and his whole buddy shutters with his approval. His eyes are locked onto where his massive hands are massaging me gently, but they flick to my face intermittently as if he's trying to fight it.

I wrap my hands around the back of his neck, giving him the silent go-ahead to stop holding back because I'm not sure I have the strength to say the words out loud. Thankfully, he doesn't hesitate to take me into his mouth and a sigh of relief escapes me.

"Oh, fuck," I moan into the night sky as he takes turns sucking on each nipple and the soft skin surrounding them. He licks and bites my sensitive flesh until I'm a burning ball of need about to explode.

But when he pauses to kiss the piercing between my breasts, I'm afraid he'll feel the way my heart skips a beat.

Chapter Thirty-Seven

Jackson

I want to fuck her. More than my very next breath, I want to rip her panties off and shove into her heat. She wants it too, I can tell. The sex at least.

"We should go inside," I choke out reluctantly.

"Okay," she replies breathlessly.

"To sleep," I clarify.

"Oh."

Before she has a chance to overthink why I am doing this, I kick the button on the fire pit, turning it off, and stand up with her legs wrapped around my waist. I carry her mostly naked body inside and to my bedroom.

"Kiss me again in the morning and I'll know you really want this."

"What?"

"You're softer at night when you can hide in the darkness. When you're too tired to fight me." I set her down on the bed but don't step away. "Kiss me again in the daylight and I'll know this is real for you."

"I don't understand."

"We already had our spur-of-the-moment night. This next

time has to mean something because I need to know that you won't run from me after. I won't be able to bear it this time if I have to watch you walk away," I tell her truthfully, searching her eyes for any indication that she's understanding me.

"This is strange," she ponders, trying to cover up with the sheet.

"Why? Because I'm telling you that I care about you?"

"Yes," she states matter of factly like duh.

"Does it have to be a bad thing?"

"I don't know. I'm used to guys harassing me about having sex until I have to give in, not making me wait."

"What the hell do you mean? No, you know what, never mind. I don't want to hear about another man touching you." I grab her by her thighs and pull her back toward me since she had managed to scoot a couple of inches away.

"I'm asking you to think about this because I want you to choose me with no underlying reason other than wanting this. Not because you're sad, angry, or needing to scratch an itch." I throw the words back at her that she used as her excuse the last time we had sex.

"What if you don't want me in the morning?" She asks, meekly.

"I've wanted you every morning, day, and night since you strutted your ass in front of me at the courthouse. What we did in my office is nothing compared to what I want to do to you now, but I need to know that you want to stay. No more running."

"Okay, fine." As she says the words I can see the tension in her body building. She's not fine, she's panicking. "Can I have another shirt?"

Her arms awkwardly hover around her chest, unsure if she

should cover her nudity until I grab her wrists gently, pinning them to the bed on either side of her.

"No, I'm all out." I eye her bare breasts hungrily because I'm still a man after all.

"You're such an ass." She rolls her eyes but smiles.

"I need to shower, do not leave this bed."

"What if I need a shower?" She tugs her hands back, but she's teasing me now, and that's a good sign.

"You know I wouldn't be able to handle it. Give me a chance to show you I'm the right choice, alright?"

"Fine, but keep the door open." She leans back on the pillows with her hair flowing down her shoulders, her panties high on her hips, and her perfect tits out. I want to kick myself in the face for ever attempting to be a good guy.

"Yes, ma'am," I grumble to the bathroom, taking my clothes off and stepping into the glass-walled shower, having the absolute best view in the world with no intention of taking advantage of it. Dammit.

I can't keep my eyes off her, though, and she watches me with equal fascination. Her siren eyes track every move I make, including as I fist myself with a soapy hand.

I only meant to tease her a bit, but when her knees widen I can't stop my hand from jerking. She slides the black cotton down her legs, flinging it away, and baring herself to me completely. My other hand grips the shower door handle but I'm not sure if I'm trying to keep it closed or throw it open.

My little fireball is trying to fucking kill me.

Her hand slides down her stomach, teasingly slow, her fingertips dancing delicately across her creamy skin like I've dreamed of doing a million times. By the time she reaches her clit, circling it with the tip of her middle finger, I'm cumming like a teenager against the fogged-up glass.

She's never going to let me live this down.

I know because she's still smiling smugly as I stalk toward her with a towel around my waist. Her legs start to close but a quick shake of my head halts her knees from moving. "My fingers or my mouth? That's all you get tonight."

Her tongue sneaks out, licking her lips, and I grip her ankles in my hands waiting for her response. "Mouth," she says with a breath and I'm already yanking her toward me. I dive in before she can blink, burying my face against her sweet pussy, and sucking her clit between my lips.

It's Heaven. It's everything.

"Fucking, shit, Jackson." That dirty little mouth. I can't wait to fuck it.

My tongue laps at her swollen bead, while my hands plaster her hips to my head, not letting her squirm an inch. She tries though, wiggling every time I work a sensitive angle, bucking off the mattress.

She can fight with me this way for the rest of my life and I'd say thank you.

Working her clit left to right earns me a whimper and the sound fuels me. I don't relent, stroking her pussy until her thighs are twitching in my hands, and squeezing my skull.

"Jackson, please, fuck." She cries out as her orgasm rushes over her, locking her legs, and pulling my hair by the roots. I love it.

Her pussy is soaked with her climax and I take my time licking every delicious inch until her knees fall open in exhaustion.

When I stand, her hooded gaze lingers on my towel where it's tented obnoxiously, staring unashamedly as I pull it from my waist. Her eyes stay glued to my erection as I wipe her mess from my face.

"Why are you allowed to get dressed?" She protests breathlessly as I pull on some underwear.

"Because I like you naked in my bed and if I don't cover up then I'll end up buried inside of you in my sleep." An eager but sleepy smile is her only response as I crawl into bed, scooping up her relaxed body, and tucking her against me. "Especially when you keep looking at me like that."

"I don't know what you mean," she whispers innocently, delicately tracing her finger up my forearm.

"You know," I grumble, loving and hating how she teases me. Regardless, with my ever-hard dick between her ass cheeks and my hand cupping her breast, I'm happier than I've ever been.

As long as she stays in the morning.

"Goodnight, fireball."

"Tell me why you call me that. Please? I won't be able to sleep."

This woman is going to play me like a fiddle in no time. She's purposefully pulling my strings, she's already too good at it.

"When I was a kid, I choked on a fireball candy. The hard red ones. It almost killed me."

She lets out a gasp in protest. "You call me that because you think that I'm going to kill you?" She sounds offended but I know deep down she is pleased with herself.

"Oh, I know you're going to kill me, sweetheart. I keep my guns locked up for a reason." I kiss her on the head to soften the joke.

"You're ridiculous."

CHAPTER THIRTY-SEVEN

"Ridiculously, into you."

"Okay, now you're being gross. Go to sleep." She wiggles against me, settling in with a sigh because despite what she says, she's into me too.

Chapter Thirty-Eight

Natalie

I startle awake when an alarm goes off, surprised because it's a Sunday, but Jackson groans as he shuts it off and gets up to go into the bathroom. I don't know if that means he has to leave or if he's just an early riser but my decision's already been made.

I silently roll off of the bed and jog down the hallway, shutting myself in the hall bathroom to stare at my naked reflection in the mirror.

The woman I see isn't someone I recognize but in the best way. I look happy and alive. I'm not the scarred girl I've been holding onto all these years. I'm more sure of myself than ever and I can't help but smile about it.

It's so cheesy but indescribably relieving.

I quickly brush my teeth and pee before tiptoeing back to his room because despite feeling confident in my decision, I'm not ready for that level of intimacy.

Not quickly enough though because he's standing at the foot of his bed, staring at the twisted, vacant sheets. He thinks that I left.

The sudden hollowness in my chest confirms my thoughts.

Choosing Jackson is the right choice.

I wrap my arms around his waist, pressing myself to his back and hugging him tightly. "It's daytime."

"Yeah, it is," he confirms with astonishment, holding onto my forearms. I twist until I'm at his front and his hands naturally settle on either side of my head.

"Can I kiss you, Jackson?" His eyes squeeze shut at my question and he takes a deep breath. "Please."

His lids snap open and his warm honey eyes look at me with gratitude. This man has no idea how special he makes me feel with a single look.

His head lowers to mine as I rise up on my tiptoes and with all the strength in my body, I choose him. I mold my lips to his because I trust him and I want him, not in a moment of spontaneity but for every moment. The good, the bad, and the ugly.

He holds me tenderly, pouring his heart out and mending mine because he wants me like no one else ever has. Somewhere between all the fighting, hesitation, and resistance, he became everything I desperately wanted.

My fingers hook his black waistband and I drag him along with me as I back onto the bed. He doesn't resist, his lips pursuing me intensely as his tongue dances with mine, and covering my body with his own.

When his cock finds its home against me I sigh in relief as my legs anchor his hips, pulling him in even closer. Desperation drives us, our hands seeking everywhere but landing nowhere specific. Our hips move in sync as he grinds his length against me.

It's torturous, it's delicious, and I'm almost certain that I could climax like this. Especially as his momentum, or maybe my hands, have managed to lower his waistband enough to let the bare head of his cock caress my clit over and over.

As his wandering lips drag along my neck, biting that sensitive spot at the base before my shoulder, I moan loudly. "Yes, yes," I mumble almost incoherently, needing him to keep going.

Our hands move in tandem, attempting to remove his boxers, until obnoxious ringing shrieks through the air, interrupting us.

"NO! Fuck!" He groans loudly, reaching over my head to grab his phone. His weight crushes me, momentarily deflating my lungs until he settles back into position between my legs.

"Malec." He snips his name out to whoever called, the phone resting in the hand of the arm holding his body over mine. His free hand fists his hard-on, lazily drawing circles on my clit with his tip while I try not to make a sound.

His eyes flick to mine then down to my pussy repeatedly, continuing to torture me. I don't know how he's able to concentrate on his phone call but he's responding at seemingly appropriate times.

My legs start twitching involuntarily as he continues to work the sensitive nub and now his hooded gaze is glued to my face as I get closer to an orgasm.

Experiencing this pleasure while he's talking on the phone is taboo and only excites me further. It's twisted and inappropriate. I can't believe he'd be involved in such a scandalous act and I love it.

The tingling in my toes matches the tingling in my chest and I know without a doubt an orgasm is imminent. I cover my mouth to hide any noise that I can't control but he drops his phone suddenly, wrenching my hands away so he can watch the release hit me and transform my face. Our eyes lock as his mouth covers mine, breathing in my silent cries, until I'm sated.

"I'm sorry, I went into the garage and the call cut out. I'll be in shortly," he speaks into his phone again as I blink back to life, chucking his phone down the bed after ending the call.

"You have to work?" I ask, breathlessly.

"Unfortunately," he says against my neck. "There's been bad stuff happening. I need to be on top of it."

"Mhm. You're pretty good at being on top of things," I murmur sarcastically. I feel his chest shake against mine with his laughter.

"Fuck, I don't want to leave."

"Sheriff Malec, I do believe that I am becoming a bad influence on your potty mouth. You never used to cuss in front of me."

"That's because I never felt anything significant enough to punctuate with curse words. You make me feel a lot of things with great significance."

His analytical response only makes me smile. Leave it to him to have an entire thesis prepared in his head regarding his vocabulary.

* * *

It's close to midnight by the time he gets back. I'm waiting in the kitchen for him because I couldn't stand to be in his bed without him. His footsteps are heavy coming through the front door and I can't help but notice a slump in his posture.

When he notices me sitting on the counter on the kitchen island, he visibly relaxes, exhaling audibly. He looks tired, more so than simple sleep deprivation. The bags under his eyes are heavy, matching the weight on his shoulders.

He beelines to me, dropping the few things in his hands haphazardly on the floor and the couch on his way over before wedging his body between my thighs. His head drops to my chest in defeat as his arms circle me.

"You should be in bed," he breathes against me, stroking my back softly.

"So should you." I tilt his head back to kiss him but he's looking at me so tenderly that I'm distracted for a moment, staring at him thoughtfully before my lips finally meet his. It's nothing like the hungry kiss this morning. This is deep and filled with longing.

This is the kind of kiss a girl would dream about on her wedding day. A passionate, love-filled promise.

His eyes find mine and I swear they're filled with the same promise. I kiss his cheek and then his jaw, erasing that thought from my brain. I'm not a fairy tale ending kind of girl, a wedding isn't something someone like me gets.

He helps me off the counter, interrupting my self-deprecating thoughts, and leads me down the hall by the hand. I don't inquire as he silently opens Dec's door, pausing to stare at his sleeping form. I watch him watch over my brother for a moment before he closes the door again and we continue to his room.

"Is everything okay?" I finally ask as he sits on the bed in defeat.

"No, nothing is okay." This time it's my turn to step between his legs, holding him while he gently sways me from side to side. "Except for you. This is more than okay."

"Then lean on me," I offer, and his head tips up to look at me. There is so much said when he looks at me, but mostly I see a man who is exhausted from life. Someone who has never had anyone to share his burdens with.

"Come on." I pull him toward the bathroom and start the bath, determined to take care of him like he's done for me. He lets me undress him without protest while I do my damnedest not to stare at his wide chest and his sculpted arms. As much as I'm dying for him to take me again, this treatment isn't about sex.

Regardless, he's hard by the time I get to his pants. I try to ignore it, but it's hard to miss as I usher him into the tub. When I turn back to him after tossing his clothes in the hamper, he's watching me closely.

"What?"

"I'm waiting for you to get in."

"This is for you, not me." I tuck my hands on my hips, intending to stand my ground.

"If it's for me then I want you in here with me."

I don't think I can argue with that logic, nor do I really want to. I throw my sleep shirt off and hear him suck in a breath at my nakedness. I didn't bother wearing underwear to bed this time.

I step in between his legs and he guides my hips down, settling me between his tree trunk thighs. There is no ignoring the elephant resting along my spine.

Despite our nudity, we behave ourselves. My fingertips skim the surface of the water, his arms, and legs, warding off the heaviness of my eyes while his hands caress me

259

everywhere he can reach.

"Do you want to talk about it?" I ask, distracting myself further as his fingertips graze my aching nipples. He cups my breasts firmly, but sighs, defeated.

"The teenage boy who had been missing for quite some time was found dead. Overdosed. He was only 16. It's the second death on my watch since Friday. The first one was a prison stabbing."

"How is it on you?"

"My job is to keep these people safe," he says blandly.

"Jackson. You can't do that to yourself." He only sighs as a response so I flip over to look him in the face. "It's not your fault."

There's an aching sadness in the depths of his eyes as he meets my gaze.

"Jackson, it's not your fault," I whisper tenderly, but with more conviction.

"Thank you, sweetheart," he whispers against my forehead, letting his lips linger there.

"You don't believe me, I can tell but it doesn't mean it's not the truth you stubborn goat."

"Wow, that's a new one. Can I have a nickname that doesn't involve an animal or insult?" He teases.

"You are a good man and a good Sheriff, Hercules," I say with all the seriousness I can muster and it makes him laugh.

"Better than stubborn goat, I guess. Come on, time for bed." We take turns drying each other off and climb into bed, settling into our usual entangled position.

"Can I tell you something?" I whisper against his chest.

"Anything."

"That first time in your office... When you heard me say no, it wasn't because I wanted you to stop, not really." He doesn't respond, but I take his silence as an excuse to continue. "You were so annoyingly good, you made me orgasm when no man had ever accomplished that before. I was mad that you were the one to do it and I couldn't stop it from happening. You're perfect at everything you do, I was pissed. And, jealous, honestly. So, you can call me a stubborn goat if you want."

"And, now?" He asks, ignoring my goat comment.

"I'm really glad that it was you. And, still you," I whisper. "I still think you're good at everything you do, but it doesn't bother me like it used to. I guess I'm starting to find you somewhat endearing," I admit, hiding my face in embarrassment. I'm not used to being so open with my thoughts but it's a sacrifice I'll make if it means he'll end his day less dejected.

He cups my face tenderly. "I think about that night every time I walk through that doorway, every time I sit at my desk. You're the only one that I've ever had in my office. In my bed. This is a unique experience for me as much as it is for you. We can navigate it together."

"You've never brought a girl here?" Not that I want a full account of his sex life, but I am curious.

"No. I always cut all my encounters short. I had no interest in playing house with anyone."

"But, you brought me here."

"You're special. I knew that a long time ago." He brushes his thumb over my chin delicately.

"Jackson, you're insane. I was mean to you all the time, how could you have possibly known that I was special?"

"Arguing with you made me feel alive again. Having you and Dec here only confirmed that. Now, I don't want you to leave," he whispers, hesitantly.

"That's a big commitment. You can't mean that."

"I don't say anything that I don't mean. You should know that. Don't worry about it though, I didn't mean to drop it on you like this."

"What if I want to stay, too?" I ask under my breath, not quite able to meet his eyes.

"Then you're home, baby." He drops his forehead to mine and I can't help but smile.

"Don't you realize how hard this is for me to believe? I've never been able to depend on anyone." *And, it doesn't seem real that anyone would actually want me.*

"I know, but I'm willing to put in the work to convince you." He pulls me in tighter, sighing contentedly.

"Jackson, we haven't even talked about what we are. Not really. Aren't we supposed to, I don't know, be in love before we live together?" I ask against his collarbone.

"We've had our own timeline, that's true, but I'm way past pretending that I'm not in love with you. I'm only waiting to say it so I don't scare you off. This doesn't count, by the way."

Chapter Thirty-Nine

Jackson

My arms are braced, preparing for her to bolt, but after a few minutes, I finally let myself relax. I sprung a lot on her and she is acting surprisingly okay.

"You're in love with me?" She whispers. We're lying so close that I can't see her face but can feel her breath against my neck.

"Hypothetically, whenever you're ready to admit that you love me too, you can rest assured that I'm in the same boat. Okay?"

"Why do you think that I will?" She asks, but curls further into me and I take that as a sign that we're good. She's not running for the hills. I've still got her.

"I hope you will. Even if I have to let you win all of our arguments," I tease, making her huff a laugh.

"Don't let me win, it's not as fun that way," she admits softly. She doesn't say anything else about the love topic so I let it be. Having her in my arms is enough for now.

In the morning I get Dec on the bus, letting her sleep, and then text Roberta to let her know I won't be in today. I worked the last seven in a row and need a day uninterrupted with the woman in my bed.

She's right where I left her and rolls back into my arms as soon as I lay down. Every time she chooses me, in her sleep or for the smaller insignificant things, I celebrate. Her vulnerability is something that I cherish because no one else gets that side of her. It's all for me.

Her leg hooks over my hip and drags me closer. "Why are you wearing so many clothes?" She grumbles against me.

"I couldn't stand naked in the driveway sending Dec to school."

"Ugh. You're so responsible." She squeals as I squeeze her side, tickling her. "Okay, I take it back. You're a child."

"I love it when you're mean to me," I tell her honestly.

She laughs and forces my shirt over my head, exposing my upper half. "Mmm, so much better." Her fingertips explore my chest and down my stomach.

"I used to have abs before you started feeding me."

"Hmm. I like you the way you are. If you had abs then everyone would think I was a lousy cook. It's bad for my reputation."

Any intelligent response dies on my lips as she scrapes her nails along the waistband of my shorts before pulling the drawstring. Her fingertips skate along the edge, barely breaking beneath the fabric. She's going teasingly slow on purpose and lucky for me, I have all the time in the world today, so I let her play.

I lift my hips to allow her to tug them down, letting her control the pace. When she palms my cock, gently wrapping her delicate hand around it, I can't control my sharp intake of breath.

She pumps me lazily with one hand, drawing my lips in with the other to slide her tongue against mine, and I'm a fucking goner.

My hand finds her breast on instinct, kneading the soft flesh until her nipples are tight and sensitive, pinching them lightly and making her squirm.

"More," she begs. "Touch me, Jackson."

"Here?" I'm already sliding my fingers through her curls, straight to her tight entrance. I enter her with ease, curling my two fingers and pumping into her at the same pace she's pumping me.

Her hand picks up speed and so does mine, making her wriggle with need. She's so sexy, moving and arching her back while she opens herself up to every sensation. She might've resisted the pleasure the first night we were ever together, but she's more than eager now.

It's getting me too worked up and I'm losing my bearings. I want this to last, needing more than a few breaths to calm myself down before I finish in her hand.

I take the reins back, slowing the momentum of our foreplay while her dark eyes blink at me curiously. She's silently begging for more and I'd be less of a man if I wasn't willing to give her everything she wants.

When my fingertips find her clit, rubbing her gently, her head falls back in relief. The look on her face, the way her long lashes flutter, makes me want to prolong this exploration all day. I want to see how every touch makes her react.

Except, she's not on the same wavelength. She's guiding the head of my cock to her pussy, holding all of the true power in this, controlling me effortlessly. I'm a ticking time bomb but I couldn't resist her if I tried.

She teases herself, teases me, circling my tip around the tight opening and I can hardly catch my breath. Anticipating what she'll do next, watching how consumed she is by her pleasure, is driving me wild. When she finally notches me at her entrance, my whole body stills, and she hesitates.

We stay like that, breathing each other's air as she takes me, barely an inch.

Every muscle fiber in me trembles, attempting to hold back, but dying to bury myself to the hilt inside of her. It's been so long since I've had her and I've been dreaming about this moment.

Her arm is anchored around my neck, keeping our heads close while we both stare at where our bodies are joined. "I'm still not on birth control," she mumbles, distractedly.

I can hardly manage to grunt as a response. I don't care if she's not on birth control, I would get her pregnant again in a heartbeat. I'm fucking ready.

"I can go get a condom, I think I have some in the bathroom," I offer, reluctantly.

"No," she blurts out quickly. "Don't leave." Her hips tilt slightly, sheathing me another inch and I groan.

"Natalie, if you want me to fuck you bare, I will. Right now. Tell me what you want, sweetheart." My heart is pounding in my chest, but she probably can't hear mine over the sound of hers.

Her eyes snap to mine, full of uncertainty, and pleading for something. Does she need me to choose for her?

I don't know but I need something from her. A single word and I'll give her anything she wants.

"Say, please," I demand, nose to nose, holding her eyes on mine. My body is locked tight with tension, embracing her with a painful grip while her nails dig into my shoulder, begging for more.

I see the answer in her eyes before she voices anything and I exhale in relief.

"Please," she breathes out the word, slamming her mouth to mine at the same time that I drive my cock into her as deep as it will go. I swallow her cries, pounding into her pussy like a man unhinged because I am. I fuck her like she's the first woman that I've ever seen in my life. Desperate to breed her.

I want to see my cum dripping out of her and I want my baby growing inside of her. The thoughts consuming me are feral. I need to pull out, that's the right thing to do but fuck, I want to fill her.

"Jackson, yes, yes," she cries, meeting me thrust for thrust.

"Where do you want my cum, baby?" I ask desperately, giving her an out if she needs one. She can tell me anywhere but her sweet pussy and I'd listen. I'd do anything she wants, but if she doesn't say anything I'm going to explode inside of her. I'm so fucking close, my thumb on her clit isn't making any type of rhythm.

"Jackson." Her voice is softer this time but filled with wanting.

"Do you want me to fill your sweet cunt, fireball?" This is the last question I have in me, so it better drive home my point.

"I need it, please!"

The last word is all it takes to tip me over the edge. I pull her hips to mine with bracketing force, spilling my release as deep as I can get it while she cries out, her pussy squeezing and contracting around me with the same desperation I felt.

Long after our climaxes ease, I'm still buried deep inside of her while she traces my back with her fingertips.

"Jackson?" She asks over my head.

"Yeah, baby."

"Are you okay?"

My head snaps to hers. "I'm great. Why?"

She laughs. "You hadn't moved and I was worried that I broke you."

"Do you want me to move?"

"No, but I wasn't sure if it was normal to cuddle like this afterward. With you still inside of me. Most guys bolt." She laughs softly.

"It's my new normal. Fuck those other guys," I mumble as I bite her neck playfully. But I hate every man who has ever been in her hemisphere.

"I know it isn't likely since I just had my miscarriage but aren't you worried about getting pregnant?" Her voice is suddenly small.

"Not in the slightest."

"Why?" Her confusion makes me hold onto her tighter. I want to squeeze all of the terrible thoughts and experiences out of her so she never underestimates me again.

"Because I want you pregnant again as soon as possible," I admit, arching my head down to kiss her stomach.

"You're not being serious." The astonishment in her voice is clear.

"I've never been more serious about anything in my life. I want as many babies as you'll let me have with you."

"You're crazy, I can't believe you just said that."

"Six? How about we have six," I suggest.

"SIX! Why six?"

"That's how many dining room chairs I have."

CHAPTER THIRTY-NINE

"Then where will you and I sit?"

Her question makes me chuckle. "I'll buy more chairs." I bring myself up to my knees, disconnecting our bodies while she stares at me in disbelief.

"You're serious?" She sits up, leaning on her hands and it makes the cum I filled her with start to leak. With two of my fingers, I push it back inside of her, making her gasp.

"I'm going to redo your room and give it to Dec. Then I'm going to call my builder and start plans on adding more rooms to the house. You're going to get a big ass SUV with a big bow on it for Christmas." I'm pumping my fingers inside of her as I explain all the plans I have.

"You're going to finish culinary school and hang your plaque on the wall. Use it, don't use it, I don't care as long as you're happy. You can spend your days cooking for our family and making big Sunday dinners."

"Jackson," she moans my name as my thumb grazes her still-sensitive clit.

"We're going to take pictures of everything, start traditions on every holiday, and fill this house with memories. Our house, sweetheart." I'm getting worked up watching her face flush with her pleasure. Her hair is wild and her chest is pink.

Her channel was already slick from my release, but it's getting wetter while I play with her. Crooking my fingers to rub her g-spot, I use my other hand to hold her thighs open because her muscles are tensed, resisting the heightened sensations.

"Relax for me, don't fight it."

"Jackson, I can't it's too much," she breathes heavily.

"Yes, you can. Let go, for me. I've got you." Her eyes find mine and I feel her body give in as her knees fall open.

"Oh, fuck. Fuck, fuck, fuck…" Her walls clamp around my fingers and she cums hard, her juices soaking my hand and the sheets. I'm staring at her pussy in amazement as her torso falls back against the bed and she catches her breath.

I want to do that again.

Chapter Forty

Natalie

He wants a baby with me. Not because we made a mistake and are making the best of it, but on purpose with full intent, he wants my baby.

It's all I've been able to think about all morning.

After our incredible re-sexification, we got in the bath and now we're in the kitchen eating lunch and I'm still tongue-tied about the whole baby thing.

"I ordered these back when I ordered Dec's birthday presents," Jackson says from the hallway, holding two small boxes. "I hoped if I had them, then you'd reconsider your decision."

I grab the box that he offers me, inspecting it carefully. It's a DNA kit.

"I don't know, Jackson. What if there are more kids out there like Dec? What if my biological father left his mark on the world and I can't do anything to fix it."

"If he did, and you have siblings out there, then it's not your job to save them."

I look at him dumbly, but he holds up his hands to stop my comment before I can make it.

"I know you would want to help them, but I'm saying that it's not your fault. You didn't deserve to be abandoned just as much as they don't. Anyone you find, if they're out there, we'll help. If you choose to connect with them then I'll be here every step of the way."

Every step of the way. He's not backing out, he's not running from the challenge of whatever my insane life might bring. He's standing his ground.

"Okay," I respond, quietly.

"Just think about it. You don't have to do it right now."

"I said okay. As long as you do it with me."

He looks stunned as if he wasn't sure he heard me correctly. "Okay? Just like that?"

"Yeah." I smile softly at him and he slinks closer to me, brushing the loose hair behind my ear. His deep honey eyes assess me affectionately, making my heart thump harder as he holds my cheek in his hand. He opens his mouth to say something but my phone rings, making me jump.

"It's Dec's school," I tell him as I answer. He watches closely as I listen to the other end of the line.

"No, I'll be right there. Don't let him out of your sight." I end the call and run to my room to get shoes with Jackson's hot on my heels. "He's there. Declan's at the school."

"What? Why the hell didn't anyone call me?" He disappears into his room for a moment and then we're both running to the door.

"I don't know, they said they called the police. He was trying to get his attention through the fence at recess but the aid made Dec go back into the building. I need to go get him."

Jackson's already grabbed his keys and I don't miss that he grabbed his badge and gun as well.

He ushers me into Suburban gently, but I can feel the tension radiating off him. He's pissed. As soon as we're on the road he's calling people, one after another, barking into the phone and trying to get answers. No one knows why the call from the school didn't get passed along to him. Until the last one.

It seems to give him the answer he was seeking but he doesn't say anything after hanging up. His jaw is locked so tight that I'm worried he'll crack a molar. When we finally pull up in front of the school he's screeching to a halt on the curb and jumping out before I can get my seat belt off.

"Uh, should you park here?" I point to the no parking signs so he knows what I mean as he holds my door open.

"Those don't apply to me." He taps the roof of his cruiser with his palm.

"Oh, right." Duh. Emergency vehicle. I've somehow forgotten the perks of Jackson's job. He's gotten my defenses down so easily, I don't see him as a blue-bleeding anti-hero anymore.

"When they called 911, it went to Lawson PD. The responding officer didn't think it was necessary to call me, even after the principal mentioned my name," he explains through gritted teeth as we rush to the entrance.

The three officers are standing in the hallway outside the principal's office when we get there, one of them I recognize from that day at the drugstore. It reminds me why I still feel justified in my hatred of law enforcement, despite sleeping with one.

"You go make sure Dec is okay. I'll be a minute." He holds the door open for me and then shuts it once I'm inside. Dec flies up to hug me as soon as he sees me.

"Hey, you okay?" I ask against his head.

"Yeah. My dad's here," he whispers like it's a secret.

"I don't think he's here anymore. I'm going to take you home though, just in case."

"Is Jackson here, too?" I don't have a chance to answer because we both hear the booming voice from the hallway.

"I don't give a damn about procedure. As soon as my name was mentioned, someone should have called me directly! This isn't about jurisdiction, that's my boy in there! The next time one of you overlooks that, I'll have your badge!"

Someone responds, bravely or idiotically. Either way, it doesn't seem like a good idea since Jackson is officially in papa bear mode, absolutely melting my heart.

"I'll go to your Chief, I'll go to the state board, I'll go to the God damn Governor. Try me!"

Dec giggles while the principal and secretary look at me with wide eyes. "Maybe next time, call him first." I shrug, trying not to laugh myself.

* * *

"We're getting a dog." Jackson's still fuming even after Dec's gone to bed for the night. "I've been wanting a k9 for the department. I'll get it trained and teach Dec how to handle it."

I appreciate his concern about Dec's well-being. His over-the-top anger is undoubtedly making my insides boiling hot for other reasons though. I love seeing the stoic put-together man with steam coming out of his ears.

"Do you think that's necessary? Declan was crossing a boundary but do you think it will get worse?" I ask, even though I know that it's not likely he'll give up quietly.

"I don't know. I'm not risking it when it comes to Dec."

"Because he's your boy?" I ask, wrapping my arms around his waist in the kitchen.

"Of course he is." He holds me tightly, pressing a kiss to the top of my head.

"You're a good man, Jackson." My admission makes his arms tighten around me.

"I love it when you're sweet to me." His hands are suddenly under my thighs, plopping me onto the counter easily.

"You said that you loved it when I was mean to you," I remind him.

"One of these days you're going to accept that I love everything about you, sweetheart." His fingertips skim up my thighs reaching the hem of my shirt, his shirt that I'm wearing, and he snakes them underneath to get a hand full of my bare breasts.

"Maybe one day." I kiss him hungrily, pouring all of my feelings from today out.

He takes all of it greedily, tugging my panties off and spreading my thighs wide before he drops to his knees below me.

He's kissing up my thighs when we both hear the click of a door down the hall being opened.

A brief look of "Oh shit" and we're both scrambling to act normal. I jump off the counter and Jackson stands up, leaping away from me like I'm on fire. He notices my underwear lying in the middle of the floor and kicks the fabric around the corner of the cabinets. Thank God my shirt's long.

"Sissy," Dec wanders into the kitchen sleepily, looking younger than he has in a while. He's growing up but he'll always be a little boy to me.

"You okay, bub?"

He shrugs his shoulders and gets into the fridge, snagging a grape from the bowl.

"Couldn't sleep?" He's a talkative kid, so when he's not saying much I get worried.

"Every time I close my eyes, I think Dad is standing outside my window or something. It's dumb. Only babies get scared." His head hanging is the saddest sight, I can't stand it.

"I have alarms on all the windows and doors. I'd never let him get to you, buddy." Jackson hugs him, tightly. "We all get scared."

"You get scared?" He asks the big man in front of him with wonder in his eyes. I tease Jackson about being Hercules, but he really is to a boy like Dec. The best male role model in the world for a little boy who has never had one.

"All the time. I was scared today when your school called because I thought you were hurt. I'm scared every time my mom gets sick. I'm terrified that your sister will stop cooking for me one day."

Dec giggles at that last one and I roll my eyes. It seems to have helped lighten the mood though so I appreciate his effort.

"You can sleep in my bed tonight, okay? We'll have a sleepover," I suggest.

Dec laughs again. "We won't all fit in your bed."

"What?"

"Jackson is too big for your bed."

"Well. Yeah, but I didn't mean all three of us," I explain.

Up until this point, I've been pretty sure that Dec wasn't aware that I was sleeping in Jackson's bed every night. It's not something I necessarily want to discuss with my little brother.

"Oh." His eyes are downcast as he shrugs and it makes my heart ache.

"Do you want to sleep in my bed?" Jackson asks, hesitantly. He shrugs his little shoulder again. The poor kid has the same fear of rejection as I do.

"Wait, so am I invited to this sleepover, or not?" It sounds like I'm the one being booted to the curb, but it makes Dec giggle again.

"It's big enough for all three of us, right Jackson?"

"Yeah, buddy. It sure is." He winks at me over Dec's head.

Suddenly, all three of us are lying comfortably in bed, Dec sandwiched between Jackson and me. It's the first night in a long time that I won't get to fall asleep in Jackson's arms but somehow this makes me feel even closer to him.

The fact that my brother chose this sleeping arrangement and took the initiative to seek Jackson out warms my heart beyond belief. For the first time ever, this place we are living in truly feels like our home.

"Jackson," Dec whispers. I keep my eyes closed and my back turned to the both of them, waiting to hear what he has to say.

"Yeah, buddy?"

"Do you think you could come the last week of school and do career day with me? All the other kids are asking their parents." His question is hopeful but hesitant. I don't even have to hold my breath to wait for Jackson's answer because I know he's over the moon right now.

"I'd love to, Dec but what about your sister? She's a cook, you know?" Jackson's question is considerate but unnecessary. I don't think anyone outside of him would consider what I do even close to a career. Not yet, anyway.

"I know. She's already done so much for me, I feel bad asking her to help me with everything," he responds sadly. It takes all of my restraint to continue playing dead. I want to turn over and tell him that I'd do anything for him. Always.

"She loves it because she loves you. We *both* do. I'll do career day but make sure you ask her if you take a field trip to a zoo or something. She loves animals." I roll my eyes under my closed lids. I make a few animal-related insults toward him and he won't let it go.

"Do you love my sister, too?" Dec asks curiously. This living situation probably is odd to him, but I hadn't thought about his perspective on Jackson and I's relationship.

"Yeah, I do."

My breath catches in my throat. It's not the first time he's insinuated his feelings for me, but I still can't quite believe it.

"Would it be okay with you if I dated her?" He asks Dec and I can't control the smile that spreads over my face.

"Like be boyfriend and girlfriend?"

"Yeah, like that. I'd take her to dinner sometimes and we'd share a room so you can have the bigger one down the hall. Would that be okay?"

"I guess so, but only if you aren't gross in front of me. Kissing is disgusting." I hear Dec's facial expression through his words. I would laugh if I wasn't supposed to be sleeping.

"I'll try to keep it to a minimum but no promises." Jackson laughs and I feel the bed shake as if Dec tried to bump him with his elbow.

278

"Are we staying here forever then?" Dec asks seriously, sobering the atmosphere.

"Yeah, you can stay forever. I'd like it if you did," Jackson responds just as seriously. It isn't until I bite my lip that I realize my jaw is quivering. It's not even about me. He's giving my brother so much with that response. It means everything.

"Okay, we'll stay then," Dec says definitively and it makes Jackson laugh softly.

"Good. It's settled then. You can tell your sister though, I'm afraid of her," he teases.

"She's not scary. She can be pretty mushy." Dec snickers.

"I know, she has a big heart thanks to you. You're her favorite person ever." The bed jiggles again as Jackson presumably starts tickling Dec and then shushing him as they both laugh.

He has to realize I'm awake because there is no way anyone could sleep through their commotion, but I'm enjoying being a fly on the wall.

"I'm her favorite kid. You can be her favorite grown-up," Dec suggests when his giggles cease. There's a silent pause while Jackson contemplates that.

"Deal." The bed shakes again and I think it's because they shook hands—my two favorite men.

Chapter Forty-One

Jackson

Declan Randolph is hiding something. I've been following him all day, watching where he's going and who he's with. He's been looking over his shoulder the entire time because he already suspects someone might be watching him.

Except, he hasn't spotted me yet and I don't think I'm the one he's worried about. Although I should be. I'm going to make sure this bastard never enters Natalie and Dec's life again.

When Declan emerges from a gas station, I follow him back to his apartment. It's the one that Natalie's mom lived in when she died, where Dec lived. When he gets out of his car, I pull up right behind him and jump out.

"Declan."

"What do you want?" The disgust is clear on his face but I don't give a shit.

"I'm giving you a warning. Don't come near Dec again. Don't go to his school," I state cooly even though I want to yank him around by his shirt collar.

"He's my son. I don't care what the fucking judge will

280

decide." He spits on the ground only a few inches from my boot.

"You didn't treat him like your son before, don't act like you're a father now. Consider this your notice that an Order of Protection has been filed. If I see you near him or Natalie, I'll throw your ass in jail."

"You're letting that piece of ass drag you around by the balls? You're dumber than I thought. That girl is worthless." He steps through a chain link gate to separate us as I step toward him, barely containing myself enough to stop from throwing him to the ground.

"It'll only be a matter of time before she ends up like her mother. I'll get my boy back," he states boldly.

"What the hell did you just say?" I shout at him as he turns toward his apartment.

"Have a good day, Sheriff." He smirks as he walks away from me because he can. I have no legal standing to arrest him, not for a vague statement like that.

I hate when I can't protect people because of the black-and-white nature of the legal code. This is one of those moments I resent the laws I've sworn to enforce.

* * *

"Why don't you drink?" Natalie asks after dinner, interrupting my thoughts about work. I've been a little more distracted since the incident with Declan. With all of the other unanswered questions about the crimes in Rollins, the pressure is building.

"My recipe called for red wine and I noticed that you don't keep any alcohol in the house," she adds when I don't respond.

"I used to but decided that it wasn't worth it after a while," I tell her honestly after I have a second to filter my thoughts. She looks at me thoughtfully so I continue.

"I drank quite a bit in my early twenties. A couple of beers after work or socially. It helped me wind down and get to sleep when I knew I had to be up for class in five hours. Then it got to the point where I couldn't remember how many I was drinking a night.

"When I almost missed my alarm the morning of my first day at the Academy, I realized how badly I was messing with my life. My mom already had a brain-eating disease. I didn't need anything else to contribute to my downfall."

"So you gave it up completely?" She asks, surprised.

"Yeah. I figured that if I only have so many good years, I should take advantage of them."

"What do you mean?"

"My mom was in her forties when she was diagnosed with early-onset Alzheimer's. If I get it, I might only have less than a decade."

That realization hits me like a ton of bricks.

I might only have less than a decade. The thought echoes in my brain.

It used to be one of the reasons that I never cared to date or have a family. I never wanted anyone to have to take care of me.

"Jackson?" Her voice suddenly sounds far away because my heartbeat is pounding in my ears. How selfish can I be?

I've inadvertently pushed that aside and jumped head first into this life with Natalie and Dec. I've been begging her to take a chance on me and I might end up losing my mind.

The stress of taking care of my mom at such a young age drained my life. I love her to death but having that weight on my shoulders was devastating. I can't do that to them.

"You don't know that you'll get it." She must see me spiraling but I barely hear her words from across the kitchen.

"It's probably a good thing that you've kept me at arm's length all this time," I laugh sadly. "You wouldn't want to be stuck with me once my mind rots." I stand up but I can't quite get my bearings.

My head is begging me to think this through logically but my body is trying to flee.

"Jackson-" She starts to say something else but I shake my head at her.

"I'm sorry, I need to…" I can't finish my sentence, I can't finish a thought. All I do is turn and walk out of the house and away from her. I hear her yelling after me but I can't even process what she's saying.

What the hell was I thinking?

She can't be with a man like me. Potentially have a baby with a man who could pass on genes for an incurable disease. I've seen the statistics, I know the chances. They're not zero.

I reverse out of the driveway, screeching the tires into drive once I hit the road, escaping before I think better of it because I've offered this woman a life I don't know that I can give her.

How can I keep her and Dec safe if I don't even know who I am one day?

* * *

By the time I walk in the front door the next day, I'm dead on my feet and it's been well over twenty-four hours since I've slept.

I barely manage to drag myself to my room, hitting the bed with a thump. I'm staring up at the ceiling when I hear my door click shut.

"What the hell is wrong with you?"

It's not the first time she's ever asked me that question, but this time I can't seem to form a response. There is so much wrong with me. The biggest is that I'm in no way deserving of having a family.

"Jackson," she huffs when I don't respond.

"I'm sorry. I've been awake all night." I speak directly to the ceiling.

"Doing what?" She snaps.

"Working."

"You were at work all night? Right. I'm sure." She storms out of my room and it takes more than a second to recognize that accusation. She thinks I went somewhere else, to someone else.

I don't have the energy to defend myself but I don't deserve her forgiveness either. She's going to hate me regardless when she realizes that I can't be the man I'd promised for her.

I roll over and face plant into the mattress. Maybe I'll suffocate in my sleep and it will solve all my problems for me.

A few hours later, I begrudgingly get up and shave the two days of stubble before exiting my room. I need more sleep but I owe an explanation to the woman I got so caught up in pursuing that I forgot I don't deserve her at all.

I can't give her what she needs.

Dec and Natalie are outside in the driveway, and I watch

while she watches him ride his bike. He's brave already, hardly needing to think about what he's doing as he rides around.

Natalie looks on like a worried mother and it makes me smile before the corners of my mouth droop. If I had died in my sleep then at least I could take care of them properly.

She must sense me because she turns suddenly, narrowing in on me in the doorway. Other than throwing daggers at me, she turns back to Dec quickly and ignores me. I deserve that.

I make my way toward her anyway as if gravity itself could keep me away.

"I was at work last night. I was in the office, by myself, doing paperwork. I promise." Her shoulders stay rigid, her head refusing to look at me. "I'm sorry for leaving the way I did but I'm more sorry that I led you on. I understand that you can't have a future with me. Dec deserves better than that, you do too."

"What are you talking about?" She finally responds, whipping around to look at me. She's so pretty and it hurts because I don't deserve her.

"I can't expect you to be with me. I would never want you to take care of me if I got sick. It's a burden and Dec needs all of your focus."

"Jackson, you act like you're already sick. You don't have Alzheimer's and you probably never will. Why are you convincing yourself that your life is over?"

"It's easier than getting my hopes up I guess. I don't deserve you guys, and never will." I clear my throat, willing away the pain. "I'm going to visit my mom. I'll be back in a few hours." This time when I leave she doesn't shout after me.

My poor, sweet mother who has had her life taken over by the disease that I'm terrified of didn't recognize me when

I walked into her room. She rarely does. This time I was greeted with the preferable confusion rather than fear.

She's rocking in her chair with a baby doll, immediately resuming her appraisal of the flowers outside her window after I enter.

Mary walks in behind me, greeting me kindly. She's her regular nurse and has taken great care of my mom while she's been here.

"How is she today?"

"Oh, she's doing great. It's been a calm week."

"Where did the doll come from?" The soft pink blanket-wrapped doll is nestled tightly to her chest.

"I assumed you brought it." Mary shrugs. "It's a helpful tool for Alzheimer's patients though, she loves it."

She exits the room briefly and returns holding a plastic bag filled with plastic Tupperware. "If you don't mind taking these home with you." She hands me the bag.

"What is this?"

"It's the empty dishes Natalie brought. Well, they were full when she brought them." She laughs to herself. "Your momma is going to gain weight in no time eating that good."

"Natalie's been visiting?"

"I'm sorry, I thought you knew. She said you guys were living together and I just assumed... I apologize," she busies herself fixing my mom's already perfect bedding.

"I didn't know."

Natalie has been visiting my mom. Why didn't she tell me?

"She comes about once a week and usually brings a couple of meals with her. She might've been the one to bring the doll." Mary looks at me thoughtfully, seeing something on my face I'm not aware of.

Chapter Forty-Two

Natalie

My hand wipes the counter down on autopilot, my brain too preoccupied to pay attention to the task. This aching in my chest is too distracting to pretend to be okay.

Dec can even tell something is wrong and has steered clear of me for most of the afternoon. He's watching a movie in the living room, only braving the kitchen long enough to grab a snack and retreat.

I'm furious with Jackson. I'm hurt. He completely shut down and shut me out without giving me a chance to communicate with him. Then he was gone all night doing who knows what. He's the one who thawed my cold dead heart and now he wants to stomp on it.

I'm back in limbo. If things are over with Jackson then we'll be back on our own. I'll have to start looking for an apartment and still be able to afford my attorney.

He convinced me that I was safe here and I was stupid enough to believe him. All it took was one hard conversation and the life he promised me is blowing up in smoke. I've turned into my mother despite my hatred of the life she gave me.

I'm so fucking stupid.

That thought nearly makes me sob. I hide the noise behind my hand so Dec doesn't notice.

"Jackson's home," Dec announces from the couch. He's only been gone an hour and I wasn't prepared to see him again so soon. The ache in my chest deepens, spreading to the depths of my stomach.

The front door flings open quickly as he comes running through it. "Dec, I'm sorry but you'll want to close your eyes," Jackson says, closing the distance between us.

"What? Why?" Dec starts to ask but immediately gags as Jackson takes my face in his hands and kisses me brutally.

My body is stiff as he holds me, my lips don't respond to his right away, but it only takes a second to forget my worries. My whole being melts against him, reciprocating his embrace, forgetting that I'm mad.

"Can you guys stop being gross?" Dec shouts from under a pillow and my body freezes again.

What the hell am I doing?

I shove Jackson away from me and wipe his kiss off my face, glowering at him with all the pissed-off nerve endings in my body. His eyes are sorrowful, but gazing back at me with intensity.

"Dec, Jackson and I need to discuss grown-up things. Do you want to stay out here or go to your room for a bit?" I ask him, continuing to glare at Jackson.

He thinks he can act how he did and then come back like nothing happened. As if.

"My movie is almost over," Dec says, dismissing us. I stomp to Jackson's room and wait as he slides past me. I shut the door quietly even though I want to slam it and spin on him, ready to bite his head off.

"You've been visiting my mom?" He asks and it halts the argument I had ready on my tongue. That's not what I expected him to say.

"Yeah. Since I moved in. I've been taking her lunch."

"And, a baby doll?"

My heart skips. I hoped he wouldn't find out about that. "I bought it for her after I found out I was pregnant. I thought... I don't know. Maybe one day if we showed up with a baby it wouldn't be so hard on her. Obviously, it doesn't matter now."

"It matters. All of it matters." He steps forward to embrace me but I put my hand up to stop him. I'm not ready to pretend like things are okay. They're not.

"Are you kicking me and Dec out?" I ask, unable to look at him.

"What? No."

"Jackson, don't play dumb. What the fuck is going on? You ran out on me and didn't come home. I waited up all night for you. Then you came home and couldn't be bothered to look at me."

"I didn't go see anyone else, Natalie. I was in my office. I promise on my life."

"I had already convinced myself that any of my doubts were because of my own insecurity, that you wouldn't do that. I wanted to give you the benefit of the doubt despite my brain telling me to hex you but you were gone for so long. Then you came home and it didn't seem like you cared. What the hell am I supposed to think?" I thump down on the bed, exhausted, with my head in my hands.

289

Every man in my entire life has mistreated me, I can't convince myself that Jackson would be any different.

"You're supposed to think that I'm a dumb ass. I panicked and ran because I didn't know how to handle my thoughts. It was never about you, not really. Only that I know you and Dec are too good for me."

I hold up my hand to stop him. "The custody hearing is in a few weeks. All I could think about is walking into that courtroom and admitting to the judge that I was wrong. I don't have any support because you walked out on me. I promised that would never happen to me and it happened. You walked out on me and Dec."

He shakes his head in response but I can hardly look at him. "I went in and did paperwork. I made you and Dec my beneficiaries. I updated my will. Liv helped me verify all of it this morning."

My head snaps to his as he gets on his knees in front of me. "What?"

"If there is any chance that something happens to me, I want you to get everything. Whether I get sick one day or die in the line of duty, I want you and Dec taken care of."

"Jackson, what the fuck?"

"I understand if you don't want to be with me because you might have to take care of me one day. I'd never ask you to, but I want to take care of you." His eyes are soft and pleading but his face is lined with worry.

"We're not married, we're not even... I don't know what we are. What if you change your mind? What if you find someone else?" He could find a beautiful, perfect woman someday. Anyone other than me.

"Natalie, if it's not you, it's no one. I don't want anyone

else and I never will. It's you, it's always going to be you." He grabs my hands in his, kissing them.

My mouth is opening and shutting but I can't make any words come out. "How can you be so sure?"

"I don't want to live without you, I can't, but if you never want to see me again, I'd leave. I'd give you the house," he says with all the sincerity in his large body, cupping my cheeks gently. "You and Dec never have to leave. You're home, sweetheart."

"Jackson…"

"It'll be official before court. The house will be in your name, it'll be permanent. Just say you'll forgive me. I know I fucked up by leaving last night, but give me a chance to make it up to you." He buries his head in my lap with his arms wrapped around my legs and I can't breathe.

I never expected this. Any of it. I don't want him to give me the house as a bartering chip. All I want is him.

This big, giant, bonehead.

"Jackson. Look at me." He doesn't move. "Please."

His head tilts up to look at me and his tired, sad eyes, watch me warily. "You know, don't you? The power that word has over me."

"You're the only person I ever say please to. You're the only one who has ever respected me enough to listen when I say it," I tell him truthfully.

"It's more than that, sweetheart. I respect you, care about you, and I-" He pauses and laughs softly. "I worship the ground you walk on. I'll do anything for you but don't ask me to leave you alone. Not yet. I'm not ready for you to be done with me." He holds my face to his and I grasp his hands in mine. For the first time ever, I see terror in the depths of

291

his honey eyes. And, genuine regret.

"Then promise me that you won't walk out on me again. Not like everyone else has."

"I won't walk out ever again. I promise." He states with confidence and I believe him. Somehow I still believe him despite how he made me feel these last twenty-four hours because I think I knew this was different.

He's only human, he's not perfect, and his fear was real.

"Watching you leave last night was unbearable because… I want this. I want to be with you," I admit with painful vulnerability. Even though I trust him, saying the words out loud terrifies me.

His eyes shut, squeezing tight while he chokes on a breath. "That's all I've wanted to hear for so long. You can't even imagine how much I want a life with you, but what if- If I get sick…"

"If you get sick then I will take care of you because I-" I hesitate, my words getting caught in my throat. "You aren't going to get sick. What happened to your mom is hard and sad, but just because she got sick doesn't mean that you will. You can't live your life thinking it's already over."

"It's not about my life, it's about yours. I can't ask you to take on that responsibility. It's too much. You're only focus should be Dec," he admits, softly.

"Stop making my decisions for me!" I demand, yanking his face closer to mine by his hair. "I can handle whatever life throws at me, I always have. I'm choosing this. I'm choosing you, so get over it." I kiss him hard, erasing any argument, and he doesn't hesitate to kiss me back.

His body crowds between my thighs where I'm sitting on the bed, allowing no space between us. His arms wrap tightly around me as if he's afraid to let me go.

"Jackson, can I order the new Batman movie?!" Dec yells through the door, knocking erratically.

The interruption bursts the seriousness of our bubble and it makes me laugh against Jackson's cheek.

"Yeah, buddy. Go ahead." He rocks back on his heels and looks at me with amusement. This is our life now. If he wants to be a part of mine, this is what it will be, but he doesn't look put off in the slightest.

"You know, I brought you back here because I didn't want to kill you in front of Dec. Our first real fight and I barely got to yell." I pout making him smile.

"We've fought a lot if you don't recall all those months you couldn't stand me. I'm positive you'll have plenty of opportunities to try to kill me, sweetheart." He grins at me, not at all worried by the words he just spoke.

"I think you should get used to this as part of the groveling process then because I expect to win every fight, fairly." I spread my knees farther apart, drawing his gaze right between my thighs and I watch his eyes darken.

"Did you lock the door?" He asks while leaning in to kiss my bare knee. Then the other one, sliding his lips higher and higher with each kiss.

"Of course, I locked it. I thought I was coming in here to punish you," I say breathlessly as he buries his face against my center. His fingers grip the waistband of my shorts and expertly tugs them off, leaving me bare.

"This is not a punishment at all." He swipes his tongue over me, making me moan quietly. It's going to take all of my strength to stay silent.

With one hand wrapped around my thigh, he spreads me

open and attacks my clit with his tongue while his other hand finds my entrance. Two of his fingers fill me, rubbing my insides while he laps at my pussy.

The way he enjoys me is the way he enjoys my food. He'd rather eat than come up for air and I am incredibly grateful for his eagerness.

My fingers curl into the top of his hair, pulling it tightly at the roots and I hope it hurts. He's a big boy, I know he can take it. This is supposed to be punishment after all.

I grind roughly against his face and his fingers, trying my best to keep my loud mouth shut. He doesn't mind as I yank him closer, his arm wrapped around my leg is holding me just as closely as I start to squirm.

It's only a few minutes before I'm feeling the build-up of my orgasm and he hooks onto me harder, not letting me go anywhere. The repetitiveness of his tongue on my clit and the deep pleasure of his fingers inside of me is too much. With every breath, I'm one wave closer to a full-blown tsunami.

"Jackson, I can't stay quiet. I can't," I whisper as best as I can.

"Bite a pillow, I'm not stopping until you cum all over my face," he insists gruffly, diving right back in and ignoring my distress. Thank God because I need this. I need to let go of all my pent-up frustration from the last twenty-four hours.

It's his fault after all, so I cover my face with a pillow and continue grinding harder against him. Fucking his face while he's on his knees for me, worshiping me like he claims that he does.

I'm so close, but the final wave I need to crest is too intense. I need it more than I need anything but my brain is overriding my body. I feel like I'm going to explode and my mind is telling me it's a bad thing.

"Give it to me, Nat," he begs, driving his fingers into me and attacking my clit while he holds me taut with his other hand pressed against my lower stomach.

That's all it takes before I'm screaming into the pillow and seeing stars.

Chapter Forty-Three

Jackson

"You called me, Nat," she whispers against my forehead. After she came, her body collapsed back onto the bed and I followed suit, draping my upper half over her. My knees are still on the ground but I'm so much taller than her it almost puts us on equal ground, our chests breathing against each other in sync.

"Dammit, I'm sorry. I didn't mean to." I bury my head against her neck, bracing for her to shove me off. Instead, she wraps her arms around me.

"It's been a while since you've used that nickname and I hadn't realized it until you said it, again." She laughs, quietly, shaking my body gently. "You don't see me as a pesky insect as much, anymore?" She teases.

"I only said that to piss you off. But, the day Declan called you Nat, it looked like he slapped you," I tell her honestly, holding her tighter.

"That's why you stopped?"

"I never wanted to be on his level."

"It's not the same. You're nothing like him." Her voice is so quiet that I can't help but tilt my head back to look at her. She's wearing a soft smile and the look in her eyes is nothing short of endearing. "I used to like the nickname until he ruined it but it sounds much sweeter when you say it."

"Do you want me to call you, Nat?"

She nods her head gently. "You care about me like no one else ever has."

"For the rest of my life, sweetheart," I promise.

"I believe you," she admits against my lips, sealing her promise with a kiss instead of words. "You're the family I always wanted, for me and Dec."

She isn't ready to tell me she loves me but I know she does because I feel it in every inch of trust that she gives me, every smile, and every window of vulnerability. To her, family is supposed to mean love and that's what she's giving me.

"Should we go back out there to Dec or do you want me to try to make him a new family member, right now?" I ask, kissing her stomach. She laughs and finally shoves me off of her.

"No way. Part of your punishment is going without for a while. You made me wonder where you were for hours, so we'll start there. You can check back in with me tonight," she says, motioning to her imaginary watch.

"You're right, I deserve that."

"Besides, I think your breeding kink is getting a little out of control." Her face is serious for only a moment before she cackles, theatrically slapping her knee.

"Call it what you want but I'm obsessed with you and I want little clones of you to fill this house," I whisper in her ear as we exit the bedroom, making her smile shyly.

My hands rest on the curve of her waist as we walk down the hall but she stops suddenly when we reach the living room and I almost plow over her. "Dec?" She says, seeing that he's not on the couch.

"Dec!" She shouts and we're greeted by silence. An eerie silence that raises red flags in my head.

"I'll check outside, you check his room." I move past her to the front door, attempting to ignore the rock suddenly sitting in my gut.

He's not on the porch or in the yard but when I jog down the front walkway, a breath of relief escapes me when I see him in the garage.

"Dec, what are you doing out here?" As soon as I ask the question, I focus in on his frown.

"Someone ran over my bike." Sure enough, his front wheel is bent at almost a 90-degree angle. Natalie comes bounding around the corner and gasps.

"What the hell?" She rushes over to Dec to examine the bike while ice courses through my veins. Suddenly, the broken bike is the least of my concerns.

"Get in the house," I demand, grabbing the bike and shoving it far enough out of the way to close the garage door.

"Why?" Dec whines, sad to leave his bike behind.

"Nat, go." My voice leaves no room for question, as soon as her eyes meet mine she's shifting into gear and tugging Dec inside.

That bike was perfectly fine an hour ago.

Which means someone was in my driveway and near my house, way too close for comfort.

Whether the bike was run over on purpose or not is what I need to find out, because Dec was a sitting duck and I let my guard down.

I immediately go from a happy-go-lucky family man back

into the Sheriff of Rollins County in the blink of an eye.

My security cameras showed a navy conversion van pull into my driveway, idle for a few minutes, and then take a purposeful three-point turn over Dec's bike. My video quality wasn't clear enough to get a license plate but I recognized the old van immediately. It's the same vehicle Declan was driving when I was following him.

I don't know how he found out where I lived, but my only guess is that his lawyer showed him the paperwork provided to the court with my contact information in it. Worse would be that someone else gave him my address which means they're not an ally of mine.

Either way, Declan does not belong on my property or near Dec. I'm keeping *my* family safe, no matter what.

Over the coming days, my hours are spent deep diving into Declan Randolph but he's M.I.A. and other cases are piling up. The number of fatal overdoses has increased and I can't help but see a connection. People are dying from a fentanyl pill that is eerily similar to how Dec's mom died.

If Declan is behind this then there is even more reason that he needs to be locked up. The custody hearing is coming up and I need to know for sure he won't be able to come near Dec ever again.

"Sheriff," Roberta greets me as I come in from the scene of the last overdose. "Prosecutor Fulton is waiting in your office."

I nod and enter my office where Fulton sits at a chair in front of my desk, staring blankly out the window. "Fulton, what can I do for you?

"Sheriff, we have a problem."

"When don't we? What is it this time?" I ask reluctantly,

sitting behind my desk.

"Vanessa Porter made a complaint. She's accusing you of conspiring to have her cousin killed. Thomas Jameson." It's been almost a month since he was shanked in his prison cell and this is the first that I've heard anything.

"You're aware that accusation is ridiculous," I state plainly. I don't have time for bullshit like this when there are real problems to deal with. "I'm being dragged into this because I hurt Mrs. Porter's feelings and accused her family of criminal activity."

"Yes, Sheriff. I agree with you but I think you need to watch yourself. The Porters are a powerful family. Once they lock in on you, they won't make your life easy," he warns.

"I don't care who they are unless they can tell me why people keep overdosing when no one seems to know where the drugs are coming from."

Fulton looks at me for a moment, introspectively, debating what he wants to say next. "I appreciate your dedication to the crime in this county. It's been a long time since we've had someone with your... Ethics."

"What aren't you saying, Fulton?"

"I think the Porter family might be exactly who you need to talk to, but tread carefully." He clears his throat as he stands. "They have a knack for making things disappear." With that ominous statement, he leaves my office without looking back.

I don't appreciate word games and context clues, I want answers. The first of them needs to come from the Porters.

I spend the afternoon breaking down their family tree.

Vanessa's cousin, Thomas, is dead.

Her husband, Chuck Donahue, is dead.

Her two brothers, Anthony and Benjamin, are dead.

CHAPTER FORTY-THREE

Her nephew, Kyle Jameson, is dead, by my firearm.

Her mother and her aunt both died when she was a child. So who is left?

Her father, Reverend Jefferson Porter, is still the pastor of a Baptist Church in the area but well into his 80s.

She has two sons, one of whom is running for Mayor of Langston. That's Randall Porter. He has a clean record like she said.

Personal information on the other one is not as openly available, but he does have a past. Jeremiah Porter has a criminal record like many others in his family. Odd that Vanessa never wanted to mention him.

Why is it that her children don't share their father's last name? Why carry on their mother's maiden name?

* * *

"Mrs. Porter, this is not an interrogation and you do not need counsel present, but if you'd like to obtain a lawyer, we'll have to put off this conversation further. I think you want to have this conversation," I state plainly. Prosecutor Fulton is sitting to my left and Vanessa is sitting across from me at the table in his office.

Her accusation of my involvement in Thomas' death already fell through because no one believed that I had anything to do with it. Now I am ready to slap her with a defamation lawsuit just to get her to talk. I don't usually play dirty but I'm over all of the bullshit.

"I don't need a lawyer, I've done nothing wrong." She huffs, clacking her fake nails on the wooden tabletop.

"Why did you accuse me of conspiring in Thomas' death?"

"Because you were asking lots of questions and then suddenly he turned up dead. What else am I supposed to think?"

"That he was a criminal and had enemies. Obviously."

"Doesn't matter now. He's dead and you're still doing your job. Why am I here?" She asks, impatiently.

"Why is your family tied so deeply with so many crimes in this county?"

"I don't know what you mean."

"Yes, you do. The majority of your family is deceased, Vanessa. Most of them related to the crimes they were involved with. You've had to notice that your numbers are dwindling."

"Are you making a mockery of the people killed in my family, Sheriff? How uncouth." She upturns her nose at me and looks away. Even I know that a woman like that makes insults when she doesn't have a real argument.

"How's your father?" I ask, watching her closely as her head snaps to mine.

"He's fine. What does he have to do with this?"

"All of his family members are dying, too. He's not concerned? What about your sons?"

"They are good boys. Leave them out of this."

"Why do they have your last name? Their father was a Donahue, not a Porter."

"My family name was much more important than Donnie's. Mine means something around here and his doesn't."

"Right. How much does it mean, exactly?"

"Enough that I don't need to sit here and listen to this. Leave my family alone. Deal with your problems in this county without my help, Sheriff. Or you'll be out of a job." She stands, huffing and puffing out the door.

"Dammit. That still gets me nowhere," I grumble. Fulton only laughs.

"I figured she would have left even sooner. Do you think she's involved in illegal activity? She's a retired southern bell, not a criminal." He stands and fixes his suit.

"I know but she knows something. She wanted me to back her son for his campaign and after a few attempts to press her on her criminal family, she's made me enemy number one. If there was nothing to my suspicions, she would have laughed me off a while ago."

"Well, good luck. Don't drag me into the pits of hell, though." He waves as I make my way toward the elevators. *The pits of hell.* Hmm.

Time to visit the patriarch of the Porter Family.

Chapter Forty-Four

Jackson

"Jackson… Who are these people?" Nat asks me in a hushed tone, looking past me. Today is custody day.

I glance over my shoulder to confirm who she means. "They're my friends. They came to support us."

"They don't even know me. Or, Dec."

"They will. As soon as I filled them in on what's been happening, they didn't hesitate. They're good people, trust me."

"I do, but what if they don't like me?" She sounds so worried that I'd make fun of her for it any other day, but not today. She has enough stress on her shoulders.

"You're a part of my life now, they know how important you are to me. They'll love you like I do." I look at her sincerely because I need her to believe it and even though I haven't said the words outright, she knows they're true.

She only rests her cheek in my palm briefly as confirmation, looking at me with those big dark eyes that own me completely.

Nathan and Callie slide into the row behind me, Jesse and Thea following suit. I haven't seen any of them since Jesse and

Thea's wedding a few months ago and so much has changed since then.

Nathan claps a hand on my shoulder when I turn toward them. "Malec," he says in greeting.

"Thanks for being here."

"We wouldn't miss it for the world, brother." Jesse shakes my hand while Thea leans against his side.

"I'm Callie, it's nice to meet you," she speaks past me, waving to Natalie behind the bar, where she's standing next to Dec. "This is my husband, Nathan. His sister, Thea, and her husband, Jesse." She points down the line to each respective person, her warm smile never faulting, silently welcoming Nat to the group.

"Thank you, for coming," Natalie responds quietly. It's out of character for her, but I suspect this type of support is strange. "This is Dec." She squeezes his shoulder but he's too busy playing a game on his Gameboy to turn around.

"I don't want to hear a peep out of you guys when I turn on my lawyer voice," Liv says from her side of the bar, meeting Natalie at their table. "Thea always makes fun of me."

"I do not!" She scoots out of her row to come closer, hugging Liv tightly. It's thanks to her that we obtained Liv as council in the first place. She was willing to travel here to Rollins from the coast to help us out and I'll be forever grateful.

Liv's smiling with her hand plastered to Thea's stomach, rubbing gently.

There's only one reason someone would do that, but Thea looks almost the same as she always does under her flowy skirt and sweater. I glance at Jesse and he nods his head with a smile.

"Congratulations," I tell Thea sincerely as she slides back to Jesse.

"Thank you, Malec." Her smile is just as sincere and I have to bite my tongue to resist telling them how eager I am about having a child now. But, that conversation can wait.

Natalie would smack me on the back of the head for sharing that information without consulting her.

When I turn to her, she's looking at Thea's stomach thoughtfully, but distantly. I intertwine our fingers and her eyes ping to mine. "You okay?" I ask her quietly.

"Yeah, I'm just ready to bring Dec home for good."

"Me too."

She smiles softly and I kiss her quickly as Judge Reisner enters the room. "Where's the petitioner?" He says before he makes it to his chair. Declan Randolph isn't here, yet.

"My client will be here, your honor. Car troubles." Declan's lawyer explains. I don't believe him but Reisner gives us a ten-minute window anyway, giving Declan a chance to arrive.

Every passing minute is agony. Natalie's feet tap impatiently while she puts on a brave face for Dec. He insisted on being here today. He made his choice, he knows he wants to stay with his sister no matter what.

Eight minutes after the original start time, Declan strolls through the doors and down the aisle to his seat without a care in the world. His usual posse follows close behind, taking up an audience in the rows parallel to us.

"Thank you for joining us Mr. Randolph, let's begin." Judge Reisner starts his breakdown of the facts, allowing the court reporter to fill in the necessary information before the lawyers begin their back and forth.

"Let's cut to the chase," Reisner interludes, throwing the

normal procedure out the window. Even Liv looks surprised, waiting to hear what he has to say. "I've been made aware of multiple instances where Mr. Randolph has stepped out of line in the last few weeks. You've only just gotten out of jail and you've already been harassing your son at school and making passive threats."

"Bullshit, claims," Declan shouts out. "Your honor," he adds as if that will soften the crudeness of his outburst.

"You trespassed at his school and his current home, you ran over his bike, and you've still not provided any concrete proof of residency or work. I've seen the video evidence. You are not a safe fit for your son. The biological parent isn't always the best choice. Custody is granted to Natalie Halstead. The Order of Protection also stands, stay away from Declan Jr. My decision is final." He pounds his gavel and the whole room is silent, absorbing the weight of his spontaneous speech.

"Thank you, your honor," Liv says, jumping up from her seat to address him properly. In an instant, Natalie is grasping Dec around the shoulders, hugging him with all her strength.

I'm dumbfounded. That was almost too easy.

"We did it!" Natalie and Dec turn to me, hugging me tightly over the bar. I hold onto them while our wall of support cheers from behind us. That's it, it's over. Dec's finally safe.

"Fuck you, this isn't right!" Declan yells, pushing past his lawyer.

One giant step and I'm over the bar and putting myself between the crazy bastard and *my* family. "Get out of here Declan, or I'll throw your ass in jail," I threaten.

"I'll hold you in contempt, son!" Reisner bellows from his stand. He looks as pissed off as I probably do.

My job is to keep the peace but I've never been more

prepared to fight. I'd enjoy knocking Declan Randolph on his ass but I'm in my right mind enough to keep Dec from witnessing it. He's a bad man, but he's still his father.

"We're not done," Declan looks at me briefly, but his gaze fully settles behind me. On Natalie.

I grab him by his shirt collar and pull him dangerously close. "Come near them and I'll make sure you disappear," I whisper in his ear just as two more deputies come into the room to back me up.

"Jackson, he's doing this on purpose. Let him go." Natalie says from behind me, tugging on the back of my shirt.

"We've got it from here, Sheriff. Stay with your family." The two deputies escort the grinning Declan and his foot soldiers out while I try to regain my composure.

She's right, he almost got exactly what he wanted, a spectacle with me at the center.

By the time I turn around to assess the rest of the room, Natalie is by the far wall, comforting Dec. Thea, Callie, and Liv form a protective half circle around them while Jesse and Nathan stand defensively between them and the rest of the room.

It's cleared out now, the danger is gone, but I've never been more thankful for the friendships that I've found. These are the people that Natalie and Dec deserve in their corner.

Chapter Forty-Five

Natalie

S omehow I've almost made it through the school year taking care of my brother. There are only two weeks left until summer vacation and I'm celebrating the milestone as if it's a golden achievement.

This past year of taking care of Dec has been the hardest but most fulfilling year of my life. I never would have guessed where we would be now, with legal custody, and living with a man who dotes on us constantly. I still can't quite accept that part.

Dec loves Jackson though, so it's hard to ignore how smitten I am. He always shows up and is kind, he never treats me poorly like Dec saw his dad do to our mom. Jackson plays with him and talks to him, never acting too busy even though he's been working a lot the last few weeks.

He's been called in multiple nights to go to crime scenes and Dec's been too uneasy to sleep in his own bed without him home. Even after Judge Reisner awarded me custody, Dec can't shake off the fear he has of his father.

He always knew his dad wasn't a good man but after having his bike run over, the outburst in the courtroom has given him anxiety. He thinks his dad is coming after him and I can't convince him we're safe.

It doesn't help that some of the kids at school caught on to his home problems and have teased him since the day Declan showed up at recess. While I thought the aide only made Dec go inside that day, she actually ended recess early for everyone and put a neon sign over Dec's head. I can only hope it will be forgotten over the summer.

Even though Jackson got called in right after dinner, I convinced Dec to sleep in his own bed tonight. He said he'd only be gone for a few hours and I've been pacing anxiously by the front door waiting for him to come home.

We haven't had any real alone time in almost two weeks. Not since the day we "fought" in his room.

It's ridiculous how consumed I am by thoughts of him. I want to be with him every minute of every day and I miss him. I can be in the same room as him and still miss him.

His headlights sweep into the driveway and I'm out the front door before he parks.

"Hey, what are you doing?" He opens his door but I'm on him before he can get both feet out. I kiss him hungrily, melting against his body where I found a home between his muscular thighs.

"I missed you," I breathe against his lips, claiming them once again. He doesn't hold back, kissing me with just as much enthusiasm. His hands are buried in my hair, holding me preciously while he attacks my tongue with his.

My hands wander across his chest and down to his thighs, gripping them with desperation. I want him so badly, I feel like I'm about to combust.

My fingers find his belt, tugging it free and popping the

button on his pants with ease. Thank God he's not in his full uniform or this would be much more difficult. The mountain of steel below his zipper is calling to me and if I don't get his pants down right now I think I might rip them off.

"Do you want to go inside?" Our foreheads are pressed together as I focus on undoing him from his pants. We're in the driveway, it's pitch black out here, and no one could see us from the road.

"No, I need this, now." One brutal tug and I get his pants and underwear down his thighs. His cock stands proudly and I don't waste a second before taking it in my mouth.

"Oh, fuck," he groans. His hands never leave my hair, holding it out of my face while I do my damnedest to fit all of him down the back of my throat. He's incredibly long and thick, but I'm not a quitter.

It's sloppy, chaotic, and absolutely inappropriate to do this to the Sheriff of Rollins County in his work vehicle but it makes it more exciting. I need him more than I've ever needed anyone in my life. More than that, I want him more than I've ever wanted anything.

The coiling of heat between my legs is so intense that I'm rubbing my thighs together for relief, but having his cock in my mouth is too addictive.

"Get the fuck up here, Nat. I need you," he pleads, mimicking my thoughts.

"No, I'm not done." I take him deeper, gagging as his crown hits the back of my throat, and he grunts in appreciation. It makes me want to keep going. I love making him crazy.

"Dammit, woman. Come here." He yanks me up from under my arms, lifting me with almost no effort, and settling me in his lap with my back against the steering wheel. Before I can protest, not that I care to, he's yanking my shirt off and exposing my bare naked body. Of course, I'm not wearing underwear, I was on a mission.

His eyes blink hazily at me for a moment in distraction and I take my opportunity to sheath myself on his waiting erection. It's still wet from my mouth and I'm dripping with anticipation. My body takes his cock easily and fully, settling onto his lap with force making us both moan.

"I needed this, so bad," I admit, softly, melting against him.

"Me too, baby." His forehead rests against mine as he thrusts into me, gently. The rush has dissipated and it feels like we're exactly where we needed to be. Connected. Together.

He fucks me slowly but I know this is something different. It's not fucking at all. He's making love to me, kissing me softly, and holding me like a treasure. It's wildly opposite from how I intended for this encounter to go but it's perfect at the same time.

A drop of moisture escapes the corner of my eye and hits his thumb where it's resting on my cheek. It's too dark for him to see, but I feel him rub it against my skin.

He knows I'm not ready to put myself out there completely but he accepts me anyway. He'll hide my tears away for now because he's a patient man, but I know it won't always be like this.

Every day with him, I can feel myself opening up more, freeing myself from my insecurities. One day, I'll expose my heart and soul for him and it will be the last time I'll ever have to do so because I know he'll keep it safe. He'll cherish all of me like I cherish him.

"Jackson," I whisper against his lips, dying to tell him the words I feel, but as usual they get stuck in my throat. I've never felt as scared as I do when it's time to be vulnerable.

"What do you need, sweetheart?" His movements stall and I know it's my fault. He needs to know I'm alright.

"I need you, forever. Okay?" I ask, grinding in his lap, still seeking the connection I can only get from him. "I need you more than anything and it scares me."

"I need you, too. You don't have to be scared. I've got you," he groans involuntarily when I increase my pace, fucking him desperately. If I can't use my words tonight, I'll use my body.

"I need this, too. Fill me, please. I want your baby growing inside of me," I beg and he breathes a sigh of relief.

"Fuck, yes." He grips my hips with brutal strength, lifting and dropping me, impaling me aggressively. It's everything I needed and all I can do is hold on as he consumes me, my fingers tangled tightly in his hair and around his neck.

"God, I can't stop but I need to make you cum," he says through heavy breaths. Having him so wild and unhinged beneath me feels too good, I don't want to slow down. All I want is for him to lose himself in me.

"No, don't be nice right now. You can make it up to me later, fuck me. Harder," I demand, yanking his head back so I can kiss him. He takes my queue, slamming into me, slamming me into him, over and over until I know the entire SUV is rocking uncontrollably.

It's like I'm on another plain, getting to experience the unrestrained force of a man and reaping all of the benefits. It's a soul-changing experience and I understand just how lucky I am to be safe in his arms.

The tears running down my cheeks now are nothing but chaotic and pleasure-filled. His cock pounds into me so hard that I can hardly catch my breath and I love it.

"So… Close," he mumbles through his exertion.

"Give it to me, baby. Please," I plead with the man who always gives me what I want and owns me entirely. The man who is going to give me a family and love me eternally.

"Fuck," he groans, stilling inside of me. His warmth fills me and makes me feel whole. For the first time in my life, I know I'm exactly where I need to be.

I kiss him lazily, pouring my heart out, wishing I was brave enough to say the words. He deserves them.

"You called me, baby," he says softly.

"Don't get used to it, Hercules, I was only testing it out." I laugh, quietly, kissing him on the nose.

"I love you, Nat. I know you're not ready to say it, but I need to. I love you enough for the both of us." He kisses me, erasing the need to respond and giving me an out because he knows I won't be able to say it back.

"You don't need to, not for the both of us," I insist, covering my heart with his hand so he understands what I mean. I have the love, I just can't say the words.

"I know," he whispers. "I know."

After a few minutes, we manage to scramble inside the house somewhat decently before he makes up for my earlier missed orgasm with two in the shower and another once we're in bed.

Always the overachiever.

* * *

"Should we go get ice cream?" I ask Dec as soon as he steps

off the school bus on his last day of school. I'm over the moon that I got him through this school year and after spending some time with Ms. Malec this afternoon in the sun, I need a treat.

"Uh. Yeah!" Dec shouts and runs to my car.

It's a beautiful day and we drive to the ice cream shop with the windows down. Dec insists we sit outside and enjoy our cones at the picnic tables to celebrate the start of summer vacation.

All of the worry over giving him a normal childhood and it's sitting at this poorly stained red picnic table, surrounded by other families, and more than a few curious bees, that I finally feel like I'm accomplishing my goal. It wasn't anything extravagant, but rather the simplicity of a basic celebratory afternoon that has me feeling like I can actually do this.

I can be a mother to Dec, I can show him how easy it is to love him, and he'll never have to worry about belonging anywhere.

"What are we doing next?" He asks out the back window of the car at our next stop while I'm pumping gas. Of course, ice cream wasn't enough, he wants an adventure.

"I don't know, I was going to head home."

"Will Jackson be there?"

"I don't know, I hope so." I smile to myself as I get back in the car. Jackson Malec has turned me mushy.

A tow truck pulls into the gas station and pulls around to park at the empty pump ahead of me before I can pull out. It's old and rusted, and the driver looks like a man you'd cross the street to get away from.

I watch through his side mirror as he reverses uncomfortably close to my front bumper. There's a smirk on his face

315

but I can't see his eyes, I can't tell if it's directed at me.

My windows are still down but there isn't any breeze to cause all the little hairs to stand up on the back of my neck suddenly.

I throw my gear shift into reverse to back out and away from this situation, but another truck pulls up behind me quickly, blocking my escape. Their windows are tinted, and I can't see who is driving but my gut is already churning.

The story Jackson told me about Callie is rushing through my consciousness like a current.

Isolated highway.

Being taken.

Being trafficked.

We're at a public gas station but it's empty and the interstate beside us is dead because we're on the outskirts of town. My fingers dial Jackson's contact without my eyes leaving my mirrors.

"Hey, sweetheart, I have one more stop and then I'm on my way home." His voice sounds far away in my ear as I watch the familiar lanky figure get out of the truck behind me.

Declan strolls to my window without a care in the world as my heart thunders in my chest.

I'm paralyzed. I don't know what to do. Especially when a gun settles on the ledge of my window, pointed right at me.

"Nat? You there?" Jackson's voice is still in my ear but no amount of strength can get me to respond. Dec's with me, I can't run, I can't fight. Not if it will get him hurt.

Declan wags the gun at me, indicating for me to end the phone call. When my mouth gaps to say something, anything coherent, he extends his arm to point the black barrel at Dec. A little squeal erupts from the back seat as my baby brother realizes what's happening.

"I'm sorry. I have to go." I choke out the final words, barely stifling a sob. "I love you."

Chapter Forty-Six

Jackson

Holiness Tabernacle. The long-time church of Reverend Porter. I insisted he be available for a meeting today because I'm ready to get answers from this family. If they're involved then the crime ends today.

My phone rings as I pull into the church parking lot and I plan to ignore it until I see Nat's name.

"Hey, sweetheart, I have one more stop and then I'm on my way home."

Silence greets me. When she still doesn't speak, I inspect my phone screen to confirm the call didn't drop. "Nat? You there?"

I glance up to the church doors where the reverend stands patiently, waiting. His white robe reflects the sun brightly, but my eyes are drawn to his face. His glasses are darkened.

Transition lenses.

I've seen him before.

"I'm sorry. I have to go... I love you."

She loves me.

Those words should fill me with endless elation... Instead,

my heart sinks. Why would she say that to me now?

Of all times, why now?

The call disconnects and I call her back instantly but it doesn't even ring before it goes to voicemail. I look back toward the church doors and the front steps are empty.

The ache in my chest deepens. Something is wrong.

I call one more time for good measure but the same thing happens. When I pull up my app to find her location, it tells me what I already know. Her phone is off. Her last location ping is at the gas station off of Rt 70. It's on the opposite side of town from me.

This could be nothing but I've never ignored my gut before. I call it in over the radio, directing the nearest deputy to the gas station until I can get there.

The entire drive there is filled with painful silence. The dread is drowning out any coherent thoughts in my mind. I hardly hear the radio transmission being directed toward me.

"Sheriff, her car is not here but we found a cell phone in the roadway. It's crushed. We're going to talk to the employee inside now."

Jesus Christ. Something bad happened. This isn't right.

"Where's Dec?" I say out loud to myself. It's after school, he should have been with her. Maybe Dec went to Charlie's house after school. Luckily, Dec's texted his friend off of my phone a few times and I have his mom's number.

"Hey, Sienna. Is Dec with you?" I ask as soon as she answers.

"No, he's not. Is everything okay?" She's a parent, she already knows that something is wrong. She hears it in my voice like I can hear the concern in hers.

"Uh, not sure. Let me know if you hear from him or Natalie. Please, it's important."

319

I make the only other phone call I can think of before I pull up on the scene. "I need you guys. Now."

My deputy comes out of the convenience store of the gas station and jogs over to me as my feet hit the pavement, heavily. "The clerk doesn't remember her, she never went inside, but she did notice a tow truck pull in about fifteen minutes ago. Assumed someone was having car troubles. The vehicles were in the far row of pumps and she couldn't see anything else. She's pulling the CTV for us now but it will take a minute."

"Dammit, we don't have a minute!" I scrape my hands over my face and take a deep breath. Behaving irrationally won't accomplish anything but can feel my self-control evaporating. I need to get it together.

"Sheriff." My other deputy waves me over to the storefront but he hesitates before he says his next words.

"What? What is it?"

"It looks like an abduction. A man approached her side of the vehicle and a few minutes later the tow truck hooked her car up and drove off. The man returned to a black Ford Ranger and then followed closely behind. There's a kid in the backseat, but it's blurry."

"Let me see. I need to see it." I watch the four-minute video from beginning to end five times before I accept what I'm seeing.

Declan took them. He took them.

A truck screeches to a stop outside and my head whips in that direction. My first breath of relief escapes my lungs. The cavalry has arrived.

"What the fuck is going on?" Nathan thunders as I approach them, buckling a thigh holster and securing his gun. Jesse's standing by the passenger door untucking his button-down shirt and pulling it off.

"Declan took Natalie and Dec. He towed their car off with them inside. That's all I know."

"Well, let's get 'em back," Jesse quips, pulling a hat down on his head with one hand, holding the barrel of a rifle in his other. "Start from the top, give us all the details."

So, I do. I tell them about every single incident involving Declan Randolph. His crimes, the drugs, and his relationship with Dec and Natalie.

"This is the drug dealer you thought might be connected to the other stuff? The 5k bombing? Callie's case?" Nathan ponders, looking at me closely.

"Yeah. Thomas Jameson was shanked in the same jail that Declan was in and I also suspected that he conspired to set Natalie and Dec's apartment on fire but I haven't been able to prove either crime. Jameson was related to Sheriff Donahue's wife, Vanessa Porter. They were cousins," I explain, trying to make sense of the pieces.

"God dammit," Jesse mumbles. "These small towns are insane."

"Vanessa Porter is involved?" Nathan asks.

"I've spoken to her. She's defensive of her family but she doesn't seem to be involved. I had a meeting with her father, Reverend Porter but..." My explanation discontinues as my brain makes sense of my thoughts.

Nathan and Jesse are looking at me, waiting for my next words.

"I was just there. I got the call from Natalie then left, and came straight here. I never spoke to him." The air in my lungs deflates. "Fuck."

"You mean you had a meeting with a man who was possibly tied to these crimes while Natalie and Dec were being taken on the other side of town?" Nathan interprets my distress clearly.

"He was in the courtroom the first day I saw Declan. I didn't think anything of it then. He's an old man, a reverend."

"Old men are often the most cynical," Jesse adds. "His sons were killed, his son-in-law was killed, his nephew was just killed in jail."

"His great nephew, too," I add. "I killed Kyle when he took you," I tell Jesse.

"I think you just found your criminal mastermind, Malec," Nathan suggests, eerily.

Chapter Forty-Seven

Natalie

"Sissy, where is he taking us?" Dec asks from the back seat. We've been pulled along by this tow truck for a few miles and it's the third time Dec has asked the question I don't have the answer to.

"I don't know, Dec. It's okay. We'll be okay." He starts to cry and I can't stop myself from crawling over my center console into the back with him. I hold him tight around the shoulders while I do my best to keep track of our surroundings.

We aren't in Lawson anymore and I'm not familiar with this area. I have no idea where Declan's taking us.

"Does Jackson know we're in trouble?" He whimpers through his sobs and I do my best to blink away the tears welling in my eyes.

"I don't think so, buddy. Declan tossed my phone before I could tell him what was happening."

"Why did my dad take us?" Another question that I can't answer.

"I don't know, Dec. I'm so sorry, I should have kept you safe."

"Should we text Jackson?"

"I don't have my phone, Dec, it's gone." I try to conceal the frustration from my voice because I know it's not his fault. My helplessness in this situation is killing me.

"I have the iPad."

Jackson's iPad always stays at home. "What? Why do you have it?"

"I snuck and took it to school, it's in my backpack. Don't be mad." His big watery eyes look up at me and I can't help but smush a kiss on his forehead.

"Dec, thank god. Give it to me, but keep it low." He grabs it out of his backpack from between his legs and sets it on my lap.

I glance subtly to make sure we're still driving in the middle of nowhere and no one is watching too closely. Declan is behind us but he'd only be able to see the back of our heads.

I open the messages icon and curse. There's hardly any service out here. I type in a message anyway, hoping like hell it will send.

HELP. DECLAN HAS US. LEFT LAWSON. DONT KNOW WHERE. TOW TRUCK AND BLACK TRUCK. HE HAS A GUN.

I hit send and wait but the message never fully sends. The green text sits in limbo while the iPad waits for enough signal. Dammit!

I copy the message and send it again after we round a curve. We're heading deeper into the mountains, which usually means worse service, but I'm desperate. After each curve, I copy and hit send again.

Finally, after a particular clear stretch of road, the iPad chimes, and the message is delivered right before we drive back into a thicket of trees. Thank God.

After a few tense, silent minutes, the iPad dings.

Jackson: The whole force is out looking. Don't let him take you to a second location. Run if you can. Describe your surroundings.

iPad: No service. Mountains. Lots of curves. No other traffic.

I hit send but again, it doesn't go through. We lost signal. We round another curve but this time I'm on alert. Jackson said to run…

Each time we go around these curves, the tow truck slows way down. It might be our only chance to escape but it's dangerous.

Less dangerous than whatever Declan has planned though, I'm sure.

"Dec, look at me." He does, with frightened eyes. "The next time I tell you to, you need to jump out. As soon as we slow down, you have to jump out of the car and run."

"What do you mean?" He's looking at me like I've lost my mind. I think I have.

"It's our only shot. We've been driving a while and might not have much time."

"What if it hurts?"

"It might, but we're not very high. Pretend there's a couch cushion on the ground when you jump and roll when you land. Then run like hell. Don't stop, even if I can't catch up. Run until your legs give out. Jackson will find us. I promise."

"Sissy," he whimpers. My jaw is trembling but I suck in a breath of air to ward it off. I need to be strong for Dec.

Another curve is approaching and I know this is it. Trees line both sides of the road. If we can get into the trees it's our best bet.

"Okay, here we go. Jump, roll, and run like hell, Dec. Don't stop for anything. Promise me."

"I promise," he whispers. I hug him tightly one last time and reach around him to make sure the door is unlocked.

The tow truck slows, rounding the sharp curve and I throw the door open as hard as I can. "Go, Dec. GO!"

The bravest little boy I know leaps from his seat and hits the ground rolling, tossing himself over and over until he comes to a stop. "GO, DEC! RUN!" As soon as the words are out of my mouth, I fling myself out of the door, too.

My body hits the ground hard, knocking all the air from my lungs and making my head bounce painfully against an unfortunately placed tree. I can't tell if Dec is up yet, I can't tell if he's running, but I can hear the brakes screeching beside me. The trucks are stopping quickly.

I knew Dec would have the advantage. If he got out first, he'd have a head start before they realized what was happening. I didn't afford myself the same luxury but I do my damnedest to pull my body up off the damp forest floor.

With a quick blurry glance, I don't see Dec anywhere. I see Declan though, running at me faster than I can react. "You bitch!" He grabs me by the hair, yanking me back toward the car. I try to fight him but it's no use, my head's spinning.

"Keep going to the farm, we'll come back for the boy after we hide the car," he speaks over me to the tow truck driver, throwing me in the back seat and pointing his gun at me. "Try it again and I'll blow your brains out."

I don't look at him, I can't. I don't even care what happens to me now, I just hope Dec is okay.

Oh God. What if I made a mistake?

What if Dec isn't any safer all alone in the woods?

My conscious thoughts are fading in and out as my head rolls around on the back seat but it's only a few minutes later when a metal gate creaks open loudly. The car is towed forward briefly before I feel it dropping, being lowered off the tow truck.

I don't bother lifting my head off the seat, I'm too defeated to care where they've taken me, but I can hear Declan speaking. "Keep her in the car. Shoot her if she tries to escape. Time for the Ice Queen to melt."

He pounds on my window and my head jolts at the noise, throbbing in opposition to the sudden movement. Declan wags a finger at me, grinning smugly before pointing his gun at me, again and mouthing, *"Pow."*

He strolls away and the sun comes beaming in through the window he was blocking, shining directly into my eyes. It's late afternoon but they parked my car out in the open.

With the windows up, the heat is stifling and I'm a sitting duck.

He's going to kill me and he won't even have to get his hands dirty.

Chapter Forty-Eight

Jackson

"We don't know what's waiting for us on the other side of that gate but be prepared for anything." I look at each of my deputies directly in the eye as I speak so I know they hear me. This is a dangerous operation because we're going in blind.

The iPad's last location pinged near Jameson's old farm. It should have been abandoned, possessed by the bank, but I know Declan must've brought them here. It's too close to be a coincidence but I'm still relying on my gut.

I look to Nathan and Jesse next, they're more qualified to handle whatever happens next compared to my four deputies but it doesn't mean I can ignore the risk they're taking.

"Let's go get your family, Malec," Nathan says with a nod.

Jesse's staring blankly down the empty road. We're about a mile from "the farm" where he almost lost his life last year.

"Jesse," I say, getting his attention.

"We should have burned this place down when we had the chance," he admits cooly.

"Yeah. Maybe this time we'll get the chance." I smack the hood of my SUV. "Let's go!"

Everyone loads into their respective vehicles and within seconds we're speeding down the road and toward Jameson's old farm. I see the entrance but instead of slowing down, I speed up. I'm not giving them the chance to expect us. Law be damned.

The brush guard on my front fender slams into the metal gate, blowing it off the hinges. That type of entrance is anything but subtle so as soon as the drive opens up to the main property, the vehicles behind me spread out to create a wall of force.

There are too many outbuildings to stay together as a group, so each side breaks off to clear their flank. Jesse and Nathan follow close behind me as we approach the main house but before I make it to the porch, I see Natalie's Honda parked off to the side.

I motion for two deputies to clear the house while my attention stays on the dark head of hair in the backseat. Her head lulls to the side of the headrest as if she sensed me and I watch her eyes widen. Her forehead is visibly damp with sweat, her hair is stuck to her temples.

She's baking alive in that car.

As we move closer she shakes her head subtly. She's warning me not to come closer but I'm two steps ahead as my shoulders swing around the corner of the house as soon as we clear it. A man leans against an old a/c unit with a gun on his lap. It's pointed in her direction, but he looks half asleep. Or, doped up.

"Sheriff's department. Don't move." My Glock is inches from his head before he realizes I'm there. "Cuffs," I direct Nathan. He does so easily, throwing the man on his stomach into the grass.

"I have one in custody," I relay into my radio, my eyes never leaving Nat's. Every cell in my body urges me to go to her, to erase the fear in her eyes. She's pleading with me to help her but I need to do so safely. Her car's parked in the open field and I don't want to walk into an ambush.

I would if it meant saving her, but drawing any potential fire in her direction only puts her at risk.

"Our side was clear, Sheriff. We'll take him." My deputy grabs our arrestee and hauls him back to one of the cruisers with his partner so my group can continue.

"Ready." Jesse claps Nathan on the shoulder.

"Ready." Nathan does the same to my shoulder.

We continue forward to Natalie's car, scanning left to right. It's a large property and there are too many places for someone to hide. We're within ten feet when I hear the telltale sound of the car door creaking open, drawing my attention to her instead of my surroundings.

"Nat. No, wait!" I yell, trying to stop her but she doesn't hear me. She runs straight for me where we have no cover.

"Gun!" Nathan shouts to my right, firing his weapon toward an old shed behind the house.

"Left side. Left side," Jesse shouts, discharging his rifle. I don't have a chance to look as Natalie crashes into my front, collapsing at the knees. My left arm wraps around her damp back on instinct to keep her from hitting the ground as I try to shield her.

"Clear." Jesse's voice reaches me almost at the same time Nathan's does.

"Clear," he echoes.

Just as Jesse and Nathan return to my position, Declan Randolph steps out from behind an old tractor drawing my attention forward.

"You motherfucker!!" He rasps from the depths of his chest, running at us full speed.

"Declan Randolph, you're under arr-" Before I can finish my sentence, his arm raises, mirroring my already raised right arm.

I don't think, I only react, dropping the woman I love and leaving her in a heap at my feet as I pull the trigger.

POW!

Jesse and Nathan are already discharging their weapons over my left and right shoulder as I step over Natalie's shrunken form, putting her behind the gunfire.

POW! POW! POW! I fire in rapid succession until my clip empties, Declan's body bearing each bullet brutally before collapsing backward.

His gun hits the grass before he does.

Threat eliminated.

"Shots fired. Send multiple EMS," my words drone robotically into the radio.

Declan Randolph won't need an ambulance. He's dead, I already know it but Nathan jogs over anyway to check for a pulse. A subtle nod in my direction is all I need to confirm.

"Jackson, we need to go. Please, let's go!" Natalie's voice reaches me but it sounds hollow in my ears. My actions are catching up to me.

I just killed Dec's dad.

"Malec. Get your head out of your ass," Jesse grips my right forearm, forcing me to lower the weapon that I haven't reholstered.

"The rest of the property is clear?" Nathan asks, communicating with my deputies for me while I'm still stuck in a haze.

"All clear."

"Jackson, Dec's not here. I told him to run and they went after him. We need to find him, please." Natalie grips my shirt, forcing my focus on her.

"Where?" Dec needs me.

"I don't know, the last curve. I don't know. We jumped out of the car and I told him to run."

"Okay, let's go. Nathan and Jesse, stay with us. Everyone else, secure the scene!" I shout, restoring my authority and flipping the switch I need to complete my mission. Find Dec.

He might hate me once I find him, but at least he'll be safe.

I tuck Natalie into my passenger seat and look at her closely for the first time since seeing her in the car. "Are you okay?"

"No, Dec's gone," she crows. Her skin is still damp from overheating and I take two seconds to wipe her hair out of her face. She has a laceration on her forehead but the blood is dried. I can already see the bruise forming but she doesn't mention it and neither do I. I know it's the least of her concerns.

"I'm going to get him back, I promise."

"I know. I knew you'd find us." She presses her forehead to mine and squeezes her eyes shut. "Declan's dead isn't he?"

"Yeah."

A soft cry escapes her throat and her body shakes in my arms. "I'm sorry, Jackson. You shouldn't have had to do that."

"Doesn't matter, I'll always do whatever it takes to keep you safe. We'll talk about it later." I kiss the tip of her nose and shut her in the air conditioning, when I turn around Jesse's standing there with a water bottle.

"She's dehydrated. The heat exhaustion is going to catch

up to her soon. Whatever comes next might be rough." He hands me the water and looks deeply into my eyes. *Whatever comes next.*

That could mean anything but I know what Jesse is insinuating. These mountains, these woods, are dangerous and unforgiving. We don't know what's out there and we don't know who Declan sent out looking for Dec already. We just have to hope that we find him first.

Chapter Forty-Nine

Natalie

"Right here. I told him to jump and run until his legs gave out," I explain to Jackson from the passenger seat. The cool air is starting to give me the chills, my body going from one extreme temperature to the other.

I was close to passing out in my car but Jackson arrived just in time. Now, Declan is dead and I'm going to have to figure out how to tell my baby brother that his dad is gone forever just like our mom.

"Stay here. Keep sipping the water," he suggests as he gets out. I scoff loudly, following suit. I was helpless before, I'm not going to be helpless now.

"I'm going."

"Nat, please. I don't know how this will go. If you're here, I'll focus better out there," he pleads but it falls on deaf ears. I don't give a shit. I'm going to help find my brother.

"I'm going."

He blows out an exasperated breath and looks to the sky, a move he hasn't done in quite some time. I can only hope he's adding a prayer in for my brother.

"Fine. Stay behind me and don't argue with me. Listen to

them, too." He points to Jesse and Nathan.

"Fine."

"Just like that?" He asks, bewildered, always expecting boxing gloves from me.

"I trust you, Jackson, but it doesn't mean I won't be a pain in your ass," I mumble the end part almost to myself.

He steps toward me suddenly and wraps me in his arms. My body melts against his in exhaustion or relief, I'm not sure. I take a deep breath to stop the tears welling in my eyes.

"I love you, fireball. You're my favorite pain in the ass." He kisses the top of my head and I push him off to break the vortex between us. He's about to ruin the hard shell I'm faking to get through this.

"Stop being sweet, please." My eyes bore into his, begging him to understand. He smirks softly because he gets me.

"Alright, get your ass in gear. Time to hike."

We trudge through thick underbrush for what seems like a mile, Jackson in front, Jesse and Nathan flanking behind me on either side, putting me at the center of their makeshift macho man triangle. I'd normally be rolling my eyes at them but I'm too weak to care.

My body is slowing down, the fatigue is far overshadowing any lasting adrenaline that I might've been storing in my body. This is probably why Jackson wanted me to stay in the truck but I'm too stubborn to admit he might've been right.

He throws a hand up suddenly, halting Nathan and Jesse in their tracks. I, however, am slow to react and smack right into Jackson's back. He doesn't budge at my collision but raises two fingers and points straight ahead, speaking some secret language I'm not privy to.

"What the hel-" Before I can ask what he's signing, Jesse's

hand wraps around my bicep, gently but firmly.

"Sorry," he whispers before he tugs me back a few feet and plants me behind his back. All three of them are suddenly standing in front of me with weapons pointed forward. I don't know what the hell is happening until two men come stumbling through the brush.

Zeek and one of his loser friends.

"Are you fucking kidding me?" I remark at the same time Jackson speaks.

"Hands up. Don't move or I'll shoot," Jackson commands with thundering authority, making me shiver. Both the idiots are taken off guard and luckily, comply immediately.

"We don't have guns," Zeek whines and that finally gives me enough strength to roll my eyes. I'm at my limit for this bullshit today. Too bad Jackson doesn't have a reason to shoot him.

"On your stomachs. Hands behind your back. Now." Another demand followed through and within a few minutes, both Zeek and his counterpart are handcuffed together around a tree.

"Dispatch, I've got two in custody. Ping my location and send the closest available units to pick up." He looks back to check on me and then nods to Jesse. "Let's keep moving." Nathan gives the handcuffs one final tug before we continue forward.

"Good luck! You're gonna need it!" Zeek quips at us as we begin walking even deeper into the woods. Whatever that means, it doesn't sound good for Dec. I turn around and give him a quick kick to the shin making him wail in pain.

Jackson quickly pulls me back into position behind him making my feet fumble while Nathan and Jesse smirk at me.

The sun is getting low in the sky and we only make it another half mile before Jackson mumbles a curse under his breath.

"What? What is it?" I peer around him and see tall metal fencing with barbed wire at the top. "What is this?"

He hasn't responded but his eyes find mine and I see clear apprehension. "What is it, Jackson?"

"This is Second Chance Sanctuary."

"So?"

"This fence probably goes on for miles. Dec had to have gone through here."

He's the Sheriff, why would that matter?

He's not saying something because even if it's private property, this is clearly extenuating circumstances.

I glance at Jesse and Nathan and realize they're both in on the inside information.

"It's an animal sanctuary," Nathan explains.

"What kind of animals?"

"Bears. Black bears," Jackson utters, drawing my attention again. I stare at him for a long time, waiting for it to click in my brain but my mind is trying to convince me that I heard him wrong.

"My brother might be in there." I point to the woods beyond the fencing. "He might be trapped in there with bears."

"He's small. He could have gotten through any hole in or under the fence line," Jesse explains. My gaze whips to his and I see the worry under his cool exterior. "Means he could get out just as easy," he adds.

"Jackson. I'm about to lose my fucking mind. What are we going to do?"

"I need to make a call but you have to trust me."

337

"You know that I do." I can't look at him, I can only stare into the trees beyond me while he makes his call.

"Lochlan, I need your help. Bring anyone you can."

We stand around for ten minutes, wasting daylight, until I hear the sound of small engines approaching. Multiple quads and a side-by-side appear within a few seconds and I'm suddenly surrounded by seven more men I've never seen before.

One of them steps off of a four-wheeler and my jaw drops. He's the largest man that I've ever seen in real life. He's taller than Jackson, who previously held the record in my mind. He's almost terrifying to look at.

I don't know if it's the furrowed brow or the aura of dark clouds around him, but it makes me saddle closer to Jackson on instinct. His ruggedness is dark and filled with disdain as if he belongs on the other side of the fence with the bears.

Jackson is as manly as they come in my eyes but he's a calm and stable force, totally opposite from this person. I never realized how much I preferred to gravitate toward stability until now.

"Sheriff," he greets, deeply.

"I have an eight-year-old boy. He's not mine by law, but he's my kid, Lochlan. I think he's in there." Jackson points through the fence and a few people around us curse under their breath. However, Nathan and Jesse are both stiff as a board, paying more attention to the new strangers and not the conversation between Jackson and this man. "He was running from bad men, he probably doesn't even realize where he is."

Lochlan scrubs a hand over his face, sighing deeply, and that's when I notice the long scar traveling from his temple straight down to just below his cheekbone. "The bears are peaceful, they don't want to be bothered. We haven't had any attacks in over a decade. If he's a smart kid, he'll be fine."

"He's smart but he's probably terrified. I didn't even know what I was sending him into, this is all my fault." I cover my face to hide my distress because I can't contain it anymore. My poor baby brother.

"He'll be fine, we'll get him," Jackson whispers against my head, kissing me just above the ear.

"Cut the fence here, we'll patch it later." A few of his guys make their way forward with wire cutters to cut the links of the fence. "Listen to me, we move in groups. No one wanders off. Make noise so you don't surprise them. If they hear you coming they'll most likely move away but if one gets curious, don't fucking shoot it." He looks at Jackson, Jesse, and Nathan dead in their eyes.

That's when I realize that no one else is armed. None of these other men are carrying anything more than normal tools.

"Do not shoot one of my fucking bears unless it already has your neck in it's teeth, you hear me?" He asks this time, expecting a response. Jackson might be Sheriff but this guy is definitely in charge. "This is their home. We respect them."

"We're only here for Dec. No one wants to cause any harm, Lochlan."

He looks at Jackson closely and then nods his head, turning his attention back to the guys working on the fence. I tug on Jackson's arm to get him to lean his head toward me. "Why don't they have guns?"

He sighs. "They're felons. Most of them anyway. They don't keep guns on the property. They can't."

My eyes bulge. We're about to go into bear territory with a

bunch of felons. Great. What could go wrong?

"Trust me?" He asks, watching the panic work across my face.

His eyes are filled with as much hope as he can muster in this situation and I see the truth in them. There's a reason he called these guys to help us, he's confident that they won't screw us over. "Yeah, I do."

A dog's bark echoes through the trees suddenly making me jump, I'm too on edge being this close to the bears. The drawl of a hunting dog continues getting closer and I look around to see if anyone else is concerned but all I see are a few guilty faces.

"I thought I told you to keep the strays locked up in the barn?" Lochlan asks one of his guys, the one that looks the guiltiest.

"I did, Boss. He must've escaped." A hound dog comes barreling into the clearing where we're standing, happily seeking attention, and pats on the head.

"What kind of dog is this?" I don't know why I ask, I need the distraction I guess.

"A mutt. Bloodhound and coonhound most likely. Someone dumped him and three others at the gate. We haven't figured out what to do with them yet. Boss doesn't want them near the bear enclosures until we know they won't bother them," one guy says. He has tattoos visible below the collar of his shirt and short cropped hair, but much kinder eyes than Lochlan.

As if the dog sensed my inquiry, he nuzzles up to me and starts sniffing my hands. His curious snuffs turn manic suddenly, snorting inhales until his reddish brown body goes taut. I barely have a chance to ponder his strange behavior when his nose hits the ground and he starts toward the fence line, whining and scratching at the metal caging until his paws meet the earth and he starts digging, rampantly.

"What were you doing before everything went down?" Jackson asks suddenly, everyone's attention is on the dog and me.

"Dec and I got ice cream."

"He's got the scent," Lochlan speaks up. "He's a hunting dog, he might be able to lead us to the boy. Let's go before he loses it."

We all take turns entering through the narrow opening, and once we're all through, Lochlan lets the dog loose. He takes off before anyone can blink.

"Spread out, stay in groups," Lochlan instructs and we make a wall. I stay right next to Jackson while Nathan and Jesse move ten feet off to my right, always keeping me in the middle.

It'll be dark soon and all I can think about is my brother being stuck here with these bears. It's all I can do to keep moving forward when my body wants to collapse, exhausted with worry.

We're coming, Dec. We're coming.

Chapter Fifty

Jackson

The amount of feet trudging through the thick brush, crushing the dried fallen leaves on the forest floor, drowns out any noise the predators that live here might be making. It's an eerie feeling, walking deeper into an unknown landscape, knowing Dec is lost and alone in the very woods that these black bears call home.

Lochlan seems confident in his stride beside me and I have no problem following his lead. I've never felt the need to assert my authority when it isn't needed. Lochlan outranks me here and I respect it.

We're only walking a few more minutes when the dog's bark pierces through the trees. He's ahead of us a few hundred yards but it seems he's stopped moving.

My heart thunders in my chest at the prospect of finding Dec. The sooner I have my eyes on him, the sooner this will be over and I can get him back to the safe zone. We haven't seen any signs of bears, but it doesn't mean they aren't here. "Let's go." I pick up speed at the thought and Lochlan keeps pace with me easily.

As we break through a thick tree line, my breath catches in

my throat and I hear Natalie gasp beside me.

"Woah, woah." Lochlan throws his hands up, commanding everyone to stop moving.

A large bear is just ahead of us in a small clearing, proudly standing on its hind legs, squaring up to the hunting dog that hasn't stopped barking at it. Its black fur is as dark as its distressed eyes, staring at all the unwanted visitors.

"Sissy!" Dec's voice comes from across the clearing and my head swivels toward the sound, but I can't see him. My eyes are frantically searching for his small frame among the trees.

"Dec! Stay right there!" Natalie yells back, dropping to her knees.

At first, I think it's in relief. Her body is finally giving out and she can't stay on her feet but it only takes a moment to realize she's looking right at him from her new vantage point.

Tucked in between a big boulder and the trunk of an old tree is his small body, right on the other side of the bear and the dog. I have to squat down to see him fully, barely listening while Lochlan takes the lead, speaking to his guys over my head.

"Hayes, call the dog back," Lochlan orders the guy with the tattoos, breaking a limb of a sapling next to him. "Everyone else, form a half circle, we'll funnel him out in one direction." The group does as he says without question, getting into position to leave the bear one route to escape in.

"Sheriff." He grabs my attention and I stand back to my height, forcing my eyes off Dec. "I'll scare the bear off. Stay behind me and grab the boy when you can. Keep your hand on your weapon but don't shoot. Even if that bear knocks me on my ass and I'm bleeding out, only if it goes toward the boy." His eyes are hard, giving me no room to question his

343

sincerity. One day I'll ask him about his dedication to these bears, but not today.

"Got it."

Standing at his full height with his arms above his head, Lochlan starts waving the limb in the air, yelling gibberish. His size rivals the bears as he marches toward it slowly, but that doesn't negate the danger. This is a wild animal and he feels threatened.

I keep pace behind him with my gun low but ready. My eyes ping from the bear to Dec, over and over.

The dog's still barking, not listening to any commands from our onlookers to stand down. If anything, he's backing closer to Dec, keeping guard between him and the bear.

"I'm coming, Dec. Hold tight, buddy."

When Lochlan's within ten feet of the bear, it mewls in distress, collectively making the whole of our group freeze. There's a deafening silence as we wait to see the bear's reaction to Lochlan's approach.

He's flailing his head side to side in defiance of being cornered but after a few seconds, it ultimately starts shifting backward, preparing to flee the area.

It lowers to all four legs very suddenly, taking off into the brush line, and I sprint the final distance to Dec. I scoop him up out of his hiding spot before I have a chance to regain my breath. "I've got you. You're safe," I strangle out through a tight throat as he cries against my shoulder.

The dog stays hot on my heels as I rush him over to his sister, dropping to my knees to lower him so Natalie can hug him.

My lungs intake a full breath of air for the first time in hours.

We've got him.

"Are you okay?" Nat fusses over Dec, checking him from head to toe. He's dirty, and his legs are cut up, but he looks fine.

"I hurt my ankle when I jumped over the fence. I couldn't run anymore, I tried." He whines into his sister's neck and I see her own eyes shining with tears. She told him to run and he was trying not to disappoint her.

"He climbed a barbed wire fence? Brave kid," Lochlan says from beside us. "Looks like you might have a new friend."

The panting red dog is lying in the dirt beside us, his nose resting against Dec's thigh. "Thanks for finding me," Dec says softly to his unlikely savior, petting the top of his head.

"Come on, let's get out of here." I lift Dec into my arms again and we head back out of bear territory the way we came.

It isn't until we're through the fence that I finally feel like Dec's safe and it's all over but the dread in my stomach stays thick. Dec's had one of the worst days of his life and I still need to tell him that I killed his dad.

"Patch that." Lochlan directs his guys and then waves me over to the side-by-side. "I'll take you guys back up to the road."

There's still work to do, I'll have to break Dec's heart tomorrow.

* * *

"It was smart expecting me here at the church so my family

would be easier to kidnap. I'll give you the credit there, Reverend." It's late, Dec and Natalie are safely tucked away at home, and now I have a case to close.

"Ah, Mr. Malec. I deserve so much more credit than that. I've been pulling the wool over your eyes for as long as you've been Sheriff." Reverend Porter sits slowly in the front pew of his church. The lights are dim and the ghostly glow of the platform lingers behind me.

I put myself in his line of sight while my two backup deputies remain on the back wall, giving us room to chat. "Why is a Godly man running a crime ring in Rollins County? Tell me that, Mr. Porter."

"Son, you have no idea what it means to be a man of God. I am only doing his bidding. Cleaning his beautiful earth of sinners."

"Sinners?"

"Sinners took my wife from me. My family."

"Explain."

He chuckles as if he's amused by my inquiry. "My sweet, Marcy was taken from this world because of sinners. High on their drugs and alcohol. They drove her off the road and we didn't find her until the next day. My wife was murdered, leaving me to raise my children on my own." He inhales a deep, rattling breath, but continues. "My sister allowed men to ruin her, bringing babies into this world out of wedlock. Men who are driven by their own sexual needs, leaving children to unwed mothers, belong in hell. Sinners have ruined this place. Rollins used to be peaceful, a place where families attended church and put their hands on the bible."

"All of this because you think you're cleaning up Rollins?"

"Filth doesn't belong here."

"Is that why people have been going missing? Kidnapping them and selling them to the highest bidder? Why my family?"

"I wasn't interested in your family, Sheriff. It only pleased me to rattle you. Declan went rogue in his attempt to pay me back the money he owed me."

"He was going to pay you back by selling a little boy and a young woman to God knows who? To blackmail me? What?"

"Don't use the lord's name in vain, son."

"I don't give a damn, Reverend." My voice is as cold as ice. I'm done with games.

"I don't know why Declan took your family, he only promised to get me what he owed me." He shrugs. "I never cared for the skin trade. Wasn't my goal. Vagrants wander into this place and ruin it. They bring drugs and corruption. Getting rid of outsiders was my only interest. My sons were greedy in their endeavors, and it got them killed."

"Where are all of the bodies then? The ones who have gone missing since Benjamin and Anthony were killed?"

He shrugs. Part of me hoped that he was trafficking these missing people somewhere else, only because it meant they might still be alive. His dismissal of their humanity leaves a heavier rock in my gut.

"Long gone, Sheriff. Don't bother. The mountains have reclaimed their souls."

It takes every ounce of strength to stand here and act unphased. I hardly blink at his detached words.

"Why the 5k bombing?" I ask, needing to tie all the loose ends I can.

"That was Thomas' idea. He thought he could get back at the military for what they did to him, but I only cared because it showed just how much power I have here. With a snap of my finger, I could have these streets cleaned up quicker than you ever will."

"Those were innocent people."

"No one is innocent, Sheriff." He coughs hoarsely into a handkerchief and lays it on the pew beside him.

"Tell me about the drugs."

"Drugs. God forgive us for the drugs."

"You said you were cleaning up, why provide Declan with drugs?" It's only a theory, but now I need to hear the reverend admit it. He's the one behind the overdoses, too.

"Mr. Randolph got one of my grandsons addicted. Hooked him years ago. When I found out it was him, I told him he could do my bidding or I'd assist in his descent to hell. He chose to do as I told him until he didn't. He was supposed to take over the drug supply, boot all the competition out, and get rid of the users. Let them die on the very addiction controlling their lives, it didn't matter to me.

"He stepped out of bounds. He mixed our business with his personal affairs. Killing his wife put a target on his back and put me in a bad way. I needed him out of jail because he was a tool. A tool who owed me a lot of money."

"Where are the rest of the drugs?"

He shrugs again. "That is the question. I'm out a lot of money now that Mr. Randolph is dead."

"How did you know he died?" It's only been a few hours since I shot Declan, the events haven't been made public, yet.

"I have ears everywhere, Sheriff."

Of course, more secrets. The information and lack thereof is making my head pound erratically. I've been asking for answers for so long, that it seems my brain can't fathom it. "Who killed Thomas in the jail?"

"Well, you did, Sheriff."

"No, I didn't."

"Ah, but asking too many questions gets people killed."

"So, it was you?"

He chuckles. "I'm an old man. I don't get my hands dirty but you know that already. I needed Declan out of jail and I needed him to take me seriously."

"So, you had your nephew murdered?"

"He was getting chatty and as a man facing a long prison sentence, he had lost his way. He was a lost cause."

"Why are you being so forthcoming about your crimes?"

"I'm tired, Mr. Malec. I can see that you are not as easy to fool like my son-in-law was. That stupid man should have never been associated with my daughter."

"Does Vanessa know you're involved in all of this?"

"She is as flippant as you'd expect. She is a preacher's daughter, she only does what she thinks will please me. Having her two boys was all she was good for. Randall will be a politician and continue my work, Jeremiah will carry on the family name in his own way I suspect."

His blatant disregard for his daughter is disturbing but not surprising. He isn't the only man of his generation with such dismissive views on women.

All the missing pieces are clicking and my disgust only builds that one man coerced and eliminated so many innocent lives.

He begins to hum, reaching for the bible on the seat next to him. A shiny silver revolver is tucked into its cut-out pages when he opens it.

My gun's drawn and my finger is on the trigger before his fingers can brush the reflective metal. "Don't fucking touch it."

"Tell my daughter to bury me in my white robes." He continues humming his tune, ignoring my command and grasping the handle in his gray and veiny hand.

"DROP IT, REVEREND!" His forearm moves, tilting the gun ever so slightly in my direction, and for the second time today, I kill a man.

With so many questions left unanswered, Reverend Porter is dead. My crime leader is simultaneously discovered and gone.

Chapter Fifty-One

Jackson

My eyes are raw with exhaustion but I push through because I'm almost done writing my reports. Discharging my firearm multiple times today, taking two lives, and explaining the actions of every other person involved has taken its toll on me but at least it's over. The crime in Rollins that I've been working to stop for over a year should die alongside Reverend Porter.

My desk lamp is on but the sun is rising through the blinds over my office windows. Today's events were actually yesterday's events, and I haven't had a wink of sleep.

A soft rap on my door surprises me and I barely manage a mumbled, "Come in," before the door swings open slowly.

"It's me." Natalie walks through the door, rousing my brain. She should be at home with Dec, sleeping.

"What are you doing here, sweetheart?"

Her eyes squeeze shut at my question and when they open again, they're filled with sorrow. "What's wrong, Nat?"

"I had to tell Dec."

"What?" I know she's referring to my involvement in his dad's death but we had agreed to talk to him together. I wanted to wait until everyone got some rest.

"He woke up screaming and wouldn't let it go until I answered his questions. He's smart Jackson, he knew something bad happened while he was in the woods." She shuffles from foot to foot, drawing my attention to her outfit. She's fully dressed for the day, not like someone who should've just rolled out of bed.

"He's angry with me?" I ask, already knowing the answer.

"He's upset. He doesn't understand why his dad had to die. I mean, I told him you had no choice but he can't wrap his head around it. He's really upset, Jackson."

"Let me talk to him." I get up from my desk, moving toward her and the door.

"No." She holds a hand up to stop me. "No, you can't. He doesn't want to see you," she chokes the words out and takes a deep breath. "We're leaving."

"Nat, don't."

"I'm sorry. He needs time and space. He needs to get away from all the bad memories here." Her first tears fall, rolling down her cheeks in thick streams. "I'm taking him to New York."

"Give me some time, I'll take a leave of absence, I'll go with you."

"Jackson, he needs time away from you. I'm sorry, but he's confused. I have to do what's best for him." Her eyes don't match the strength of her words but it doesn't matter, it's a punch to the gut anyway.

All I can picture is my favorite eight-year-old boy devastated by what I've done. The hurt he's feeling is tearing me apart and it's all my fault. I killed his dad.

My entire world is crumbling and I have no power to stop

it. It feels like Declan won after all.

"You guys are leaving me," I utter the realization, losing any lasting strength keeping me upright. My knees hit the floor hard.

She embraces me then, holding my head against her stomach. The place where I thought we'd be growing our family but instead, it's over.

"I don't want to go, Jackson. Please, believe me. I don't want to leave you but I need to do what's best for Dec. You have to understand. Please, don't make this harder on me, I can't take it," she begs, crying through her words. "I lo-"

"Don't," I beg. "Don't say those words, not now. Not if you want me to let you go."

"I don't want you to let me go," she whispers sadly against the top of my head. "I wanted a home with you, but I have to do this. We have to leave, please believe me."

This is it, my heart is being ripped from my chest and the prophecy is fulfilled. I'm losing them and it's killing me.

She kisses the top of my head gently and releases her hold on me, but all I can do is slump further to the floor as she walks away from me.

Watching her walk away from me is worse than death by a thousand cuts.

I'm losing the woman I love.

I've lost Dec.

I've lost my family.

Everything.

* * *

Natalie

We've barely made it a few hours north when my phone starts vibrating excessively in the passenger seat. After my phone got destroyed by Declan yesterday, I was lucky to have an old spare tucked away. It's one of those survival techniques that I thought I was past by now. Always have a backup for when life turns to shit.

I glance at the screen, hardly containing the sob threatening to leave my throat. I can't believe after everything we went through, it ended like this. I always assumed that he would screw up and break my heart, I never thought I'd be the one to break his.

Jackson: Missed Call

Jackson: Missed Call

Jackson: Let me know when you make it to NY safely. Tell Dec I'm sorry for everything and I love him. Please.

He loves Dec. I know he does but it doesn't change the reality. Jackson killed Dec's only living parent and now my brother is left to deal with the emotional aftermath. Even after explaining to him that it was my life or Declan's, I know this is too much to expect a child to process.

That's why we had to leave. I wasn't going to force Dec to stay in a house with a man that he can't even stand to look at. My mother did it to me numerous times growing up, but the situation was never quite as complicated as this.

So, I continue navigating to New York and hope that I'm making the right decision. I'll get Dec the help that he needs to process his grief and I'll give him time.

My feelings for Jackson are greater than anything I have ever known, but Dec will always be the priority.

CHAPTER FIFTY-ONE

I only hope he can forgive me for choosing my brother over him.

Chapter Fifty-Two

Natalie

"Dec, we're here." The nerves in my stomach are wound tight, I haven't been able to eat at all today. Dec's in the backseat sleeping and I'm relieved for the silence. It's been *two months* since I've pulled into this pristine driveway.

New York offered ample distractions but the time passed painfully, for me.

I got Dec into an almost free summer camp sponsored by a local church and being around other kids helped him immensely. He didn't have the chance to let his thoughts run away with him.

He's a brand new kid, and his joy for each day is bright and infectious, so far from how he felt right after we left Lawson.

Luckily, I was able to contact my former culinary school counselor and she helped me re-enroll to get my missing credits. While Dec was at camp every day, I finally finished my culinary certification.

We talked about everything but we talked about Jackson a lot. It took Dec a few weeks to admit it, but he missed him.

I missed him terribly.

Between my classes and taking care of Dec, I didn't get many chances to talk to him without my brother's ears listening in. Especially when it seemed like everything felt worse after each phone call.

My heartbreak was amplified by the distance, not knowing if our separation would end.

Every day, I wanted to tell him it was only temporary but the truth was that I didn't know if it was. It was Dec's decision. I had committed to sacrificing my feelings for my brother's sake, even though I was crumbling inside.

But last week he admitted he wanted to see his friends at school again and didn't want to enroll in New York. When I asked him about coming home to Jackson he only needed a day to think about it before giving me the okay.

He was ready to come back to our home, here.

My fingers fidget nervously on the steering wheel as I park in the same spot I used to. His spot is empty because I didn't tell him we were coming. Part of me wanted it to be a surprise, the other part was afraid that he'd tell me not to come.

He could have changed his mind. He told me once that he didn't want me running anymore and that's exactly what we did. We left him.

Dec yawns dramatically, stretching out in the back seat. He's grown at least an inch since we've been gone, I can only imagine how much faster he'll grow in the coming years. He glances out the window toward the house but we both sit in thoughtful silence for a few more minutes.

He wanted to come home but I know this might be hard for him.

"I'll go see if the door's open, grab your bag from the trunk and meet me inside when you're ready," I tell him gently, pushing aside my own nerves.

My steps to the front door are hesitant.

I never had a key, I only ever used the keyless entry. What if he changed the code?

What if there is a woman here? It's been two months, he could have moved on...

I punch in the only numbers I know and exhale roughly when the lock flips automatically.

I push the door open and it's exactly the same, smells the same, and the kitchen looks untouched. It's like coming home after a long vacation.

I creep down the hallway to my old room and pause in the doorway. The yellow room is as bright as it was before.

"Sissy, what is this?" Dec asks from beside me, near his old room. A large, plush, cushion sits on the ground next to the computer.

"It looks like a dog bed." The words are barely out of my mouth before I hear the unmistakable sound of a dog scampering across the hardwood floors.

"I got a dog," Jackson's breathless voice announces from the end of the hallway. "I saw your car pull into the driveway on my cameras. I broke every speed limit to get here," he admits.

He looks exactly the same, except maybe ten pounds lighter, as if he hasn't eaten properly in two months.

I choke back a sob just thinking about him being all alone in this house without us. "I should have called..." I breathe with relief as he takes a hopeful step toward me.

Jackson. Our Jackson.

"I'm just glad you came." He takes another hesitant step in my direction but stops when Dec squeals with laughter. The red-haired hunting dog who found him in the woods that day is licking his face without mercy.

"You adopted him?"

"It's actually a she. No one bothered to check before I guess." He rubs his palms nervously down his sides as if he doesn't know what to do with his hands.

"What's her name?"

"She doesn't have one. I was waiting, hoping you guys would come home someday so Dec could name her." His eyes have always conveyed so much, and I can see just how much he truly missed us. It breaks my heart and heals it at the same time.

I reach out and take his restless hand, gently tugging him toward his room so we can have a moment to talk without Dec's ears listening in.

As soon as I'm in the room that I missed terribly, that reminds me of the man I longed for desperately, I turn and spring into his arms.

"I missed you, so much," I utter into his neck. His arms embrace me desperately, holding me almost too tight to breathe.

His forehead presses to mine and he inhales deeply. "You have no idea, sweetheart. I was losing my mind without you."

"So much that you adopted a dog." I laugh at the absurdity and he smiles gently.

"She saved Dec's life, it was the least I could do."

Of course, Jackson's big heart couldn't bear to leave the dog without a proper home. He's a regular at taking in strays.

"We are ready to be home if you'll still have us," I whisper against his lips.

His eyes squeeze shut, embracing my words before his lips take mine. He kisses me with all the raw aggression he's bottled these last two months, consuming me entirely. There's nothing gentle about it and it's exactly what I needed.

My back hits the wall as his lips drag down my jaw and my neck, tasting me, remembering me. "Don't ever leave me again, fireball. I barely survived." He bites my sweet spot and soothes it with another kiss.

"It would kill me, too." I tug his head up to look at me. "I love you, Jackson. I'm never leaving, again."

His breath catches in his throat and nothing but pure love is staring back at me. He needed to hear those words as much as I needed to say them, again. I meant them the day that Declan kidnapped us, but this is the moment I wanted. I needed to look Jackson in the eyes and finally be able to say the words out loud.

"I want to get married," he replies, stunning me. "I have a ring because I need you to know how serious I am, but I need to do something first." He moves away from me, leaving me slack-jawed.

He pulls a ring box from his nightstand and comes back, opening it to show me. It's a beautiful, shiny, giant diamond. It's meant for a princess. "Jackson…"

"I want you to have the wedding of your dreams. I bought the most classic ring I could find because you deserve something that will last forever. Something timeless, traditional, and hopefully one day you can pass it down to one of our kids. I want it to weigh your hand down so you always think of me, and I want you and the world to know that you belong to someone. To this little family we have, and the bigger one we'll create. I want you to marry me, Nat…"

I'm not even sure I'm breathing, but he continues. "But I need Dec to be ready first."

CHAPTER FIFTY-TWO

"What?"

"I'm not asking for his blessing because honestly, I'll risk his anger if it means I won't lose you, again, but I need to make sure that he's ready for me to be a part of your family. We can wait until he is, but I swear I'll put in the work to earn him again. Just like I did with you."

I touch the diamond delicately, testing that it's really there. It's as smooth as it looks. It's everything I could have ever dared to dream of.

"Let me talk to him then I promise I'll get down on one knee like a proper gentleman and ask for your hand. I'll do it in a much cooler place than this so you aren't embarrassed to tell the story of our engagement. I'll hire a photographer, it'll be perfect."

"This is perfect." I wrap my arms around his neck and kiss him with all the love in my heart. "I don't need the elaborate story."

"You might not need it, but you deserve it." He places my left hand over his heart. "From here on out, I am giving you the life you've always wanted."

"All I want is a life together, Jackson. A family with you."

"Me too, but I want Dec to want it, too, or it will tear you apart," he utters.

"Well, go. Go! I don't want to wait anymore." I push him toward the door and it makes him laugh. He spins on me quickly, kissing me fiercely. "I love you, sweetheart. Wish me luck."

"Good luck," I respond breathlessly. He winks at me before he heads down the hall to Dec.

Chapter Fifty-Three

Jackson

I just laid my heart out to the woman I'm in love with, telling her my intentions to marry her, but I'm more terrified for the conversation that lies ahead. I want Dec to accept me again. I need him to.

"Did you really wait to name her so I could?" Dec asks from the living room. He's sitting on the couch with 'girl' between his knees. It's the only temporary name I could think of to call her these last two months.

"Yeah. I wanted you to know she was your dog as much as she's mine." I sit down hesitantly next to him. "That means you'll have to work with her. Let her outside, play with her, and make sure she's always taken care of."

"I can do that," he states confidently.

"I took her to some training and she's going to help me out at work, but she's our dog. She's a part of our family."

Dec looks at me thoughtfully but doesn't say anything. He's usually so affectionate, I miss the kid who would attack me when I walked through the front door. It's been a long two months without it but I don't know if we'll ever go back to how we were before.

"I'm sorry about your dad, Dec. I wanted to be the one to tell you what happened that day. I never wanted to hurt him. I promise that it was never something I wanted to happen."

"Natalie told me. She said that if you wouldn't have shot him then he would have killed you guys."

"It wasn't a good situation. You were the first thing I thought about. I didn't want to break your heart, buddy. I'm sorry."

"I didn't want him to die," he utters so softly that I can hardly hear him. "But I know he was bad. I would have chosen my sister, too."

"What do you mean?"

"If I had to pick who to got to stay alive. I would pick my sister. She always loved me more than my dad did."

It's so complex for an eight-year-old to consider that it stuns me silent. He's had to see too much in his life; I only want to give him a better one moving forward.

"Are you going to feel okay staying here? I don't expect you to forgive me for what I did, but do you think it would be okay if I stuck around?"

He ponders my question, silently petting the dog on the head. I can hear my heart pounding in my ears. His trust and acceptance mean everything to me; it's a big ask after what I did. No matter how justified the shooting was.

"I'm scared, Jackson," he whispers and it cracks my chest in two.

"Scared of what, buddy? Me?"

"No. I don't know." He buries his head in his hands and I notice his shoulders trembling slightly. "I've been keeping a secret and I don't want you to be mad at me."

"Anything you tell me is safe, Dec. You're always safe with

me."

"I lied to Natalie."

"About what?"

"She asked me once if I saw Mommy taking drugs and I told her no. She asked if I ever saw my dad with any pills and I told her no."

"But?"

"I watched my dad give Mommy blue pills that morning before school. He left and I didn't want her to take any more, so I took them."

My heart is thundering again, making it hard to hear his words. "What did you do with the pills, Dec?"

"I don't want to get in trouble, Jackson. Natalie didn't know, I don't want her to get in trouble either." He starts to cry, his little body shaking uncontrollably.

"I am on your side, Dec. I'm always on your side. You are not in trouble, I promise. I just need to know what happened." I wrap my arm around his shoulders on instinct and sigh in relief when he leans into me instead of pulling away.

"I hid them. They're in a little treasure chest I gave Mommy one year for Mother's Day. She used to put her rings in it." He wipes his cheeks, regaining his composure. That means the biggest of his secrets is out, everything else probably isn't as bad.

"Where is it now?"

He shrugs. "I don't know. It used to be in my special box." *The one that I've had in my office for months.* "That's what he wanted that day at my school. He knew I had them I guess but I didn't know where they were. He was so mad."

That bastard. He was never interested in a relationship with his son, he only wanted his drugs back. He took Dec and Natalie that day because he wanted his drugs.

I can't believe they've been in my possession this whole time. I could be angry that I missed the opportunity to put Declan behind bars the proper way, but I'm glad that the drugs haven't been on the street. They aren't in any hands that would spread them.

"I'll take care of it. Thank you for telling me, it took a lot of courage." I squeeze him to my side. "I'm sorry you had to bottle that in for so long, buddy."

"Natalie was doing so much for me and I was afraid she would get arrested. I was so scared. If I just told him where they went then maybe he would have left us alone a long time ago," he stutters through his words, the guilt weighing heavy on him. It's a dilemma he should have never had to navigate alone.

"You guys are both safe now. No more secrets, okay? I'll take care of everything."

He nods his head against my arm. "We're really staying here forever, now?" He asks, never moving from my side.

"Yeah, as long as it's okay with you." I clear my throat, my earlier nerves coming back. "I want to marry your sister and become a real family. Do you think you're ready for something like that?"

"You would be her husband?"

"Yeah, I would."

"What would that make me then?"

"You would be my brother. You're Natalie's brother by blood and you'd be my brother by law, but you'll always be my boy. You're my favorite kid. Nothing will change that."

"What if you guys have babies?"

"Then you'll be an uncle but it might even feel like being a big brother."

"I could be a big brother and an uncle?" He asks so enthusiastically that I can't help but laugh.

"Absolutely. You'd be the best at both jobs."

"Thanks for picking us, Jackson."

"No, Dec, thanks for picking me."

"Oh my God, I love you guys," Natalie squeals, running into the living room. Her face is streaked with dried tears. She was definitely listening the whole time.

She launches at us both, forcing a group hug over top of the dog's head, making both Dec and I crack up.

"Sissy, you're squishing me," Dec utters through his giggles.

"Sorry, sorry." She releases him and plops herself onto my lap. Her head rests against mine as Dec starts rolling around with the dog on the floor.

"What are you going to name her, Dec?" She asks.

"I don't know."

Nat turns to me, looking at me closely. "What about, honey?"

"Honey?" Dec asks.

"Is that supposed to be a Winnie the Pooh, bears like honey reference?" I ask.

She runs her fingers through my hair and smiles. "Can be, but that's not why I picked it."

I watch her curiously as she looks at me mischievously.

"Not going to tell me, are you?"

"Mmm, maybe eventually."

Epilogue

Jackson

"Are you ready to look?" I ask Nat while we're standing in the kitchen. It's been a month since she and Dec have been back home. He started school a few weeks ago and we've established our new normal.

"I'm ready as I can be, I guess. Read it for me, I can't look." She takes a deep breath and palms her belly.

She hasn't taken one of *those* tests yet, but neither of us has been shy about our eagerness to have a baby. She insists that it might take a few months depending on ovulation but it doesn't stop me from taking her every chance that I get. Many of my lunch breaks are spent bending her over this very countertop while Dec's at school.

She closes her eyes as I open her DNA test results, scrolling until I find the ethnicity breakdown. I've been sitting on the results for a while now and she's finally ready to tackle whatever information comes forth.

"Natalie Halstead, you are... German, Finnish, and Persian." She gasps. "Persian? How much?"

"About 16%. The other European stuff is greater but it's a mix. Persian could explain the dark hair and dark eyes."

"Yeah, it could." She smiles brightly, looking at me with relief. "That's so cool. I've never made any Persian foods... I should look up some recipes!"

All I can do is smile at her. This woman is so special to me. I'll never be able to express how much I needed her in my life. Nothing I've ever done compares to sharing these experiences with her.

My plans for our proposal are set. She's clueless and I've never been more excited about keeping a secret from someone.

I've planned a private five-course meal to be served in one of my mother's favorite gardens. It's on a rolling estate not far from here. She still brings up its vast rolling meadows and elaborate fountains on her good days. I know Natalie will appreciate the personal touch and the family connection.

Sienna already offered to help Dec decorate the house after we leave so he can be a part of the celebration when we return home. He doesn't know it, but I'm asking him to be my best man.

"What about possible matches?" She asks suddenly, her worry returning over her test results.

I scroll down to familial matches but the page stops short. "There aren't any. There are a few possible census connections but nothing that looks real. If you have family out there, they aren't in this database."

"Oh, thank God." She laughs again and I can't help but gravitate toward her. I plop her up on the counter so I can wrap my arms around her easier. "Thank you for helping me do this," she whispers sweetly.

I kiss her gently, fully intending to take it further until she pulls back. "Wait, what does yours say?"

"I don't know, I didn't look."

She sticks her hand out motioning for my phone to look at my results. She scrolls for a few seconds, finding what she needs and I watch her eyes go round.

"Jackson…"

"What?"

"You have a match."

"What? What do you mean?"

"It says you have a possible sister. A half-sister."

I snatch the phone out of her hand frantically, making it tumble over in my palm. Natalie clasps her hand over the screen before I can look again. "Take a deep breath. Don't panic. Whatever happens, we'll do it together. Remember?"

I nod briefly before looking at the match screen, but seeing the name associated with the account makes my blood run cold. "Montgomery."

"What?"

"Her last name is Montgomery."

"So?"

"That's the Governor's last name." Natalie's hand covers her mouth as she gasps.

If this woman is truly my half-sister then the current Governor would be my father…

My mom wasn't making up the affair, I just never believed her.

Until now.

Thank you for reading!

The next book will take us to Second Chance Sanctuary and the rugged mountain man, Lochlan Dane. You'll find out just how deep the chip on his shoulder goes and why he prefers life among the bears.

About the Author

Amber Cassidy is a new indie author whose current focus is the small-town romantic suspense genre. This author has a Bachelor of Science in Psychology and a Minor in Sociology. Previous work as a Mental Health Specialist has enabled her to observe the intricacies of the human mind and how it is affected by significant events in one's life.

You can connect with me on:
- https://www.tiktok.com/@ambercassidy_author
- https://www.instagram.com/@ambercassidy_author

Also by Amber Cassidy

Check out the Chance Encounters Series on Amazon!

First Sight
Book One of the series introduces us to the crime happening in Rollins County with Nathan and Callie's unlikely meeting and their struggle with corruption.

First Touch
Nathan's little sister, Thea, is a small-town librarian struggling with trauma from her past. She never expects the mysterious new stranger in town to be the one to tear down her walls, or how they are connected more than either of them realize.

First Chance
Book Four - Release Date TBD